A TALE OF TWO ENCLAVES

A TALE *of* TWO ENCLAVES

WWII Stories and Mussolini's Internment Camps

CARMINE VITTORIA

Newly revealed historical events intertwined with personal stories in this book make it paramount that the horrors of WWII are never to be repeated.

TABLE OF CONTENTS

PROLOGUE

Quoting philosopher George Santayana: "Those who cannot remember the past are condemned to repeat it." This quotation has been repeated by many others in slightly different forms but it has evolved into this often-quoted one: "Those who do not learn from history are doomed to repeat it."

The essence of this book is that unless and until historical events are factual or truthful and all-encompassing to people's lives, it may be rather difficult, if not impossible, to learn from history. If an event does not impact people's lives, it may not be considered historical. As such, there isn't much to be learned from history.

But, we believe there is still much to be learned from the events of WWII. Most books on WWII, usually emphasize military operations, rather than people caught in a war zone. In my previous book, *Hidden in Plain Sight*, I introduced a cross-spectrum of characters to show how people in a small town in Southern Italy were affected during WWII.

This time, I have introduced characters representative of people in Vienna, Austria, and Avella, Italy. Their economic standings range from the poor to the affluent and classes in between. This comparison is made to show how people's lives, in two very different towns and social structures, were affected in WWII. Hence the title, *A Tale of Two Enclaves*.

I conducted a tremendous amount of research to present this historical fiction before you. During the process, I uncovered new historical facts that shed light on some of the puzzles of this particular war. Nevertheless, *A Tale of Two Enclaves* is not about reporting historical events per se, but, rather, what effects it had on people's lives. This is important to future generations so as not to repeat the fatal mistakes of WWII. I hope my contribution helps.

ONE

One Enclave of Friends

Avella is an ancient Italian town and is proud of its history. It dates back to the Paleolithic Period which is roughly 2.5 million years ago, the Old Stone Age. Archeological remains have shown human presence along the Clanio Creek. Water in the creek flows from the top of Monte Avella to the valley below and the town of Avella. The valley extends from the sweeping foothills of the Apennine Mountains to Naples and is sometimes referred to as Naples' backyard.

In ancient times, the name of the town was Abella due to the abundance of hazelnuts there. The Abella hazelnut is one of eighteen species. The town of Abella was under the heavy influence of the Etruscans and Greeks who had settled in Paestum and Neapolis (Naples) in the eighth century BC, as well as the fierce Samnite tribes of the Apennine Mountains. There is strong evidence that the Samnites were natives of the area. The common denominator between the descendants of the Stone Age and Samnites was that they were nomads, hunters, and shepherds. To our knowledge, there is no evidence linking the two groups to modern-day shepherds. In the third century BC, Abella became a principality of Rome while also being surrounded by Samnite settlements. As such, the town was rewarded with an amphitheater by the Roman Emperor Sulla in 89 BC, when the Romans invaded and conquered the valley.

*View of the valley and Mount Vesuvius from the top of Monte Avella.
The town of Avella is at the foothill below. Courtesy of Piero Busiello.*

An antique map of the region may be seen in the Vatican Museum in which the name Abella can be discerned, although the year is not displayed. However, by the turn of the fifteenth century, the name of the town changed to Avella. As in most small towns in Southern Italy, Avella, in the 1920s, was split into two distinct classes of people: the gentry and the peasants. This description of the classes is well documented in Carlo Levi's book, *Christ Stopped at Eboli*. It suffices to say that these two classes of people in Avella did not mingle very well, and they lived in different parts of town. The gentry lived mostly in the center of town, usually surrounding a piazza or main square, and the peasants lived in the periphery, toward the foothills of the mountains.

As in Aliano, where Carlo Levi was exiled, the gentry in Avella may be best described in relation to the ruling establishment—the carabinieri or police, mayor, city hall workers, artisans, landowners, etc. Farmhands, shepherds, and unskilled workers made up the peasant class. Socially and economically, these two classes didn't have much in common. They simply ignored each other. The clash between the haves and have-nots is as old as time itself and is universal.

The shepherds took their sheep to graze on the fields of Monte Avella as far as the Calabria region, commonly known as the boot of Italy. It was arduous work. The reward was the bountiful food supply along the many trails on the mountains, and the ability to sell dairy products and wool. Farmers toiled the land of rich landlords, who resided in cities like Naples and Rome.

The central government in Rome only catered to the gentry. As for the peasants, they didn't exist in the eyes of Rome. Thus, the division and resentment between the two classes grew with time, culminating in the delay of civilization in small and remote towns like Aliano and Avella. The same side effect didn't occur among the gentry, however, because they had the opportunity to visit civilized cities such as London, Paris, Rome, etc.

Fast forward to the late 1920s. The tumults of World War I, the Spanish flu, and economic and political upheavals still lingered in people's minds. Is Benito Mussolini the one to take people out of their misery? The general feeling among the people of Avella at that time was that at least he got the trains running on time. Unfortunately, trains throughout Italy never ran on time. But, if a lie is repeated often enough by the regime, people start to believe it. Those were the underlying thoughts among the peasants and gentry in the town of Avella at the time. It was well known that he was running around with mistresses and was corrupt, but as long as they felt that his heart was with the people there was hope. As it turned out, belief and hope superseded realities then and thereafter.

With the outbreak of WWI, shepherds withdrew to the mountains of Avella, as did their ancestors in other wars. Sergio Cortone and Dario Di Marelli were the only shepherds recruited by the Italian Army into the special division of the Bersaglieri or mountain division in the Alps. Other shepherds escaped to the surrounding hills and mountains and emigrated to the United States and throughout the world, initiating a tenacious search by the carabinieri for shepherds in the hills.

During WWI, the Italian Army consisted mostly of conscripted peasants who were malnourished while fighting for a cause few could understand. About 470,000 conscripts resisted call-up and 300,000 deserted. Now fifty years later, a shepherd who emigrated to the United States was still on the carabinieri's list of people to be recruited for Army duty! Since childhood Sergio and Dario fantasized themselves in the uniforms of Bersaglieri with that plumed helmet. They behaved like brothers, Sergio being slightly older, and their families lived in the same building for many generations. Sergio and Dario saw the Bersaglieri when they visited Avella on their recruitment tour of Southern Italy. The soldiers ran up and down the street blowing trumpets and bobbing their helmets from side to side, somewhat theatrically, enough to impress them. The Southern Italian boys were soon cured of their fantasies after serving duty on the tundra of the Alps.

Sergio was the main cog who guided the herd of sheep to grass fields atop the mountains and hills from the south of Rome to the boot of Italy. He knew where all the small lakes, creeks, grass fields, resting places, and wild boars were, like the back of his hand. Shepherds loved that feeling of being able to roam around without the interference of local governments in the valleys below—total freedom. In some sense, they were divorced from governments—anarchists at heart. Typically, the crew of shepherds consisted of three to four shepherds and one of them was responsible for procuring the food here and there while guiding the sheep along the journeys to the grass fields. Dario had the dual responsibility of procuring the food and assisting in guiding the sheep. On short journeys, the young ones were introduced to shepherding. Yes, it was arduous work, but that was the price of independence and total freedom.

Sergio was assigned to the infantry group of the Bersaglieri. He was stationed in the trenches atop a mountain in the Dolomite Alps. Dario was lucky. He was stationed about five to ten miles west of the trenches, where he served food in a cafeteria at the Officer Club. One year after the Italian Army's catastrophe in the fall of 1918 at Caporetto, now Kobarid in Slovenia, both were injured and captured by the Austrian Army.

In his wake, Sergio left behind a pregnant wife, Imalda, who had been his soulmate since kindergarten. They shepherded together, helping out their parents in search of grasslands in the mountains. It was inevitable that the two would get married. In those days, one married within their respective class. Of course, there were some exceptions, but not many. Marriages were not arranged per se, but it was understood that one married within one's social stratum. Furthermore, women's rights didn't exist as they do today.

Imalda was fiery and a go-getter. When she was barely ten years old, she and her sister helped their parents shepherd on the high mountains. Often, they were left alone with the sheep, as their parents were on the hunt for wild boars and grassland.

Whereas her sister was afraid to be left alone, Imalda took charge and loved the opportunity to impress her parents. She would often arm herself with a special heavy wooden stick, so she was ready to take on the wolves.

Marriages in the shepherd community were arranged based on how many sheep each of the families could bring to the prospective marriage. In the case of Imalda, she had her eye on Sergio since they both left elementary school in fifth grade. As far as shepherds were concerned, third grade was usually good enough for them to be able to sign their names on documents or ballots during election times. Sergio, however, was no blooming flower ready to be picked. He was just as wild and proud as Imalda. It was only natural that the two of them would eventually get married. Their parents, in this case, had no choice but to let love take over.

However, there was a new leader in the Avella shepherd community. Imalda had become the matriarch and, therefore, their leader. In particular, the community chose her to represent them in the business of interfacing with the gentry in the valley. Besides settling disputes among shepherds, she sold all of the products produced by the community: goat cheeses, wool, milk, wooden utensils, etc. Imalda sold their wares mostly at Avella's farmers' market every Monday, and in Nola on Wednesdays. The market at Nola featured a much larger crowd. The town was about ten kilometers west of Avella toward Naples, and accessible by train. Imalda would display her cheeses at the most advantageous spot in the marketplace and nobody dared to challenge her. She would even shush away little children.

While there was no tenderness when it came to business, Imalda was very soft-hearted with family and friends. Sergio and another shepherd helped her load goods on the train to transport them to market and back. The train usually arrived punctually at 8:11 a.m. and stopped for only five minutes. However, on Wednesdays, the train master made an exception for Imalda. He allowed extra time for her to load all her produce onto the train. He was too intimidated by Imalda to enforce the five-minute rule. The train master made up time by speeding faster between stations. As such, she exercised power and demanded respect as the leader of the community. In some sense, most of the shepherds were still in the Stone Age. But on the other hand, they were well ahead of their time as women were still not recognized or allowed to lead in many countries then. But Imalda's mother relinquished her mantle to Imalda after WWI, with the consent of the shepherd community and Imalda led the community from that day forward.

In those days, it was not easy for a shepherd to change his career since the average shepherd lacked the education to do so. There was even less chance for a shepherdess. However, in comparison with other shepherds, Sergio's credentials looked good. He and Imalda finished elementary school, which was more than what most did. Nevertheless, he was not deterred from his dream of becoming a Guardia di Finanza or a finance officer. Usually, finance officers are employed in airports, train or bus stations, and department stores, and are charged with taxation issues, price fixing, taxation of mountain properties, and any transactions involving money. Upon graduation from the academy, Sergio was issued a uniform and pursued his dream. He enrolled at the Police Finance Academy in Naples to train as a guardia di Finanza specializing as a mountain policeman. This allowed him the luxury of distancing himself from the drudgeries of shepherding while still maintaining his friendship with the shepherds up on the mountains.

Sergio and Imalda soon owned an old building, circa the eighteenth century, with a large portone or huge entrance door. Within the confines of the building, there was a semi-circular courtyard adjacent to a large field of grass. Fourteen to fifteen apartments surrounded the courtyard evenly distributed from the ground floor to the third floor. The property was handed down from generation to generation by shepherd descendants. It was located at the edge of town, next to a business farm that cultivated hazelnuts and green olives. It is interesting to note that the farmer and farmers before Sergio were able to hide a Roman amphitheater for an exceedingly long time by placing foliage, shrubbery, and trees next to it. He could not divulge the existence of the amphitheater for fear of losing the farm to the state as keeper of antiquity.

Across the street from Sergio's building, his family cultivated a beautiful garden consisting of fruit trees, a small fish aquarium, grapevines, and flowers. On the ground floor, the apartments of Sergio's Don Nicola and Claudio resided right next to each other. Don Nicola's music studio was located on the second floor, next to other temporary tenants. Don Nicola and Claudio lived there for many years and were very good friends of Sergio's family. In the winter, Sergio rented the field to shepherds who fed their sheep at a minimal cost.

Don Nicola was a cellist employed by the Teatro di San Carlo or San Carlo Opera House in Naples. He was proud to have learned to play the piano on his own, as opera composer Puccini did. He met Giacomo Puccini at the San Carlo Opera House when *La Boheme* was presented to a Neapolitan audience for the first time. At that time, Puccini was still revising his opera, although it had premiered much earlier in Turin, Italy. The sudden death of Puccini in 1924 shocked Don Nicola as well as the rest of Italy and the opera world. It was claimed later by some journalists that the composer was a Fascist. Being a socialist at heart and versed in the doctrines of Karl Marx, Don Nicola knew better, as he and the composer shared similar views of Italian politics.

Don Nicola's family consisted of himself, his son Nicola Jr., and his daughter Flora. His wife, Gelina, died of the Spanish flu. He fervently wanted his son to follow in his footsteps as a musician, but Nicola Jr.'s interest was elsewhere in canvas painting. Nicola Jr. was only at the beginning of his adulthood but already an accomplished artist. He was beginning to attract the attention of churches that were in need of upgrading old paintings. Somehow, he escaped the wave of impressionist art, exceedingly popular at that time, and concentrated on classical paintings, which was a rarity then. Don Nicola realized that his son was a talented artist and was truly proud of him. Flora was Papa's favorite and attended his music studio. She was a mezzo-soprano and specialized in singing light operas, like Puccini's and Mozart's.

Claudio and Francesca were the parents of their only child Dario Di Marelli. Claudio owned an all-purpose store that sold everything from kites in the spring to Christmas toys in the winter to soap all year round. Of course, Claudio wished for Dario to take over the business and, perhaps, expand the business to many other items that he had in mind. However, Dario was of a different mindset. He and Sergio often would go on long trips to the mountains in search of grass fields and talk about what they would like to do with their lives. Dario was hooked on nature and his true passion was cooking. He cooked at home and on those long trips. At that time, no restaurants could generate enough business to succeed in a small town like Avella. But that wasn't true for a big city like Naples.

There was love and respect between Sergio's, Don Nicola's, and Di Marelli's families, despite their different backgrounds. All of the children referred to the elders as uncles. Their children would enter each other's apartments as if it were their homes. In short, there were no formalities between families. The friends and their families complemented each other and they were at ease in each other's company.

Sergio admired Don Nicola's and Di Marelli's political passions and intellect, although he was apolitical. As a shepherd, he didn't care much for government interferences of any kind. Returning the sentiment, Don Nicola and Claudio admired Sergio's commonsense approach to life and the spirit of a goat (fiercely independent) which was earthbound and proud. Whereas Sergio's descendants were local

Samnites, Don Nicola's were the invaders, Romans. To be precise, they were Roman Jews who resided in Rome around 100 BC and migrated to Abella since Abella, Pompei, and Naples or Pozzuoli were then the only towns allied with Rome. Don Nicola's descendants came from that migration of Jews to Abella. Claudio was a Sephardic Jew whose descendants came from Spain via Sicily in the sixteenth century. His last name, Di Marelli, implied that his descendants came from Sicily after leaving Spain. Most likely, the town in which they settled was located near the sea as implied by the name.

Like Sergio, but unlike Don Claudio due to his age, Don Nicola volunteered in the Italian Army during WWI. Don Nicola's duties were far removed from the fighting fronts near the Alps Mountain ranges. His duty was to rally support for the war locally. He was a conductor of the Army's band which traveled from town to town playing military marching music. The band consisted of musicians who joined for the purpose of not being sent to the front. One of them was Don Nicola's drinking partner Erminio, who owned a wine store in Avella. Often, Don Nicola would stop at Erminio's store coming home from the San Carlo, near the train station, to chitchat about anything under the sky. Being a socialist at heart, Don Nicola innately detested those duties as well as the band. He was a classically trained musician after all. What's more, the Socialist Party was against Italy entering the war. Nonetheless, he didn't have a choice unless he shirked his duties and was sent to the Alps.

The neighborhood where Don Nicola, Sergio, and Claudio lived was located on the edge of the foothills, the eastern periphery of town. Mostly shepherds and farmers lived there. Although Claudio and Don Nicola's families were well-to-do professionals and respected in town, they felt comfortable living there. Across the street from the building where Sergio, Claudio, and Don Nicola resided, their dear friend Alvaro lived. Alvaro was a lawyer and an accountant. His job, shortly after WWI was that of a public notary at the post office. He represented people in court, managed the wealthiest accounts, notarized important documents, assured delivery of mail without delay, and signed off on immigration papers for those emigrating.

The name Alvaro is derived from the Spanish name Alvarez. He was a descendant of the Jewish denizens who left Sicily during the infamous inquisition of the 1500s. A royal decree was approved in 1492 by Queen Isabel and King Ferdinand II which aimed to expel from Spain any free Jewish person who did not convert to Catholicism. Over 200,000 were converted and about 100,000 were expelled. The ones who were expelled emigrated to Italy, Greece, and other countries along the

Mediterranean Sea basin. They took surnames representative of their former towns in Spain or their new towns.

There were two migrations of Jewish people to Sicily. The first one occurred in 63 BC when Emperor Pompey expelled Jews from Jerusalem. Most likely, there was migration throughout countries in the Mediterranean Sea, including Spain for example. The second migration occurred during the Inquisition period in Spain whereby Jewish people were expelled from Spain for not converting to the Catholic religion. This wave emigrated to Sicily, Greece, the Balkans, etc. The Jewish population reached 30,000 to 40,000 in Sicily and they assimilated very well into the framework of contemporary society. For instance, they matriculated in philosophy, medicine, artisan pursuits, and farming. Some of the expelled chose to move inland to the Calabria and Naples areas. Alvaro's last name, Da Alia, is derived from the town in Sicily from which his descendants came from. Alvaro's family included his wife Felicia, son Mario, and twin daughters, Serafina and Filomena.

Alvaro was the lawyer who represented two shepherd brothers hiding in the mountains of Avella during Italy's conscription period in WWI. Alvaro was well known in the shepherd community since he lived in their neighborhood. Fortunately for the brothers, there was a national amnesty for all deserters in 1920. In Avella, being a small town, no secret remained a secret for long. Alvaro's reputation came to the attention of the only royal family in town, Garcia Alvarez de Toledo. He descended from a Spanish royal family dating back to the 1500s. As a result, Garcia's son, Ramiro, employed Alvaro as an accountant for their global financial affairs.

The relationship between Garcia Alvarez, head of the family, and Alvaro Da Alia was like that of father and son, especially when Garcia discovered Alvaro's Spanish background. They would converse in Spanish in the library study where Alvaro worked one day a week putting together accounting files. How ironic was it that Garcia's descendants chased the Da Alia's descendants out of Spain! Now, both resided in the same town in harmony. Garcia was proud of the fact that his ancestor, Ferdinando, was the conquistador who, for the first time, captured Naples in 1555 for the Spanish Crown. As a reward, the King of Spain appointed Ferdinando Viceroy of Naples. Alvaro was quick to remind Garcia that his ancestors arrived in Naples' backyard well before Ferdinando established the first Jewish-Spanish settlement. In a strange turn of events, Alvaro and Garcia were both thankful that their ancestors settled in the same town of Avella, and both got a big chuckle out of that bout of irony. Spanish influence in the Naples area was and remains strong to this day. The Neapolitan dialect, the cultivated food, and architecture are just some examples.

Once a year, children of the Palazzo Barone workers, including Alvaro's, were allowed to swim in the only pool in Avella, located in the garden adjacent to Garcia's palazzo. The palace was built in the sixteenth century by the third Duke of Alba, Ferdinando Alvarez de Toledo, when he was Viceroy of Naples. The garden was dedicated to Princess Livia Colonna as a token of love from her husband, Fernando Alvarez de Toledo, Count of Caltabellotta. The Colonna family had been a powerful one for the past ten centuries. It has produced six popes, was one of the wealthiest families in the world, and continues to exert tremendous political influence. In 1880, Livia married her long-distance cousin of yesteryears, the Alvarez dynasty. Their two grandsons, Ramiro and Alvaro, were mayors of Avella during the early days of fascism.

Alvaro Alvarez married Anna Maria Dupont. The Dupont family founded Dupont Chemical Company which is located in the United States, in the state of Delaware, and today boasts factories all over the world. Their children, Fabrizio, Ferrante, and Francesca-Chantal sold the palace to the municipality of Avella in 1989 for 800 million lire, about $1–2 million dollars. The city of Avella has converted the palace into a museum. The three offspring now reside near Rome where they currently manage an agro-tourism farm.

By the 1920s, a new leader, Benito Mussolini, appeared on the horizon as prime minister of Italy. In those days the Fascist government provided many perks to relieve the misery of the people. For example, stipends were awarded to families with children. In addition, military veterans were given preferential treatment for government jobs. But to foster population growth, the Fascist regime taxed heavily unmarried men over a certain age.

One of the first acts of Mussolini's Fascist regime was to abolish elections. This decision allowed the prefect in the province to appoint mayors with the approval of the interior minister in Rome, who was a Fascist. However, the prefect might not have necessarily been a Fascist, as was the case in Avellino—Avella being in that province. The prefect is a public servant and is the state's representative in a province. It was a position created in ancient Rome.

During those hopeful and happy times, Mario, and his twin sisters, Serafina and Filomena, the accountant's children, were schoolmates of Sofia and Paolo, Sergio's children. Living next to each other, it was convenient to walk to school together.

The private school was located downtown and it fostered a bond between the children. Mario and Sofia were the elders. Kindergarten and elementary schools were managed by the nuns. Even at a very young age, Sofia was fiercely independent and proud, much like her mother Imalda, and protective of her brother Paolo. Her hair was blondish-brown and curly, like the painting of Ginevra Benci by Leonardo Da Vinci. Initially, these two groups of children didn't get along. They bickered on the way to school. But their parents not only insisted that they get along but also protect each other from unruly Fascist schoolchildren. The Fascist Party placed a special emphasis on indoctrinating the minds of children.

Mario was a serious student who excelled in Greek and Roman history. He admired the art behind Greek mythology. The nuns favored him to lead in school presentations to outsiders. That did not sit well with Sofia. She was forever competing with Mario. In due time, the two arrived at an impasse—they ignored each other. After school, Sofia, Serafina, and Filomena apprenticed at a seamstress shop managed by two sisters who specialized in dressmaking. Much was expected of them, if they stayed with it. The seamstress shop was one block from school, near the main piazza. Sofia took the responsibility of taking the sisters to and from there. Mario took Paolo home after school so they could study together. Today, Mario would be considered a nerd, as he was often invited by other parents of school children to study together at their homes.

Felicia took up piano lessons at Don Nicola's studio. The name Felicia derives from Felice, which in Italian means happiness, and that she was full of. Blessed with a beautiful family, she had much to be grateful for. She became an accomplished pianist who specialized mostly in Chopin.

In the fall, when the harvest season was in full swing, Sergio would invite the four families—those of Don Nicola, Di Marelli, Alvaro, and Ramiro—to pick Moscato grapes from the garden and to partake in a typical shepherd dinner that included wild boar, lamb, and porcini mushrooms. Of course, Erminio supervised and suggested the date best for picking grapes, as he was the guru of grapes and wine. At these social get-togethers, it was a smorgasbord gathering of the classes: shepherds, socialists, lawyers, members of the royal family, and musicians.

Usually, after one of these dinners, Sergio would invite the guests to visit his private collection of antique Roman statues, Greek vases, fresco paintings, etc. The guests knew the origin of these artifacts since the area surrounding Avella was full of them. Sergio knew all of the burial grounds of Etruscan, Roman, and Greek art treasures. The garden abuts the farm where the owner had been hiding the Roman amphitheater for many years. Today the site has been discovered and turned into a museum site. The whole town may become a museum one day, like Pompei, as archaeological digs have been discovered with complete town settings below the farms' grounds.

Yes, those were happy times. The worst of times was just around the corner, and it was embodied by a terrible countenance: Fascism. In the early 1930s, the Don Nicola, Alvaro, Claudio, and Ramiro families were well aware of where Fascism was headed. They hoped that the bad dream was going to be over soon so they could resume their lives. In effect, they put their lives in a holding pattern until better times. As for Sergio, it made no difference to him as his family could always retreat to the mountains. Alvaro and Ramiro were immersed in global business ventures, almost immune from Fascist interference. Don Nicola did not like what was happening in Avella and the rest of Italy as he was a purebred Socialist who detested Fascism. The other four families were afraid for Don Nicola's life because of his outspoken views as Fascist thugs were beginning to roam the streets of Avella. Fortunately for Don Nicola, many in town empathized with his views.

After a four-year stint, Mayor Ramiro was replaced by his brother, Alvaro Alvarez, as appointed by the same prefect. Under the new administration, Alvaro Da Alia, in turn, was appointed chief magistrate of city hall, again in charge of everyday civil affairs. Thus, not much changed in city hall. However, the same could not be said about the safety in the streets of Avella. By then, everyone in town was aware of the Blackshirt members of the Fascist Party. These thugs looked for political dissidents, Socialists, and especially Communist agitators. As a result, people ventured into the streets only for emergencies during this time. The social evening walk, or passeggiata, was now a thing of the past, as some of these thugs were unruly, festering for a confrontation. Their purpose was to make their presence felt and to intimidate the citizenry into submission.

The timing for a new shop in the middle of town couldn't have been better. Sofia and the sisters were ecstatic at the prospect of launching careers of their own. Initially, they were going to concentrate on knitting sweaters and making dress uniforms for school children. For one thing, Imalda no longer had to sell wool in Nola. Now, she would let Sofia sell her wool, meaning that Sofia could tap into Imalda's clients and vice versa. Imalda envisioned that someday Sofia would take over from her, representing the shepherd's goods at the market, but Sofia's inclination was more toward dressmaking.

At that time, new fashion styles were appearing in newspapers and magazines. The jitterbug era appeared on the scene globally sporting new chic styles for both men and women. There was a revolution in the fashion of women's apparel in sports and formal dress. For one thing, dresses and swimsuits were a lot shorter. The girls envisioned an opportunity to get involved with the new trends in fashion. Before the fashion revolution, there was barely enough business to support two dress shops in Avella—the girls' and one other shop owned by their mentor. After the fashion revolution, the two shops would be in a cooperative mold rather than a competitive one, working under the same umbrella.

Don Nicola and Mario would often take the 8:11 a.m. train to Naples. Don Nicola would head to the opera house for rehearsal and Mario to the university. However, Mario was getting more than a university education. He was being indoctrinated by Don Nicola about politics—Socialism versus Fascism. For a change, Don Nicola didn't have to worry about being confronted by the thugs. Mario admired Don Nicola for his insightful observations of the political upheavals in Europe and Italy. In particular, Don Nicola advised Mario to enroll in the Navy to make up for his obligatory military service. The Italian Navy was not yet infiltrated by Fascists. At the Naples train station, the two split to go their separate ways. At the university, Mario would attend a lecture or take a final exam. As for Don Nicola, he went straight to rehearsal at the opera house. However, the university was within walking distance of the opera house. When Mario finished with school work or attending lectures and Don Nicola had no evening performance at the opera house, they would return home together. Again, politics was on the agenda.

TWO

The Other Enclave of Friends

In between the times that Sergio and Dario joined the Bersaglieri and Mario attended Naples University, much happened in Avella. Imalda gave birth to a daughter Sofia. Butchers were selling cat meat for rabbit meat and the town was totally void of enthusiasm for WWI. Up in the Alps, Sergio and Dario were cured of their infatuation for the Bersaglieri. It was early October 1918, when the Italian Army went on a counter-offensive to regain territories lost the year before in the Veneto region, north of Venice. Sergio was stationed in a trench in the Alps, east of Bolzano, and Dario in an Army cafeteria nearby. Both positions were overrun by the Austrian-German Army.

Sergio and Dario were injured and placed in the same Austrian Army hospital north of Bolzano on the border between Italy and Austria. The Army converted a rundown hotel into a makeshift hospital. Sergio was exposed to poisonous gas used by the German Army in trench warfare. Dario was injured when a bomb exploded in his kitchen, as he was about to serve breakfast at the Italian Officers Club. Dario's chest and stomach areas were pockmarked with shrapnel wounds. Sergio developed a fever and cough. Upon further medical examination, Sergio had contracted the Spanish flu. Immediately, he was placed in a special hospital. The mortality rate was rather low if the flu was detected early.

The second wave of the Spanish flu caused the most deaths in the Italian Army's hospitals. The flu claimed the lives of 100 to 150 people in the town of Avella alone. Sergio was lucky to be alive since he had contracted the flu one month before the end of WWI in October of 1918. Frankly, it was not clear at that time whether a particular army group or the flu won the battle in the final push by the Italian Army toward Venice in 1918. Sergio was eventually released after a one-month stay. Hospitalization gave him plenty of time to think about his imminent future. By then, Sergio was exposed to the world of the gentry and felt comfortable with the thought of doing something other than shepherding. Sergio also looked forward to seeing the new arrival to his family—his four-year-old daughter Sofia.

Forever acting like the big brother to Dario, Sergio paid a visit to see how he was doing. Dario was so happy to see his dear friend Sergio visiting him. The first thing that Dario did was to motion with his hand toward the cabinet next to his bed. Sergio opened the small drawer to see a letter addressed to Dario's parents. Sergio wanted to embrace Dario assuring him that the letter would personally be delivered, but Sergio was too afraid to hurt him by doing so. Dario was bandaged from head to toe. Sergio slightly turned his head so that he could hide his emotions, and, instead, gently shook Dario's hand.

By the time WWI ended, the Austrian Army discharged Sergio from quarantine quarters and transferred him to an Italian Army hospital in Bolzano. He was looking forward to going home to see his first-born child that he had not yet seen and to reassure Dario's parents that Dario would be fine. Anxiety built up to the point that at every train stop, he would ask the train master how many more hours to Naples. In between stops, he occupied his mind by trying to picture what his child and wife looked like, and how the rest of his neighborhood friends were holding up.

The Austrian Army hospital staff transferred Dario to a modern-day hospital in Vienna equipped with advanced surgical tools to perform the delicate surgery to remove the shrapnel embedded all over his body. There was no X-ray equipment in the Army hospital to precisely locate each shrapnel, especially the tiny ones. In particular, the Vienna General Hospital—Allgemeines Krankenhaus der Stadt Wien— ranked at that time as one of the leading university hospitals in the world and, most importantly to Dario, was equipped with the latest X-ray equipment. The hospital was located about five miles West of the Danube River and near the center of Vienna. On the way to Vienna, Dario could identify himself with the mountains surrounding the Brenner Pass. After all, he was still a shepherd at heart. He pictured himself carving a living there. However, not as a shepherd. The only problem with that thinking was that he most likely would be shipped back to Avella after surgery. Shipping Dario to Avella before surgery would have been tantamount to putting him to death and no Viennese doctor would want that on their conscience, especially when the source of the shrapnel came from an Austrian bomb.

Surgery was scheduled the day after Dario's arrival. Guided by the X-ray pictures, his surgery was broken down into two stages: critical and non-critical. In the critical stage, the chief surgeon operated in the morning removing two shrapnel near the heart and artery. During the non-critical stage in the afternoon, medical interns removed all the shrapnel from Dario's torso and legs. While still under sedation, the wounds were washed and cleaned by nurse Anneliese. She knew from whatever limited information available that Dario was a shepherd but was surprised that he could also be Jewish. That was not very common in the Jewish community in Vienna. She ought to know since she was Jewish. Her family resided in the Alsergrund District of Vienna hugging the western side of the Danube Canal. Mostly, lower- and middle-class Jewish people lived there—manual laborers, craftsmen, and small-scale businessmen such as café owners and traders.

Anneliese surmised that Dario was a Sephardic Jew since his name implied the region or town adopted by his family when Jews were expelled from Spain during the Inquisition period. The following morning, Anneliese served breakfast, and she was all smiles. Dario knew why. She had every reason to be thankful to God for having introduced Dario to her—he was Jewish, a shepherd, and all alone. She was on a mission to find out more and take care of him.

But culturally, they were as different as night and day. Dario was not familiar with procedural matters in hospitals. For one thing, shepherds didn't reach that level of sophistication or modernization. In some sense, Dario entered the twilight zone of modern civilization. He was not religious, but Anneliese was. Academically, he completed five years of elementary school, whereas Anneliese attended the gymnasium school in Vienna, which was equivalent to thirteen years of schooling in the United States, besides nursing school. Fortunately, Anneliese could converse a little in Italian, as she took Latin and Italian courses in school, but it didn't help much as Dario spoke with a Neapolitan dialect. Yes, there were many barriers between the two, but she was on a mission to overcome them.

Once Dario overcame his shyness, he too was on the same mission. Their conversations became more personal. Anneliese admired Dario's honesty and humility, as well as his physicality. Being a shepherd, Dario loved all mountains, including the ones in Austria, in particular the Brenner Pass. He also had a passion for cooking. In short, Anneliese wanted to pack him in a gift box, take him home, and introduce him to her parents. That had to wait until the hospital released him, another modern regulation not well understood by Dario as he was raring to go and explore

Vienna and visit Anneliese's parents. Indeed, love removed whatever barriers that may have existed between the two.

On the day of his hospital release, Anneliese dressed Dario in a suit and tie which was something of a new experience for Dario, but he went along with it only to please Anneliese. She was all bubbly about the occasion about to happen. Dario was going to ask her parents, Gisella and Martin Levy, for her hand in marriage. The family belonged to the Ashkenazi religious group which predominated in Vienna in comparison to the Sephardic, Orthodox, and other Jewish denominations. Of course, she would translate it all. Yes, the parents loved him within a second of his entry to their apartment. They could tell from his body language that he was a man brought up with proper manners and respectful of others. Also, they sensed that Anneliese could not be any happier. Of course, Anneliese had been telling them everything about Dario.

But then all of a sudden, Dario began to stutter. He had never been that nervous before. What's more, he had rehearsed what he was going to say numerous times. However, the Levy family just chucked it off and celebrated the occasion. Dario wanted to convey in the strongest terms that he planned to reside permanently in Vienna with Anneliese. They were all smiles as this was what they wanted to hear. Furthermore, he planned to follow in Sergio's footsteps and embark on a new career as a cook. When Gisella and Martin heard that, it was like hearing music to their ears. However, the two of them heard different tunes.

Martin owned a bakery about a city block from their apartment. On the way to school, Anneliese would often stop by her father's bakery to munch on a pastry with a chocolate drink. On weekends, she would work as a cashier. His immediate thought, regarding Dario's announcement, was that he was going to help him launch a career as a baker and keep the business in the family. As to Gisella, she was thinking along a similar line but slightly different. She worked as a maid part-time for a very wealthy Jewish family in the Dobling District where affluent residents lived. The district was located slightly north of the Alsegrund District, but still west of the Danube Canal.

Most Jews in Vienna settled in the Leopoldstadt, Brigittenau, Alsergrund, Dobling along the Danube Canal, Innere Stadt in central Vienna, and Hietzing, which was about five miles west of the canal districts as of 1919. Jewish people made up about 10% of Vienna's population of 2 million. This did not include about 3% of mixed marriages between Jewish and Christian couples. If one were to analyze the correlation between class standing and the location where Jews resided along the canal, one would discover that the poor class was located at one end of Leopoldstadt and the wealthy ones at the other end of the Dobling District, almost a linear correlation. About 400 BC, Celtic tribes invaded the eastern Alps and established the kingdom of Noricum, the first state of Austrian territory. Romans appeared in the kingdom about 100-150 BC and the region became part of the Roman Empire.

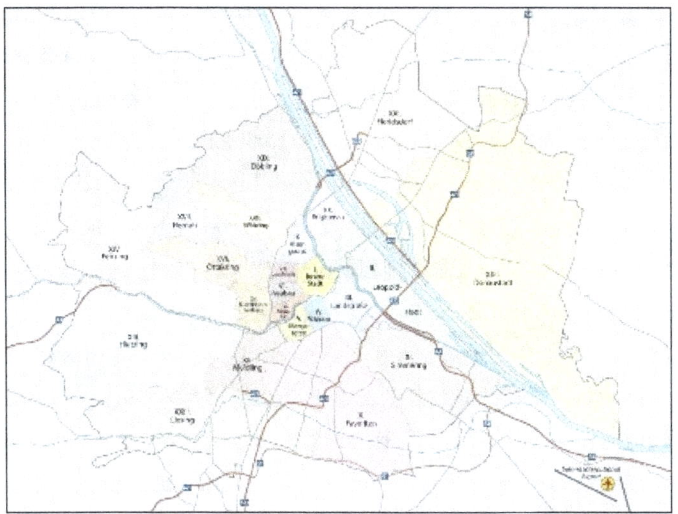

Map of Vienna's districts, courtesy of www.dreamstime.com

As usual for the Roman occupiers, an extensive road system opened the territory to the rest of the Roman Empire. Most likely, the road system connecting to the rest of the Roman Empire in Italy went through the Brenner Pass as it is called today. The history of Jews in Austria began with the transport of Jews from Judea by the Roman Centurion armies. Romans discovered an advanced civilization of scholars, doctors, writers, craftsmen, etc.

Roman legions had much to learn from this advanced civilization and, therefore, transported Jews to various Roman colonies and Rome as slaves. However, it didn't take very long for these slaves to gain full Roman citizenship—Plebeians. The first Jewish-Roman war occurred around 62 BC when Pompey was the emperor. About 1,000 and 1,500 years later, there were second, third, and other waves of Jewish immigration to Austria, including Sephardic Jews from Spain, for example. Jewish communities prospered throughout Europe and enjoyed political equality. But during other periods, Jewish communities suffered pogroms, deportations, mass murders, and anti-Semitism—in the Middle Ages, for example.

Gisella worked as an all-purpose maid to the Herzog family in the Dobling District which included father Harold, wife Sarah, and daughters Nanna and Suzanna. Sarah and Gisella were long-distance cousins by marriage. Whereas Harold was Jewish and an Austrian citizen, his first Jewish cousin Herbert Herzog kept his Polish citizenship. Their ancestors flip-flopped residences between Poland and Austria depending on the political climate against Jews in the two countries. Herbert's villa was located across the street from his cousin's estate. He was a gregarious and charming playboy. He was married to Ala with two children, but it didn't stop him from having mistresses in Cortina D'Ampezzo, St. Moritz, Berlin, Warsaw, etc. It's almost impossible to estimate how many illegitimate children he fathered all over Europe.

On the other hand, Harold was just the opposite—a settled-down family man, civic leader, and respected by his peers. However, they had something in common. They were real estate speculators who bought rental properties, land, abandoned buildings, etc. Herbert specialized in the search for opportunities or speculations since he was the one who traveled all over Europe. Harold did the research on potential investments proposed by Herbert. The contract between the two was just a simple handshake. But for some strange reason, they decided that properties in Austria should only have Herbert's name on it and in Poland Harold's. This may have been a way to protect themselves against political turmoil against Jews in those two countries. Clearly, they were well aware of past turmoil.

The Herzog cousins were employed by the Ruhrchemie Company whose headquarters was located in Dusseldorf with branches all over Germany and in Vienna. The CEO of the Vienna Branch was Bernhard Worten. Bernhard, Herbert, and Harold were classmates at Vienna Technical University. Bernhard and Herbert majored in business administration with a minor in accounting, whereas Harold majored in chemical engineering. Harold aspired to be a research scientist with the purpose of developing new applications, but the other two were something else. It was a mystery how they were able to graduate and have a good time all over town. All three were employed in about the same year. The company dealt mostly with the export of coal throughout Europe. Bernhard rose through the ranks because his father-in-law groomed Bernhard to replace himself as the next CEO. His buddy Herbert came along for the ride to the company's board of directors, whereas Harold kept his nose close to the grindstone on coal research and development. Life was good for the cousins as they moved to the Dobling District next to Bernhard's estate. Forever the speculator, Herbert suggested to Harold that they should invest in real estate and land since there were many abandoned buildings after WWI due to unemployment and economic turmoil. Harold was taken aback since he didn't know beans about real estate and neither did Herbert.

Prior to the twentieth century, Germany possessed an abundance of coal reserves in the Ruhr Valley to fulfill commercial, industrial, military, and home heating needs. With the appearance, soon after, of automobiles, airplanes, motorcycles, etc., it changed Germany's fuel requirements. Petroleum was the fuel of choice in the early 1920s. A crash program was initiated then in Germany to convert coal into synthetic petroleum. Coal hydrogenation produced high-quality aviation, motor gasoline or benzene, diesel fuel, and lubrication products. The main chemical companies that produced synthetic fuels were IG Farben and Ruhrchemie. Not much changed in the duties of Bernhard, Herbert, and Harold, except Herbert and Bernhard had to search for new markets utilizing the new fuel in Europe. This meant that both Herbert and Bernhard had plenty of opportunities to revert to old times by taking excursion trips to resort towns in Europe.

In particular, Gisella had double duties as a maid and a cook in the Herzog household, since the previous cook died soon after the war due to chest wounds at the Battle of Veneto/Venice in North Italy. She explained to her cousin Sarah that while she was cooking there for the Herzog family, a professional chef was doing the same at her household. For example, she elaborated that he could cook the most exquisite dishes of Hungarian goulash, in addition to French, Italian, and Scandinavian cuisine. Gisella mentioned Hungarian goulash only to entice Sarah since she knew that it was Sarah's favorite dish. Gisella suggested that it would make sense to have him cook for the Herzog family so that she could return to cooking for her family. Without hesitation, Sarah said, "Bring him over, and let's see what he can cook."

Dario's menu at the Herzogs was vast. Ricotta cheese was produced in the morning and fed to the family hot and fresh with marmalade. The family truly enjoyed the unique taste. Hard cheese was produced by curing the ricotta cheese in smoke. For a shepherd, this was rather routine, but it impacted the family greatly. The eggs were prepared in many different ways with various condiments. Variety was the order of the day in preparing the meals. Dario prepared the big meal in the early afternoon when the girls and the father came home from school and work. Sarah gave Dario a day's notice as to what she wanted for the big meal and potential guests' wish list. In the evening, a light meal was served. The wines of choice were produced in the Dolomites region, east of Venice. Refrigeration was a problem in the summer which was another reason to serve fresh food every day.

In all, Dario's dream came true. He was able to practice his passion for cooking, which he held since childhood, and be with a woman he loved surrounded by mountains. Yes, Dario and Anneliese got married and started a family in Vienna. Dario's parents were introduced to the Levys at the wedding. Dario's father was proud of his son's achievements, returning to Avella a happy man.

As in Avella, there were four close-knit families within five city blocks of each other in Vienna—the families of Harold, Herbert, Bernhard, and Martin. It was amazing how life changed in mysterious ways in those days in both enclaves, as some members of the Vienna enclave eventually would meet the other enclave of friendly families in Avella. In both towns, it came down to a life-and-death struggle for survival. Sarah managed the purchased properties while the two men, Herbert and Harold, argued the pros and cons of the next purchase of property. In addition, she collected rent and interest from bank deposits and other investments, and disbursed payments to the gardeners, plumbers, maids, the cook, and whoever made up the additional help. Her taste for clothes was impeccable—the latest fashion from Paris, Milan, and Berlin—which included dresses, coats, and shoes made to order.

Once a month, sometimes more, there was a dinner party in which the guests included family members, close friends, the usual gang of three—Herbert, Martin, and Bernhard—as well as such dignitaries as musicians, poets, painters, politicians, government officials, and special guests of honor such as a singer or piano player. The dress was formal with the men wearing tails and the women gowns. Gisella borrowed a gown from Sarah only for that night in case Sarah changed her mind on a later occasion. The children were placed in a separate quarter in the garden area. They were cared for by Anneliese whose four-year-old child was among them. The two teenage girls, Nanna and Suzanna, were only there to compare notes with their mother Sarah about people attending the gala night. They were into boys and people in general. Nanna was more of an extrovert, like her mother, who liked to socialize at these dinners.

Nanna had been taking piano lessons from a young prodigy cello player, Ehrlich Wolf, who worked at the Vienna State Opera or Wiener Staatsoper, where the Herzog family had season tickets. Herbert arranged for Ehrlich to play Chopin's piano compositions at one of those gala receptions. As usual, Uncle Herbert was up to something mischievous. He induced, perhaps, bribed, Ehrlich to give piano lessons to Nanna since he heard so much from his friends in Warsaw about Ehrlich's piano competition there. Ehrlich won the Chopin competition in Warsaw in the junior class. True to his devil-may-care attitude, he contacted Ehrlich directly about giving lessons to his niece. He did not consult Harold knowing full well that he would frown upon it. The truth of the matter was that Nanna had a crush on him after a couple of lessons.

Ehrlich belied his delicate and angel face. He was a strict disciplinarian but otherwise respectful and very gentle. Nanna would attend those dinner parties with the hope that the mother would invite Ehrlich to play some of Chopin's beautiful piano concerts. The mother was well aware of Nanna's sentiments, but she didn't want to rush things. Ehrlich demanded adherence to what was composed, including every note. Sometimes Nanna would wander off into some other tunes just to break the monotony of repetition. Her interests were more of the personal kind. She was looking for a little smile or tenderness from him. But there was no compromise with him. Until they reached a stalemate.

After a couple of hours of constant badgering for perfection, Nanna wilted like a flower and walked out of the lesson. Sarah called Herbert to patch things up between the two until the next session. Again, there was no give on either side. This went on for quite a while until Uncle Herbert, forever the mediator, negotiated peace between the two—no more Franz Liszt piano compositions. Clearly, they were artists with a preference. The fact that they got together again meant that they were willing to give it a go, expecting some tenderness from either side. Of course, after a while, it went beyond artistry. Once again, Uncle Herbert came to the rescue for he could see that they were made for each other. Nanna and Ehrlich eventually happily married.

However, Suzanna was an introvert, much like her father, and a serious student of classic literature—Dante Alighieri, Shakespeare, Greek philosophy, etc. She and Nanna attended a private girls' school. In the summer, both girls went to summer camp near Innsbruck and enjoyed boating and swimming in a river nearby. In the winter, they went skating and, on the way home, they stopped at their favorite cafe to enjoy their favorite dessert, apple strudel with chocolate. Also, it was a stop-over for other teenage skaters.

This idyllic life came to an abrupt end by the mid-1920s. Antisemitism was strongest in Vienna during times of political turmoil and economic hardships. To what extent these turn of events in Vienna were correlated with the rise of the Nazi

Party was not clear. All political parties and private clubs were anti-Semitic, except for the Socialist Party. One law demanded that since Jews made up 10 percent of the population in Vienna, they should only fill 10 percent of the positions in commerce, law, medicine, banking, newspaper publishing, and higher education. It just so happened that these were the fields in which Jews predominated.

This presented quite a dilemma to the Jewish population. They made up 65 percent of Vienna's lawyers, 59 percent of physicians, and 50 percent of journalists. Jewish students made up 30 percent of the student body of the Viennese gymnasium. The fact that more and more vacation spas and hotels excluded Jewish guests contributed to them taking more vacations abroad. Italy benefited from this boycott. In particular, Dario had the dual role of being a cook and a tourist guide. Of course, he would guide the close-knit family of Vienna to meet the one in Avella and also guide them along the Sorrentine Peninsula or closer to the beaches of Rimini or the Italian or French Riviera. But things were getting nastier by the day.

In 1927, public violence entered the political discourse. Austria was now on the road to civil war, creating a Fascist Corporate State. In 1929, Nazi hooligans roamed the streets of Leopoldstadt and attacked cafés and small business establishments, as instigated by the Christian Social Party and the Greater German People Party.

About this time, Herbert insisted that his wife take the children to Palestine while they could because the streets were no longer safe in Vienna. Most likely, Bernhard, who was a gentile, advised Herbert to do so. He had a much better view of things to come. He promised that his company would protect him and Harold as long as possible, and, if necessary, the two of them would be warned when to panic. In the 1930s, Vienna Jews were divided politically. One group voted for Social Democrats and the other for strictly Jewish parties. Eventually, both groups voted for the Social Democrat Party, unifying their votes against the Fascist parties. Unfortunately, the votes were not sufficient enough to make a difference.

Jewish students at the University of Vienna were confronted with violence never encountered before. The German Student Organization of Vienna demanded enrollment restrictions for Jewish students, as enacted at universities in Vienna. Austrian Nazi thugs escorted Jewish students out of classrooms and threw them out in the streets, often injured. Jewish professors were regularly harassed during lectures. Not only were the streets unsafe, but the whole administration turned its back on what was happening. All of this occurred while the police stood by without interfering.

In 1933, the Enabling Act gave Hitler and his German ministers all legislative control. This meant that if things were bad before, they could only get worse soon after the passage of the act in Austria and in Sudetenland. In Austria, parliament was dissolved and in February of 1934, as civil war broke out, the Democratic constitution was suspended. Vienna no longer had an elected legislature. A Fascist authoritative government—Standestäat—took over the government instead. By then, Nanna and Ehrlich were married and expecting a child soon.

Bernhard warned the two cousins that the worst had yet to come. In a somber mood, he said: "The nut case [Hitler] had adopted in his book, *Mein Kampf,* the measures of King Albert V in 1420, when the king imprisoned, killed, deported Jews and expropriated Jewish properties". So, Bernhard advised them to do the trivial matter of transferring money from Austrian banks to ones in neutral countries like Switzerland, the United States, England, etc. Herbert organized the transfer of the entire Herzog family deposits since he did many business transactions in Switzerland and to a lesser extent in the United States and England. Thus, Herbert took care of the family and the money, but the real estate acquisitions remained to be a big problem. Hope vanished with the enactment of the Nuremberg racial laws.

The Nuremberg Law stipulated that only "pure" Germans could hold German citizenship. This meant that Jews could not be citizens of Germany and forbade intermarriage of "pure" Germans and Jews. Applications of the law excluded Jews from employment not only in Germany but also in Austria. Harold and Herbert worked for Ruhrchemie headquartered in Germany. The two cousins understood the implications to their real estate holdings. So, they acted fast before the law was implemented in Austria. Herbert sold their holdings in Austria since he was a Polish citizen. In Germany, they didn't know anyone they could trust to maintain the holdings. In Poland, the law was yet to be applied, not until Germany occupied that country after 1939. Basically, they put their real estate holdings in Germany and Poland in their names with the hope that they would not be noticed since they resided in Austria. At worst, they may have to reclaim their properties in Germany via the courts.

Herbert truly appreciated his friend's tips or warnings about Nazi's intentions, but, being the instigator of irregular ideas, he felt that the Herzog family should have a plan in hand to escape from the clutches of the Nazis. The idea was to stay one step ahead of the Nazis' intentions. His ace in the cards was none other than his old friend Bernhard who had provided so far very insightful information which the Herzogs had utilized. In the meantime, they hoped to remain in Vienna until better times. They were cautious of street stormtroopers and minimized any contact with city officials who were Nazi sympathizers. Ehrlich still played the cello at the opera house, but he could sense that the selection of operas drifted toward the Wagnerian type of operas favored by Nazi sympathizers. It was time for him to bail out of Vienna.

During a break in the opera season, early in January of 1938, Ehrlich's and Dario's families, including wives and children, visited Avella for dual purposes. Dario needed a vacation and Ehrlich explored possibilities of living in Italy until this Nazi madness blew away. In addition, Dario wanted to introduce his son, Sergio, to his parents and introduce Ehrlich to another famous cello player, Don Nicola. It was too premature to start looking for employment. In the opera world, Ehrlich was well-known and respected. He and Nanna left their three-year-old daughter, Arya, to grandmother Sarah.

In Avella, Ehrlich and Don Nicola got along splendidly. It was not every day that two world-famous cello players went out of their way to meet and talk about operas. How could they not, they were both avowed Socialists. Don Nicola was overcome with emotions because for once he didn't have to argue too hard about the virtue of Socialism. Also, he knew very well why Ehrlich was there. Don Nicola informed Ehrlich that soon he would be promoted to conductor at the San Carlo Opera House and that management would be delighted to replace one cello player with another world-famous one like him. That was music to Ehrlich's ears.

Dario's parents hugged and kissed Sergio to the point that Sergio Jr. was embarrassed by it all, as any child would. When the adult Sergio was introduced to the child, he broke down in tears embracing him. Naturally, he was honored to have a child named after him. Nobody ever honored him for anything. He kept looking at his, not so little anymore, adopted brother, Dario, as if to say thank you. After these acquaintances, it was time to meet the rest of the clan. As usual, Sergio invited the rest of the clan to welcome the guest of honor—Nanna and Ehrlich, Anneliese, and one of their own, Dario and his son—to a dinner get-together in the courtyard. Erminio pitched in to bring spumante wine from his shop for the celebration. Usually, Sergio invited the clan into the garden, but, in the wintertime, it could get somewhat nippy. Winds off the mountains can be more than a nuisance.

The list included the four musketeers—Ramiro, Don Nicola, Da Alia, Di Marelli—as well as Mario and Sofia, Filomena and Serafina, etc. The Viennese guests were overwhelmed by this spontaneous welcome from total strangers. Of course, Dario helped out in preparing the food. The music was provided by the local band of five musicians and the singing of Neapolitan songs by the four musketeers, drunk by then.

The next day, Don Nicola escorted the guests to a guided tour of Naples' historical sites and, of course, the San Carlo Opera House. They boarded the 8:11 a.m. train from Avella station to Naples. Most often, the 8:11 train was not on time, as advertised by the local Fascists. However, Don Nicola was a happy man because he could converse with someone, besides Mario, about Socialism and Fascism and discovered someone who was an extremely competent cello player to replace him when promoted to a conductor. In an interesting factoid, most opera conductors are usually former cello players. They rented a horse-drawn carrozza or carriage and headed toward the most beautiful scenery—the Posillipo District of Naples and the Baia Bay. The sun was smiling upon the passengers, as the carrozza made its way through the Spanish, French, and Arabic quarters of antiquity and finally to the Baia Bay where Roman senators, emperors, and generals vacationed.

Don Nicola loved to compare the different styles of architecture and the interesting personalities of Roman times. He loved to say, "I am more Roman than the modern-day Romans." His Jewish descendants were in Rome well before Saint Peter appeared on the scene asking for directions to downtown Rome. At the smaller bay in Baia, the carrozza waited for the passengers to view the whole Bay of Naples and in the opposite direction, the islands of Procida, Ischia, and Capri.

Posillipo District: It hugs the coastline of Naples to the smaller bay, Baia.
Courtesy of Pomona Pictures.

Lunch was prepared for them at Zi Maria restaurant courtesy of management at the San Carlo Opera House. They had local mozzarella from Ravello and lettuce for antipasto, a pasta dish of macaroni and porcini mushrooms in white sauce, fresh octopus in red sauce and mussels, and finally spumoni ice cream with fresh strawberries doused with anisette. The San Carlo management office was located across the street from the restaurant. They wanted to know about Ehrlich's experience at the Chopin competition in Warsaw, not so much about the cello experience, since they knew all about Ehrlich's reputation as a passionate player of the cello. Don Nicola must have done some prior brainwashing of the management. They wanted to know if Ehlich could adapt to Naples or vice versa. It was not an interview per se. They all felt that this was the man that they hoped to get interested in San Carlo.

After that brief exchange, the visitors headed back to Avella. The Viennese group was left alone to do whatever they wished—visit historic sites in Avella or go to a tourist town like Ravello or Amalfi. They decided to roam around Avella and get to know the people and character of the town in the few days left on their visit. Dario and Sergio served as their guide. Since the Viennese group loved mountains as much as the shepherds, they opted to go hiking on a hill nearby to search for wild porcini mushrooms which also grow in the hills of Vienna. However, at that time of the year, most of the mushrooms are poisonous. Both Dario and Sergio could easily identify which ones were poisonous, usually the colorful ones. They enjoyed being in the mountains, especially when hotels and resort places in the mountains of Austria were not very accessible to the Jewish people in the late 1930s. In general, harassment by stormtroopers and Nazi sympathizers in the streets of Vienna was building to a crescendo.

Where the street turmoil was heading in the streets of Vienna, it was difficult to predict at that time. People knew it was going to be bad for the Jewish residents. Yet, they did nothing about it. Harassment by Fascist thugs in the streets of Avella peaked in the early 1930s, but, in Vienna, it went unabated. In the Leopoldstradt and Innere districts, where the Jewish population was mostly concentrated, the harassment by stormtroopers increased daily. Non-Jewish residents and police officers looked the other way. Jewish residents were identified with the yellow Star of David on their garments. Districts in the suburbs of Vienna also suffered the indignities of the thugs, such as being forced to clean the streets with a small brush. Again, most of the Viennese residents seemed to enjoy the spectacle. Of course, Jews feared for their lives even then.

The trip back to Vienna was uneventful. Ehrlich returned in time for the resumption of the opera season. They could tell from the intensity of harassment in the streets of Vienna, as compared to Avella, that something was brewing and it was not very pleasant. Indeed, on March 12, 1938, German troops entered Austria. A formal referendum vote on April 10 was announced to formally annex Austria as part of German territory. Referred to as the Anschluss referendum, it also forbade Jews and Romanis from exercising their right to vote.

Herbert sprang into action. He and Bernhard arranged for everyone to leave Austria before April 10 because after that date German Nazi laws such as the Nuremberg racial laws applied to the citizens of Austria and it would be pure hell. He made sure that the clan of friends had their visa papers in order and travel arrangements. Herbert departed for Poland, and Harold and Sarah left for St. Moritz. The Wolf family—Ehrlich, Nanna, and Arya—returned to Avella to reside in one of Sergio's apartments. The Levys left together with their son-in-law's family to settle in Palestine, via Brindisi. Bernhard remained in Vienna, sad to see his friends depart. Claudio Di Marelli and wife joined his son's family later in Palestine. Their dream was to someday return to Vienna. Unfortunately, thereafter, catastrophe hit the Jewish people of Vienna.

Suzanna, the daughter of Harold and Sarah, did not want to leave and stayed with a farmer family near Vienna. By then, Suzanna was recognized as a scholar in classic literature and the first one in the Herzog family to receive a Ph.D. in sociology from the University of Vienna. She hoped all the harassment, physical intimidation, and persecution of Jews throughout Vienna and, especially, at universities would end. Jewish students were physically prevented from attending classes at universities and, sometimes, dragged out of classes and beaten up. Jewish attendance in the gymnasium schools in Vienna reduced from 30 percent to much less than 10 percent.

It was too late to leave the agony behind after the Anschluss. The Jews of Vienna suffered immensely. To leave Austria, they had to pay taxes in the order of 50 percent to 75 percent of the value of their properties. To add insult to injury, the Nazi regime took over possession of their properties and other valuable items. In other German-speaking territories, Jews suffered the same consequences. Alternative European nations were quickly dwindling. Except for one: Italy was the only country in Europe that did not require an entry visa.

THREE

Run for the Hills

In the 1920s, Mussolini regarded Italian Jews as Italians. On several occasions, Mussolini spoke favorably about Jewish contribution to Italian society in general and the Zionist movement. Italian Jews occupied important jobs in Fascist courts, police departments, and the armed forces. For example, Da Alia was chief of city hall. Don Nicola and Da Alia's families never felt threatened by the Fascist government. Nevertheless, Don Nicola had to be very selective as to whom he addressed his Socialist diatribes against Fascism.

It was not until November 1938, that Hitler prevailed on Mussolini to introduce racial laws in Italy. As for the shepherds and farmers, it made no difference what imposition the Fascist government put on them. They were going to do things their way and that was the end of it. As for the artisans, professionals, and the gentry in general, they were a threat to Fascism. They had the means and, perhaps, the incentives to rebel against Fascism. In short, the thugs did not want Don Nicola to wake up a sleeping giant.

The other purpose of the thugs was to quell any local insurrection against the regime and to keep tabs on anyone who acted too aggressively against the regime. In some sense, the locals were held prisoners of these street Fascists. People could not speak their minds. There was no love lost between Don Nicola and them. His friends were forever warning him to keep his distance from them. The thugs knew very well about Don Nicola's Socialist views against Fascism. They were forever goading him whenever they met in the streets and they would have loved nothing better than to have him incarcerated. Don Nicola was a marked man. He had to be more selective in unloading his diatribes on the people of Avella. However, he did have an outlet;

musicians at the opera house in Naples were all anti-Fascist.

At the end of the day, he took the train in Naples to go home. He often would stop at Erminio's wine store/restaurant before going home and chit-chat about the latest gossip of that delusional man, Mussolini. The Fascist thugs were well aware of Don Nicola's routine. They planted a Fascist detective in civilian clothes to eavesdrop on their conversations. The purpose was to label Don Nicola as a political dissident and, therefore, a security risk to the state. Eventually, they would have placed Don Nicola in jail, losing the key to the jailhouse.

All came to naught when Erminio recognized the detective as a Fascist from the nearby town of Sperone. Erminio lived in Sperone where everyone in town knew everybody else. It was a very small town on the other side of Avella's train station. Erminio shouted at the detective, "Eh guaglione, va fa Napule!" That's the universal language in Naples for what a person could do with himself. The word guaglione implied an immature punk, as the detective scampered away like a rabbit. That was the end of chasing down Don Nicola all over town to frame him.

Before Fascism showed its face in Avella, the gentry and the peasants tended to be apolitical. But with Fascism on the horizon, they split up into various party affiliations. For example, the peasant class was divided between the apolitical shepherds and farmers on one side and the unskilled laborers who worked as handymen in farms, cafés, and at odd jobs, and who sympathized with Communism on the other. Thus, the peasant class was mostly apolitical or Communist. Similarly, the gentry was split between the professionals who were mostly Socialists, and the very wealthy Monarchists. Overall, the gentry couldn't care less, as long they were left alone to do their thing. They flip-flopped depending on where the benefits resided. The shepherds, in general, were too proud to be intimidated by Fascist thugs roaming the streets. They disappeared into the mountains, waiting for better days to return to the valley. Professionals and Socialists detested the Fascist Blackshirts as well as the Communists. There was no happiness in the streets of Avella.

As such, the Communists, the shepherd community, and the Socialists truly loathed each other. Whereas shepherds were apolitical but fiercely independent, more like anarchists, not depending on anyone or the government for a living, the West end crowd of Communists expounded forever the virtues of a revolution. They believed that only through a revolution could the upper class and the church be forced to share their wealth. The Socialists didn't believe in revolution, but their aims were similar to the Communists. The role of the Fascist Blackshirts was basically to separate these groups of people from each other, as they cordoned off the riffraffs on either side of the Piazza—east and west. The Blackshirts aimed to protect the industrialists, landowners, and other wealthy people who financially supported their movement in the early stages.

By then, everyone in Avella was aware of the Blackshirt members of the Fascist Party. They consisted of Army veterans, former or retired police officers, and unemployed bullies. The Fascist Party, headquartered in Rome, paid for their employment. But they were everywhere. In short, there was no place to hide.

Besides keeping the opposition parties at bay, the Fascist Party concentrated on converting the young. In the spring, a Fascist official visited local schools to talk about the grandiose projects of Fascism. Children dressed in school uniforms applauded every word the man delivered under the direction of their teacher, although the children had no idea what the man was talking about. Fascists appealed to the young ones with festive appearances, sporting events, and parades. Parents had no choice, but to acquiesce to the propaganda being staged.

The Main Street of Avella, Corso Vittorio Emanuele, runs east to west; Nola and Naples are south and southwest, relative to the street, respectively. At the east end, toward the foothills, the neighborhood consisted mostly of shepherds and few professionals. The few political ones tended to be Socialists. They advocated social changes within the framework of a democratic government—no revolution. As Main Street wound toward the west, more artisan stores appeared, as did tailors, convenience stores, cafés, bakeries, pharmacies, professional offices, etc. City hall and the main piazza were located roughly halfway through Main Street. Well-to-do families, industrialists, land owners, doctors' offices, politicians, and elitists lived there. At the other end of Main Street, the west end, lived mostly farmhands, and unskilled workers whose allegiance leaned toward the Communist Party. They also advocated social changes but, through a revolution of the classes, much like the Bolshevik revolution.

One thing the Blackshirts could not prevent was the gossip in the streets of Avella about Mussolini's love life. Mussolini's new mistress, Clara Petacci, was in her mid-twenties when she met Mussolini, who was in his mid-forties. They met at a beach resort in Ostia, east of Rome, as Mussolini's car traveled with his caravan on his way to give a speech on the Pontine Marsh project south of Anzio. The caravan stopped as people cheered and waved along the side of the road. Mussolini, forever looking for adulation and his next conquest, was mesmerized by Clara's blonde hair and her exuberance to meet "Il Duce," the leader.

He did oblige. Her mother was also equally an avid supporter and admirer of Mussolini. Not long after, Clara arranged for her mother to meet the Duce. Mussolini did not discriminate between young and old, as long as they adored him. The next meeting with Clara was in his huge office located in Piazza Venezia. There he seduced her on the carpeted floor. Gossip about the new mistress was running wild in local newspapers and popular magazines. It was perplexing that those stories appeared publicly, given censorship, and how he secretly hand-picked the editors of national newspapers and magazines.

Clara Petacci kept a detailed account of the time she spent with the Duce in a personal diary which was seized by Italian authorities in 1949, and was released for public viewing only in 2009. It is now considered an important record of the private life of the dictator and sheds light on a side of his character that was long unexplored by historians. Her records conform to his image as a man of power and physical daring, which was central to the virile cult of Fascism. However, it also exposes the fact that he was a boastful man who often needed others to pamper his ego by telling him how handsome or virile he looked, how much women and the Italian people loved him, and how he was a genius much like Napoleon and Caesar. Interestingly, it was Clara who recorded how dull a conjugal life Mussolini had with his wife Rachele and how he kept up to five lovers at one time when he was younger.

Claretta Petacci was born on February 28, 1912, in Rome, Italy, to Dr. Francesco Saverio Petacci and his wife Giuseppina Persichetti Petacci. Her father was a primary physician of Pope Pius XI. She was genteelly reared in an upper-class Catholic family and, as a child, studied music with violinist Corrado Archibugi, a family friend. By the time she became romantically involved with Benito Mussolini in 1932, she was engaged to a man named Riccardo Federici, a lieutenant in the Air Force. Her family reportedly supported her affair with the dictator to climb the social ladder. She married Federici in 1934, but they separated soon after.

There is a myriad of history attached to Mussolini's love life. For one thing, people in town did not want to praise Fascism because they knew that it was corrupt. Castigating the man or the Fascist government would have landed that person in jail. Thus, by default, the safest thing to talk about was the love life of Il Duce. One could just imagine the rumor mill in those days in Avella and other small towns. Any political conversations would have had repercussions. One favorite topic of conversation then was the emotional state of Mussolini's wife, Donna Rachele. His previous marriage to Ida Dalser produced a son whom he never acknowledged. When he became prime minister, Ida and their son were incarcerated. Other love affairs included the ones with a Russian Jewish emigré, Angelica Balabanoff, and a married woman, Fernanda Facchinelli. He then married his first mistress Rachele Guidi and they had five children, two girls and three boys. Thereafter, Mussolini had several mistresses and brief sexual escapades with female political supporters. In the end, he died in the arms of Clara Petacci.

The people of Avella, as well as the rest of Italy, viewed Mussolini as vain and corrupt and their patience was running out. To counter this mood, the Fascist government instituted a program in which it financially subsidized large families. However, the real intent was to reach an artificial goal of a population of 60 million people. Only then could Italy support a viable army large enough to fight in Europe, as argued by Il Duce. The population then was forty million.

Il Duce also argued for people to donate their gold wedding rings, necklaces, earrings, jewelry, etc., to the government. Thus, the Fascist government gave in one hand and received in the other. People were fed up and had no choice but to wait and see if improvements to their living conditions were forthcoming from the regime. The other choice was to spend time in jail or be publicly ostracized by the thugs. It is not clear at what stage submission entered people's minds.

During the Ethiopian War from 1935–1936, Mario was assigned to a transport ship by the Italian Navy. Mario and Sofia were married and lived in the Naval station's apartment complex. When the ship was away transporting troops to Libya, Sofia returned home. Sergio made an apartment available to the couple in his building since there were empty apartments. She didn't feel safe being alone among all those sailors. However, Sofia welcomed Mario with open arms at the Naval station when he was on furlough. They were in a hurry to make up for lost time. The couple still had Posillipo in their dreams and, for their three-day get-togethers, they romped all over Posillipo and visited Roman and Greek sites along the coastline of the smaller Baia Bay, just like old times when Mario courted Sofia.

Mario had total confidence in Imalda delivering their baby. She delivered thousands of babies in the shepherd community as well as in the neighborhood. Mario planned to be home at the time of delivery since his discharge from military duties would have coincided with the delivery. Whenever Imalda performed the procedure, she took on the persona of a field marshal. Everything had to be in order: hot water, towels, people in proper places, and no distractions. Children were chased out of the room. Windows were wide open for fresh air. Imalda demanded no less. She requested, actually demanded, that Sofia move into another room where there were three windows. She was meticulous in the delivery of her first grandchild. The only thing that she could not plan for was the sex of the baby. In those days, there was no technology to do so. But it didn't prevent Imalda from predicting the sex of the baby correctly 90 percent of the time. She never revealed her secret but correctly predicted a baby girl for Sofia.

Serafina and Filomena initiated a new trend in women's fashion design besides knitted sweaters. The new changes in fashion caught the fancy of the world, including Avella. However, few in town could afford the new dresses except, perhaps, residents of the Piazza neighborhood, royal families, and members of the Fascist hierarchy. Like her mother, maternity was not going to hold Sofia from expanding their pool of customers. She had collected a list of potential clients from the days when she and Mario frolicked around Posillipo, meeting neighbors near the Naval station and visiting Don Nicola at the San Carlo Opera House. These were customers who could afford the high-end fashion designs. Alvaro and Felicia, the twin sisters' parents, were proud to inform the Alvarez family that the girls were in a position to pay rent. Ramiro owned the building where the shop was located. It took only about six months to reach that milestone. Ramiro's wife ordered three dresses, each in different pastel colors, and all of the same style. The former seamstress shop where the girls, the twins, and Sofia apprenticed, assisted each other when overloaded with work. In effect, the two shops had a monopoly in dressmaking, since they were the only two shops in town and they shared the patterns of the new fashions. Both shops developed the fine art of modifying the original patterns to fit the sizes and shapes of their customers. The girls were aware of Don Nicola's scorn for Fascists in town, but they had no choice but to serve the wives of important Fascists. Otherwise, the thugs would have found a way to shut down the shop.

Mario's discharge from the Navy occurred on June 1, 1936. The war in Ethiopia ended about a month earlier. Mario hurried home to his wife for the birth of their child. Remarkably, that same morning, Don Nicola, huffing and puffing, knocked on the door of Mario's apartment. By the intensity of the knocking, Mario surmised that Sofia was at the door. So, he purposely delayed opening it. He hurried to pack heavy items, as he didn't want Sofia to pack anything, knowing that she was in no condition to do so. By now, Don Nicola was frantically shouting, "Open the fucking door! Sofia is going to have the baby soon!" Mario looked at his watch and it was 12 minutes before the next departure of the train from Naples to Avella. Usually, he would take the tram just to enjoy the scenery of the neighborhood, but not this time. He ran to the station and arrived in Avella one hour later. Don Nicola trailed with all the packed suitcases on the next train. He didn't mind as he knew that it was for a good cause.

From the station in Avella, Mario took the dirt road through Erminio's winery and farm, a shortcut to home. As a schoolboy in Nola, he would often stop there to climb a fig tree, but not this time. The farm consisted of a parcel of land dedicated to fruit trees and the rest to grapevines. In early fall, Erminio produced a variety of wines, but his specialty was prosecco and spumante—Italian sparkling wines. He was the first one to buy a motorized grape crusher in Avella. In the old days, either it was manual labor or a donkey was tied to a rotating wooden rod to crush the grapes. When Mario arrived at Sergio's house, Alvaro and Sergio's families were waiting for him outside the locked door where Imalda was delivering the baby. He knocked on the door but Imalda refused to open it. He then got on his knees to peek through the keyhole to observe the birth of his child, Lena.

Don Nicola arrived at the station in Avella at a later time and asked Erminio about Mario's whereabouts. It seemed that the whole town knew about the impending arrival of Sofia's baby. Erminio, without hesitation, offered to drive Don Nicola to Sergio's house. He could see that Don Nicola was exhausted with all those suitcases. As in any other small town, few things remain a secret for long. By the time they arrived, a crowd had already gathered to celebrate the birth. Erminio came prepared. He brought bottles of spumante to add to the happy occasion.

Fortunately, Mario left the Navy just in time to avoid being recruited to transport Italian troops to fight in the Spanish Civil War. Naval transport was vital to the Italian participation in the war in Spain. Mario received an inquiry from the Navy, as to whether or not he was interested in re-enlisting as a lieutenant commander, a promotion from his previous assignment.

Mario had no desire to work in the local Fascist government or to teach at a public elementary school, for which he qualified. However, the Italian Navy didn't need much of a convincing story, since they operated almost independently of the Fascist directives. Mussolini was embroiled in the Spanish Civil War in which the Republicans, Communists, and Socialists were pitted against the Nationalists and Spanish Fascists. Roughly 100,000 Italian troops were transported to fight in Spain to help Francisco Franco, who eventually became the Fascist leader of Spain.

What Mario really wanted to do was get involved in music but still stay within his specialty—ragioniere, serving as a lawyer and accountant. This decision had a lot to do with Don Nicola. Of course, he exposed Mario to the idea of seeking a job at the San Carlo Opera House. Don Nicola just wanted company on those long rides to Naples. But besides that, Mario was the most qualified of the candidates. During the little time spent at the Naval station, Mario was so relentless in pursuing the job that he became a good friend of its general manager. Mario cultivated the art of being charming and unyielding when he needed to. This time, it paid off. To strangers, Mario appeared distant and devoid of emotions. However, mentally, he was as active as a volcano, especially on things that mattered to him. He lit a fire under the dream of the two of them someday settling in Posillipo. Whereas Sofia wore her emotions on her sleeve, Mario hid them. The two complemented one another like hand and glove. Mario became the main accountant/lawyer at the San Carlo Opera House with Don Nicola running interference in his getting the job.

The San Carlo Opera House lost money each year during the 1930s. The ticket office generated only 45 percent of its budget. Few of the so-called upper class and/or nobility were able to donate, but that still wasn't enough to make up the difference. In 1835, Alexandre Dumas, who spent time in Naples, described the upper class thusly: "Four families enjoyed great fortunes; twenty lived comfortably and the rest had to struggle to make ends meet. It mattered to them to have a well-painted carriage harnessed up to a couple of old horses and a private box at the San Carlo. They lived in their carriages or the theater, but their houses were barred to visitors." This was the situation before WWII, but more so during the war.

Management tried to squeeze the salary of orchestra players or to reduce the size of the orchestra, but not that of singers. Mario came up with a brilliant idea. Instead of expecting people from the valley to travel to Naples to attend a performance, he suggested that performers visit small towns to stage operas. Mario concluded that such performances did not have to be first-class. The entry fee would be commensurate with the quality of the performers. Singers had not been in a habit of taking a pay cut even when performing in a small town. However, orchestra players could be recruited locally. Churches, schools, and civic centers provided acceptable outlets for staging an opera. Relatively speaking, the availability of places to stage an opera in the valley far outnumbered the number of performers. This meant that Don Nicola's music studios needed to produce many more performers to cover all those outlets in the valley. Not an easy task. Don Nicola saw an opportunity to expand his studio. In addition to his accounting job, Mario started a talent agency in collaboration with Don Nicola. Whereas Don Nicola trained new performers, Mario represented promising talent for San Carlo as well as other opera houses in Europe.

Don Nicola staged the opera, *La Boheme*, in Saint Peter's Church in Avella for the first time. He conducted the orchestra and directed the performers. The orchestra consisted of musicians from the local band. He recruited popular local singers, who were known for singing Neapolitan songs, and trained them to be adequate opera singers. To the audience, it made no difference. They were starved for opera music. It was hard work, but he believed in the cause and knew very well that the locals would be humming those tunes long after. He hoped to neutralize all that gossip about Il Duce's sex life and have people concentrate on the overthrow of Fascism. The opera in Avella succeeded beyond expectations.

Mussolini had a dream to be the modern Caesar of his time by mobilizing his army to invade Ethiopia in 1935 to bolster his ego. Yet the two characters, that of Caesar and Mussolini were very different. Caesar was a born strategist and leader of the military. Mussolini forever tried to measure up to generals and military officials. He spent more time posing than trying to understand warfare and, most importantly, preparations. As usual, the shepherds smelled a rat on the warpath and began to run for the hills to avoid conscription in the Italian Army. This much they knew: Grass did not grow in desert countries. They didn't understand what the fuss was about Ethiopia and didn't particularly want to know.

At five in the morning, Nino woke his aunt, Imalda, to ask permission to use her cottage and to take a herd of sheep up the mountains. "Of course, you can, but there is no need to get me up so early in the morning," she answered in a soft voice not to wake up Sergio. Nino was the oldest child of three children of Imalda's sister, Gioconda. Imalda loved her nephew for his proud, untamed, and impeccable spirit to survive, much like a goat. If caught by the police in town, the Fascist thugs would put tremendous pressure on the carabinieri to detain him for Army duty. Nino didn't want to take that chance to get stuck in Avella. Up on the mountains, he could easily hide and escape from the clutches of the Fascists.

The sound of small bells attached around the neck of the sheep woke up Giacomo. Most likely, Sergio permitted him to sleep there. His duties as a carabiniere were to apprehend shepherds eligible for Army duty. At least go through the motion. Nino asked Giacomo if he wanted to come along in the search for fields of grass. "I could use some help," Nino quipped, and Giacomo responded, "Why not." They have been friends since elementary school-days. He was not about to turn Nino or any other shepherd to Fascist authorities. Yes, there was some animosity lingering between the carabinieri and Fascist authorities. The attitude of the prefect fostered that attitude in the carabinieri force.

Thus, by the late 1930s, the Fascist thugs were losing grip of Avella's streets. But just the opposite was happening in Vienna. Whereas local laws in Austria were influenced by laws in Germany, Italians were immune to what was happening north of the Alps. The local prefect in the provinces interpreted laws as he saw fit in his locales and the politicians in Rome couldn't do anything about it because they had bigger fish to fry.

For example, for small towns, like Avella, politics was controlled by the prefect— mostly career civil servants, who retained their traditional dominance over local governments—and the new Podestas were Fascist mayors. The Podestas were mainly landowners, retired Army officers, or influential local politicos rather than Fascist enthusiasts. The prefect in Avellino appointed Ramiro as the temporary mayor of Avella. The purpose of the appointment was to clean up a mess at city hall. The Fascist Party was not sufficiently organized in small towns, like Avella, to mount an objection to the appointment. To the peasants, shepherds, and, in general, the people of Avella, Rome might as well have been some remote place on the moon, where all decisions affecting big cities were made.

In effect, Ramiro became a podesta by default, ultimately in name only but not in spirit. Ramiro was doing a favor for the prefect by taking the post. In effect, the prefect owed him one. The first appointment that Ramiro made was to put his friend, Alvaro Da Alia, as chief administrator of city hall. The job entailed the issuance of birth certificates, payroll, immigration issues, public school administration, issuance of licenses and ordinances, etc. Ramiro wanted to eradicate corruption at city hall, as the outgoing and retiring Fascist mayor was embroiled in bribery charges. Sergio made Ramiro aware of all the details of the fraudulent acquisition of the land. He wanted someone there whom he could trust. Ramiro, being the mayor, was protected by the prefect and, therefore, immune to all the fuss raised by the local Fascists.

FOUR
Laws of Inhumanity

The Wolf family arrived unannounced at Avella train station. They didn't have time to put the word out. As they moseyed over to the wine store to ask for directions to Sergio's place, Erminio shot out of the store like a bullet to meet them. How could he misjudge who they were with their standout light complexions? Besides, Erminio had previously met Nanna and Ehrlich numerous times at Sergio's get-togethers. He surmised that the blond child must be theirs. Erminio grabbed their suitcases and led them into the store babbling something incomprehensible to the Viennese couple. Nanna and Ehrlich, who spoke little Italian, tried to explain to him that they needed to go to Sergio's place. All the while, Erminio kept interrupting Nanna by making the universal sign for food. He gestured with his cupped hands. Erminio's wife quickly cooked a pasta dish that Arya enjoyed immensely while Erminio drove his car around to the front of the store.

Don Nicola and Sergio couldn't believe their eyes when the Wolfs arrived. Everyone pitched in to help get the apartment ready for their occupancy. It didn't take long for Arya and Lena to run around in the courtyard and the adjacent grass field playing games. At last, the Wolf family arrived at their adopted home knowing that they were loved and wanted, a very dark contrast to the streets of Vienna and the terrible things still to come.

The clan of Avella friends knew very well that the Wolf family went through hell at the hands of Nazis and that it must have taken tremendous courage to leave their home in Vienna. At least life was more tolerable in Avella since the Fascist thugs spent more time up in the mountains searching for deserters rather than in the streets. The carabinieri provided little to no assistance to the thugs in the search.

The clan wanted to make the stay of the Wolf family in Avella as pleasant as possible. At Sergio's garden, Ramiro did the honor of welcoming the Viennese couple and child, since he was the oldest person and respected in town. "You are among friends," he concluded. He then turned to Nanna and said, "You are too beautiful not to embrace." Then he turned to Ehrlich, "As for you, you are too ugly to embrace, but I will just shake your hand." They all got a big laugh out of that. He then invited all the children to his indoor pool to cool down.

Between 1935 and 1938, the relationship between Mussolini and Hitler changed dramatically. It changed from Mussolini being scornful of Hitler—almost to the point of contempt—to one where he played second fiddle to him. The turning point in their relationship occurred in September of 1937. Mussolini paid a visit to Germany, where he reviewed a long parade of troops, artillery, and other military equipment. It blew his mind. He recognized for the first time that Germany had built a powerful army with advanced weapons. This German buildup was a no-no under the peace agreement of Versailles in 1919. These Army demonstrations of strength were intended to impress the Italian leader, Il Duce, and they did. Mussolini realized, then, that Hitler would go to any lengths and means to achieve his goal of war. Mussolini envisioned an opportunity for himself, as always. He would ride Hitler's back and take whatever colonies were left by Hitler after the war.

The final coup d'etat in their relationship occurred when Hitler occupied Austria, although Italy was Austria's protectorate until March 1938. Austria and Italy signed a treaty in which Italy would protect Austrian territory against foreign invaders. Also, in 1938, Il Duce assisted Hitler in fooling Prime Minister Neville Chamberlain of Britain into acceding Sudetenland to Germany during a so-called peace conference in Munich. Il Duce served as a translator at the meeting! By that time, Hitler could have placed a collar around Mussolini's neck and led him around like a puppy. The flip-flopping on the part of Mussolini in less than a year showed his unscrupulous character.

One month after the Anschluss vote in Austria, Hitler visited Naples to review the Italian fleet, not too far from the Naval military station where Mario had trained as a naval officer. There was a large crowd along the coastal road organized by the Blackshirts. Mario, Ehrlich, and Don Nicola wanted to see the madman up close since the Naval station was within walking distance from the San Carlo opera house. Although Ehrlich had been in Avella less than a month, he wanted to be there in Naples to explain to Mario and Don Nicola the sham in front of their eyes. According to Ehrlich, Hitler was the personification of evil. In a somber tone, he declared to the others, "My friends, it's going to be a lot worse than you think. Eventually, he will gobble up Italy just like he did Austria. Those Nazis surrounding him are here to assess the military capabilities of the Italian Army and Navy." Mario and Don Nicola tightened their asses and looked worried. They never imagined that it could happen to Italy. That possibility frightened them. They were Neapolitans who loved life to the fullest.

The three of them noticed that Hitler was doing all the talking while Mussolini looked away, rolling his eyes as if to ask, "When will he stop talking?" Hitler's entourage mostly snickered about the poor condition of the Italian fleet. At that time, Nazi Germany had an operational radar and kept it a secret from their supposed ally. It was obvious to anyone there that each of the two countries was marching to a different drum. Germany was marching to war and Italy was not. The arrogance and body language of the Nazi entourage seemed to say as much. Mario and Don Nicola walked away with a lot of questions, one of which was, "Why was Il Duce so subservient to Hitler and the rest of them?" Ehrlich had no doubt about Il Duce's role. This was not an equal partnership. The only thing that Il Duce didn't do was kneel in Hitler's presence. They felt that something terrible was brewing and Mussolini had no clue as to the real intent of his guests. Mario and Don Nicola asked themselves, "Who is fooling whom?" They felt uneasy and apprehensive but couldn't put their fingers on what disturbed them the most. But not Ehrlich. He was a man of few words but very precise and insightful about the situation at hand, much like his style of music presentation.

It wasn't long before bad news reached its way to Italy through a special proclamation exported from Germany. On July 14, 1938, Mussolini embraced the "Manifesto of the Racial Scientist," and between September 2, 1938, and November 17, 1938, Italy enacted a series of racial laws, only to appease Hitler. The gist of these new laws in Italy included the following: foreign Jews were forbidden to settle in Italy; Italian Jews were banned from jobs in government, banking, insurance, education, the entertainment industry, and the practice of law. The manifesto was shocking to all Italians, especially when, a few years back, Mussolini declared that the Italian Jews were the glue that bound Italian society together.

It was no surprise that the racial laws in Italy pretty much reflected the ones in Germany enacted exactly four years earlier. On September 15, 1935, two laws were enacted in Nazi Germany—the Nuremberg Laws. These laws declared that only

Germans of German or related blood would be allowed to hold German citizenship. This meant that Jews could not be full citizens of Germany and had no political rights. The other law banned intermarriage between Jews and people of German or related blood. In addition, Jews were no longer permitted to work in the civil service or government-regulated professions such as medicine and education. Many middle-class business owners and professionals were forced to take menial employment. Emigration was problematic, as Jews were required to remit up to 60 to 90 percent of their wealth as a tax when they left the country.

The Nuremberg Laws were applied not only in Germany but also in Austria and Sudetenland. This was nothing more and nothing less than a rehash of laws of persecution enacted during the fifteenth century under King Albert which were by then rejected by all countries of the civilized world. But by 1938, it was almost impossible for potential Jewish emigrants to find a country willing to let them in because of the visa requirement.

With the issuance of the manifesto, there was no more hope for many Italians that things would get better under the Fascist regime. They would be lucky if it stayed the same in the coming war. Suspicion ran rampant about Mussolini's motives. People began to talk openly about all the corruption in the regime. Most Italians followed their consciences and resisted the unjust treatment of Jews and did so at great personal risk to themselves and their families. This resistance took many forms. Some Italian Jews transferred businesses and other sources of wealth to trusted Christian friends for safekeeping. In addition, some Jewish lawyers continued servicing non-Jewish clients with the assistance of non-Jewish attorneys. Other examples of non-compliance included bankers who overlooked or ignored Jewish bank accounts thereby protecting their assets from being confiscated.

In a panic, Ehrlich asked Imalda to deposit the family's money in her bank account knowing full well that Sergio had no clue about bank deposits, since she was the business manager of the whole shepherd community. Apparently, Ehrlich must have learned a lot from Herbert to stay ahead of potential problems. Most shepherds like Sergio did not trust banks. Basically, they didn't like banks to fondle whatever little money they had. This allowed for the Wolf family to hide their money from authorities. Imalda was very proud to do that for a dignitary like Ehrlich. Ehrlich was employed as a substitute cello player in the San Carlo Opera House until Don Nicola assumed the duties of the orchestra conductor. He was required by law to register with the local authorities to obtain a work permit in Italy. Presto, Ramiro and Alvaro intervened on behalf of Ehrlich to obtain the permit. Racial laws were somehow put on hold at the San Carlo as well as many other establishments. The San Carlo opera house was becoming a nest of Socialists with Don Nicola being their leader.

There were other acts of sympathy. Since Italy required no entry visa, a Polish Jewish family decided to leave Warsaw just before the outbreak of WWII on the advice of their next-door neighbor Herbert. They left much behind—friends, family, a chocolate factory, a house, bank accounts—everything. They arrived at their usual summer vacation spot, the hotel in Florence near the Ponte Vecchio bridge. The family explained their ordeal to the hotel owner, Giacomino. His answer was reassuring, "Don't worry, I will take care of it." The family enjoyed their stay while feeling assured. The hotel owner drove the family to the French Riviera and on to Paris. He refused a single lira of payment and that included their stay in the hotel. Eventually, the Polish family emigrated to the United States. One member became an influential advisor to President Reagan on Russian affairs. Also, Herbert anticipated that Germany would invade Poland soon and convinced his family to transfer all of their money to a U.S. bank in New York City before traveling to Italy. Herbert did the same, always one step ahead of trouble.

Not only was the populace in Italy unhappy with the racial laws, but so was the Catholic Church. As is common in the Catholic Church, their views are usually expressed by the Pope, but sometimes there are exceptions. And there was a serious exception prior to WWII. A chronology of time events that took place in the Vatican before and after the publication of the racial laws in Italy follows.

MAY–JUNE 1938

Pope Pius XI deliberately planned to be out of the city while Hitler was in Rome on May 3. On June 25, he sought the American Jesuit journalist John LaFarge and summoned him to Castel Gandolfo, the summer residence of the Pope, about 30 miles south of Rome. It is located on the Alban Hills overlooking the Tyrrhenian Sea and Lake Nemi. The pope told the Jesuit that he planned to write an encyclical denouncing racism, and asked LaFarge to help write it while swearing him to strict silence. The title of the encyclical was, "Humani Generis Unitas" or "The Unity of the Human Race." A papal encyclical is one of the highest forms of communication by the pope and usually deals with some aspect of Catholic teaching—clarifying, amplifying, condemning, or promoting one or many issues. Historically, a papal encyclical is addressed to bishops and priests of a country or region or all clergy. LaFarge took up this task in secret in Paris, but the Jesuit Superior-General Wlodimir Ledóchowski promised Pope Pius XI and LaFarge that he would facilitate the encyclical's production. This proved to be a hindrance since Ledóchowski was privately an anti-Semite and conspired to block Lafarge's efforts whenever and wherever possible. The basic notion of the encyclical was to argue that because of the existence of one natural law and one creator, the human race was also one. Pope Pius XI advocated for this point of view.

JULY 1938

Pope Pius XI addressed the students at Propaganda Fide with words that were to provoke Mussolini's wrath: "It has been forgotten that the human race, the entire human race, is a single, large, universal human race. The expression ***human race*** denotes, precisely, the human race... However, it cannot be denied that in this universal race, there is no room for special races or for a multitude of different variations or even many nationalities that are even more specialized... One might well ask why Italy ever needed to imitate Germany... We must call things by their name if we do not wish to incur grave dangers, including the risk of losing the name and even the notion of things."

SEPTEMBER 1938

On September 6, Pope Pius XI received members of the Catholic Radio of Belgium on pilgrimage and gave a speech that has remained famous: "Listen carefully. Abraham is definitely our patriarch, our forebear... Anti-semitism is a hateful movement... We Christians must have nothing to do with it... Anti-Semitism is inadmissible. Spiritually we are all Semites."

On September 15, the Holy Father related to the Vatican Ambassador to Italy Father Tacchi Venturi: "But this is gross! I am ashamed... I am ashamed of being Italian. And you, Father, please tell Mussolini! Not as pope but rather as an Italian, I am ashamed of myself! The Italian people have become a flock of stupid sheep."

In late September, the Jesuit, LaFarge, had finished his work and returned to Rome, where Ledóchowski welcomed him and promised to deliver the work to the pope immediately. LaFarge was directed to return to the United States, while Ledóchowski concealed the draft from the pope, who remained wholly unaware of what had transpired.

FALL 1938

LaFarge realized that the pope still had not received the draft and sent a letter to Pius XI where he implied that Ledóchowski had the document in his possession. Pope Pius XI demanded that the draft be delivered to him at once, but did not receive it until January 21, 1939, with a note from Ledóchowski, who warned that the draft's language was excessive and advised caution. Pope Pius XI planned to issue the encyclical following his meeting with bishops on February 11, but he died one day before both the meeting and the encyclical's promulgation could have taken place. After Pius XI's death on February 10, 1939, Cardinal Eugenio Pacelli was elected his successor as Pope Pius XII in a short conclave on March 2. Pius XI's encyclical was returned to its authors by the new pope. According to Peter Eisner's book, *The Pope's Last Crusade*, and Giuliana Chametes' article in *The Jesuit Review* in 2013, Pope Pius XII withheld publication during his tenure as pope. It took about fifty years for the encyclical to "see daylight."

1986

A copy of the encyclical was discovered in Paris, France. The 1997 book by George Passelecq and Bernard Suchecky and translated by Steven Rendall, *The Hidden Encyclical of Pius XI*, tells the story.

These episodes have raised several questions. How many copies and/or drafts of the encyclical existed and who possessed them? How was it possible that all copies were hidden for nearly fifty years? The first two questions can now be answered: Pope Pius XII had them. Whose draft or copy was discovered in 1986 long after the death of Pope Pius XII? The unknown outweighs what is known. Could the publication of the encyclical in 1938–39 have changed the course of WWII? There have been many speculations about the medical condition of Pope Pius XI at the time of his death.

The implementation of the racial laws in Italy was applied unevenly by the Fascists, depending on where one lived. In big cities like Rome, where visibility was high, the Fascist government strictly implemented the laws with the hope that the visual or the application of the law in the streets would be seen in Berlin. Mussolini, being a journalist at heart, believed strongly in the power of the visual. However, at the San Carlo opera House, the Jewish general manager was fired as well as some Jewish members of the orchestra, including Don Nicola, Ehrlich, and Mario.

The same was repeated at military installations, like the Naval station in Naples.

Whereas before the proclamations, the Italian Navy was divorced from Fascism, afterward, the Navy was forced to obey Mussolini's whim. In small towns like Avella, nothing changed. Alvaro still worked at city hall. The Jewish community just ignored the proclamations, since the thugs did not have the authority to enforce them. Only the prefect could do that, but, being apolitical, he was not about to.

The winter of 1939 in Avella brought brutal tornado-like winds. The cold and the snow flurries felt like daggers to the bone. The weather matched the posters of the racial laws splattered all over town. People did not want to give in to the weather so they stayed indoors, but it didn't stop the Fascist thugs from putting up the posters. Still, people did not want to come out, because townies knew that Fascists were usually the bearers of bad news. Indeed, that was the case. The news traveled as fast as the wind. The town was dumbfounded. They were a homogenous society and comfortable with each other. Besides, their neighborhood had been established for millennia, long before Fascism. Hence, they looked at the proclamation with disdain, asking themselves, "Who in the hell are they talking about?" It never entered their minds about the distinction of anyone in town.

The Jewish community had contempt for the proclamation. They were part of the fabric of the town. It was inconceivable that this new movement of Fascism was going to separate people and communities that had lived together for centuries and, some, for millennia. The proclamation made no sense to them. The town rallied behind their friends and neighbors.

Don Nicola, Ehrlich, and Mario were able to operate the studio and Mario's talent agency. By then, Ehrlich felt at home and contributed much to the joint efforts to foster operas in small towns. Since Alvaro held onto the city hall job, he relinquished the part-time accounting job at the Alvarez residence to Mario. The seamstress shop managed by Filomena, Serafina, and Sofia was unaffected by the proclamation. In effect, not much changed in Avella. Also, both Don Nicola and Mario realized that as soon as things quieted down, they could go back to San Carlo to resume their jobs. However, Ehrlich was of a different mindset. Although he was surrounded by nice people sympathetic to his needs, his dream was to return to his beloved Vienna and opera house once the nightmare was over.

In times of peril, Neapolitans have learned over many years how to adapt to survive. The motto, "Ci arrangiamo" or "We make do," has been instilled in Neapolitans from the day they were born. Don Nicola and Mario felt the same. Being superstitious, like most Neapolitans, they had premonitions about the future. The year 1939 was the time for all those emotions. An entry in Ciano's diary best summarized the feelings of most Neapolitans and the rest of Italy about Hitler. Ciano was the Italian Foreign Minister and the son-in-law of Mussolini. He married his older daughter, Edda. Between August 11–12, 1939, he had conferences with his counterpart, von Ribbentrop, and Hitler in Salzburg, Austria.

CIANO'S DIARY ENTRY FOR AUGUST 13, 1939

"...I return to Rome completely disgusted with the Germans, with their leader, with their way of doing things. They have betrayed us and lied to us. Now they are dragging us into an adventure which we have not wanted and which might compromise the regime and the country as a whole. The Italian people will boil over with horror when they know about the aggression against Poland and most probably will wish to fight the Germans. I don't know whether to wish Italy a victory or Germany a defeat. In any case, given the Germans' attitude, I think that our hands are free, and I propose that we act accordingly, declaring that we have no intention of participating in a war which we have neither wanted nor provoked.

The Duce's reactions are varied. At first, he agreed with me. Then he says honor compels him to march with Germany. **Finally, he states that he wants his part of the booty in Croatia and Dalmatia."**

Don Nicola, Ehrlich, and Mario had every reason to worry about the future. Their intuition was right on the mark! WWII would take place within a few days. Germany invaded Poland on September 1, 1939.

This turn of events had a profound effect on Herbert's lifestyle in Warsaw. Herbert lived in one of the apartments in a building owned by Harold on Chopin Street in Warsaw, Poland, after leaving Vienna in early April 1938. The cousins decided after the war to formally divide their holdings for the sake of their children and grandchildren. He had an elegant appearance complemented by a deep voice. He was a very compassionate man who extended himself to help any way possible others who went through rough times with the Nazis. Herbert adorned his apartment with classical and avant-garde paintings. He enjoyed walking in the Ujazdowskie Park in Warsaw, visiting family and friends, and the Chopin competition held at the Warsaw Philharmonic. He kept in touch with Bernhard in Vienna and his cousin Harold in Switzerland by phone. However, his favorite sport was to be in constant communication with his investment brokers in New York City and Switzerland for investment opportunities.

On August 31, 1939, Herbert Herzog boarded the Queen Mary ship in South-ampton, England, on the way to New York City. Yes, he got away just in time, as usual, with the help of his friend Bernhard who had put two and two together, when he perused the accounting books at his company. Bernhard discovered that the inventory of benzene fuel was unusually low, almost empty, and surmised that an attack on Poland was imminent, because Poland occupied the front page newspa-per coverage in all countries of Europe. Also, the main customer for the benzene was the German Army. What a beautiful friend! He passed the information to Herbert who in turn surmised that the attack would be on September 1, because he under-stood Nazi mentality more than he liked to admit. Without packing a suitcase, he left for England well ahead of the invasion. Thanks to his dear friend, he got away.

FIVE

Victory Rescued

The battle of Dunkirk has been studied, analyzed, and dissected by the military officers, historians, and scholars of WWII. It is the thesis of this chapter that, of all the battles of WWII, this one was the turning point of the war. It turned total defeat by Britain into ultimate Allied victory. This specific period is re-examined given recent revelations of communications between Hitler and Mussolini which directly affected the outcome of the Dunkirk battle. There have been many explanations for the pause by the German Army toward Dunkirk, allowing for the escape of British, Belgian, and French troops by sea across the English Channel. In the book, *A Soldier's Record*, Albert Kesselring, who was general of the Luftwaffe in 1940 and field marshall of the Army in 1943, said the pause was a "fatal error" on the part of the German Army. This chapter addresses that puzzlement. It chronicles day by day, for the first time, the background that precipitated Hitler's order for the German Army to pause for three days and allowed Allied soldiers to escape the encirclement at Dunkirk. The pause saved lives, and it gave the Allies the confidence to persist and to fight another day. Historical books about WWII have reported on what led to the encirclement in the first place at Dunkirk. We will not dwell on this.

The evacuation inspired Churchill's world-renowned speech: "We shall fight on the beaches." The evacuation at Dunkirk bought time with the hope that the day of reckoning would come. It did come at Stalingrad, at El Alamein, at Sicily, and at Normandy. It showed that the German Army was not invincible but, more importantly, it gave people in small towns like Avella, and the rest of the world, hope and motivation to take on Fascism and Nazism in their inimical ways. As to how and why the British, French, and Belgian armies were trapped at Dunkirk, refer to the historical references for details. According to references, it is clear that the German Army followed the so-called Schlieffen Plan from WWI.

One German Army Group was commanded by General Gerd von Rundstedt and the other Army Group by General Fedor von Bock. The latter Group attacked Belgium, while the former attacked south, toward the Ardennes Woods, and then swung around to the English Channel. The German Army deployed the Schlieffen Plan of WWI in which the German Army pivoted toward the English Channel in the heat of battle. It trapped elements of the British Expeditionary Force (BEF), and the French and Belgian armies in Dunkirk and vicinity. Paris is about one hundred miles south of Amiens. The French Maginot line of defense is about 100–150 miles east of Reims. The situation was rather dire for the Allied Armies, especially for the British Army. The British contingent at Dunkirk represented the best-trained troops and more than 50 percent of their active army. Even with the recovery of their troops, it affected their war strategies for the rest of the war. The British hierarchy thereafter was reluctant to commit British troops indiscriminately but prone to commit colonial troops in battles.

On May 22, 1940, Winston Churchill convened the War Cabinet to discuss the Dunkirk entrapment and what to do about it. After two days of intense discussions, on May 24, War Cabinet members Neville Chamberlain and Edward Woods, the First Earl of Halifax, prevailed upon Churchill to contact the Italian ambassador to Britain, Giuseppe Bastianini, in London to mediate a peace conference, similar to the one in Munich held on September 30, 1938, among the belligerents then. By normal circumstances or by protocol, an ambassador reports an important message directly to his foreign minister. At that time, it would have been Mussolini's son-in-law, Ciano. By default, Bastianini must have contacted Mussolini, since Ciano was absent from Rome from May 22 to 26, according to his diary. He was dispatched by Mussolini to Albania.

According to Ciano's diary, Mussolini sent his foreign minister to Albania to instill the Albanians to eat two meals a day instead of one, although Ciano was privy or aware of what was happening in Dunkirk as a result of communications with Italian ambassadors at different capitals and Ciano. Indeed, it was very strange, to say the least, to dispatch a foreign minister to worry about diets in another country. According to Ciano's diary, he was reluctant to go to Albania, when the military situation in Dunkirk called for him to be in Rome communicating with Italian and foreign ambassadors. He had no choice but to go. Was it possible that Il Duce was up to no good? Yes, he was. He didn't want Ciano to be in Rome during the critical stage in Dunkirk.

It also showed that Mussolini had little confidence in Ciano representing his interests which were paramount to him. Ciano alluded in his diary to the many disagreements with Mussolini about Italy's alliance with Germany's wars. In short, Mussolini didn't trust Ciano's involvement in communicating with other foreign dignitaries at that time, especially directly with Hitler. Ciano alluded in his diary to terse conversations that he had had with Hitler and Ribbentrop in the previous year. The fact that Churchill called for a meeting implied that something important was brewing and Mussolini didn't want Ciano to share in the limelight. Dispatching Ciano to Albania on a whim also indicated to Ciano that his days as a foreign minister were numbered, especially when the CEO and father-in-law didn't trust him to be around at critical times. What follows are communications between Italian and foreign ambassadors with the Foreign Office in Rome during those pivotal times.

REFERENCE: LS-I, I DOCUMENTI DIPLOMATICI ITALIANI, NONA SERIE (1939-1943), VOLUME IV (Aprile 9 - Giugno 10, 1940).

Reference Item 510
The Italian Ambassador to Paris Raffaele Guariglia to the Minister of Foreign Affairs Galeazzo Ciano

Paris, May 20, 1940

Ho l'impressione che Governo francese voglia orientare attuali operazioni ad un concetto manovra tendente battere avversario con forze provenienti da Belgio ed altre riserve per cercare così di impedire o ritardare avanzata verso mare ma nello stesso tempo coprire la capitale.

I have the impression that the French Government wants to orient operations to a maneuver concept tending to beat the enemy with forces from Belgium and other reserves in order to try to prevent or delay the advance towards the **sea** but at the same time cover the **capital.**

Reference Item 516
The Italian Ambassador to Berlin Dino Alfieri to the Minister of Foreign Affairs Galeazzo Ciano

Berlin, May 20, 1940
Ho avuto l'impressione che, se gli eventi lo permetteranno, i tedeschi punteranno principalmente su Calais per agire direttamente sull'Inghilterra, nella convinzione che, piegata Londra, anche Parigi sarà costretta a sottomettersi.

I had the impression that, if events permit, the Germans will be able to approach mainly **Calais** in order to act directly on England, with the conviction that, once London is subdued, **Paris will also be forced to submit**.

Reference Item 518
The Italian Ambassador to Berlin Dino Alfieri to the Minister of Foreign Affairs Galeazzo Ciano

Berlin, May 21, 1940
Questo Ministero degli Esteri informa che le operazioni militari procedono con successo e che l'avanzata verso il mare ha fatto notevolissimi progressi. È in tale direzione che si accentua l'azione tedesca per separare le armate franco-inglesi del Nord da quelle francesi del Sud.

This Minister of Foreign Affairs Joachim von Ribbentrop informs that the military operations are proceeding successfully and that the advance towards the **sea** has made considerable progress. It was in this direction that the German action to separate the Franco-British armies in the North from the French armies in the South was accentuated.

On May 26, 1940, Ciano returned to Rome. However, Mussolini did not mention Bastianini's call on the 24th; for that matter, Bastianini also did not report to Ciano about the call from the British War Cabinet. If Ciano had discovered insubordination on the part of Bastianini, he would have recalled Bastianini and sent him to jail. Bastianini's only choice was not to report or tell anyone. Otherwise, he would have caught the wrath of both Mussolini and Ciano for different reasons, one for disclosing and the other for insubordination. Nevertheless, he caught the wrath of Mussolini. He double-crossed Bastianini anyway, as he did with Dumini in the Matteotti affair, not surprisingly. Mussolini ordered Dumini to kill Matteotti. Quoting Ciano's diary of May 31, 1941, "Bastianini was terminated from his job by Mussolini, who explained it by saying that his [immediate] family doesn't like him and also reproached him for having built a villa at Rocca di Papa—a victim of the campaign started against him by Donna Rachele." Donna Rachele, by this time, ruled her household, including her husband, Mussolini.

That was unusual, to say the least! It was as if Ciano lived in a vacuum purposely created by Il Duce. Why? Given the fact that the two disagreed about the alliance between Italy and Germany, there was no incentive for Mussolini to inform Ciano, since there was no trust or agreement on anything between the two. Therefore, it is surmised that Mussolini must have contacted Hitler on the same day that Bastianini informed him of the call from London, on May 24, and advanced the idea of a peace conference as proposed by the British. It is claimed here that, on the same day, Il Duce urged Hitler to call for a halt, or a pause, in the German Army's advance to Dunkirk to show goodwill. Only Hitler had the power to stop the advance on Dunkirk. No general would have dared to challenge the Fuhrer.

It is argued that both Fascist and Nazi leaders had much to gain from a peace conference like the one in Munich in 1938. Remarkably, the same individuals, who pushed for a peace conference in Munich, were also the same ones, Lord Halifax and Chamberlain, who initiated another peace conference. Mussolini and Hitler recognized those players as weak, who would deliver anything on the platter in the name of peace. Given the personality of Mussolini and his deep desire to gain colonies at no cost and let the German Army be the conduit to his dream, he must have called soon after he received the message from Bastianini. Also, it would not have committed Italy to enter the war, since Il Duce was advised by the Italian general staff that Italy was not ready for war until 1943. See Ciano's diary.

Evidence has come to light to indicate that communications between Bastianini and Mussolini and between Mussolini and Hitler on May 24 must have taken place, see documents from the archive of the Italian Foreign Office of May 24 and 25, 1940. Communication between members of the British War Cabinet and Bastianini was reported in McCarten's book, see References. The order given to the German Army by Hitler is cited in many references.

Reference Item 565
The Italian Ambassador in Paris Raffaele Guariglia to the Minister of Foreign Affairs Galeazzo Ciano

Paris, May 24, 1924 (Memo from French Foreign Office to Guariglia)
unica strada per parlare con Hitler
Esclude che possa farlo il Governo attuale. Dubita che possa farlo un Governo Reynaud con Lavai agli Esteri. Considera invece possibile un contatto con un Governo Pétain-Laval, onde ottenere da Mussolini un intervento presso Hitler.

only way to talk to Hitler
It excludes the possibility of the current government [French] doing so. He [Pierre Laval] doubts that a Reynaul government with Laval as foreign minister will be able to do so. On the other hand, he considered it possible to contact a Petain-Laval government, in order to obtain from **Mussolini an intervention with Hitler.**

Reference Item 584
The Chancellor of the Reich Adolf Hitler to the Head of Italian Government Benito Mussolini

May 25, 1940
Prima che io dessi l'ordine di rompere nella direzione del Canale, io fui dell'opinione che doveva farsi una pausa al nostro movimento in avanti anche se vi fosse il pericolo di un arrivo o di un ritorno di forze anglo-francesi.

Before I gave the order to break in the direction of the Canal [English Channel], I was of the opinion that we should **pause** at our forward movement even if there is danger of an arrival or a retreat of the Anglo-French forces.

Thus, the common denominator for all communications centered around Mussolini and Bastianini. Interestingly, Mussolini rehired Giuseppe Bastianini to replace Ciano as foreign minister in February 1943. Ciano was banished to the Vatican as ambassador there. Could this appointment have been a payoff to Bastianini for keeping quiet for approximately three years about their conversation on May 24,

1940? Yes, indeed!

The pause lasted from May 24 to the late afternoon of May 27, almost three and a half days. It saved many lives, see the plot below.

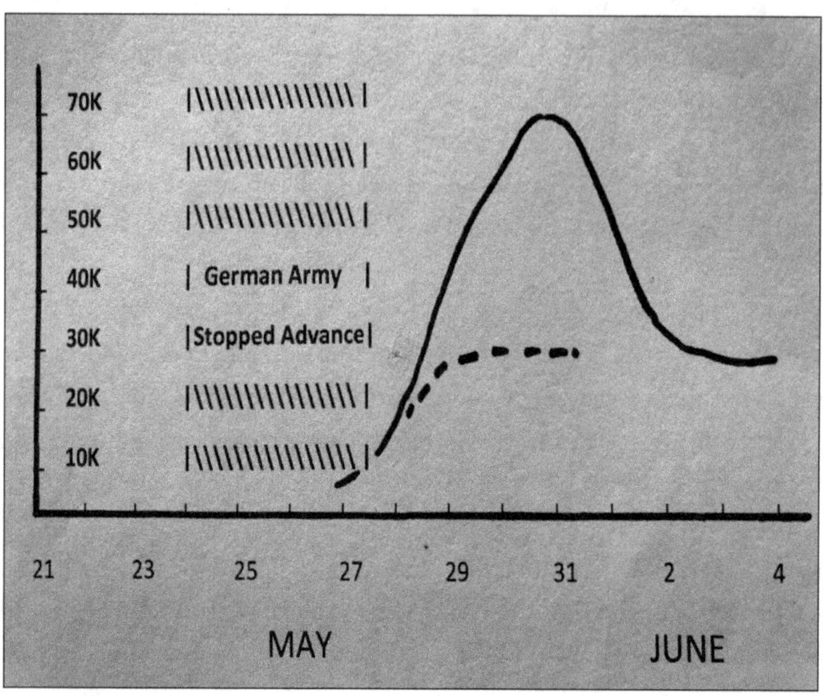

Plot of soldiers rescued on a daily basis from the beach of Dunkirk in May – June of 1940. Data obtained is from actual reports of soldiers rescued. The dotted curve represents an estimate of soldiers rescued, if there was no pause in the German Army's advance toward Dunkirk. Courtesy of Anmarie Vittoria.

The top curve indicates the number of soldiers rescued daily in the thousands starting on May 27. The evacuation peaked at about May 31 and it ended on June 4. The German Army reached Dunkirk on June 4. The fact that Mussolini proposed to Hitler to enter the war on June 4th, according to Ciano's diary, demonstrated that he was well aware of the end date when the German Army would arrive at Dunkirk. He was itching to get into the spoils of war and wanted to be first in line for the crumbs.

Had there been no pause or halt, the German Army would have been at Dunkirk between May 31 and June 1. It is estimated that 125,000 soldiers would have been evacuated instead of 358,226. No matter, Allied soldiers at Dunkirk lived for another day to return to the battlefields of North Africa, Italy, France, and Germany.

Political dissidents, like Mario and Don Nicola took to the streets and mountains to fight Fascists and Nazis throughout Italy.

Soon after the Dunkirk debacle, Mussolini entered the war on June 10, 1940, allied with Germany instead of his preferred date of June 4. In addition, he initiated the internment camps in Italy at that time, only to impress the Fuhrer. Clearly, the intent of the Duce was to reap the spoils of war. From the German hierarchy's perspective, they achieved much without the assistance of the Italian Army. Thus, Hitler advised Mussolini to enter the war much later than the fourth. Clearly, Hitler did not want to share the spoils of war or the glory of marching on Champs-Elysees in Paris with him.

By then, Il Duce should have realized that the gig was up, and the Nazis knew it. As such, Hitler was onto him with the ruse. This was like a poker game in which the player with the high hand calls the bluff and wins it all. Yet, this loser did not walk away from the table, in this case, walk away from the war. It didn't make sense, since he would always have a poor hand. His army was not prepared for war until 1943, according to his general staff. Perhaps, madness or desperation may explain. Thus, his persona changed from a con artist to a beggar. People in Avella and the rest of Italy didn't have to be told. They sensed that Mussolini exercised his will, not the people's.

The day after the arrival of German troops at Dunkirk, the German Army turned ninety degrees toward Paris, only about 100 miles south. The sixty remaining French divisions and the two British divisions in France made a determined stand on the Somme and Aisne but were defeated by the German combination of air superiority and armored mobility. German armies outflanked the intact Maginot Line and pushed deep into France, occupying Paris unopposed on June 14. After the flight of the French government and the collapse of the French Army, German commanders met with French officials on June 18 to negotiate an end to hostilities.

On June 22, 1940, the Second Armistice at Compiègne was signed by France and Germany. The neutral Vichy government led by Marshal Philippe Pétain replaced the Third French Republic and German military occupation began along the French North Sea and Atlantic coasts and their hinterlands. The Vichy regime retained the free zone in the south. Following the Allied invasion of French Africa in November 1942, the Germans and Italians took control of the zone until it was liberated by the Allies in 1944.

Italy declared war on France and Britain on the evening of June 10, 1940. The two sides exchanged air raids on the first day of the war, but little transpired on the Alpine front at the border between France and Italy, since France and Italy had defensive strategies. On June 17, France announced that it would seek an armistice with Germany. On June 21, with a Franco-German armistice about to be signed, the Italians launched a general offensive along the Alpine front, the main attack coming in the northern sector and a secondary front advancing along the coast. The Italian offensive penetrated a few kilometers into French territory against strong resistance but stalled before its primary objectives could be attained; the coastal town of Menton, situated directly on the Italian border, was the most significant conquest.

On the evening of June 24, an armistice was signed in Rome. It came into effect just after midnight on June 25, at the same time as the armistice with Germany, signed on June 22. Italy was allowed to occupy the territory it had captured in the brief fighting. A demilitarized zone was created on the French side of the border, Italian economic control was extended into southeast France up to the Rhône, and Italy obtained certain rights and concessions in certain French colonies. An armistice control commission, the Commissione Italiana d'Armistizio con la Francia (CIAF), was set up in Turin to oversee French compliance. Italy reclaimed the birthplace, Nice, of their famous hero of the Italian Revolution of 1860, Giuseppe Garibaldi. Most historians regarded the invasion of Italy into France as a stab in the back of an old friend. At that particular time, France was fighting for its dear life against the onslaught of the German Army near Paris. The world had never witnessed an army move so rapidly with their armored divisions. It came to be known as the blitzkrieg. The Italian Army was not as powerful, as it amassed a huge army just to gain a few inches of territory. That was how much Mussolini was blinded by his ambition and delusion of himself. The Germans saw him as an opportunist at their expense.

The people of Avella were anxious about Italy entering another war against France, besides the ones started by Germany in Poland and France. They felt that they had tolerated Mussolini for too long. The gossip in town was no longer about the love life of Il Duce, the clown, but when the next round of warfare would be. They didn't have to wait too long. The town was in shock when they heard about the invasion of France. Both France and Britain were allies of Italy in WWI. If anything, their mindset was to repeat WWI on the side of France. Of course, Fascist thugs were parading up and down Main Street drumming up support for the war. If townies were anxious before, now, they panicked, hiding their true feelings from the thugs about the war. Don Nicola could not help himself from draping the statue of Garibaldi in the Piazza with a black cloth, implying the death of Italy. It was prophetic. Garibaldi is to Italy what George Washington is to the United States. Fortunately for him, no one saw him doing it in the middle of the night. He was treading on dangerous grounds. He could not afford to antagonize Fascist thugs. They didn't need a reason to put him away. As usual, shepherds were heading for the mountains, as they had done for centuries in times of war and turmoil in the valley.

As for the Wolf family, there was no other place to go. Ehrlich expected the war would, sooner or later, come to Italy and, perhaps, even to Avella. Their best bet was to stay put and take the lumps with the rest of the locals. However, if worse came to worse, Imalda suggested that shepherds would be happy to make room for his family up on the mountains. The Wolf family liked that option since they missed the Austrian Alps. As such, Ehrlich was assured that he would get to play his cello either in Naples or in Vienna. It never entered his mind to flee to Palestine, since instability was the order of the day in many parts of the world.

SIX

Hidden in Plain Sight

By June 1940, Europeans knew exactly what the intentions of the Fuehrer were—to occupy the rest of Europe. Il Duce's short attention span prevented him from being cognizant of the ramifications of his friend's conquests. Only a year earlier, Ciano warned Il Duce about the untrustworthiness of the Nazi leadership. The only country in Europe that could have challenged the Fuehrer's advances then was Russia, but it wasn't long before they too became a target in 1941. In the meantime, the Fuehrer bribed Stalin by allowing Russia to occupy half of Poland, making the Communist State dormant temporarily. However, Europeans should have also known about the Fuehrer's not-so-hidden intentions—the elimination of Jewish people throughout Europe.

Extermination camps were explicitly built throughout Western Europe for the sole purpose of eliminating the Jewish population. Jews in German-occupied territories began to emigrate to Italy as early as late 1939 because an entry visa was not required. The rest of Europe required one. However foreign Jews were eventually interned by the Fascist regime in small hilly towns of Southern Italy around June of 1940. As of 2009, forty-eight such camps have been reported to have existed throughout Italy, of which sixteen were located in Southern Italy. However, these reports do not represent the full account because, in some cases, records of internees' registration forms at city halls disappeared and were never recovered. Hence, there may have been more than forty-eight such camps. Personal stories of internees escaping to Italy are introduced in this chapter to elucidate how foreign Jews found themselves in internment towns in Southern Italy and survived the harsh living conditions there. Italian Jews were rounded up only if they were involved in political activities against the state.

Among other agitators and political dissidents, Carlo Levi and Communists were exiled to Aliano, Basilicata, and other small hilly towns in remote regions of Southern Italy in 1935. These towns were so isolated because modern civilization hadn't reached there yet. Hence, the title of Levi's book, *Christ Stopped at Eboli*. It was a common complaint among the peasants in the Piazza of Aliano, "Gesu Cristo si ha fermato a Eboli," implying, in a jokingly way, that modern civilization must have stopped at Eboli. Thus, the locals equated Christ with civilization. The divide between the peasant and the gentry classes in Aliano was even deeper than in Avella. Political exiles there endured a secluded, harsh life in a malaria-infested region of Italy. As a journalist, Mussolini knew firsthand the power of the visual—out of sight, out of mind. He did not want to draw attention to the plight of political dissidents by putting them in places easily accessible to outsiders and, especially, to the media. He wanted to convey to the Italian people that there were no dissidents and that everyone was fine with Fascism in Italy. He succeeded to some extent. The only escape from one of these God-forbidden places occurred in 1929.

Carlo Rosselli, a Socialist, was exiled to the island of Lipari, about ten miles north of Sicily. Lipari was so remote that escape was considered impossible. Carlo Rosselli escaped by boat to Tunisia and on to France. He and his brother, Nello, were later killed by Fascist thugs in 1937. Certainly, the rest of Italy was not aware of those remote places. Mussolini learned that he could be successful in hiding political dissidents from the rest of Italy and the world and, icing on the cake, there was no need to pay for jails, guards, and maintenance. He applied the lesson learned in 1935 with the creation of so-called internment towns in 1940. He hid the internment towns in Italy like the town of Aliano, where Carlo Levi was interned. Not even people in towns bordering the internment towns became aware of the internees.

More importantly, Mussolini wanted to convey to Hitler that Italy also had internment camps, as in Germany. So, what if he mislabeled camps as towns? Just a small lie. The impression on Hitler's mind mattered more than the lie. But the Fuehrer knew that Italy was unprepared for war and that Mussolini depended on his goodwill and there was none to be had. Camps in Germany were extermination camps. The ones in Southern Italy were not. In fact, not a single Jewish person, political dissident, nor Roma died there during WWII, except from sickness such as malaria, influenza, and typhoid due to lack of medicine. Internment towns in Southern Italy were liberated by the Allied Army in late 1943. After 1943, the Nazis rounded up Jewish internees in towns of Northern Italy and deported them and other internees—LGBTQ and Romanis—to extermination camps in Germany and elsewhere to be killed.

Convents, monasteries, abandoned churches, castles, and old villas were utilized to house internees. In some cases, they were housed in regular run-down houses or apartments. Internees would walk around town incognito. Locals were too busy trying to survive a war to notice a stranger in town.

The Fascists interned anyone deemed to be dangerous to the party, especially political dissidents, foreign Jews, nationals of enemy states, Romani, and many others. As such, the Fascist government ordered the arrest of all German, Austrian, Polish, Czechoslovakian, and stateless Jews between the ages of eighteen and sixty and transferred them to internment towns. There is no proof of any discussions on record between the Italian and German authorities about the disposition of those internment towns.

The internment camps were classified into two different categories: One was for foreign-born civilians who were detained according to war laws. The others were detained for public safety reasons. For either category, one could be detained as internamento libero or free internment, which obligated the internee to remain in small towns, usually remotely located. The internee didn't report to anyone. He was free to move about town. However, the internee was responsible for his own food and lodging. The other type of internment camp forced the internee to live in barracked camps or, more often than not, in a town designated by the prefect.

Nevertheless, internment meant severe restriction of personal freedom, similar to prison. People were separated from their families, housing, familiar social and occupational surroundings. They were arbitrarily put together, depending upon the capacity of the camp or internment town. The towns were loosely guarded and not by barbed wire. Only for urgently needed medical treatment was an exit permit issued by the mayor or magistrate. Resistance to regulations usually led to a transfer to a stricter camp or town, as on one of the islands off the Italian mainland, like the island of Lipari. That is the largest of a chain of islands in a volcanic archipelago situated between the well-known Volcanos of Vesuvius and Etna. The internees were also not permitted to work but received a daily allowance of 6.50 lire, which is about one dollar today. The amount scaled to the needs of the poor rural populace and was increased several times to compensate for progressive inflation.

INTERNMENT IN THE TOWN OF CAMPAGNA

The news about Dunkirk's encirclement by the German Army reached the world. Realization began to creep into the people of Paris that their city was vulnerable to occupation. It initiated an exodus to any place outside of France. Jewish residents of the Le Marais District next to the Notre Dame Cathedral were apprehensive, to say the least, because they had heard much about racial law enactments and implementations in neighboring countries. Jean-Claude Almand owned a kosher butcher shop in that district along Rue du Renard. His father, Jorge, opened the shop soon after he escaped Spanish Fascists during the civil war. Jean-Claude changed his name from Juanito, as his father fondly called him. The family came from a poor background. The shop was their only means of making a living in France and they didn't want to part with it. Jorge was born in the Spanish Basque region of Bilbao which borders the Atlantic Ocean. Although Dunkirk was about 150 miles north of Paris, the thought of relinquishing the shop and the indignities associated with the racial laws weighed heavily on their minds.

They decided to transfer ownership of the shop to a trusted Socialist non-Jewish friend from Basque. Jorge returned to Bilbao with his wife Rosalina, since the civil war in Spain had ended. But Jean-Claude headed to Portofino, Italy, since Italy had no entry visa requirement. Besides, he often visited his childhood friend from Bilbao there, who also owned a butcher shop but it was not kosher. With the help of his friend, he established another kosher butcher shop near the marina side of town. The shop flourished beyond expectations, to the point that he was going to invite his father to join him in Portofino. He missed hearing his father call for his Juanito with that staccato voice. His mother would rush over to admonish his father for that authoritative voice.

Another reason why Jean-Claude wanted his parents there was to introduce them to his fiance. Before he could even plan for the big day, the local carabinieri showed up in his shop. He didn't think much of the visit, because often they would stop by the shop and simply shoot the breeze with him. But not this time. In a very apologetic way, they requested his presence at the office of the Maresciallo at 7 a.m. the next day. "About what?" Jean-Claude inquired. The carabinieri walked away shrugging their shoulders. He had taken care of the paperwork to obtain a license for the shop. Other than that, he couldn't think of anything else to worry about.

The Maresciallo explained to Jean-Claude the new order imposed on him by the Fascists. The manner in which he referred to the Fascists, it was clear to Jean-Claude that there was no love lost between the Maresciallo and the Fascists thugs in town. He said the new order required Jean-Claude to be detained overnight at the station and to be transported to an internment town for the duration of the war. Explaining the whys of the order didn't alleviate the shock of the sudden change in Jean-Claude's life. "Is there anything that you want me to do for you while you are gone?" Maresciallo added. Jean-Claude recovered from his shock and asked him if he could tell his friend Corrado to close his shop and apartment and hand him the keys.

That evening, he was incarcerated with five other foreign Jewish prisoners at the police station. Very early in the morning, the six Jewish prisoners were escorted by two carabinieri guards to the train station. Their anxiety subsided to some extent, when they realized from the track number that the train was headed to Naples and not toward the German border. Still, they couldn't comprehend why Naples. At Naples, they switched to a local train to Eboli, the town made famous by Carlo Levi. The guards from Portofino were replaced by two from Naples. At Eboli, they boarded a bus to their final destination: the town of Campagna.

The bus miraculously navigated the circuitous road and dangerous curves up the mountain to the town. The road was barely wide enough for the bus to travel on, especially around the curves and large boulders protruded from the top of the mountain. Then a deep gorge came into view, enough to drive the heart into rapid palpitations. The six internees were exhausted by the time they arrived at the piazza, where the city hall of Campagna was located. They were then escorted to the magistrate, who informed them of the rules by which they were interned and assigned to a convent or a monastery. Written instructions in various languages were handed out.

There were two internment sites in Campagna. The town is located about twenty miles east of the city of Salerno in the Picentine Mountains of the Cilento area, and about five miles north of Eboli. The criteria for the location of such internments, in addition to being remote, was that they were not near any ports, important roads, railway lines, airports, or munitions factories. Campagna met those criteria and the prefect of Salerno chose two religious buildings in the town to be inhabited by the internees, the Convent of the Osservanti dell'Immacolata Concezione and the Dominican monastery of San Bartolomeo, both of which already had been used as training facilities and barracks for officer candidates in the Italian army. The San Bartolomeo monastery was built in the 1400s on a steep slope of the Girolo Hill in the valley near the Atri River. At the time, the building had three floors and sufficient room for 450 people plus guards. The Concezione or Conception Convent dates back to the 1500s and was somewhat smaller than the monastery. The internment buildings were for men only.

Since the internees lived in close quarters, the Fascist rule of not socializing didn't apply. Normally, the rule applied in town settings whereby internees were housed in different parts of town, as in the case of Carlo Levi interned in Aliano in the Basilicata region. This allowed for some social freedom enough to make the lives of internees in Campagna tolerable.

The San Bartolomeo Church is immediately adjacent to residential buildings in what was, and still is, a small mountain town. Prisoners were apparently at liberty to wander around and make friends with the populace and even accept hospitality, such as meals. Two inmates died of illness in three years and were buried in the local cemetery with Jewish rites. There were two rabbis among the detainees. A number of the inmates were also doctors who provided medical attention. Internees had a soccer team that played against local amateur teams, and they had a camp bulletin. Jean-Claude played goalie for the team which competed in Serie C level soccer, equivalent to third-level soccer in Italy. The team representing Campagna was a former minor league team of Naples, Serie A. Also, a small synagogue was set up in San Bartolomeo church. For a while, a pianist among the prisoners played the organ for Christian services on Sundays.

While the Jewish internees did have curfew to adhere to, they had the same rations as the local population. The camp was never a concentration camp in the Nazi sense. Internees were allowed to receive food parcels and visit sick relatives. In addition, there were no mail restrictions. None of the internees was killed or subjected to violence. In fact, the internees were constantly protected from deportation to Germany, as Nazi Gestapo police and SS troops often requested. Local Fascist authorities kept the activities of internees hidden from higher authorities. However, during the retreat of the German Army from Sicily in August of 1943, a German major asked permission from madre superiora to inspect the San Bartolomeo Convent as possible quarters for German officers. The major promised to be back the next day. That evening, all the internees fled to the mountains with the help of the guards, nuns, and the locals. Upon inspection, the Major decided that the convent was not suitable for officer quarters. The major was really in search of Jewish Internees. The fact that he promised to return the next day may have been, perhaps, a not-so-subtle way to warn the nuns.

That was not the last attempt by German troops to search for Jewish internees. Days before the German Army retreated from Salerno, the same major returned to the convent. But this time, he didn't ask for permission. The day before his appearance, a patrol stopped in front of the convent for an hour or so, which served as a warning. Soldiers usually just forced their way into the convent. For whatever reason, religious or a woman's intuition, the nuns anticipated that the major would return and prepared. The internees returned to the hills when the Germans finally retreated north to Rome. The camp operated from June 16, 1940 to September 8, 1943. Thereafter, the guards walked away from guarding the internees. The guards were not paid and they had to take care of their own starving families. Jean-Claude decided to stay put until the end of the war. There was still a war waged north of the Alps.

Between late 1943 and 1945, the people of Campagna, or any other internment town in Southern Italy had a common desire—to survive this war. After the warring armies headed north, another enemy appeared—starvation. The only recourse for the people of Campagna was to forage the nearby hills for food and wild animals such as wild boars, rabbits, foxes, and deer. Jean-Claude was right at home on the mountains, as his father used to take him along as a young man on the Pyrenees to hunt for wild boars. These are ferocious animals that test a hunter's moment of truth—him or the boar—as boars will charge at a hunter, if challenged. Either the hunter climbs a tree nearby or stands his ground and kills the boar. Those lessons came handy, as Jean-Claude survived the starvation period and looked forward to resuming his life in Portofino after the war.

When he returned to Portofino, his parents and his friend Corrado were waiting for him with open arms at the butcher shop. The shop was in full swing serving local customers. Apparently, his parents had had enough of Franco's regime in Spain, since both Jorge and his wife were avowed Communists at heart and Franco a mixed-up Fascist. The Liguria and Reggio Emilia regions of Italy represented the stronghold of Communism in Italy after the war. People there voted predominantly for the Communist Party. As far as the parents were concerned, they came home, knowing their son would soon join them. Not only did they revive the shop, but also Jean-Claude's apartment. They decided to give Jean-Claude breathing room by renting an apartment on the hills overlooking the marina, where Jean-Claude's shop and apartment were located. Life was beautiful once again. There were no plans to go back to Paris.

INTERNMENT CAMP IN FERRAMONTI DI TARSIA

By August of 1939, the Polish territory of Danzig occupied the attention of European media. Government officials of Britain, France, Italy, and the rest of the world worked feverishly to prevent a war. It didn't matter what was proposed to appease Hitler. He was hell-bent on invading Poland. His argument was that the German-speaking people of Danzig needed protection. Everyone knew that the argument made enough sense to kill a horse.

After the Stockholm reception receiving the Nobel prize in physics, Fermi and his wife didn't return to the University of Rome, as most colleagues expected. They hightailed it to Columbia University in New York City. However, in retrospect, it was not a surprising move by the Fermi family. The Fascist government had just enacted racial laws in Italy in July of 1938 which didn't please Fermi's wife, Laura, who was Jewish. They braved the terrible sea conditions of the Atlantic Ocean in December instead.

David and his wife, Olga, decided to leave Poland for the only country in Europe that didn't require an entry visa: Italy. David Puzkarski was an aspiring young assistant professor in the physics department at the University of Poznan in Poland. He admired the work of Enrico Fermi, who, the year before, had received the Nobel Prize in Physics for his work in splitting an atom. The experiment cost him $160. Today, any high-energy experiment costs well above $15 billion.

The Puzkarski family traveled to Ghezzano, a small town near Pisa in the Tuscany region of Italy, only because Fermi was once a student there at the University of Pisa, Scuola Normale Superiore. During Fermi's tenure, the school's emphasis was more on classical literature and liberal arts. The university hired David as a part-time lecturer as he was an international scholar of physics. The racial laws were not implemented yet at small universities. Rather, universities in big cities such as Rome or Milan drew the attention of Fascists. That was the hope of the administrators at Pisa University anyway. Just the thought of being in Pisa, where David and Olga wanted to be, and away from an imminent war, was comforting.

After the invasion of Poland by Germany, there was a brief lull in warfare until Germany invaded France. However, a dark cloud soon appeared on the horizon. As David prepared for his morning class, a knock on the door interrupted his train of thought. Two carabinieri appeared dressed in formal uniforms with black triangular hats, as in a funeral procession. They requested his and his wife's presence in the general meeting room at city hall in Pisa at 7 a.m. After they arrived, many hours passed before they were moved to the local prison, where they were placed in close proximity with others as well as with common criminals. The cell was overcrowded, lacking the most basic sanitary facilities, and infested with lice and fleas. After hours of excruciating wait, the carabinieri escorted the Puzkarski couple to the train station where they boarded a train scheduled to arrive in Cosenza, in the Calabria region, that evening.

The carabinieri never explained their actions. Only during transport did the couple realize that they were traveling south and not being shipped to the German border. They thought they finally learned of their destination when they arrived in Cosenza. But then a transport guard escorted them to a bus full of prisoners. The bus stopped at a camping ground full of recently built barracks, the Ferramonti camp, the only camp housing both men and women. The camp was more like a town, much like the ones built for American soldiers after the war in Long Island by William Levitt.

Ferramonti was the largest internment camp in Southern Italy. Established in the summer of 1940, it stretched over an area of sixteen acres and was made up of ninety-two barracks of various sizes, with many of them built in the classic "U" shape and equipped with kitchens, latrines, and common sinks. The Italians began building Ferramonti on June 4, less than a week before Italy entered World War II. The arraignment of foreign Jews began on June 15, and prisoners began arriving at the camp on June 20. From 1940 to 1943, over 3,800 Jews were interned at the camp—3,682 were foreign-born Jews, and 141 were Italians. In general, Italian-born Jews were not imprisoned unless they participated in anti-Fascist activities. At first, upon arrival, the Puzkarskis were designated a barrack and assigned a mattress, a pillow, two blankets, two sheets, and a towel. However, they were so tired that they slept on the wooden floors. The distribution of quinine, essential for the treatment of malaria, was prohibited, although this measure was later amended.

The camp was located about twenty miles north of Cosenza, in the Calabria region of Southern Italy, the boot. It had been erected on a swampy, mosquito-infested site near the Crati River. After heavy rain in winter and spring, the terrain turned into mud and temperatures hovered around 105–110°F in the summer. According to an American report written after liberation, from the arrival of the first internees to the end of 1943 there were 820 cases of malaria and 109 of jaundice. Fortunately, this type of malaria was not severe or fatal, and so no deaths resulted. But the feverish victims were forced to lay for weeks on their cots without the necessary nourishment or medications.

Ferramonti was under the direction of a police chief or questore who was directly responsible to the Fascist minister of the interior in Rome. Under this supervision there developed a self-governing system by the internees which, as surprising as it may seem in a Fascist country, was based on democratic principles. A meeting of the barrack representatives was held to elect the camp spokesperson and the persons responsible for the various commissions such as health, school, and culture. The camp administration granted considerable latitude to prisoner self-government and was concerned as well as feared that the Ministry of the Interior would intervene. The Jewish community in turn began to organize an internal parliament representing members of various barracks. A soccer team was organized and coached by a former major league soccer coach. It competed against local competition but all games were played at the Ferramonti camp.

Gradually the internees set up a school, pharmacy, medical station, three synagogues, and one Catholic and one Greek-Orthodox chapel. With donations from a private philanthropic relief organization in Milan, a concert grand piano was acquired. David Puzkarski volunteered to organize a piano competition in which he participated. He had to play his beloved Chopin piano compositions. The audience was starved for beautiful inspiring music as played by David. Each Sunday, David was compelled to play the piano for them. Not even a fly was allowed to distract with David's playing. An active cultural life developed, with theatrical performances and musical events that were attended by police officials along with their wives and children.

Initially, piano recitals were attended by neighbors and friends. With time, they grew to larger audiences and took place in the general purpose room where movies, theater, and musical events took place. Local people were invited to these events. In particular, Stefano, the local band leader, was invited by the Puzkarskis. They had much in common. Besides the piano concerts, Stefano was also using the occasions there to recruit farmhands for his extensive farms in the vicinity. Most, if not all of the local young men, weren't around to tender the farms. Olga and David had lived in their youth on farms in Eastern Poland where farms stretched as far as the eyes could see.

The year 1943 was the most difficult for Ferramonti internees. Between August and September, the German Hermann Göring Army Division retreated from Sicily, and passed a few meters from the camp. To avoid potential danger, the guards ordered the evacuation of the camp and all the internees who could, fled to the surrounding countryside, and were hosted by farmers in the town of Tarsia. To avoid a Nazi intrusion and protect the ones who remained in the camp because they were too old or sick, a yellow flag was hoisted at the entrance of the camp with the presence of a priest to recite the last rites and to explain to the Major the presence of a typhus epidemic inside the barracks. A Jewish rabbi dressed as a monk recited in Latin. Fortunately, the Major didn't know any Latin. Thanks to these stratagems, Ferramonti was unscathed by the retreating German troops.

Even though the Ferramonti camp was freed by the British in September 1943, many internees remained there in the ensuing years. David and Olga decided to stay put because there was still a war going on in Poland. Germany fully occupied Poland at this time. They also felt a true kinship with the locals. A considerable number of marriages, in fact five, were celebrated in Ferramonti di Tarsia, many motivated to obtain one of the sought-after family barracks. In addition, twenty-five children were born there, legitimately or otherwise.

It was, perhaps, also Ferramonti's location in Italy's deep south, far away from Rome's Fascist radar, that kept people safe. People in Ferramonti were unaware of the atrocities occurring in other camps, such as at Auschwitz in Poland. Though inmates went hungry, nobody starved. One way or another, with the help of the locals, the internees managed to survive that terrible ordeal, war, starvation, and extermination camps.

Chronologically, it was the first camp to be freed and also the last to be formally closed. A total of thirty-eight Jews and five Gentiles lost their lives in Ferramonti. Ironically, the only internees to die from machine gun fire were those from an Allied plane which flew over the camp and mistook it for a hostile military site. The aircraft fired on the occupants, killing four people and injuring sixteen others at the end of August 1943. After September 8, the Italian guards left the camp, and, on the morning of September 14, 1943, the first British military trucks entered the camp. The camp was officially closed on December 11, 1945.

By late 1943, there was no food except, perhaps, in the farms. Deserters flocked to farms in Calabria and Basilicata, but still there were not enough farmhands to alleviate the food shortage. Stefano was happy to oblige and invited the Puzkarskis to help themselves on the farm and, for that matter, stay on the farm if they wished. They flip-flopped between barn and barrack living. Occasionally, David gave a piano concert at the general-purpose room where Stefano brought his family and friends along. Physics took a back seat to everything else until the war was over in mid-1945. The main priority now was food.

When the Puzkarskis returned to Poland, the country was in total shambles. Russia was now occupying Poland instead of Germany. As in other countries occupied by Russia, most valuable goods, agriculture, and art were transported to Russia. That left occupied countries in starvation and ill-equipped to compete in the market. The object was for these countries to depend on Russia. Half of the faculty staff at Poznan University was missing. Laboratories were non-functional. It was a university only in name. Nevertheless, David returned to his post and resumed his studies to help build the university to its former days. At least, he exercised his freedom to do what he always wanted to do.

INTERNMENTS IN POTENZA, BRIENZA, & TITO

German Jews took the brunt of persecution much earlier than any other country in Europe long before WWII. It didn't help that Rolf Horstman's father, Peter, fought with the German Army in WWI where he was injured and received the Iron Cross for bravery. Stormtroopers made life miserable for Peter anywhere in Hamburg. It only got worse with Hitler in charge of the government, especially when the Nuremberg racial laws were ratified. Rolf took over the bakery in the Niendorf District of Hamburg, as his parents emigrated to Palestine. After the event of Kristallnacht in late 1938, Rolf finally capitulated and decided to leave Germany.

The biggest headache for Rolf was giving up the ownership of the bakery to a total stranger whose only qualification was that he hated Jews. This process of transfer of properties was often referred to as Nazi Aryanization. To add insult to injury, Nazis transferred him to the Dachau concentration camp. It defied logic and civilized laws in any country of Europe. Rolf was released from Dachau with the proviso that he left Germany immediately with his wife and son. Furthermore, the Nazi government required Rolf to pay an exit tax equivalent in value to about half the prize of all the properties he owned including his house, jewelry, paintings, etc.

The Horstman family had just enough money left to take a train to Bolzano, where in the past, they often had vacationed and skied on the Alps. Rolf had often traveled to Bolzano with his father as a young boy. That was where his father spent time in the trenches during WWI. With the help of the Jewish community there, Rolf was able to settle and eventually open a bakery specializing in carrot cakes.

In the fall of 1940, two carabinieri visited the bakery and requested that he and his family appear early the next morning at the maresciallo's office. The request reminded him so much of how things were done in Germany, when he was sent to Dachau. Rolf immediately locked up his bakery and apartment the next morning. As expected, and without much explanation by the Maresciallo, the family was escorted to the train station where they boarded an express train to Naples. At least, the train was not heading north toward the Alps but south to warm Naples. Rolf had always wanted to go there, but now he had no choice but to go there with family, how ironic.

Besides the Horstman family, another Jewish person from the former Sudetenland boarded the train toward Naples. He too was escorted on the train by the same two carabinieri. He introduced himself to the family as Herr Karl Shultz. The same Aryanization process had taken place after the night of Kristallnacht whereby ownership of Shultz's leather handbag store was transferred to a non-Jew. Like them, he emigrated to a town near Bolzano. At the Naples train station the two carabinieri from Bolzano were replaced by two from Naples. They then all boarded a local train to Potenza in the Basilicata region, the poorest region in Italy then and now. Once there, a guard escorted Karl by bus to a small town about ten miles east of Potenza, called Brienza. A civilian employee from Potenza's city hall escorted the Horstman family to the Magistrate Office, a short walk from the station.

Upon entering the office, Rolf signed a registration form which he was required to sign every day promptly at 9 a.m. The magistrate then explained the rules governing their stay in Potenza and handed out instructions in German and Italian. A translator stood by as the magistrate explained the rules in German. They were told that a subsidy was available for them to help pay rent for an apartment. They were free to roam around the city but they could not socialize with other internees. The magistrate then escorted them to the apartment and proudly displayed running hot water in the apartment.

However, the subsidy barely paid for the rent. A resourceful Rolf convinced a bakery to employ him part-time serving coffee to the morning crowd on the way to the train station. Karl was not so lucky. His single room apartment in Brienza had no running water in a remote small hilly town infested with mosquitos. His only consolation was that he could freely walk around town, on one street.

The German troops camped in Potenza after retreating from Sicily in mid-September 1943. They occupied the town for about ten days. That was not enough time for SS troops and Gestapo police to organize a raid. The internees scampered to the mountains and hid in the lofts of barns with goats and cattle beneath them. Others didn't venture into the streets in order to avoid either meeting the troops or the daily Allied bombing. Rolf stayed put in his job at the bakery. Through it all, not one local informed the troops about the internees' whereabouts. The fact that German troops were in town in a retreating mode and the Fascist leader was incarcerated reminded them that the curtain was about to come down on them at any moment.

The main purpose of German troops being in Potenza was to defend the retreat of the main contingent of the German Army to Salerno and eventually to Rome. Locals were forced to dig ditches and perform other manual labor. British planes dropped leaflets to warn residents of the impending Allied bombing there, especially around the railroad station. Allied bombing devastated the station and part of the city resulting in many deaths.

Besides Potenza, German patrol troops camped in Tito and Brienza. These two towns were located five and ten miles east of Potenza, respectively. The patrols served as a lookout for Allied troops in that area, giving German troops in Potenza an escape route north. After a gallant effort by Canadian troops from west of Potenza, German troops in all three towns were forced to hightail it north in late September via the city of Avellino.

Being small towns, the internees in Tito and Brienza fell under closer scrutiny by German patrol troops. In one particular incident in Brienza, there was a foreign Jewish family interned in town and the daughter had long blond hair. She looked Germanic. One day, she and a friend were walking, and two German officers commented on how Aryan she looked. They pretended to speak Italian so that no questions could be asked of them. However, there was a happy ending to this incident. The interest of the soldier was only of the amorous kind. One of the girls and one of the German officers married after the war in Italy. It was that marriage certificate which eventually proved the existence of Jewish internees in Brienza. How many more internment towns were like Brienza?

After the Germans left Potenza, there was freedom at last for the next two years. The Horstman family was counting the days when they could get back home. There was no reason to rush home, because the war was still raging up north. In the meantime, the family and the people in town were just trying to stay alive and healthy until better times. As in other internment towns, lack of food predominated everything else, including stoppage of subsidies, since the Fascist government ceased to exist.

In the beginning of the summer of 1945, the family headed home. The city of Hamburg was unrecognizable after the heavy Allied bombing. The Blankenese District, near the Elbe River, was totally wiped out. Damage in the Niendorf District was significantly less. However, the bakery that the family once owned no longer existed. Government assistance helped out in the search for an apartment. The ultimate goal was to re-establish a bakery in the same Niendorf neighborhood as before.

The Wolf family hunkered down in Avella for a couple of years while other Jewish families tried to escape to Italy during that time to avoid being trapped by the Nazis north of the Alps. By then, internment towns sprouted throughout Italy like mushrooms. Avella was not selected by Rome as an internment town, although it had all the requisites of an actual one. Ehrlich had a premonition that sooner or later Fascist thugs in Avella would be coming for him and the family.

Ramiro paid a visit to the Wolf family household together with Don Nicola. Both looked very somber. Ehrlich had anticipated pretty much what the visit was all about. News of internment towns began to leak because there were just too many to keep bottled up as in the times of Carlo Levi. The somber mood suddenly changed as Arya jumped into the arms of Don Nicola shouting for her uncle, "Zio! Zio!" Both Don Nicola and Ramiro planted a soft kiss on Arya's beautiful blond hair, and handed a baby doll to Arya. Arya enjoyed being in the children's party arranged by Ramiro at his indoor pool.

Ramiro explained to Ehrlich and Nanna in a direct manner that living in a small town like Avella is very different from a city like Vienna. For one thing, there are no secrets in a small town. Everyone in town knew all about your presence and background, especially local Fascists. As Ramiro stared at Don Nicola, he added that they identified Ehrlich as a protégé of Don Nicola, who they hate with a passion as well as anyone associated with him. This was a warning for Don Nicola to stop barking at Blackshirts and at local Fascists.

"Hence, the local Fascists have labeled you as a security risk to the Fascist State, because you are a foreign Jew," Ramiro went on. "The Fascists have reported you to the Maresciallo requesting for your family to be sent to one of the internment towns in Southern Italy. The prefect and I have strategized as to which one. The town of Tito is ideally suited to your needs as well as being near to us. Your family will be cared for by another mother hen like Imalda. Her name is Vera Strega and she is the matriarch of the shepherd community there. She will find proper housing accommodations and food, and protect your family from the Fascists."

The Wolfs arrived in Tito where Strega lived. Strega's apartment was situated across the piazza from her son-in-law's barber shop. Male clients went there to gossip and get a shave. But most customers were women, since the barber had also kept up with the latest women hairstyles. The son-in-law's professional name was Ottavio, as he felt the Roman name gave him respectability. However, his lady customers called him Bambolone, a big boy doll. Upon arrival, Strega could see from her apartment's window that a big Maserati auto parked outside the front door. She recognized who the driver was and rushed out even though her hands were filled with ricotta. She had to drop everything and greet her old friend, Ramiro. Strega often joined Imalda on the mountains of Avella and Tito in search of grazing fields for their sheep. Strega had met all of Sergio and Imalda's friends in the neighborhood, including Ramiro. She loved Ramiro for his humility. It also helped to be very wealthy.

Strega jokingly embraced Ramiro only to make her husband jealous knowing full well that Ramiro would recognize the ruse. However, her husband didn't bite, and instead smiled at Ramiro. Ehrlich and Nanna were amused, realizing then that they were in good hands. They recognized in Strega a loving woman who was tough as nails when she had to be. So, everything that Ramiro had said about Strega was true. They felt at ease. Immediately, Strega returned to her apartment to put some hot ricotta in a fig leaf for Arya. Ramiro's last words to Strega were: "Ti raccommando," implying to take care of the family. Strega replied, "Ma fa a Napule." The gist of her joking reply was, "No need to remind me, be assured that they will be taken care of." Ramiro got a big chuckle and smiled as he walked away.

Usually, the phrase, "Ti raccommando" is used by a Mafioso or Camorristo or the equivalent in Southern Italy, which is Ndrangheta, in order to ask someone for a special favor that carries a lot of weight. However, Strega knew very well that Ramiro was not a Mafioso, but his request came from the heart and was sincere. In turn, her reply was to reassure Ramiro, in a loving and not derogatory way, that she understood the nature and seriousness of what was at stake. Of course, no offense was taken, but it evoked a smile from Ramiro as he walked away.

The first thing that Nanna inquired about was the whereabouts of a local doctor. Strega noticed that Nanna was pregnant. There was no local doctor but Strega delivered all the babies in town. That was the beginning of a beautiful friendship. The first thing that Strega did was to find housing for the Wolf family and made sure that it was close enough to hers in case of emergency. At least, Nanna could shout loud enough for Strega to hear.

Coming from Vienna, Tito was quite a shock for the family, especially when they discovered that there was no running water in the house. But, at least, they were in a position to exercise their free will. No one around them imposed their ways on them, as in Vienna. The people were friendly and extremely helpful. In effect, the townies and the new emigres were all in the same boat, whether they liked it or not. The next day, Strega registered the newcomers with city hall. Ehrlich and Nanna were impressed with the way she demanded and received respect from the officials. Ehrlich was required to sign in every morning no later than 9:00 a.m.

Strega delivered a baby boy, Werner, about four months after the arrival of the Wolf family. It was 3 am. when Mr. Wolf knocked on the front door of Strega's house in full panic, as his wife was about to have a baby. By then, he had learned enough Italian. Strega knew exactly what to do and calmly walked over to his house. The Wolfs and Strega got along splendidly.

Whenever there was an issue with food as it became less available, Strega came to the rescue. For example, Strega made available goat milk routinely to the baby, as she easily had access to it. She thought that whatever the reason the Wolf family was exiled it must have been a silly one because the Fascist government was silly. Nanna learned from Strega how to cook local delicacies and, often, socialized together for a picnic which also included Bombolone's family. Often Arya and Bambolone's children played with other children in the Piazza inventing new games every day. The war meant nothing to them. Fascist dignitaries stopped coming to schools in Tito and other small towns to indoctrinate young minds. People could see through the propaganda.

There may easily have been more internment towns since registration records were destroyed by fleeing Fascist mayors or had not been kept at all. According to Elizabeth Bettina's book, *It Happened in Italy*, the mayor of Potenza denied the existence of internment residences there, although there were as many as 450 internees in town. In fact, one former internee couldn't find any records in Tito after the War. Birth and death certificates were the only proof that Jewish internees indeed lived among the populace of Potenza, Tito, and Brienza during the war. However, there is even less information about Brienza.

Overall, there was much empathy between the townies and the internees. The internees couldn't believe how backward the locals were, as they, themselves, were professionals and highly educated. Yet they could see that life was hard for the locals who never had tasted modern civilization as they had. The locals could not understand why these cultured people were in town and in the middle of a war. "Who put them here?" they would ask. But they had something in common. Both groups had to survive this war. They helped each other as best they could.

INTERNMENT CAMPS IN NORTHERN ITALY

After September 1943, the German Army occupied Italy from Rome to the

Alps. As such, the Nazis imposed their racial laws on Italian territory, including the internment towns and camps. Many of the prisoners in the north and central regions did not have an option to leave and emigrate someplace else as those in Southern Italy. The Nazis quickly established an SS and police apparatus and did not distinguish between Italian and foreign Jews. They were shipped to extermination camps instead. In the fall of 1943, German authorities rounded up Jews in Rome, Milan, Genoa, Florence, Trieste, and other major cities in Northern Italy. They established police transit camps at Fossoli di Carpi, approximately twelve miles north of Modena, at Bolzano in Northeastern Italy, and at Borgo San Dalmazzo, near the French border, to assemble internees in one location prior to deportation.

In general, these operations had limited success, due in part to advance warning given to the Jews by Italian authorities and locals, and in part to the unwillingness of many non-Jewish Italians to participate in or facilitate the roundups. For example, of approximately 10,000 Jews in Rome, German authorities were able to deport 1,023.

Giacomino lived in the Jewish Ghetto, so named in the Middle Ages, near Via Ottavio and the Jewish Library. On October 16, 1943, he woke up early and decided to smoke a cigarette along the Tiber River. The morning breeze was so soothing that it seemed like he could have walked forever. When he returned to his apartment building, he saw his furniture strewn in the street and smelled diesel. He ran up the stairs to investigate. People's clothes, suitcases, and furniture were spread all over the stairs. His heart pumped faster and faster as he approached his apartment on the top floor. No one was there. His wife, daughter, son, and nephew were all gone. Vanished in thin air, never to be seen again. To say that he was a broken man did no justice. That scar lived forever in his mind.

Settimia Spizzichino was one of the sixteen who survived Auschwitz. In 1995, she gave an interview to the BBC in London in which she said: "I came back from Auschwitz on my own. I lost my mother, two sisters, a niece, and one brother. Pius XII could have warned us about what was going to happen. We might have escaped from Rome and joined the partisans. He played right into the Germans' hands. It all happened right under his nose. But he was an anti-Semitic pope, a pro-German pope. He didn't take a single risk. And when they say the pope is like Jesus Christ, it is not true. He did not save a single child. Nothing." For more details, refer to the books, *Bitter Chicory to Sweet Espresso* by Carmine Vittoria, and *The Battle for Rome* by Robert Katz.

SEVEN
Neapolitan Law 101

The most critical aspect of internment was the interior condition of the apartments. Most, if not all internees, were not accustomed to antiquated housing styles of the Middle Ages. It must have been a traumatic experience to be exposed to such living conditions whereby families had to share bathroom facilities and sometimes no running water. In addition, overcrowding soon became critical as more internees came to Tito. Strega saw to it that the Wolf family didn't have to share their bathroom.

As the war became more and more of a burden to the Fascist government, the subsidy to the internment towns and camps diminished considerably. In fact, most internees were on their own to support themselves. Indeed, that was exactly the situation during the Abyssinian/Ethiopian War, when Dr. Carlo Levi, exiled in Aliano, had to pay for everything, including room and board and even medical supplies needed to treat the locals.

In addition to Poland, Germany gobbled up part of Central Europe and Mussolini was rewarded with the Balkan countries and the French Alps, which he craved. World leaders did what they do best, nothing. They accentuated only the fears of renewing the war. Germany shipped raw materials such as iron, nickel, coal, wood, and benzene to Italy, to upgrade the armaments of their army. The consensus among the Italian general staff was that the army was poorly equipped even with the addition of those raw materials from Germany. They needed to modernize their army to a much higher standard. Most of their weapons were from WWI. Their tanks were so small that British soldiers called them match boxes as one rifle shot could blow them up. Naval ships lacked radar, although German, American, and

Britain's navies had been equipped with it since the mid-1930s. Needless to say, the morale of soldiers and sailors was rather low. According to Ciano's diary, Italians would have preferred to fight Germany, if at all. Hitler's intentions were clear to any country in Europe—war at any time and at any place.

Fascist extremists like the Blackshirts clamored for more war. They plastered posters with pictures of Mussolini all along Main Street of Avella and sang the Fascist song "Faccetta Nera" or "Black Face" in the streets. People refused to look at the posters to the point that they no longer took their passeggiate in the evenings. The consensus among the locals was that the less said and seen of Mussolini the less likely they were to think about him. Gossip in town was no longer about the love life of Il Duce, but about the Ciano family's profiting from the armament industries.

The Communists on the west end of Main Street would take the posters down or paint over them in the middle of the night. They were itching for a fight with the Fascists since there was no popular support for any war, especially one allied with Germany. Their goal was to incite riots, or at least a disturbance, at any cost. There was no peace in the streets. For a change, Communists instigated brawls with the Fascists. The carabinieri tried to keep the peace between them by cordoning off the piazza area from both groups. The well-to-do and middle class kept their distance from both belligerents. The shepherds at the other end of Main Street appeared to be indifferent to all the commotion since they focused on ways to avoid both of them and conscription. They didn't believe in wars or revolutions, since it would only lead to more wars and revolutions. Simply put, the mindset of the shepherds was that all they needed were mountains to provide food for all seasons. Shepherds in small hilly towns of Southern Italy felt the same way.

Between the fall of 1940 and the spring of 1941, there was a lull in warfare in Europe. The people of Europe, including those in Avella, hungered for peace and normalcy. They enjoyed whatever little peace they had at that moment rather than entertain the thought of another war. Trains ran sort of on time, there were financial perks for having children, men were encouraged to marry and start a family and Mussolini was welcome to bullshit all he wanted. Hence, no reason to complain. In the shepherd neighborhood, Imalda and Felicia were basking in the winter sun as they cared for their granddaughter, Lena. By then, Lena was five years old and was chasing baby sheep all over the courtyard. Sergio was on his last inspection tour of the mountains before the winter snow. Sofia was pregnant, but that didn't stop her from working with Filomena and Serafina at the seamstress shop next to the Alvarez

Palace. Brothers Ramiro and Alvaro Alvarez were no longer mayors, as they concentrated on their personal and global businesses. Alvaro Da Alia continued managing city hall as before. Every Sunday afternoon, the four musketeers—Sergio, Alvaro, Don Nicola, and Ramiro—gathered to play cards under the shade of grapevines at Erminio's wine factory. Only Erminio was allowed to chit-chat with them. They wanted to put as much distance as possible between themselves and all that talk about the next war. A bomb could have exploded next to them and they would not have budge one centimeter. Life was beautiful, at least for that moment and at that place.

The prefect, who had been in office long before Fascism appeared on the scene, handpicked the new mayor. In effect, he acted as the liaison between the Fascist government in Rome and the province. Similarly, the office of the questore linked the national police force, the carabiniere, with the province. Sometimes these two offices acted more like a buffer between Rome and the province, as was the case in towns like Avella. In many towns in Southern Italy, peasants viewed Rome as the real enemy. However, the responsibilities of these two offices changed over the years. For example, today, the Office of the Questore also serves as the liaison between the Office of the Carabinieri, local police, and Interpol or Europol, the international police force, implying that the Office of the Questore will be around for the next 2,000 years.

Like the Alvarez brothers, the new mayor was apolitical. This was a reflection of the prefect. The other responsibility of the questore, in consultation with the prefect, was to appoint the chief of police, Maresciallo of the carabinieri, equivalent to a rank of sergeant. The enforcement of law and order at the local level was thus shared between the carabinieri who were, by and large, apolitical, and the Blackshirt Fascists, who answered to the Fascist interior minister in Rome. The questore threaded a fine line between the two extremes of law enforcement at the local level. The prefect had a free hand in appointing the mayor since the Fascist Party abolished elections and the interior minister couldn't care less about the appointments. In addition, the Prefect superseded a Fascist judge's recommendation concerning the assignment of a political dissident to an internment town or camp. All judges were accountable to the prefect since Cicero's time.

Mario managed the accounting office for the Alvarez family at the Palazzo Barone, Ramiro's estate. However, he practiced law out of his home, next to Sergio's apartment. Don Nicola was the local music impresario getting ready for the next opera performance in town. Both Mario and Don Nicola awaited word from the San Carlo opera house about returning. The racial laws prevented them from working in Naples, but not in Avella. Big cities were under the watchful eyes of Fascist judges for violators of the law. That was Il Duce's way to impress Nazi hierarchy—with the implementation of Italian racial laws in big cities. Italian people sensed where he was headed and didn't like it one bit. More war.

Don Nicola rejoiced at the stalemate between the Communists and Fascists in the streets. He could then speak his mind and not be afraid of getting beat up or sent to jail. But still, he had to be careful to pick the place and audience to exercise his newfound freedom. He was a loose cannon but dearly loved by his friends. By this time the Di Marelli family emigrated to Palestine to join Dario's family via Brindisi and the Middle East. Don Nicola represented everything that they believed in—he knew that war was imminent and that there was no way to prevent it. What's more, that Socialists and Communists had no impact on the Fascist government.

Mussolini claimed privately that the Italian people needed a bloody nose to toughen them up for the next round of wars. According to him, that was what it took for the Roman Empire to expand in Caesar's time. Needless to say, it took more than a nosebleed to build the Roman Empire. For one thing, it took powerful Centurion Armies and the backing of the Roman Senate to raise the money. Mussolini's war effort was short on both accounts. What made it more intolerable to the Italian people was his allegiance to Hitler.

It took two years after WWI before the carabinieri searched for Army recruits. Shepherds expected the same response from the carabinieri. Besides, their friend, Sergio would warn them about future raids. Sergio was privy to gossip in the carabinieri's quarters, since he was the mountain policeman sharing the same barracks. In reality, the carabinieri purposely informed Sergio about any coming raid, since, like Sergio, half of the shepherd community was related to the carabinieri.

The Fascist thugs rallied the people on Main Street to join the army. Italy was already on a warpath in Libya as the Fascist Army, under the leadership of Field Marshal Graziani, attempted to invade Egypt. The next country on the list to be invaded was Greece. Mussolini had upstaged Hitler for the first time. Prior to that, whatever invasion was planned in Europe by Italy required permission from Hitler, but not the other way around. In some sense, it was a one-way street relationship in which orders could only come down one way, from Hitler on down. The sad part of it all was that their personal relationship and one-upmanship games affected many people's lives. It was incomprehensible but true.

Some in town signed up to join the army. Others donated gold wedding rings and jewelry to the war effort. The Blackshirts were on to the shepherds. They would reconnaissance the shepherd's neighborhood from time to time for unusual activities. Regardless, shepherds were not going to sign up. The feelings among them were contempt and disdain. Besides, they didn't want to catch the wrath of Imalda. She would warn them when to hit the mountains. For the shepherds, it was also a trivial matter to avoid both the carabinieri and the thugs. They knew the infinite paths to the mountains like the backs of their hands. Plus, the two groups, carabinieri and Blackshirts, differed in their definitions of law and order. Whereas the carabinieri would go through the motions of capturing young shepherds and find a myriad of excuses to fail at that, the Fascists were earnest in trying to capture them. As such, there was no cooperation between the two police groups.

The upper class in the piazza area couldn't care less whether or not Mussolini declared war. They had bribed their way before and they would do it again to have their sons avoid enlistment or obtain special favors from the system. Their connections went all the way to Rome. Thus, the burden fell mostly on the middle class and the peasants of the west end, who were mostly Communists, and they were the ones complaining the most about the war. There was no fairness on Main Street.

The declaration of another war would not have surprised Don Nicola or the Alvarez family. For one thing, the Ramiro family had nothing to do with city hall or the Fascist Party. Don Nicola and his son were too old to be enlisted and Da Alia's two girls were ineligible for the draft. Don Nicola regained his former position in the orchestra at the San Carlo Opera House as the novelty of the Italian racial laws was beginning to ebb even in big cities. It was just a matter of time before Mario could resume his former position at the San Carlo. Even though there were fewer performances at the San Carlo, Don Nicola would find any occasion to snoop around for news about the war in Libya. He had direct access to the latest news as the port of Naples was located nearby. The port was the main one for transporting troops to and from Libya. He didn't trust the national newspapers since editors heeded Mussolini's party line.

In the meantime, Mario and his father, Alvaro, were able to hold on to their jobs as lawyer/accountant and chief of city hall, respectively. Overall, the main preoccupation of the four musketeers was to stay as far away as possible from the war, the Fascist Party, and the Fascist thugs. As for Sofia, Serafina, and Filomena, they and their seamstress shop were still in business and they catered mostly to the elites of the Fascist Party in Avella and the upper crust of the piazza crowd. Sofia was also looking forward to the birth of the next baby, a boy, as Imalda predicted this time.

All were caught up in a whirlpool of madness generated by Mussolini, but they couldn't get away from it. The locals were powerless to change things. As such, people did the best they could under difficult circumstances. Unfortunately, the nightmare lasted five more years. As in life, there are always happy moments, irrespective of the times. Exactly five years after the birth of Lena, Sofia gave birth to a baby boy, Paolo, named after Sergio's grandfather. Again, Imalda delivered the baby and this time Mario was there for the birth.

From 1940 to 1941, the German Army was forever bailing out the Italian Army in Greece and North Africa. The Italian Army was taking a shellacking from the smaller Greek Army. Hitler came to the rescue, and in doing so, he occupied the Balkan countries. He didn't leave any crumbs for Il Duce. Also, Hitler thereby had to postpone his plans to invade Russia to June. Initially, the invasion of Russia was scheduled for the spring of 1941. The delay turned out to be crucial in the defeat of the German Army in Russia.

The specter of Napoleon loomed larger and larger in the minds of Hitler and his staff of generals as the war in Russia raged on and on. The German Army command had predicted an eight-week campaign. The war situation in Russia served as an impetus for the two nemeses—the Communists and the Blackshirts—to be at each other's throats in the streets of Avella in the summer of 1942. Now, the roles were reversed. The Communist thugs were in pursuit of Fascist thugs. Partisan groups began to appear on the mountains of Avella-Baiano, free to move around. They consisted mostly of Communists, Socialists, former Army conscripts, farmers, and shepherd youths. For the first time, Communists and shepherds joined forces to fight a common enemy—Fascists. They hid in caves commonly found in the mountains. Thus, the tide had turned not only at the local level but throughout Europe and North Africa. The shadow of Dunkirk loomed greater and greater over the minds of Nazis and Fascists as El Alamein and Stalingrad were just around the corner. The myth of an invincible army was about to hit the dust.

The need for more recruits to join the Fascist Army in Libya heightened to the point that the carabinieri were forced by Fascists into action looking for any male on two legs. The only potential source of recruits was to be found in the shepherd community, as they escaped to the mountains. It was no secret where to look. The carabinieri knew in their hearts the day of reckoning was coming and the Fascists would try to impose their will on them. However, they still went through the motions to appease the Fascists. Young shepherds seemed to be one step ahead of the carabinieri, thanks to Sergio's collaboration. However, there were no more recruits to be had in Avella, as Italian troops were engaged from Stalingrad to Al Alamein, including the Balkans, with approximately 2-3 million soldiers.

Many soldiers from Avella never made it back to their girlfriends, fiancees, wives, brothers, sisters, mothers, fathers, and friends. A handful came back home from the campaigns in North Africa. Only one soldier returned from Russia. There were about 100 casualties and many others injured. One of the hardest parts of all this was not knowing what was happening to loved ones in faraway lands. Letters from the front stopped coming soon after the soldiers arrived at their destinations. The people in town became emotionally drained. Those days were the saddest period in the lives of the people of Avella. The hurt was truly unbearable. For some, the mental scar lasted a lifetime.

People sensed that Europe was on the verge of either catastrophe or liberation. As such, people were anxious. Food was becoming more and more scarce to the point that there were no more cats in the streets. For example, coffee beans were replaced by dried chicory buds. The daily diet consisted mostly of polenta. On Sunday, tomatoes were squeezed on polenta to give the appearance of a pasta dish. Butcher shops exhibited fewer meat varieties. Cat meat was sold as rabbit meat. Shops boarded windows to save glass or to discourage looting, despite there not being much to be had in the shops. The lira was worth next to nothing. Salt could be had at 150 lire per kilogram on the black market. Its original price was one lira. Sugar was unattainable and only one hundred milliliters of olive oil was allowed or just over three ounces. Green vegetables, fruits, potatoes, milk, meat, fish, eggs, tea, and coffee were impossible to obtain. Thank God for wine. It was still in abundance.

Shepherds didn't suffer as much, as the mountains provided all the food they needed. Hunting for wild boars was becoming profitable. Hence, Sergio was on the lookout for poachers to protect the food availability for people in Avella. Specifically, Sergio made sure that the clan was taken care of. The carabinieri's main preoccupation was to avoid daily conflict in the streets between Communists or partisans and Fascists. Don Nicola informed Mario that the management at the San Carlo would welcome him back to resume his former position, as soon as Mussolini disappeared from the scene. In the meantime, opera performances were curtailed for a short time. People were in no mood to be entertained.

Mario and Sofia were awakened early one morning by a loud knock on the door. Flustered and upset, Imalda pleaded, "Please help me, they have detained my nephew, Nino, on a raid in the cave of San Michele." The Blackshirt Fascists raided the cave and apprehended a group of partisans including Nino. They did not inform the carabinieri before the raid. Normally, the Fascists would request the carabinieri to raid a specific location based on their intelligence, but not this time. Mario visited Nino the next day in jail. He learned that the Fascists also discovered partisan literature, pamphlets, and posters advocating the overthrow of the Fascist State. At best, Nino would be sent to an internment camp. At worst, he could be shipped to Libya to join the Italian Army and become a casualty of war or be injured for life.

At the trial, a Fascist judge presided over the court. Mario argued that Nino couldn't possibly have written the posters or anything else, since he could barely sign his name. Besides, Nino had taken refuge in the cave, as a violent rainstorm came down on the hills. Thereupon, the judge asked Nino who was responsible for the literature. Nino declared that he needed the paperwork to start a fire. It was getting cold. Finally, Mario presented medical evidence that Nino was handicapped. Nino's left toe was mutilated, as it was bitten by a wolf. Hence, he argued that Nino should be exempt from Army service. Mario invented a cock and bull story to diffuse the issue on hand that Nino was a partisan. It must have been exasperating for the Judge to decipher fact from fiction. Neapolitans love that type of talk. It is in their nature to take things with a grain of salt when it does not involve life and death matters.

Mario's violation of the racial laws never came up during the trial, as he was Jewish and practicing law. The Fascist judge purposely stayed away from bringing it up, since the local prefect would have reprimanded him and most likely have annulled whatever decision he made in that regard. The judge instead asked Mario if he was aware of the pamphlets hidden in the cave. Mario alluded that there were rumors in town about partisan activities in the foothills. Mario knew very well that Don Nicola might have written the posters. Thereupon, the judge said, "Avella is a small town. There are no secrets here, so who did it?" Mario just shrugged his shoulders and raised both hands in the air in the typical Neapolitan gesture.

The judge sentenced Nino and Mario to internment camps. Nino as a partisan saboteur against the state and Mario as a political dissident. Interestingly, Mario did not deny the charge, because he had much to hide and did not want to produce evidence against himself and others, like Don Nicola.

The trial had nothing to do with justice. It was a search for potential threats to Fascism. The judge was amused by Nino's bullshitting as Neapolitans love that, and concluded that Nino was harmless. On the other hand, he considered Mario the real danger to Fascism in the future. Mario was a marked man, ever since he submitted a letter in an obscure naval military newsletter criticizing Fascist leadership on the poor condition of Navy ships and their lack of radar. He alluded to corruption at the highest level, and that it prevented the modernization of Italy's Navy ships.

The snooping into the Navy's magazine was nothing new by the Fascist government's intelligence agents, OVRA. Fascists were watchdogs for any institution that was not committed 100 percent to Fascism and in particular the Navy. For one thing, the Navy, in contrast to the Army, was not an early supporter of Fascism, although it was subordinate to the Fascist government by no other choice. During the Ethiopian war, political dissidents were sent to internment camps just based on what they wrote or read in personal letters. In one case, a prominent medical doctor extolled a book that he read about Socialism in a letter to a friend. The local mailman made the letter available to the Fascist agent for review of its content. The Fascist agent warned the doctor that there might be consequences in reading books of that nature. The implication of the threat was rather obvious.

Sentencing was the purview of the Fascist judge, but the implementation of it fell to the local administration, the prefect. Thus, there was a way to soften the blow of the judge. As such, the prefect had the option to consult with anyone he wished. At least, Nino avoided conscription in the Army. It was a small price to pay for Mario. He believed that the war was soon going to be over and Fascism overthrown for good. His ace in the cards was his close connection to the Alvarez brothers and indirectly to the prefect, who was the final arbiter of his fate. Mario's family was none too pleased with the outcome of the trial, regardless of the location of the internment town. Sergio, Don Nicola, and Mario's father, Alvaro, soon prevailed on Ramiro to intercede on behalf of Mario and his family.

The judge recommended sending both Nino and Mario to the internment camp at Ferramonti di Tarsia in Calabria region, a mosquito-infested place in obscurity, although he had no jurisdiction as to which internment camp to send Mario or Nino. He over-extended himself. The Alvarez family at the palazzo could not afford to turn over tons of paperwork to another accountant. They wanted to keep their finances private. Also, the family desperately needed Mario to be nearby and easily accessible. Ramiro Alvarez interceded on behalf of Mario by suggesting to the prefect where his dear friend and accountant, Mario, could be interned to alleviate pain to the family and to his global business. After all, this prefect recommended Ramiro to be mayor at one time when the Prefect needed an apolitical person like Ramiro to clean city hall of corruption. Thus, the Prefect owed Ramiro a favor.

As Fascism became more and more of a nightmare, Ramiro could take liberty with the Prefect by suggesting a camp accessible by train from Avella. Some camps in Campania, Basilicata, Calabria, and Sicily regions were remotely located and not easily accessible. Towns like Campagna and Ferramonti could only be reached by train to Eboli, then by bus and, finally, by other means of transportation. The desired option would be for Mario's family to travel readily back and forth from Avella to the internment town by a single mode of transportation, preferably a train. As such, they could visit Mario regularly, even though inconvenient to all concerned. It could have been worse. The only camp that satisfied Ramiro's criterion was the one at Tito near Potenza, which was reachable by train. Besides, it was the town where the Wolf family was interned and Ramiro was well acquainted with many people there, including Strega.

Mario was looking forward to meeting the Wolf family and the locals at Tito, but Sofia and the children were in shock. They wanted to have their papa stay home. Of course, he would have loved to stay home, but that was a quirk of life that needed to be endured. An official representative, or a carabiniere, escorted Mario when he traveled by train to Tito. The family could visit Mario any time. It could have been much worse.

EIGHT

Here Comes the Band

In July of 1942, Mario reported to the maresciallo's office in Avella for his internment in the town of Tito, Potenza Province. It was at that time that the invincible German Army was about to experience defeats for the first time at El Alamein, Egypt, and at Stalingrad, Russia. Tito is located in the Basilicata region of Italy. During the Middle Ages, Calabria and Basilicata (Lucania then) were under Byzantine rule, and the region was an important commercial center. The Jewish population then was estimated at 12,000. It flourished and influenced the commercialization of the region. Many Jews were prosperous merchants dominating such industries as silk trading and cloth dyeing. Money lending was also an important source of revenue. However, by the 1940s, the towns were poor, isolated, and infested with malaria-carrying mosquitos. Modern civilization had bypassed these towns. They were ideal remote small towns for the Fascist regime to hide political dissidents and people who may be a security risk. There was vagueness by the Fascists as to what constituted a risk. It allowed them latitude in apprehending whomever they wanted to put away into obscurity.

Sofia dreaded this day. Time seemed to fly when the family wished so much for the time to linger. Mario was accompanied by a group of shepherds, his wife and family, Don Nicola, Alvaro, and friends. They clamored for the Maresciallo not to let Mario leave Avella. Ramiro assured friends and concerned family members that Mario would be in good hands. His assurance went a long way in soothing the feelings of all those who were there, but it was time to let him go.

The Carabiniere accompanying Mario sat incognito at the opposite end of the train compartment from Mario. Everybody could see that he was a guard, as he was wearing that black robe uniform. He kept his distance from Mario so as not to draw attention to Mario and regarded himself as more of a protector than a guard. He was a veteran of WWI who had served in the Army with Sergio. He and Sergio knew each other a long time, having spent their youth up on the mountains shepherding. The relationship between the Carabiniere and Mario was very cordial and respectful. Certainly, Sergio made sure to give him an earful, as to how to take care of Mario.

At Nola, farmers, shepherds, and vendors got off the train and left the compartment looking like a barn, but it was a welcome relief. At Naples, Giamo purchased the transfer tickets, as they changed trains. Mario soon learned that Giamo paid for the tickets out of his pocket. Giamo had that swarthy appearance reflecting his descendants of millions of years ago and had a heart as big as Mount Avella. The Fascist State no longer subsidized internees for travel, food, and lodging. The government couldn't even feed its troops in Libya or any other place in Europe. The regime was bankrupt of money, soldiers, and armaments, but still pretended everything was fine and under control.

The same occurred in the Ethiopian War. Mario didn't know what to expect once he arrived at Tito, but he trusted Ramiro that everything was going to be fine. At the train station in Potenza, two carabinieri guards from the town of Tito, wearing the usual black robes and triangular hats, were waiting for the train to arrive. The two guards never greeted Mario or Giamo or checked whether or not the right internee was handed over to them. Giamo embraced Mario, planted two kisses on his cheeks, and said, "One kiss is from Sergio and the other from Imalda" and left to catch the next train back home. Without uttering a single word, the two carabinieri proceeded toward the train station in Potenza to catch the train to Tito. This time, Mario had to pay for his transfer ticket.

As the train approached the station in Tito, Mario heard faint music. His first thought was that someone important had to be on this train. He recognized the song, "Parlami D'Amore, Mariu," ("Talk to me of love, Mariu") which was a favorite Italian song and the personal anthem of Mario and Sofia. Ramiro found himself standing next to a three-piece band as he waited on the platform. One player played the trumpet, another the clarinet, and the third sang the song. Hidden behind big and jolly Ciccio was none other than Sofia. Ramiro had driven Sofia and the three musicians to the station in his beautiful Maserati. As Mario and Sofia ran into each other's arms, Ciccio sang the beautiful melody with all his heart. As for the two, the song was too short. They wanted to stay in each other's arms forever. Mario was moved to tears. At the same time, he felt that he should never have doubted Ramiro and whispered as much to Sofia. He had learned an important lesson: Faith and hope are important aspects of life. It was time to break up the party. Mario thanked Ramiro for having Sofia come to Tito. However, Ramiro, forever the gentleman, said that the song was Sofia's idea and she organized it all. As always, he preferred to stay in the background letting others take the credit for his good deeds.

He instructed Mario to meet him in front of the Palazzo Colonna, in the main piazza, after Mario's visit to city hall. Mario was required to register with the magistrate. In the meantime, Ramiro needed to send the band back to Avella before the last train departed for Naples. Otherwise, it would have been a logistical nightmare for him and Mario. There were no hotels in Tito and city hall did not register ordinary citizens to living quarters arbitrarily as political dissidents without the consent of an owner. Mario recognized the members of the band. The short and heavy-set member, Vito, played the clarinet; the tall and slender one, Peppe, the trumpet, and the swarthy-looking one, Ciccio, sang. Ciccio was the same one who delivered warm ricotta to town early in the morning on his donkey. Sergio couldn't get his mojo going unless he had that ricotta in the morning. Often, Ciccio was hired for pay by young lovers to serenade their lady friends. This was a ritual of the times before the war. His repertoire was old Neapolitan love songs.

Ramiro sensed that Sofia was apprehensive about Mario being away from the family in a strange town. Then again, everything was topsy-turvy in small towns. There were many questions running through Sofia's mind: Is it a jail? Is Mario going to be placed in a barrack? Will Mario have to do heavy work? It never entered Sofia's mind that he was going to be interned in someone's house or in a monastery. Things were moving too fast for her to comprehend the situation. She had to see for herself what was going on in Tito. Ramiro's intent was to remove all those lingering thoughts, assuring her that the family would have access to Mario at any time. Also, Strega would take care of him just like Imalda would. Besides, Ehrlich's family was there next to Strega's apartment. Sofia broke out with a relieved smile because she had heard so much about Strega from Imalda since she was a baby, thinking that any friend of Imalda must be unscrupulous and tough as nails. Ramiro wanted to convey to her that life would go on as before except Mario was required to be in Tito instead of Avella.

The two guards, who came for the ride from Potenza to Tito, scampered away during all that commotion. Apparently, they were not paid for the extra duty of accompanying Mario to city hall. No official from city hall showed up to receive Mario at the station. It befuddled Mario as to what to make of it. His first thought was, "Perhaps, if I hurry, I could go back home with Sofia, Ramiro, and the band." No such luck. He could see, from the corner of his eye, a man walking toward the station. It looked as though he didn't want to fight that hot breeze blowing off the Sahara Desert.

"Signore Da Alia?" the man said, approaching the station platform. The clerk was a short, heavy-set man wearing a typical cap and a thin jacket over his shoulder. No doubt, the man was suffering from the heat.

On the way to city hall, the streets reminded Mario of the poor section in Avella. Main Street in Avella became narrower and the housing more shabby as it approached Castle Longobardo on the hill. Tito was a carbon copy of Avella, except there were irregularly spaced steps every so often. It only made the climb to city hall more tiring. There was something about the locals that he could not relate to, at least from his first impression. He was looking forward to seeing the Wolf family and meeting and engaging people in the streets of Tito, just like he did in Avella.

Whereas in Avella, Main Street was paved and had sidewalks, in Tito, Main Street was a cobbled street with no sidewalks. The few locals who looked him over appeared to be suspicious, as if he were from a distant land. By then, Tito had many out-of-town internees. As Mario and the clerk walked up Main Street, they crossed paths with a herd of sheep heading for the hills. Mario thought that it was an unusual sight unless the sheep were headed to a body of water to cool down. Usually, sheep headed to the hills in the early morning and headed back in the evening hours. Then, immediately after that incident, a donkey loaded with farm equipment followed by a woman balancing a heavy basket on her head followed in the same direction. Mario was encouraged by what he saw. My kind of people, farmers and shepherds, Mario surmised.

Stray chickens and goats roamed all over Main Street. A pudgy woman dressed in black vestments came out of her house, leaving her front door open, shouting to no one in particular that someone had stolen her chicken. She walked from street to street raising a fuss. She didn't find her chicken. Someone must have needed that chicken more than she. Food was also scarce in Tito. A quick glance into the woman's house revealed the makeup of her house: one room consisting of a bedroom, kitchen, and barn, no different from some shepherd homes in Mario's neighborhood. There were few young men in the streets.

The town of Tito could relate to other nearby towns where internees were housed. The people's customs, lifestyles, and traditions in the Basilicata, Puglia, and Calabria regions have remained the same since the Middle Ages. In some sense, their behavior had been frozen in time. In comparison with other regions in Italy, the town, as well as many towns in the Basilicata region, were sheltered from modern civilization. Political internees, like Mario, in isolated towns like Tito placed their lives on hold until the War ended. In some sense, time was becoming irrelevant to internees and the locals. Interestingly, the great scientist, Albert Einstein, commented on the relevance of time, "...the distinction between past, present and future is only a stubborn illusion." In other words, time is an illusion, as it was then for a lot of internees and locals.

Finally, the clerk and Mario reached city hall in the piazza, across from San Vito Church. The clerk was out of breath. He needed something to drink and rushed ahead to get some water from the fountain, near Palazzo Colonna. Duke Ferdinando (Fernando) Alvarez de Toledo, Ramiro's grandfather, had married his long-distance cousin, Princess Livia Colonna. The Colonna family was a powerful family from the Middle Ages to modern times. They exerted tremendous political influence from Rome to Southern Italy including the Basilicata region. Prince Colonna of Basilicata was the biggest landowner of the whole region and owner of the Palazzo Colonna, a relative of Ramiro through marriage.

The clerk directed Mario to the third floor to see the magistrate. Normally, the clerk directed an internee to either the mayor's or the Maresciallo's office, depending on who was available. Since Fascism was out of favor with the locals, and especially with shepherds in 1942-1943, these two officials wanted no part of the internment camps. They felt that whatever association, direct or indirect, with Fascism could be detrimental to their political futures.

In 1935–36, Fascism in Italy was popular as a result of the conquest of Ethiopia. So, every Maresciallo and mayor wanted to take credit for the success of Fascism. They walked around town like peacocks trying to get attention from the populace and to exert their authority. Times changed and, as such, the mayor and the Maresciallo of Tito were sitting on the fence as to which way the political wind was blowing.

The magistrate, Pasquale, was apolitical and he was clear about the rules of internment in Tito by which Mario had to follow: no government subsidy, sign the register every morning at nine, no socializing with other internees, and stay within the confines of town. Pasquale didn't define where the confines of town were located, since he did not want to pay for guard details stationed at the confines. When Mario entered the Magistrate's office, he had the feeling that everyone in that office, including the Magistrate, had a scornful look. All that posturing between the two stopped once Mario asked the whereabouts of Strega in town. It was clear to both that shepherds made up the majority of the population in Tito.

Pasquale recognized, by the nature of the question, that Mario was cognizant of where to look. Mario explained to him that his mother-in-law was also a matriarch of the shepherd community in Avella. That brought one big smile from Pasquale. He was impressed and attentive thereafter to Mario's needs. "One of our own," Pasquale thought. It was clear from the ensuing conversations that both were anti-Fascist and sympathetic to the causes of peasants. There was a kindred spirit between the two.

Pasquale was raised in a shepherd family dating back for millennia. Early in life he had shown an aptitude for schooling. He was highly motivated in school, self-contained, and scorned trivial pursuits. He was mentally and physically more mature than most other children in school. Thus, he entered the world of wonderment and knowledge. Being bottled up in the world of poverty and peasantry for all those years, Pasquale looked forward to turning the page over on the past. The family recognized as much and sacrificed to put him through advanced schooling.

At the Lyceum school in Potenza, Pasquale majored in classic languages, Greek, Latin, and Italian. He continued his studies at the University of Cosenza, Calabria, where he earned degrees in law and accounting, and became a ragioniere (lawyer) or accountant. As with most ragionieri, he was unemployed for four years until the mayor of Tito, a Fascist friend of Pasquale at the university, appointed Pasquale as an errand clerk in the mayor's office, delivering mail to various offices. It only meant one thing to him, no turning back. From there on, he moved to city hall to distance himself from his Fascist friend.

The town of Tito consisted mostly of shepherds and farmers and they represented the peasant class. As in Avella or any other town in Southern Italy, the eternal conflict between the haves and the have-nots or between the peasants and gentry dates back as far as time itself. The conflict between the classes is inherent in human nature. No legislative or political action can regulate this natural conflict. Rallying the lower class toward Socialism and/or Communism, as in the 1930s, would have generated only another lower class and it would have been back to square one—the eternal conflict. Thus, peasants in Southern Italy have masqueraded their animosity toward the local gentry under the pretense of complaining about rulings in Rome. In their view, Rome had empowered the upper class to govern, subjugate, and control for centuries the unskilled workers, farmers and shepherds, and peasants to do menial work and produce food to feed the country at measly compensation.

Due to the turn of war events in North Africa and the Balkans, the mayor of Tito was in a quandary as to which way the political wind was blowing. Should he remain a Fascist or go through a conversion? He was sitting on the fence, forever procrastinating as to what to do. He minimized public exposure to hide his allegiance. The Maresciallo was too stupid to realize what political options lay ahead. Pasquale loathed both of them. However, Pasquale could not tip his hand, to Mario or anyone else, about his true allegiance. Mario surmised as much from his demeanor and body language when he first appeared at Pasquale's office. It was then a game of cat and mouse between officeholders and the public to save their asses in those days.

At this point, Mario had the courage to inquire about the whereabouts of the Wolf family, knowing full well that it was a no-no in the rules that Pasquale had just declared. Pasquale broke into one big smile and said, "Why didn't you ask me that in the first place? Strega's apartment is next door to city hall and the Wolf family's apartment is next to Strega's. Don't worry about the rules. That's for people I don't like. Now, I like you."

Mario seized the moment by inquiring if he could rent an apartment next to the Wolf family. Pasquale acknowledged that Strega owned only two apartments and, besides that, internees have occupied the rest of them in town. He added, "Ramiro has informed me that he has permission from his cousin to house you in the farmhouse of the garden within the palazzo."

By then, Mario was exhausted from all the traveling for that day. He decided to postpone his visit to the Wolf family. He felt like his life hung on a thread, but things were evolving for the better. Finally, he moseyed across Main Street to Palazzo Colonna, where Ramiro would be waiting to meet. The piazza was crowded with people. Old farmers and shepherds sat on benches made of stones or large rocks on one side of the piazza smoking rolled-up cigarettes and staring at no one in particular. They seemed to enjoy the morning sun and retelling the same stories over and over again until they evoked a smile or a laugh or a repeat of another old story. The gentry mostly stood in the middle of the piazza, indifferent to the peasants and vice versa. They behaved as if the ones sitting on stones came from some uncivilized world that had nothing to do with theirs. The topic of conversation among the gentry was complaints about other gentries. Their hatred of each other ran deep. That was typical of the piazza crowd, as in most small towns of Southern Italy then.

Ramiro and Sofia waited anxiously in front of the large fountain abutting the palazzo. He asked Mario, "How did the bullshit go? Sooner or later all those clowns are going to catch hell."

"I heard rumors that the mayor will be the first one on the chopping block," replied Mario. However, Mario wanted very much to clear the air with Sofia regarding Imalda, as there were some hard feelings between Sofia and her mother. He explained that the episode in court was unavoidable. It had nothing to do with Imalda and her nephew Nino. The Fascists wanted to stop Don Nicola from yapping away at them and the printing of pamphlets. Then Mario added, "They used me to silence Don Nicola. They accused me of being a political dissident only because I represented Nino in court." He continued, "So, Sofia, please tell Don Nicola not to yap at the thugs, especially now. Sooner or later, they will get their dues."

As Ramiro and Mario entered the library in the palazzo, Ramiro turned to Mario and said, "You may resume your accounting work here, but this part of the palazzo is usually inhabited by relatives of the Colonna family, but, for now, they decided to live in a safer place. Pasquale has my consent for you to stay here. A courier from Avella will bring accounting papers from Avella from time to time. However, you may want to stay in the farmhouse during your internment." The farmhouse and the garden were adjacent to the main building of the palazzo. The farmer who managed the garden was thousands of miles away, stationed north of Stalingrad, Russia. The German, Italian, and Romanian troops had been encircled at Stalingrad by the Russian Army for over three months. A custodian was left in charge of the palazzo.

The garden in the palazzo was not the only garden devoid of its farmer. In fact, most farms in Southern Italy had not been cultivated for over two years. All, or most of the young and middle-aged farmers, were in faraway lands, from Libya to Russia, fighting wars. There were many broken-hearted women in small and big towns. These towns became women-dominated.

The farmhouse was located in the middle of the garden and Tito in the middle of nowhere, remotely carved in the hills of Basilicata. The garden surrounded two swimming pools, similar to the ones in Palazzo Barone, Ramiro's residence. Mario would have access to the library and the farmhouse. The farmhouse was a typical one consisting of a barn on the side of the house, but no animals at that time. On the ground floor, farm tools, machinery, and electrical items were stored in one room. The bedroom on the second floor, with large windows, had a splendid view of the garden. In the same room, there existed a small dining table, kitchen cabinets, a small stove or burners, and a place to wash up. Bathroom facilities were located next to the barn on the ground floor. A wooden picnic table took up most of the patio outside the farmhouse. The only redeemable feature of the place was that he could walk to city hall a short distance and sign the register every morning and maintain his privacy among friends-to-be. He had a feeling that he knew them, since the neighborhood in Avella, where he had lived, got along very well with shepherds and farmers.

Mario made a mental note to ask Ramiro, if he had permission to invite Nanna's and Ehrlich's children, Arya and Werner, to the swimming pool, especially when Sofia came to visit with the children, Lena and Paolo. Ramiro thought about it and responded thusly, "The short answer is no. However, it is just a question of bribing the custodian which I am about to do now. In the meantime, relax and enjoy the summer sirocco storm from your room." The sirocco is a weather condition in Southern Italy induced by the winds of the Sahara Desert. When it rained, it deposited small sand particles from the Sahara Desert. Folklore stories of yesteryears told that this weather condition drove people to insanity. However, the sea breeze reverses the wind directions in the fall as the Siberian cold wind tries to warm up in the southern shores of Italy.

Politically, Main Street in Tito was more homogenized. Shepherds and farmers dominated both ends of Main Street. Communist and Fascist sympathizers were sprinkled here and there but never amounted to many in any part of town. Also, they were not in a position to rally their respective troops. There were not enough of them to make a difference politically. The war stretched Italy to the limit in terms of manpower and armaments. The well ran dry. People expected that, as food was getting scarcer by the day. The farmers around town had a bigger problem, no farmhands.

After the exhaustive day, Sofia and Mario retired on the terrace, above the bedroom, and gazed at the stars. It was a lonely place with no one around. The only pleasant visitor in the evenings was the cooling breeze from the Tyrrhenian Sea replacing that daytime heat. Mario and Sofia missed their children terribly as well as the four musketeers, their family, and friends. Sofia declared with vigor that she and the children were determined to visit every weekend to run the household.

The next morning, Mario accompanied Sofia to the train station. They embraced and parted. The occasion didn't call for much talking. They were left in their own thoughts. Mario thought: "The old man is a man of his word and a true sentimentalist." Sofia had peace of mind, as she learned Mario was in good hands locally due to Ramiro. As for the old man, he was happy to put the young couple at ease with the impossible family situation. By and large, internment was not much of an encumbrance to Mario's family, but an inconvenience.

All of a sudden, Mario was all alone. The people of Tito were nice and Pasquale very accommodating, but he needed a friendly person or family to lean on like the Wolf family. He and Ehrlich got along just fine in Avella, as sometimes they went hunting for wild boars in the mountains. Sergio served as a guide. Finally, he had to meet the famous Strega. He moseyed across the piazza to Strega's apartment. He introduced himself to Strega as Imalda's son-in-law. Strega's body language changed from one of being cold and curious to warmth and full of sunshine.

"I know your mother-in-law, Imalda, from way back when I was a child," Strega blurted out. She wanted to know everything about him and his family and why he was in Tito. "Quelli strunzi (those bastards) put me here in Tito," Mario pointed toward City Hall.

She didn't want to hear sad things anymore, because she had heard the same sob stories from many internees. With the warmest smile, she said, "I am here to help you, because Imalda and Ramiro would kill me otherwise and also because you are my lawyer defending me against those two," and laughed. Mario asked her if the Wolf family was home. "They should be home because I can hear the little boy screaming." Mario rushed over to the Wolf's residence and didn't bother to knock on the door. As he entered the front door, Arya came running toward Mario screaming, "Zi Mario" and jumped into Mario's arms. Arya had spent more time in Avella and Tito than in Vienna so was able to speak some Italian, at least more than her parents. The little one followed.

As this was happening, Mario fantasized how it would be when his children and Sofia planned to visit him soon. They all embraced Mario as if he were the lost uncle or brother. Ehrlich asked him, "What brings you to Tito?" Mario responded, "The same reason that you are here, except the Fascists labeled me as a political dissident." Mario went through the whole spiel of what happened to him. However, he was also there to bring good news. "Ramiro set it up so that our children and other children could use the swimming pool in the palazzo."

On the way back to the farmhouse, Mario tried to picture what the children or Sofia would say at the train station when they arrived for the weekend. He had so many questions to ask and yet he was gone for only a couple of days. One pressing need was to secure some food before the family arrived. Mario contacted Pasquale in the morning when signing in at the register and inquired as to whom to see about food. Without hesitation, Pasquale suggested that he should see the local barber in the piazza, known in town as Bambolone. Of course, everyone in town loved him. He got involved with everyone in town, from anyone's love life to inconsequential things. The only problem with that was his house was across the piazza where his wife had a good view of anyone coming and going from the shop. It raised havoc in his family. His wife was jealous of anyone, especially women, coming near him for consultation. However, Pasquale warned Mario not to call him Bambolone but Ottavio, short for Octavius.

No one in town knew his real name. As a young man, Ottavio saw an opportunity to break away from the drudgeries of shepherding. He apprenticed in a barbershop as an assistant, as the barber's son wanted no part of the barbershop business. Usually, apprenticeships were reserved for family members. In a way, Ottavio was lucky to latch on. This move derailed his plans to marry his fiancée, Carolina, whose mother, Strega, was the matriarch of their shepherd community. As a matriarch, she could not condone the marriage, since her first duty was to preserve and expand the community of shepherds. In cases like that, love always wins over the personal obstacles of others. Eventually, they married and settled in the quarters above Strega's house with a direct view of the barbershop across the Piazza.

The older men asked for a shave and the younger ones a haircut. On his own, he began to style women's hair which did not sit well with his wife. However, soon, he had more women customers than men, as the young ones left to join the Army. After a couple of years, he was drafted into the Army and shipped to Libya to fight in the Ethiopian War. Most likely, Ottavio may have been transported there by one of the Naval ships in which Mario was a Naval officer. The Army assigned Ottavio to one of the field hospitals where he learned the skills of a nurse assisting medical doctors in operating rooms. He saw enough suffering to last him more than one lifetime. It had a dramatic effect on his outlook on life. He became more jovial, and compassionate toward others, and always looked for the bright side of life. By the time he left the Army, he learned many skills and had become a true Figaro, skillful in many things but master of none.

Although the population of Tito diminished, food was scarce, farms were unattended, and people were anxious for the next news about the war. As a result, the barbershop became more of a psychology ward. Ottavio would console women whose boyfriends or husbands were away to war, American expatriates who made the mistake of returning to Tito, and people in general. He was a cheerleader and someone on whom to lean. Besides performing barbershop chores, he was also a matchmaker. Women would pass on messages to would-be suitors via Ottavio.

When Mario visited the barbershop, Ottavio already knew everything about him, symptomatic of a small town. By then, Mario was the main topic of conversation in the shepherd community, as Pasquale's big mouth told Ottavio of Mario's special connection to the shepherd community in Avella and especially to Strega. The first thing he said to Mario was, "You can call me Bambolone, but only you. My mother-in-law told me to take you to her about anything that you may need." He closed the shop and proceeded to walk with Mario across the piazza toward Strega's house. As in Rome, all roads in Tito led to Strega's house, especially when it came to food. After all, she had access to all food generated by the shepherd community in the hills nearby. She was still active as a matriarch.

Her apartment consisted of two rooms: an all-purpose room on the ground floor and a bedroom one floor above. The downstairs room served as a kitchen and dining area and had an open fireplace where cheeses were concocted. The room was gloomy and the walls over the fireplace were dark with soot. It looked more like a witch's hovel. Whatever hard feelings there may have been in the past between Ottavio and his mother-in-law, evaporated away. On many occasions, Strega had to arbitrate arguments between Ottavio and his wife about women visiting the barbershop for consultations. She was happy to see Ottavio and it showed in their body language and in their manner of speaking with each other. Strega admired Bambolone as a good-hearted person who could easily commensurate with other people's misery and do something about it, much like her.

That Friday, Mario went to the train station early in the morning knowing full well that Sofia and the children would not be there until around noon. He kept watching the clock above the train station entrance. In the meantime, he paced in and out of the station. Time became irrelevant as emotions took over. It seemed like an eternity for the train to arrive, but it finally did. Lena ran toward the platform and jumped into the arms of her papa. The little one, Paolo, trailed behind Lena and grabbed his papa's leg, wanting to be picked up as well. And Sofia was left holding the suitcases. It seemed that they stood on that platform embracing each other for-ever, trying to make up for lost time.

People waved and smiled, as the family walked past the houses on the cobbled street up to the piazza. The locals were just as happy to see the family together. It completed, in their minds, their picture of Mario, like a dossier of the man. For them, family was everything. News of the family's arrival spread up and down Main Street. At the entrance to the palazzo, Bambolone stood next to the circular foun-tain inviting himself to be with the family. He behaved like the acting mayor wel-coming them since the locals hadn't seen the mayor in a while. It was a gesture to assure the family that Mario was in good hands. He also informed Mario that some locals wanted to celebrate the arrival of the family so that all the children could frolic around the garden in the palazzo, and that permission from the palazzo's custodian was secured for Sunday afternoon. How could Mario say no to such benevolence? Bambolone was a mover and a shaker, but the custodian cashed more bribe money, besides that of Ramiro and Mario. The source of money didn't matter to the custo-dian, as long as there was more of it. No pride in those days.

When Mario's family first arrived at the palazzo, the children were excited to see the pool, the garden with grapevines, and fruit trees, very similar to their grandfather Sergio's garden. Normally, the big meal in Italy is consumed right after noon. The hot air in Tito did not cooperate with the locals' natural inclinations or preferences. So, the big meal on Sunday was pushed to the evening hours, when the cool breeze would make its appearance. Bambolone, Pasquale, Strega, Ehrlich, and their families came to the farmhouse. They brought local wine, roasted rooster, all sorts of cooked vegetables, cheese, and their children. There were children all over the place running around in the garden. That was what the people needed, a feeling that things were normal.

As always, Bambolone behaved like a master of ceremony. He loved to create happy occasions to dilute the sadness. At heart, the shepherd in him dominated his personality. He had seen enough war to last him a lifetime and wanted to erase this terrible war in people's minds. It reflected the mindset of most of the shepherds. Bambolone thought wars were meaningless. It never settled anything. It just post-poned arguments. Therefore, he tried to create a peaceful atmosphere among peo-ple, right in the middle of town, isolated from the rest of the world. In summary, Bambolone was the ringmaster of the circus as well as the clown. In a toast to the hosts and guests, Pasquale invited Sofia and the children to visit Mario anytime, with no need to formally request permission through the prefect. He said with in-dignation, "You are one of us!" slamming his hand on the table. Pasquale assumed enormous responsibility which had no precedent then. They all drank to that. After dinner, Mario's family looked forward to relaxing in the evening breeze and gazing at the stars from the terrace.

That upcoming fall of 1942, dramatic news about the war broke out around the world. Field Marshal Bernard Montgomery stopped the invasion of Field Marshal Erwin Rommel into Egypt at the border with Libya at El Alamein. The combined Italian and German armies were in full retreat to Tobruk. The Russian army overran the German positions at Stalingrad. These two battles showed the world that the Axis armies were over-extended and beatable. There was a sigh of relief in the Allied democracies. The specter of Dunkirk came back to haunt the German and Italian armies, as Winston Churchill envisioned, and Field Marshal Kesselring feared.

The effect of these two battles had a tremendous impact on Fascists, especially in small towns. Fascists became either more fanatic and died gallant and glorious deaths according to their self-images, or changed the colors of their black shirts to a more neutral color to confuse people of their former allegiances. Other Fascists took a hint from the results of the battles and left town altogether, to return in better times.

The Italian Army was in total shambles with no hope of ever regaining its for-mer strength, which was not much to begin with. This meant that the populace in Italy took the brunt of the food shortage. Germany was not going to bail the Ital-ian populace out of their misery. Germany had enough problems of its own. These turns of events brought dramatic changes at the local level. In one of the morning signings, Pasquale informed both Mario and Ehrlich that, henceforth, there was no need to come to the registry and sign in. Basically, they were on their own, no differ-ent from the locals, but their presence in town was required. There were still fanatic Fascists in everyday control.

Also, with the impending fall, the people in Tito and other small towns in South-ern Italy were preparing for the harvest. Unfortunately, the problem remained: there still weren't enough young farm hands to help out with the harvest. The absence of farmhands accentuated the shortage of food everywhere. Fortunately, there was not much to harvest in the farms inside Palazzo Colonna in Tito, or Palazzo Barone in Avella. Those farms were devoid of crops because no seeds had been planted in the spring since no one was around. However, the grapes in the garden cried for attention as they required harvesting.

This was a unique time in Fascist Italy. The top echelon leadership in government, either Fascist or traditional, were reluctant to make controversial decisions that may affect their political careers in the future. Hence, they were just as happy having the underlings make those hard decisions. Pasquale understood that and so did Mario. For example, Mario went through the motion of going through requests formally without expecting any response from anyone at city hall. They operated in the usual Neapolitan way, with a nod and a wink. Mario desperately wanted to go home at harvest time to be with Sofia, his children, and his friends in Sergio's garden, as in the golden days.

He made a formal request to visit Avella with the purpose of helping out with harvesting grapes at Sergio's. Pasquale reacted accordingly, "Can I come along?" They both laughed and filed the request away so that no one could hope to find it in a waste basket. This way no one signed off on the request, as the staff at city hall preferred. However, Mario was required to pay for the guard's extra duty, food, lodging, and travel costs. For him, it was a bargain, compared to the joy it brought to his family and friends in Avella. Obviously, Pasquale had learned a lot from Bambolone. Mario made the point that the harvesting may need more help and asked Pasquale, if the Wolf family could come along. Pasquale just shrugged his shoulders as if to say, "Why not bring your good friends, Strega, Bambolone, etc. along? Of course." Pasquale didn't mind doing small favors, as long as he appeared impartial to other internees. In those days, no one covered your back.

Word in Avella spread rapidly about Mario and the Ehrlich family's visit. People welcomed any good news, especially after all those years of being careful of what to say publicly or fearful of antagonizing the local Fascists. It was a new experience to be able to speak frankly. The Fascist thugs were no longer roaming the streets of Avella. Most of them had disappeared. Others did their best to cover their tracks and indiscretions of the past by leaving town. After the war, about 15,000 to 20,000 Fascists were hunted down by partisans and Communists and killed by trial or no trial. Whatever minute administrative connection between Rome and small towns in the South ceased to exist. As such, these towns were on their own for survival. That also applied to internees residing in those towns. As far as the peasants were concerned, that was good news because they felt that only bad news emanates from Rome. Not to hear anything from Rome was therefore a blessing and a plus.

Erminio, Sofia and the children, the four musketeers, Mario's sisters, school friends and some town people came to the train station in Avella to welcome Mario, the Wolf family, and the hired escort guard, who kept his distance in the train. The guard didn't want to spoil the reception by intruding, portraying authority, or as an enforcer of Fascist rule; though, those were duties that he was paid to do. He chose to present himself as a bystander. He was in no-man's-land, not here nor there. During the long train ride, the internees and he got along very well and arrived at an understanding in which he would be out of sight of the townspeople. He would sleep in the carabinieri's barracks in Avella. Normally, guards were required to be in full sight of prisoners, even during resting.

The moment was magic. The people in Sergio's garden were concentrating only on each other's company. Don Nicola was bubbling with emotions as he wanted to tell Mario and Ehrlich all about what had happened in town since their departure. Imalda came over to Nanna and introduced her to all. Mario's parents were so proud of their son that they followed him wherever he went. Mario and Ehrlich profusely thanked Ramiro for making their stay in Tito livable, with an opportunity to meet new friends. Sergio, the master of ceremony, was meticulous in arranging everything just so. Imalda, forever the protector, had a watchful eye on the children, who were running all around the garden. The twin sisters and Sofia gathered in one corner to gossip. Erminio was as bubbly as his spumante wine served to the guests. Finally, Imalda introduced the guest of honor, her dear friend since childhood, Vera Strega who had arrived the day before the internees. The place went wild applauding incessantly, knowing full well her role in Tito. Ramiro handed a bouquet of blue violets to Strega along with a big hug.

All of them had one thought in mind, "When is Mussolini going away?" In fact, a short time later, King Victor Emanuel III declared, in Mussolini's presence, "You are the most hated person in Italy." The question that remains to this day: Why were there internment camps when Fascism and its creator were so discredited in 1942–1943? Where was the logic? The only plausible answer was that the few ministers surrounding Il Duce were rabid fanatics who fought tenaciously for their survival and to hold on to their power or else.

After a sumptuous dinner, Don Nicola, Ramiro, Alvaro, and Erminio stood on the dining table and sang the beautiful melody, "Parlami D'Amore, Mariu" a cappella in honor of Sofia and Mario. The four of them put a lot of emotion into it, to the point of evoking some moist eyes. They had rehearsed the song in secret at Don Nicola's studio. As in life, all good or bad things come to an end. Mario and

Sofia's good dreams were short-lived. Ehrlich and Nanna wanted that moment to last forever. Nightmares created by Il Duce seemed to go on forever, but the end appeared to be on the horizon. The internees had no desire to return to Tito, but had no choice. At least, they had a tiger in their corner to fend off potential problems—Strega.

The war in Libya reached a stalemate, localized between Tobruk and El Alamein. The Axis Armies were under the command of Field Marshal Rommel and that of the Allies under Field Marshal Montgomery. Both armies did not have sufficient manpower or firepower to induce a major breakthrough either way. After Dunkirk, the British and colonial armies were not in any position to dictate the pace of war in Libya but were sufficiently strong enough to repel Rommel at El Alamein. The German High Command treated the Libyan campaign as a secondary front, just to keep the Allied Army away from the European theater. The purpose of the German Afrika Korps was to prevent the routing of the Italian Army by the British in Libya.

In the spring of 1943, people didn't have to read the newspapers to know the status of the war in Libya. Food was becoming more and more scarce, farms were abandoned, there were no more passeggiatas (walks) in the evenings, and no more young men. The mayor of Tito, a Fascist, left town never to return. Sofia's visits to Tito were becoming fewer and fewer, as train schedules were becoming more and more problematical due to daily bombing from Allied planes. Sofia did come with the children for Christmas in 1942. Mario, with the help of Bambolone and Ehrlich, put together a nativity scene with small statuettes for the children. Two shepherds played the bagpipes from house to house with children in tow on Christmas day. The war was getting closer and closer to home. It was no longer there but here at their doorsteps. Allied bombing earmarked railroad tracks and supply routes and loomed larger and larger in the minds of the people in Southern Italy. Sofia's visits were becoming less frequent and eventually stopped. On top of all this, terrible atrocities in concentration camps north of the Alps were beginning to be reported in newspapers.

The first two years of the war in Libya were characterized by chronic supply shortages and transport problems spanning from Egypt to Tunisia. The coastline stretched for approximately 1,300 miles with few ports to unload soldiers and supplies. Hence, control of the central part of the coastline was contested by the British and Italian Navies, which were equally matched and exerted a reciprocal constraint on supplies. As such, a stalemate was reached. With the entry of the U.S. Army in the North African theater, it tipped the balance of supplies, armaments, and soldiers over to the Allies. It was just a matter of time before the American soldiers adapted to desert warfare and could help out the Allied efforts. They paid a heavy price for the lessons of war at the Kasserine Pass located between Algeria and Tunisia.

The German and Italian Armies were in full retreat to the Tunisian port of Tunis, about 100 miles from Sicily. In Tunisia they were hemmed in from the east by the British eight Army commanded by Field Marshal Bernard Montgomery and from the west by the U.S. II Corps commanded by Lieutenant General Lloyd Frendendall. In February of 1943, they were confronted by a German Army consisting of soldiers from the Afrika Korps and soldiers from the Russian Front.

Field Marshal Erwin Rommel of the Afrika Korps saw an opportunity to seize the American supply depot at Tebessa, Algeria, near the Tunisian border. His focus was to consolidate their military position in Tunisia and expedite an orderly retreat to Sicily. To reach Tebessa, the Afrika Korps had to advance through a narrow corridor of about one mile wide referred to as the Kasserine Pass in the Atlas Mountains. It was such a bold move that it came under heavy scrutiny by the German general staff. The concern was that limited manpower and equipment put the Afrika Korps at risk. Rommel argued for raiding the American supply base in order to gain time for a measured and orderly retreat.

On February 14, 1943, armored units from General Erwin Rommel's Panzer Army and the Afrika Korps launched an offensive directed against the Kasserine Pass, lightly held by inexperienced American troops with some British and French support. On February 19, a veteran German-Italian assault group smashed into the U.S. troops holding the pass. The German Panzer IV and Tiger tanks were vastly superior to the U.S. M3 light tanks and light anti-tank guns, and soon the Americans were retreating along the pass in disarray. The American soldiers and the general staff were unprepared for the Axis onslaught. Once through the pass, the Axis forces continued their advance, but severe winter weather, increasingly mountainous terrain, and stiffening Allied resistance slowed progress. Simmering disagreements between Rommel and his colleagues as to how the advance should proceed then came to a head, and on February 22, Rommel called off the offensive. Two days later, after an intense U.S. air attack, Allied troops reoccupied the pass.

Soon after the battle, the leadership of the US II Corps changed hands when Lieutenant General George S. Patton took over the command. The rationale of the American general staff was that it would take a tank of a man like Patton to defeat another tank of a man like Rommel. However, Patton was more than a tank. He was also a poet and a scholar of ancient Greek and Roman classics and history. He was overheard at the site of Roman ruins in Tunisia saying, "I have been here. Oh, how much I love being here. I can see where the Roman and Carthaginian Armies lined up in the Punic wars." In fact, he had never been there before. Patton went on to say, "I got him." Of course, he was referring to Rommel, as both must have been of the same mindset. After the battle, there was only one option for the Axis armies, to exit as quickly as possible through the port of Tunis with as many soldiers as possible and equipment. On May 13, about 300,000 German and Italian soldiers were taken prisoner. According to estimates, two to three German and four to five Italian Army divisions escaped to Sicily, where they re-grouped to defend the island.

This turn of events in North Africa shattered Mussolini's dream of becoming a modern-day Caesar. He was no longer that cocky, arrogant, self-assured man making those long and haranguing speeches in Piazza Venezia. For the first time in his career, he was forced to listen to others as to how to remedy his disasters. Doubts began to surface, from the King of Italy on down to the people in the streets. Mussolini and his son-in-law Ciano no longer trusted each other and rarely spoke to each other. Ciano was demoted from the post of foreign minister to the ambassadorship to the Vatican. He was replaced by Giuseppe Bastianini in early 1943, former ambassador to Britain, as payment for the Dunkirk imbroglio.

Conspiracies and accusations among Fascist ministers mushroomed overnight. The council of Fascist ministers was polarized, pro or against Il Duce. In Mussolini's household, Donna Rachele, his wife, was taking over as the main advisor and supporter of Benito. The literal translation of the word donna in Italian means woman, but, in the case of Mussolini's wife, it implied authority and power, much like a don in the Mafia. Mussolini trusted no one else. Still, he believed in his dream.

At least the situation on Main Street in small towns ameliorated. No longer did Fascist thugs roam the streets intimidating the populace. Now most local Fascists denied that they were affiliated with Fascism. They no longer wore black shirts or left town. In Tito, the Maresciallo came out of hiding to show some form of authority. After all, the Questura, the carabinieri administration, did not fall under the jurisdiction of the Fascist government.

In Avella, both the mayor and Maresciallo were apolitical. As such, they were safe from the growing partisan and Communist activities in the hills. As in Tito, Fascist thugs seemed to have disappeared. However, a day of reckoning was not too far away. Communists and partisans kept score as to whom to do away with after the war. While some sort of normalcy returned to small towns, there was still no food, no young men, and no commercial activities.

When flowers bloomed all over the mountains in 1943, it reminded the shepherds that it was time to tend to the sheep. Townspeople as well as those from Naples headed up to the foothills to scavenge for fruit in farms left abandoned by farmers. They also foraged chicory and other edible plants that grew along the dirt roads and snails among the stonewall partitions. Wild boars and other wild animals roamed the high grounds of the mountains. Hence, the shepherds by example provided the solution to the food crisis.

The mountains provide the shepherds a variety of foods. Cheese and milk are derived from sheep. Up on the mountains, assortments of green wild vegetables and berries may be found at any place where one's eyes can feast on. In Avella, Porcini mushrooms blanket the hills. The problem is that not all other mushrooms are edible. Some may be poisonous. However, shepherds are taught from childhood which ones are poisonous. As for meat, shepherds hunt for wild boars, rabbits and other small animals. Like nomads, they prefer lamb meat on special occasions (Christmas). In the hills of Avella, wild horses run wild, since the Samnites appeared in the Clanio creek during the stone age. The horses are considered to be sacred and, therefore, off limits in hunting for them. There is no law preventing the hunt, but it is understood by everyone in town. There was one exception in which the culprit caught the wrath of the town and was jailed for one year.

As for Sergio, he was oblivious to the war, although he sensed that it could soon come to Avella. He had participated in WWI and he had no room in his mind for those memories. But with the shortage of food, he spent more time in the mountains looking for poachers and removing the metal traps they placed to capture any animal, including sheep.

By this time, the country was in no mood for levity. High fashions were out of style, the movie industry was non-existent, most opera houses closed down, and, for the first time, fewer Neapolitan songs were being composed. Sofia, Filomena, and Serafina reverted to knitting sweaters and securing wool from Imalda. Sofia stopped taking the train to Tito for fear of the train being bombed. Rumors in town placed Allied planes around the Bay of Naples and as far north as Livorno, the two biggest Italian Naval ports on the Tyrrhenian Sea. Imalda's and Sofia's concerns were for the safety of the children. The four musketeers still got together as much as they could, more to check on each other. The uncertainty kept everyone anxious. Throughout their history, they had witnessed catastrophes in the valley, but nothing compared to what was yet to come.

Mario was now getting more worried, as he hadn't heard or seen Sofia and the children for over seven months. News about the war rarely reached Tito and its picturesque scenery just accentuated Mario's loneliness. For a social outing, he would visit Bambolone for a haircut and shave, and the latest gossip about the Maresciallo and the mayor's whereabouts. Often, he would visit the Wolf family for a picnic outing in the nearby hills and search for porcini mushrooms and snails. It was cozy, but not enough to distract him from his loneliness. He had no inkling about the threat of war locally.

On July 9, 1943, the Allied Army invaded Sicily with two-pronged attacks from the south of the island. The Eastern Task Force was led by Field Marshal Sir Bernard Montgomery which consisted of the British Eighth Army. The American Seventh Army commanded by General George S. Patton attacked the western side of Sicily. The two task forces reported to Harold Alexander as commander of the Fifteenth Army Group. Altogether about eight to ten army divisions were involved in the Allied invasion to cut off the retreat of the German Army to the mainland at Messina. The Italian Army stationed in Sicily presented no threat to the Allies. Historically, Sicilians have always rebelled against occupiers of their beautiful island including Italian soldiers.

The culture of Sicily dates back before the ancient Roman and Etruscan civilizations. Sicily is to Italy what California is to the United States—fruits basket of their country and more. They consider any police and military presence in Sicily, ordered by Rome, as either an interference in their lives or an invasion. To add insult to injury, the so-called Italian invaders were accompanied by German soldiers. The relationship between the Axis soldiers and the Sicilians was rather strained, to say the least. The German Army didn't have to call for curfews at night. The streets were deserted by evening hours. No woman dared to walk in the streets at any time. The men would have sacrificed their lives to defend the honor of their women. According to a soldier from Avella stationed there, Sicilians would not share their delicious farm bread with any of the invaders who ate dark bread that was hard enough to bounce off of a wall.

Italian Americans were very helpful in the planning and execution of the invasion of Sicily. In particular, the Mafia was involved in assisting the U.S. war efforts. Associates of Mafia boss, Salvatore "Lucky" Luciano in New York City, contacted numerous Sicilians to help the Naval intelligence acquire maps of Sicilian harbors and its coastline. Vito Genovese, Luciano's underboss, offered his services to the U.S. Army and became an interpreter, advisor, and sergeant. He quickly became the Army's most trusted employee and was instrumental in replacing Fascist mayors throughout Southern Italy with his recommendations. In some sense, it was like putting the foxes in charge of the chicken coops. Through the Navy's contacts from Operation Underworld, the names of Sicilian underworld personalities and friendly Sicilian natives, who could be trusted, were obtained and used in the Sicilian campaign. The joint staff planners for the U.S. joint chiefs of staff drafted a report titled, "Special Military Plan for Psychological Warfare in Sicily" that recommended the "establishment of contact and communications with the leaders of separatist nuclei, disaffected workers, and clandestine radical groups, i.e., the Mafia, and giving them every possible aid." The report was approved in Washington on April 15, 1943.

The island was defended by about 200,000 Italian and 32,000 German troops, and 30,000 Luftwaffe ground troops. The main German formations were one Panzer Division, Hermann Göring, and the Fifteenth Panzergrenadier Division. By late July, the German units had been reinforced, principally by elements of the First Parachute Division, Twenty-Ninth Panzergrenadier Division, and the XIV Panzer Corps, bringing the number of German troops to around 70,000. The Axis Army plan was for the coastal formations to form a screen to receive the invasion and allow time for the field divisions further back to intervene, as needed.

The invasion of Sicily had a deep psychological impact on Mussolini. During the evening of July 24 and the early hours of the 25th, the Grand Council of Fascism and the Fascist government met to discuss the immediate future of Italy. By now, Donna Rachele was the major force in the family and in charge of the government. She advised Mussolini not to attend the meeting because nothing good could come of it. While all in attendance were jittery about their intentions or purpose of the meeting, Mussolini was sick, tired, and overwhelmed by the war reverses suffered by the Italian military. He seemed to be looking for a way out of power. Grand Council Member Dino Grandi, leader of the Council and the Fascist Party, proposed a vote of no confidence. A vote was held on the night of July 24–25, 1943, and passed with nineteen votes for, eight against, and one abstention. Among the nineteen votes of no confidence was that of Mussolini's son-in-law Galeazzo Ciano, who had been the minister of foreign affairs. The motion was passed, with Mussolini barely reacting. While some Fascist extremists balked, and would later try to convince Mussolini to have those who voted with Grandi arrested, Il Duce was too stunned and unable to choose any course of action.

However, the next morning, Donna Rachele advised her husband, Mussolini, to arrest the nineteen and not to report to the king about the council meeting. She warned Benito that the king would have him arrested. Mussolini scoffed at the idea of being arrested. Groggy and unshaven, he kept his routine of a twenty-minute meeting with the king, during which he normally updated Victor Emanuel on the current state of affairs. After the presentation, the king said that he, Mussolini, was the most hated person in Italy. The king then informed him that General Pietro Badoglio would assume the powers of prime minister and that the war was all but lost. Mussolini offered no objection. Upon leaving the meeting, he was arrested by the carabinieri, who had been secretly planning a pretext to remove the leader for quite some time. They now had the council vote as their formal arrest, since the interior minister voted for the dismissal.

The prefect and questore reported directly to the Interior Minister Luigi Federzoni who voted for the dismissal of Mussolini. To what extent the king was the mastermind of the council's vote is not clear. When news of Mussolini's arrest was made public, relief seemed to be the prevailing mood. There was no attempt by fellow Fascists to rescue Mussolini. The only remaining question was whether Italy would continue to fight alongside its German ally or surrender to the Allies.

News of the incarceration traveled at the speed of light. Large crowds in small towns and big cities gathered in their piazzas to celebrate. They thought that the nightmare was over and the buffoon, Il Duce, got what he deserved. In Avella, for the first time, Communists, partisans, Socialists, and Social Democrats gathered together with the rest of the people in town to celebrate. The crowd extended to side streets and they cheered every word politicians now spoke. All of a sudden, every politician was anti-Fascist, but people didn't care what they said. For a change, they were happy. All was forgiven, except that the Communists were preparing a hit list of Fascists. In ancient Rome, it was called the proscription list to do away with political opponents. In two thousand years not much has changed. The same gatherings were occurring in Tito. On the one hand, Mario and Ehrlich envisioned the end of the internment. On the other hand, there was a war not too far from where they were.

From July 25, the day Mussolini was incarcerated, to September 8, 1943, when Italy surrendered unconditionally to the Allies—a total of forty-five days—must have been the most confusing time for Italians. How was it possible to jail the leader of one form of Fascism and still fight along with a leader of another form of Fascism—Nazism? What about all those Italian soldiers dispersed from Russia to Libya? Who thought this out? Obviously, the king and Badoglio couldn't see past their noses. They saved their asses by fleeing to Brindisi, Puglia, which was occupied by the Allies. So, who in hell was in charge in Rome? It proved what peasants have thought about Rome for generations, "They were and are a bunch of useless strunzi." Local administrations in small towns didn't know how to proceed in those forty-five days. It was like living in no-man's-land. In the meantime, the German Army was at their doorsteps, hovering over them! On the one hand, they were happy, but on the other hand, everything appeared so confusing and hopeless.

As the war raged in Sicily, there was much disagreement between Montgomery and Patton as to the conduct of the invasion. There are many books written about their disagreements on the battlefield. It came down, basically, to a conflict of personalities. The upshot of it was that the bird escaped from the cage. More than 100,000 Axis troops escaped through Messina to the mainland of Italy. Axis troops took ferry boats to travel at night from Messina to Calabria. Countless Italian troops were taken prisoners by the German Army and loaded onto trucks to be deported to Germany for forced labor. They would be part of the vanguard of a new workforce in German factories geared for armaments. Contrary to other historical reports, the first imprisonment of Italian soldiers by the German Army occurred on August 17, 1943, not on September 10, 1943, in Rome, when Germany occupied Rome.

The retreating route of the German Army is illustrated in orange color. The internment camps are highlighted in yellow. Courtesy of Anmarie Vittoria.

Italian soldiers were rounded up and loaded onto trucks heading north along the old Roman road. In ancient times, Rome imported salt, wheat, corn, oranges, and other farm products from Sicily. The road from Sicily splits into a fork junction at the town of Lamezia, one toward a coastal road, which had been the original road since the Roman days, and the other toward the mainland, which was a relatively newer road. Thus, from Sicily to Lamezia, the German Army traveled on the old Roman road. Caesar must have turned over in his grave.

The pace of the convoy of vehicles traveling north was necessarily slow, because Allied planes strafed them randomly from time to time and from place to place, such as rail lines, main roads, industrial centers, and Army and Naval stations. In fact, the internment camp at Ferramonti, which was located within a stone's throw of the old Roman road was strafed by an Allied plane. The camp was mistaken for an Italian Army base. Fortunately, the internees scampered to nearby hills with the help of the guards and the local people. Yet still, there were four casualties and fifteen to twenty reported injuries. The internees had left the barracks as soon as they heard from the local carabinieri about the German convoy heading their way. German troops did show up at the barracks and inquired about its nature and the purpose of the camp. It would have been devastating if the German troops decided to accommodate themselves there. A story about a yellow fever pandemic was concocted to drive them away and no internment person was rounded up. Most of the convoy traveling was done at night due to extremely hot weather and the strafing by Allied planes during the day. The weather in mid-August can be excruciatingly hot and sticky in the Calabria region. The beaches of Lamezia must have seemed very inviting to the troops. The pattern was always the same. No matter what type of vehicle, soldiers would park on the beach, take off their clothes, and run to the beach in the nude.

Twin brothers, Dimitri and Vladimir, born in Ukraine, were part of the convoy as designated truck drivers. They had joined the German Army in the battle of Kiev in Ukraine. The German Army recruited Russian farmers who were disgruntled with the economic system of collectivization. Farmers were poorer after the implementation of the Communist policy because there was no incentive to produce more wheat. Collectivization aimed to integrate individual landholdings into state-controlled farms to increase grain production for the urban population. It instead resulted in more shortages of food for all. In that sense, they all starved equally, a Communist credo. In fact, according to Gareth Jones who was an adviser to former British prime minister David Lloyd George after WWI and a journalist, millions of people in the Ukraine died of starvation as a result. Wheat grain produced there was shipped to Moscow instead.

Russian soldiers, recruited by the German Army, soon learned that whether people died of starvation in Ukraine or at Nazi extermination camps made no difference. Either way, the victims didn't receive proper burial. The logical conclusion was that both governments, Nazism under Hitler and Communism under Stalin, were equally bad. The two brothers desperately wanted out after being sent to Sicily as part of the reinforcement group to the Afrika Korps from the Russian front.

The two brothers were assigned to drive a truck loaded with Italian soldiers. In addition to them, three other German soldiers served on guard duty, riding in the back of the truck with prisoners. When they arrived at Lamezia, the beach was too inviting to bypass. The truck was parked near the beach and the road junction. No sooner had the truck approached the beach, that the clothes came off, and the three guards on duty ran nude toward the water. That was the brothers' intent all along. Vladimir shouted at the astonished prisoners, "Out!" The prisoners fled north, south, and east of the junction. The brothers knew exactly where the German convoy was headed because they had the map for the destination, Salerno, Naples, and further north.

Their best chance of avoiding capture was to keep their distance as much as possible from the pre-planned route of the convoy. This meant that they should proceed along the Roman coastal road to the town of Sapri and then pivot east toward the mainland, arriving in the hills near Potenza. From there, they would have the time to re-examine what to do next. The hope was that there would be no German troops in the area of Potenza. However, as it turned out, that was a miscalculation. The Germans deployed a small contingent of soldiers in Potenza to protect the flank of the retreating German Army traveling along the modern coastal road to Salerno.

The German Army feared that the Allies could have approached Potenza from Taranto, on the Adriatic Sea. The two brothers arrived at Sapri well ahead of the convoy and turned into a secondary road, walking along the foothills, avoiding the town of Brienza. They still were wearing German Army fatigues covered with oil and grease and did not want to draw attention to themselves. Besides, Brienza was too close for comfort to the convoy route. In late August, apples, pears, grapes, and figs are plentiful. They helped themselves to the fruit along the way since the farms were unattended and entered an empty farmhouse to change their clothes. Their body frames were so big that the farmer's pants came only to above their ankles. But by the time they reached the outskirts of Tito, they didn't care about their appearance. They desperately needed water.

They rushed to the fountain in the piazza. Bambolone could see from his barbershop that these strangers were not local farmers as they were too big and too light in complexion. They walked, smelled, and looked like deserters. How ironic. These two deserters were looking for a remote place in the hills to hide, the same place chosen by Mussolini to hide internees! Bambolone concluded that they were German soldiers, but the big question in his mind was, "Where were the rest of them?" The people of Tito were starving for information about the whereabouts of either army. They felt comfortable, as long as they didn't see any military activity thinking that the war must be far away. But when they saw Allied reconnaissance military planes flying over the Calabrian coast, that comfortable feeling evaporated. It had gentries and peasants talking to each other in the piazza for the first time in centuries as to which army was closest to Tito.

Bambolone saw an opportunity to decipher from the two soldiers the whereabouts of the German Army. It was useless for him to talk to them in Italian. In a stroke of genius, he thought of Ehrlich. How to get them together? He cupped his hands together to mimic eating. The two Ukrainians would have followed Bambolone to the moon to get something to eat. Strega was observing the whole spectacle from a window in Wolf's apartment, as the three of them approached the front door. She was there to teach Nanna how to cook a tripe dish favorite of the shepherds, and Mario was helping Arya with homework. Strega, with that defiant look, swung the door open before they could knock, as if to protect the people inside.

Bambolone, forever the charmer, said, "Vera, these poor souls are hungry, can we feed them some bread and cheese?" Mario and Ehrlich realized quickly what Bambolone was up to. Both would also like to know where in the hell was the German Army for different reasons. Mario wanted to escape to Avella before German soldiers showed up in Tito. Ehrlich wanted to hide as far away as possible from German troops. Ehrlich rationalized that the children could not have survived the ordeal of escaping to Avella with the family, Mario, and the two Ukrainians.

After much exchange between the deserters and Ehrlich, there emerged a bleak picture on hand. The deserters estimated that the German convoy was about fifty miles near the Tyrrhenian Sea. The Germans were retreating toward Salerno and Naples on the way to Rome along the old Roman road, Via Appia, and their aim was to destroy the port of Naples. As a standard practice, the retreat would be covered by a flanking group of soldiers stretching to Potenza, near Tito, and Avellino, near Avella. As such, there was no place for people to hide, since Tito, sooner or later, would be in harm's way. The best that they could hope for was to move all livestock to the mountains, away from the German Army, because the town would need the animals later to survive. The message was clear: grin and bear it for a short time and keep your mouth shut. The brothers from Ukraine explained that there was no time to waste if they wanted to arrive in Salerno before the German convoy. Otherwise, they would be surrounded by German soldiers.

At this point, Mario told Ehrlich to tell the two Ukrainians that staying put in Tito, may have put them in a more dangerous situation than being in Avella, if the German troops showed up in Tito. At least, in Avella, they could easily hide in the mountains with the shepherds. Without wasting any more time, Bambolone, the two Ukrainians, and Mario headed back to the water fountain in front of the Palazzo Colonna.

Word spread like wildfire, as people were drifting more and more toward the piazza. At this critical time, they were looking for a leader, since the mayor was no-where to be found. The Maresciallo did what he did best, disappear, at crucial times. By default, Bambolone took charge of the situation. He inspired confidence and determination. Bambolone delivered the bad news to the crowd in the piazza which was nearly full. An eerie silence fell throughout the piazza. Then all of a sudden, a surge of people came toward Bambolone proclaiming him mayor and carried him on their shoulders. Strega followed with Nanna. Whereas before Bambolone's wife was jealous, now she was hysterical and worried over what the Germans could do to him. They carried Bambolone on their shoulders all the way to city hall whereby Bambolone declared himself the new mayor and that all personnel at city hall hence-forth must report to him. Of course, they were friends and played a game of who can bullshit the most, him or Pasquale.

But he had a serious problem on his hands: how to keep German troops away from the limited supply of food in town when they showed up. Bambolone in-structed Strega to put her carmunity of shepherds on alert and to start moving sheep to the high mountains. Similar instructions were given to the few farmers in town. The two brothers changed into decent shirts and pants. The plan was to arrive at the Salerno train station before the German convoy and onward to Naples and Avella. Mario didn't have the time to say hello and goodbye to all those well-wishers in the piazza, including Pasquale, Strega, Ehrlich, and Nanna who waited outside the palazzo for Mario. The last parting words from Pasquale to Mario were, "In case the Germans arrive in Salerno before you, you may want to visit the church of San Bartolomeo in Campagna," another internment camp in a nun's convent. However, the trio had a train to catch to Potenza.

As they arrived in Potenza, they saw, from a side street, two German soldiers patrolling Main Street. Quickly, they entered a house, scaring the dwellers. Mario explained the situation and the woman availed herself to guide them in a roundabout way to the train station. Finally, all three of them were sitting pretty on the train on their way to Naples. However, when the train arrived at the station in Salerno, they heard, over the public announcement, that the railroad tracks between Salerno and Pompei were bombed by Allied planes and extensively damaged. Fortunately, the convoy reached only the outskirts of Salerno. What to do? The brothers knew the route that the convoy would follow. There was only one choice to get to Pompei and then on to Naples to avoid the convoy—over the mountains that overlooked Amalfi. The convoy planned to travel later on a road east of Amalfi, eight to ten miles from where they were about to walk along the mountain pass.

The convoy arrived in Salerno a couple of hours later. It was a desperate situation for all. The problem was how to get around Amalfi without drawing attention from the locals, especially when the brothers looked so conspicuous together. They decided to split up three ways, crisscrossing streets every so often until they arrived at the foothills of Amalfi. After the convoy crossed the mountain pass, the main convoy split into two convoys. One convoy circled left around Mount Vesuvius on the way to Pompei and Naples, and the other circled right toward Nola.

Both Naples and Nola had communication and railway centers. From Naples, trains could reach as far north as Germany. The German Army in Naples intended to create a collection center in which Italian soldiers, deserters, foreign and Italian Jews, Neapolitan residents, and Romani were rounded up and transported north to Germany. Nola has always been a conduit to the Adriatic Sea via Avellino ever since Roman times. Telegraph, telephone, and other forms of wireless communications have been routed through Nola. Roman statesmen, politicians, and emperors traveled from Rome to Nola on the way to Brindisi on the Adriatic Sea; the final destination being Greece or the Middle East. Emperor Octavius and his son Augustus settled in Nola. Thus, by occupying those two cities, they controlled all communications and railway centers heading to Southern Italy.

By this time, news of the German retreat along the coastal road reached Avella.

Sofia was anxious as to what was happening in Tito and in particular about Mario. She prevailed on her father, Sergio, Alvaro, and Don Nicola to intercede for her and ask Ramiro to find out about Mario. Word came back that he had left Tito and was on his way to Avella with two surprise guests. Sofia was overjoyed. She started to hum her favorite song.

There was no time to enjoy the scenery in and around Amalfi, although the two deserters fell in love with the city. After what they had been through, it was understandable why they let their guard down. Mario reminded them to stop gawking at the place. At the top of the hill, they stopped at the town of Ravello to purchase buffala mozzarella at Mario's favorite deli. The deserters were in heaven as they ate a sandwich of mozzarella, salami, and tomatoes while overlooking the view below of Amalfi and the sea. Again, Mario had to remind them that they were on a mission, and to get out of there alive. Mario's leadership as a Naval officer came in handy. However, he behaved more like a mother hen than a military officer, protecting the two new friends like a hen, except these wandering chicks were a lot bigger than the hen. Mario wanted desperately to get home and count on Sergio and the shepherds to hide the two brothers up in the mountains. He had a feeling that the brothers, being of a peasant stock, would be comfortable in the company of shepherds. After that, the brothers would be on their own.

View of Amalfi atop the mountain on the way to Pompei. Courtesy of Irpinia Avventura Club.

NINE

No Time for Octopus

After an arduous climb on the mountains atop the city of Amalfi, Mario, Vladimir, and Dimitri arrived on top of Mount Faito, where Mount Vesuvius and Pompei came into view. From their vantage point, they could see below that the two convoys toward Naples and Nola hadn't arrived yet. The descent to the valley was rather steep and dangerous, but they made it safely to the train station in Pompei. This railway system originated in Sorrento and continued through Naples on the way to Avella–Baiano, referred to as the Circumvesuviana, meaning that it circled Mount Vesuvius. Their plan was simple: Arrive at the train station in Naples before the convoy and depart for Avella via the Circumvesuviana train.

View from the north edge of Mount Faito. Amalfi is on the opposite end of the mountain. Pompei is just below in the valley and Mount Vesuvius is in the background. The coastal town of Torre Del Greco (Greek Tower) is on the west edge of Vesuvius, toward the coastline. Nola is on the north side of Vesuvius. There was no funicular railway, as seen on the left, at that time. Courtesy of Irpinia Avventura Club.

As the train approached Torre Del Greco, the railway was elevated above the street. Greek settlers settled there long before Romans appeared on the scene. In Roman times, Torre del Greco was a suburb of Herculaneum, characterized by patrician or upper-class villas. After the 79 AD eruption of Mount Vesuvius destroyed Pompei and the two villages, Sora and Calastro, none were known to have existed.

The famous Italian comedian, Toto, was among those who made Torre Del Greco his annual summer retreat. The reason for Torre Del Greco's popularity as a resort town was its fine beaches, coral jewelry, and the rural setting of lush farmlands and vineyards, as well as its proximity to Mount Vesuvius. As the town nearest to Vesuvius, Torre Del Greco is the main starting point for tourists wanting to scale Mount Vesuvius. This was facilitated by a funicular railway, Vesuvius Funicular, which took tourists to the crater from the town. During World War II, the city was used as an ammunition depot by the German Army and consequently suffered heavy bombing by the Allies.

Coral art and jewelry remain a mainstay of the city's economy. Diving for coral has taken place in the Mediterranean Sea ever since Roman times. Already in the fifteenth century, Torre del Greco became known for its coral diving and harvesting of red coral. However, it wasn't until the seventeenth century that the first cameos were produced from shells. At present, there are several hundred companies and several thousands of people employed in the manufacturing of coral and shell cameos. Coral is now mainly imported from Asia since increasingly areas in the Mediterranean are becoming protected. The total industry is estimated to have a turnover of about $225 million.

Torre Del Greco Coastline. The railway line is above the coastal road and Mount Vesuvius is in the background. Courtesy of Irpinia Avventura Club.

Like children, the three of them peered and marveled at the majestic Vesuvius. Unbeknownst to them, the German convoy was traveling on the street below, in the same direction, on their way to Naples, a short distance from where they were sitting. The first one to notice the convoy was Vladimir and he turned different shades of paleness. The good feelings among them vanished. All those efforts, struggles and planning were all for naught. Dreams of freedom had to be postponed. What to do? Panic? That was the worst thing to do. Mario had a plan, as he was very familiar with the area and the local fishermen. He had often bought coral items for Sofia and the family, when he was stationed in Naples during the Ethiopian War. He looked at the situation from a positive perspective. So far, they had traveled a long distance safely. Home was within sight. He rationalized, "We have to travel only a short distance to be home." The glass was more than half full.

Mario and the two Ukrainians gingerly got off the train at the next stop in Torre Del Greco, and spent time in the station until evening, pacing back and forth, peeking every so often at the convoy from a concealed opening in the window. Soldiers in the convoy appeared exhausted and their faces covered with sweat and sand. It appeared to them that the convoy spearheaded straight ahead to Naples and beyond. Therefore, Torre Del Greco was not the convoy's final destination or plan, at least for the time being. They decided to sit tight in the station until dark. Still, the remnants of the convoy were outside the station. They decided to roll the dice and head for Mount Vesuvius. The station master led them to a back door staircase leading toward the foothills of Vesuvius, as the convoy was still moving slowly along the road to Naples. Mario concluded that even if they were spotted by the soldiers, they would have been too exhausted to give chase. Halfway up on Mount Vesuvius, the trio tried to sleep on the ground. Naples looked so near, but yet so far. Mario could almost smell home cooking from Sofia's kitchen in Avella. The panoramic views of the Bay of Naples, the islands of Capri and Ischia, and the coastal town of Sorrento were mesmerizing. It motivated them to try harder to escape capture. So much beauty awaited them. They were determined more than ever to make their escape.

In their retreat, the German Army concentrated their troops in large cities such as Naples, Salerno, and Avellino to the east, and Caserta to the north, as well as railway and communication centers such as in Naples and Nola. Nola and Avellino were the gateway to the East. Thus, the main strategy of the German retreat was to create a safe escape north toward Rome. They stationed troops in Salerno in order to stop or delay the Allied advance from the South. They occupied Avellino for the sole purpose of protecting the flank of their retreat from Allied advances in the east and south. The city of Caserta provided the linkage to the supply line from Germany. This meant that German checkpoints controlled the only rail connection to Avella, at Naples and Nola. So, even if the trio were to bypass the train station in Naples, the German checkpoint at Nola or other stations along the railway line could have stopped the trio on their way to Avella. So, they had to scrap the original plan.

Traveling in the valley by daylight or at night was problematic. Sooner or later, the two Ukrainians would draw attention from Fascist sympathizers. There were still a few of those around. Mario decided that the best option was to forge ahead to Naples and wait until the Germans left if they could ever get there. He felt that the Germans would not stay very long in Naples, as the Allies were chasing the German Army to Naples or anyplace north toward Rome.

In the meantime, the Germans were hell-bent on the way to Rome. The troops were led by "Smiley" General Albert Kesselring. He approached every military situation with a smile. He had inherited remnants of the proud Afrika Korps. His main ambition as a general was to prove to Hitler that he was a better tactician in utilizing the Afrika Korps than the popular Field Marshal Erwin Rommel, who commanded the German Army stationed in North Italy. Hence, Ehrlich's warning to Mario and Don Nicola, when Hitler visited the Naval station in May 1938, came, unfortunately, true. Ehrlich had emphasized then that the Nazis' reason to come to Naples was only to assess the weakness of the Italian Navy and Army so that they could occupy Italy at a later date.

Italy was treated no differently from other countries colonized by the German Army in Europe. Having started out as a Luftwaffe officer didn't help Kesselring's psyche. Hitler promoted Kesselring to field marshal and commander of South Italy on September 8, 1943. Once Kesselring's troops joined with Rommel's troops, he would have to relinquish his command. Hence, he took his time in doing so. Unfortunately, Southern Italians were caught in the middle of a deadly tug-of-war between two egotistical German generals. Direct collateral damage was so extensive that it took more than fifty years to partially rebuild towns and cities in Southern Italy. Indirect collateral damage, the resurgence of the Mafia, has survived to this day.

To give Kesselring military credit, he was able to, somehow, maneuver his army in Southern Italy to the high grounds, forcing Allied soldiers to fight uphill, as in Salerno, Monte Cassino, and Anzio. No general conquered ancient Rome by attacking from the south. Most successful invasions of Rome derived from the north. Due to the terrain in Southern Italy in the fall and winter, it was and is very difficult for an Allied soldier to climb steep mountains and fight looking up, whilst the enemy can observe every move from the top. The mud was knee-deep in places and it took a valiant effort just to be able to trudge through it, let alone fight uphill. Apparently, Polish troops were caught in such a quagmire at Monte Cassino. Allied generals must not have learned much from war tactics in Southern Italy from Roman history. All they had to do was to talk to a local shepherd.

The common denominator between Rommel and Kesselring was that both were raised in a society whereby being systematic and dogmatic was a religion. As such, it is interesting to note that retreats of the German Army from North Africa, Sicily, and mainland Italy were characterized as being systematic and orderly. The purpose was to conserve strength, control the pace and places of battles, and prevent a helter-skelter retreat from Italy. In fact, Rommel's pre-emptive attack at the Kasserine Pass was nothing more than what he was taught since childhood, a systematic approach to a retreat from Tunisia. Also, Kesselring practiced the same religion as Rommel in Italy which helped him being promoted to a Field Marshall.

Superior firepower and brute force overcame all obstacles presented by the German Army and they forged ahead all the way to Rome. Unfortunately, the Italian people were caught in the middle of two insane military strategies led by two egotistical generals. In Rome, some Allied generals took photos of themselves next to the statue of Emperor Aurelius to symbolize their conquest of Rome. Absurdity ruled over common sense. The same generals justified all that devastation in Southern Italy in terms of collateral damage. Certainly, the victims, Italian people, and Allied soldiers didn't share in that feeling. The battles of Salerno, Monte Cassino, and Anzio resulted in enormous war casualties for all warring countries. Devastation from the bombing of towns and cities caused unimaginable misery, injuries, and deaths to the civilian population. Some towns were bombed out of existence back to the Stone Age. This was an example of philosopher George Santayana's expression, "Those who do not learn history are doomed to repeat it," except, at that time, the people who were doomed were civilians and soldiers, not Allied generals.

The only way to arrive in Naples from Torre Del Greco, without being discovered by German patrols then, was by sea across the Bay of Naples. At 4 a.m., the three of them descended to the shoreline where fishermen gathered for their morning fishing outing. At parts of the coastline at Torre del Greco, there is no beach. Large boulders take up most of the shoreline instead. The fishermen descended to a small clearing area next to the boulders. Usually, fishermen started early in the morning for the sole purpose of fishing for octopus. Once an octopus is spotted by a fisherman, a flashlight is directed into its eyes, and it is picked up with a net.

Mario knew some of the fishermen there, as he had bought octopus from them in the past in Posillipo when he was stationed at the Naval military base. He made an offer that they could not refuse. He offered them three times more money, compared to selling all their octopus in Naples, if they could transport them to the Naval station across the Bay, about five to six miles away. All the fishermen there volunteered to take them over at no cost. The fishermen put two and two together and concluded that Mario's party was running away from the convoy. They made themselves available to help out, knowing full well that they were endangering their own lives. That gesture impressed Mario immensely. Money meant nothing to the fishermen and, yet, they could barely carve a living fishing for octopus.

By the time the trio arrived at the Naval station in Naples, the morning sun welcomed them. The station was completely demolished by the Allied bombing. Mario searched for his old apartment. It was barely livable. Later in the morning, scugnizzi came out of their hiding places—big and small buildings, storage rooms, garages, classrooms, auditoriums, etc. A scugnizzo was typically a male war orphan who roamed and hustled in the streets for food, stole anything that brought something in return, and pimped their sisters or mothers. Their ages ranged from five to twenty years. Most times, the mothers threw them out of the house—one less mouth to feed. Prostitution accounted for about 30 percent of their business.

It didn't look like a Naval station anymore. Remnants of sunken ships drifted at sea near the harbor. All the food and utensils in the kitchen area were gone. Food existed only in their minds. Neapolitans scavenged anything that was edible in nearby farms and towns. It was a mess all around the neighborhood of the Naval station, but a beautiful mess to hide from German soldiers patrolling the streets. The only recourse for the scugnizzi and the trio was to stay there and hide. They made for strange bedfellows.

The San Carlo Opera House was nearly intact, barely damaged by the Allied bombing. Opera performances were intermittent at that time, which was a downer for few Neapolitans, but most welcomed the reprieve. Nevertheless, Mario moseyed over to the opera house to look for former colleagues. He hoped that, perhaps, Don Nicola could be there, knowing full well that he was not about to go through two checkpoints at Nola and Naples. Of course, it was wishful thinking. The routine was the same every day. He would go to the opera house and ask for Don Nicola's whereabouts. Most times, janitors and maintenance people were there waiting to tell him the bad news. He looked for anyone who could pass a message to his family in Avella, but no luck.

As for food, the Ukrainians went fishing every day catching enough fish to put food on the table. The scugnizzi traded tomato jars for fish and a modus operandi was reached whereby each party contributed to the search for food. The biggest problem was the availability of potable drinking water. The scugnizzi took care of that need by raiding gardens with small pools full of small non-edible fish and boiling the polluted water. Fortunately, the rainy season was just around the corner.

Badoglio's abandonment of his troops, and his failure to order them immediately to fight the Germans, resulted in the German capture of 600,000 soldiers, including 22,000 officers, and a huge amount of war materiel, extending from the Italian mainland to Southern France, Yugoslavia, and the Greek islands. Italian soldiers were loaded into railroad cattle cars, taken to Germany, and interned in slave labor camps for the duration of the war. More than 7,000 Italian soldiers died when British bombers sank German ships transporting Italian soldiers from the island of Crete to Greece and eventual internment. Those who did not drown, the Germans machine-gunned, prompting Mussolini to send a message to a German garrison commander thanking him for "his kindness to Italian soldiers." Indeed a sick man. German General Hubert Lanz received a twelve-year sentence for the killings in cold blood at the Nuremberg War Crimes Tribunal in 1948 and was released after five years.

An additional 600,000 Italian troops were either killed or taken prisoner in the tundra of Siberia. Only about 10,000 returned home. Most of them vanished in the Russian gulags. Others married and started families in Siberia. Most of them died in the battle of Stalingrad. A few of them were deported to Germany to work in armament factories. Similar stories can be recounted in other countries of Europe as well. It was doubtful that the king and Badoglio thought of these poor souls when they signed the Armistice. It is safe to say that they were thinking of their own political futures. It was a sad period of time for the soldiers, parents, wives, children, friends, and women in waiting.

King Vittorio Emanuele III and his family, Badoglio, and other ministers escaped very early in the morning of September 9 through a German checkpoint at Tiburtina, Rome. To this day, there is no satisfactory explanation for how it was possible to escape the clutches of German guards at the checkpoint, when it was well known within the German hierarchy that Hitler hated the king with a passion and vice versa. Hitler wanted their capture at all costs. Somehow, they made their way through the checkpoint on the way to the city of Pescara on the Adriatic Sea and headed directly south, along the coastline to the city of Brindisi, in the province of Puglia, occupied by the Allies at that time.

On the same day, local administrations in Southern Italy abolished internment camps. Freedom at last for the internees. At Ferramonti, some chose to stay until the end of the war. Internees at Potenza, Tito, and Brienza decided to do the same. For example, Nanna and Ehrlich decided to stay put in Tito in the care of Strega. Any place else invited danger or being captured by the Nazis. Other internees didn't have that safety net and felt that the risk and danger of traveling through parts of Northern Italy and North Europe, still under Nazi control, far outweighed the freedom and kindness of townies that they enjoyed at those internment towns in Southern Italy. However, the convent near the Church of San Bartolomeo at Campagna, near Salerno, where roughly 450 internees resided, had an uncomfortable feeling, since it was located near a large concentration of German troops in the Salerno area. Government administrations in Northern Italy were caught off guard by the announcement of the Armistice. As such, no decision on their internment camps was made. Besides, they had no control over their own destiny. They were forced to bite the bullet and smile.

The Allied Army invaded Salerno, on September 9, 1943, code-named Avalanche, to the surprise of no one. The U.S. Fifth Army (General Mark Clark), and Canadian and British Armies spearheaded the attack at Salerno, while the British Eighth Army under General Bernard Montgomery advanced slowly from Taranto toward Potenza, the site of an internment camp, encountering minor opposition. On September 10, the German Army occupied Rome and rounded up Italian soldiers to be deported to Germany, and deployed as laborers in factories.

TEN

Not Here nor There—Purgatory

While Mario, Dimitri, and Vladimir waited to extricate themselves from the clutches of the Nazi occupiers in Naples, the German Army paid an uninvited visit to Avella in the middle of the night. Townies became aware of their presence as the rumble of tanks and motorcycles scurried about town at the same time as the sound of roosters. The German Army occupied Avella from about September 1 to mid-October of 1943. News spread by word-of-mouth that German soldiers and tanks had arrived suddenly in Baiano from Nola; they traveled on the only asphalt road, Via Appia. According to the rumors, their tanks were headed on the only dirt road from Baiano, toward Avella, but it didn't stop their motorcycle drivers from buzzing around the farms at the foothills and in the town itself. One purpose of those drivers was to announce their appearance, but most importantly, it was to strike fear in people's hearts. The cemetery in Avella was located on a dirt road halfway between the two towns, one mile apart. The other connection between Baiano and Avella was via the railway line, the Circumvesuviana. Discussions in the piazza centered on which farm the German soldiers might be camping on and what their intentions could be. Speculations ran wild because no foreign Army, either in WWI or WWII, ever camped in large numbers this far south of Italy, besides Sicily.

To add to their anxieties, confusion reigned as to whether or not Italy was still allied with Germany. Prime Minister Pietro Badoglio on July 25, 1945, declared that Italy was still allied with Germany in the war. On September 8, he declared the opposite, an alliance with the Allies. Hitler never believed him in the first place, as he made plans to occupy Italy either way and, indeed, Italy was occupied by the German Army soon after Mussolini was incarcerated. How could the people of Avella or any other town nearby possibly know the mess created by Badoglio and the king? Not knowing the disposition of the German Army disturbed the locals more than anything else.

The locals were clueless as to the reason for the visit. They wondered why Avella, and not the towns of Baiano or Nola, hosted them. The answer was simple. From the top of the hills of Avella, one could see the entire valley and the Bay of Naples. German soldiers of the Fifteenth Panzer and Hermann Goring Divisions camped atop a hill next to two caves. The camps had a panoramic view of the valley below, including Avella, Baiano, Nola, Mount Vesuvius, Caserta, and the Bay of Naples. Besides that, Baiano, Avella, and Avellino formed the first line of defense to the Allied advance from the Adriatic Sea. It was vital for the German Army to have an uninterrupted escape route to Rome. Also, hiding in caves neutralized the Allies' aerial firepower.

These two divisions were part of the convoy that retreated from Sicily. Via Appia passed through Baiano, which served as the main supply line to Salerno and also as an escape route to the North. A secondary road was built for quick access of the two Divisions to the Via Appia escape route from the two camps. This road was paved as a way to avoid the dirt road, which could become muddy during the rainy season in October and November. After a couple of weeks of rest, these two divisions were committed to battle in Salerno. For military reasons, the Germans wanted to keep the location of the camps secret from the people of Avella. No one in town dared to try to find out the location. Of course, the shepherds knew, but they were not about to tell anyone. They were perched well above the hills, on the high mountains.

The valley has been invaded by every country surrounding the Mediterranean Sea and countries north of the Alps since Hannibal showed up in the valley in 217 BC. Even a group of gladiators led by Spartacus ransacked the valley and the town of Nola. In later years, religious crusaders built Castle Normanno in Avella as an observation post during their crusades in the Middle East. An interesting statistical factoid stands out from these invasions. About every one thousand years, a country or a combination of countries from North Africa have invaded the valley since 217 BC: Hannibal (217 BC), Saracens (900 AD), and the French Expeditionary Force (1941). The French Expeditionary Force consisted of Moroccan, Algerian, and Tunisian soldiers. Could there be another invasion from a North African country in the year 3000?

The hope among diehard Fascists in town was that, perhaps, the Germans would come to town to help ease the food shortage. That was delusional. All doubts and the few good vibes were removed when German motorcycles appeared unexpectedly from out of nowhere, whizzing and aiming at people in willful acts of intimidation. German soldiers in heavy trucks and tanks, and on motorcycles with side carriages arrived along the cemetery dirt road to Avella. Tanks were so big that they took up the whole dirt road. In order to get around them, one had to walk in a drainage ditch abutting the road. The soldiers moved about with purpose and looked busy putting up posters in the piazza to declare a new order. One word often repeated on the posters was verbieten, meaning to forbid.

The mood in town was somber. People didn't want to be caught in the streets with soldiers, especially when they were drunk, and that was most nights. Sometimes they would march from their camp to city hall and back, with their guns at the ready, singing German marching songs in the middle of the night. The message was loud and clear, "Get off Main Street" at any time of the day. One could not even breathe air from the mountains without having to share it with a German soldier. They were all over town. They didn't come to help nor did they have regard for the plight of the people who were near starvation.

The worst feeling was not knowing what was coming next. The attitude was: to expect the unexpected and get out of the way. Most people in Avella locked the doors to their houses and didn't go outside once they realized that these soldiers would not hesitate to shoot anyone. Even to see a medical doctor was an adventure in avoiding them in the street. People were afraid of being shot when venturing into the farms and hills searching for anything edible because they didn't know how far into the farms they could go before encountering a German patrol or checkpoint. Sofia and the twin sisters shut down the dress shop in the piazza. She hibernated with the children in one of Sergio's apartments. The whole Da Alia family also moved into another apartment in the courtyard where Don Nicola, Sergio, Sofia, and their families resided. Altogether, there were eleven extra people taking refuge there. At night, the portone to the courtyard was locked and secured with long steel bars.

Sergio no longer inspected the mountains for poachers, because German patrols around the camps would not permit it, and he was not about to test their will. The camps were located on the hills near the east end of Main Street, about a mile east of Sergio's residence. Whatever little food was secured by the shepherds on the mountains for Imalda's family, Ciccio transported it on a donkey, circumventing the camps approaching Main Street from the west end of town. This meant that he had to travel along the edge of the high mountains an extra two or three miles in a westerly direction toward the Castello Normanno, also known as Castello Longobardo, and then pivot down to Main Street toward Sergio's residence. That food went a long way in sustaining the bare minimum to satisfy the hunger of those four families in the courtyard. In the morning, soldiers were seen running nude in the streets surrounding Sergio's building toward their camps for their daily exercises.

The mayor left town, running from the Germans. He was afraid that they would discover that he was a podesta, a Fascist mayor, in name only, since he was not affiliated with the Fascist Party. The apolitical prefect appointed him. Again, he didn't want to be in a position to guess what they would do to him. Simply put, he did not want to give them the satisfaction of dictating orders to him. In general, many mayors in the area began to leave towns for that reason. As for Alvaro Da Alia, he left the Magistrate's Office as soon as he heard that tanks were headed for Avella. By then, news of atrocities at the German extermination camps was being reported globally. As for Don Nicola, he decided that the San Carlo didn't need a cello player after all, since it shut down. The war spread from Salerno to Naples. Neapolitans began to put up resistance to German soldiers' demands to deport their few young men to Germany. The Alvarez and Colonna forebears had survived wars, revolutions, civil wars, and plagues for centuries. As such, the surprise visit by the German Army in Avella had no effect on Ramiro and the family. Interestingly, the very rich and the shepherds, the two extreme ends of the social class, seemed to be immune to social unrest and wars. Neither of those need a government to survive.

This period of time marked the end of Fascist governance and the beginning of lawlessness in Avella and in other small towns in the Naples area, since local authorities disappeared. The Maresciallo was as useless in maintaining civil order in town. His main preoccupation was to find a place to hide, because, sooner or later, he would have to be accountable to the locals. In the meantime, more and more deserters, not necessarily Italian, were showing up mysteriously in the mountains banding together with partisans. Some had good intentions as they became involved in sabotaging the German war machinery. Others were just brigands involved in the black market and thievery in towns.

Farms were raided for livestock, as the Germans needed horses to pull heavy equipment up the hills and for food. Even farms owned by the churches were raided. There were four to five wine stores in Avella. Fortunately for Erminio, his winery was located near the train station, sufficiently away from the camps to be noticed by German soldiers. Nevertheless, he too skipped town to a neighboring one on the Circumvesuviana line. Desperation was beginning to set in, and the true nature of the visitors' intent was clear to all: serve our needs or get out of the way. The problem was that there was nothing to give or serve, except for wine. The people of Avella were not aware of the debacle of the Italian Army in Sicily and there was no one to help them out of this mess. When there is no hope, desperation sets in. That was the situation in Avella as well as in other small towns.

Germans were not about to share any road with the locals, especially the escape roads to Via Appia in Baiano which led to Rome. The bridge on the west end of Main Street was bombed and destroyed by the partisans of the Baiano-Avella area operating in the high mountains which meant tanks could not traverse that part of town. As such, the two remaining roads were constantly patrolled by the Germans. Anyone from Avella or Baiano traveling on those roads would have drawn a lot of attention at checkpoints on the way to the cemetery and were most likely detained for questioning.

The German soldiers couldn't even leave dead people alone. Funeral processions on the way to the cemetery were stopped at checkpoints. Often, soldiers would inspect an opened casket. The priest would remind them each time that what they were doing was sacrilegious. Did they expect the dead to invade the camps? It made no sense and was just another way to intimidate the people.

At the foothills near where Sergio lived, there were five narrow dirt roads heading toward the hills and the high mountains, which were all blocked by German checkpoints. Most likely, the German camps were located on one of those hills within sight of Sergio's building. Certainly, Sergio knew very well where the camps were located, but he was not about to share that with anyone in town. Ciccio volunteered that information only to Sergio and to his donkey. It was the type of information that didn't do anyone any good if the Germans caught wind of it.

The location of the caves, where German soldiers hid during Allied bombing raids, was no secret either. There were only two caves in the foothills and every farmer knew their whereabouts. One other cave, San Michele cave, was located in the high mountains. German troops did not utilize that cave, because the road to the cave was often flooded. The Germans surrounded the town and there was no way in or out or of running to the caves in case of Allied bombing. Only German troops could utilize the caves.

Obviously, there was no recourse to complaining about the Germans' iron-clad encirclement of the town. Local Fascist officials had no leverage with the German occupiers. German soldiers did not trust anyone from the previous administration since the Mussolini debacle. Besides, there was no incentive for Alvaro to come out and confront the Germans. He would have been shot on the spot. It was such a helpless feeling to have German trucks, tanks, motorcycles, and soldiers interrupt normal life in town. That special Neapolitan spirit was snuffed out of them.

The occupation presented one hell of a problem for the Jewish community of Avella. News of extermination camps was beginning to filter through newspapers and radio, though details were scant. Whatever little news there was shocked people to their core to the point of not wanting to talk about it. They didn't want to believe or store that type of inhuman behavior in their minds. Others believed that it couldn't occur in Italy. However, what they didn't realize was that they could be deported out of Italy to those extermination camps. Alvaro saw to it, before leaving city hall, that all personal records were hidden in the cave of San Michele. Shepherds, with Imalda's insistence, helped Alvaro hide the records in a deep, dry well. The cave was located halfway up to the top of Mount Avella. As for Don Nicola, he was vulnerable. The fear was that one of those fanatic Fascist thugs might be revengeful enough to turn him in to the German authorities.

Of particular interest to the German Army in Avella was the capture of deserters who were to be sent to Germany to work in the armament industry. Also, the Gestapo police showed up much later in Avella to do the dirty work for the SS troops. However, they didn't need the Gestapo to flush out deserters. Former local Fascists pointed the finger at where to look. German security guards apprehended one deserter and immediately sent him to Germany. The only other deserter was never discovered. These types of searches were suspended soon after the Allies began to force the German Army from the beaches of Salerno. The small Jewish community of Avella breathed a sigh of relief.

All employees of city hall also left their jobs. They didn't want to be accountable for the missing records. The Maresciallo pleaded ignorance of the records, since he had nothing to do with city hall. Ramiro kept tabs on Italian and German authorities via gossip from the elites in town. Imalda, with Sergio's assistance, provided liaison between the shepherd community and the needs of the people in the neighborhoods, mostly shepherds. The consensus among the four musketeers was to lay low, especially Don Nicola, until more news came.

With the demise of Fascism, there was no more singing of the Fascist song, "Faccetta Nera," and propaganda on the radio. Newspapers splashed the report that the German Army was in full retreat at Potenza which was the back entry to Salerno. This implied that the Germans would soon leave the area. The feeling that they were leaving Avella was so overwhelming they forgot that they were hungry. Potenza and Tito, which still had about 500 internees, were occupied in late September by the German Army with the aim of preventing Field Marshal Montgomery from entering Salerno from the Adriatic Sea. The Field Marshal never advanced within rifle shot range of attack, but a Canadian regiment did and relieved Potenza. However, the other internment camp at Campagna was weathering most of the attacks and counterattacks by both Armies. With Potenza in Allied hands, it was inevitable that the German Army would soon retreat from Salerno.

As usual, the German Army controlled the pace of retreat. Their retreat was methodically planned to stymie and pin down the Allied Army as long as possible in Italy and away from Germany. The Allies then reacted to whatever defensive scheme concocted by General Albert Kesselring. As such, Kesselring chose the terrain and where the battles took place, always choosing the high ground. With the fall of Salerno, the handwriting was on the wall. The German Army had no other choice but to retreat north to Naples and eventually to Rome. In the meantime, they chose to make life miserable for all.

Back in Avella, the two German divisions camping on the hill were no longer there, undoubtedly they were heading north. Everything began to quiet down in the streets as fewer and fewer soldiers appeared in town, but enough to cause some concern in the Jewish community. When things appeared to be rosy with the news of Salerno, the Gestapo appeared in Avella near the end of September. Policemen in civilian clothes, most likely Gestapo policemen, abducted a teenager, his sister, and his mother in their house. They were carried away in the back of a truck. The father had died in Albania during an invasion by the Italian Army. The raid was timed with the full retreat of the German Army from the area since transportation north was readily available.

The people in Sergio's building realized that these belated actions were those of desperate Fascists before the curtain came down on them. In particular, there were old scores to settle between Don Nicola and Fascist fanatics who were willing to do terrible things to people who didn't agree with their political philosophy. Hence, the musketeers moved fast for the sake of Don Nicola's and Alvaro's families. Obviously, the Gestapo must have had pertinent information about the teenager's family, since it was such a surgical operation. What worried the musketeers was the precision and timing of the operation. So, where did the information come from? The four of them thought that having Don Nicola dress in a monk's garb would not work for he would be easily recognized by the Fascist thugs.

The only recourse was to find either a secluded place up on the high mountains or an isolated place among the many hills surrounding Avella. The first option was out of the question. Don Nicola, Alvaro and Felicia could not possibly climb up the high mountains, although, once there, shepherds would make a home for them. The old fox, Imalda, knew exactly the place not too far from town. There were still checkpoints toward the hills where the two German divisions left camps, as injured soldiers were left behind temporarily. Imalda had a plan as to exactly how to circumvent the checkpoints. She exuded confidence and the families would have followed her to the end of the world, if necessary. Her stewardship was impeccable and she knew those hills like the back of her hand. There were no checkpoints on the way to the castle, as Ciccio discovered, which was about two or three miles west of the checkpoints. Effectively, all the checkpoints were in the east end of town near Sergio's residence. The only possible problem was that, in the beginning of October, the rainy season commenced, and the Clanio Creek flooded. Under those conditions, some in the group might not be able to cross the Clanio Creek.

This meant that Imalda needed to move faster than she liked in implementing her plan. A group of eleven people saddled up and were ready to follow Imalda. It included seven of Don Nicola and Alvaro's families, Imalda, Sergio, Lena, and Carlo. Sofia was left at home in case Mario showed up. Lena and Paolo stayed close to their grandmother. It was in the middle of the night. The mountain air was cool and refreshing in early October. The group walked with a herd of sheep down Main Street toward the Communist section of town, away from the five checkpoints, and turned right toward the Clanio Creek, the same spot where the bridge was blown up earlier.

The only problem with that scenario was that sheep rarely were herded on Main Street and, especially, toward the west end of town. The high mountains are located in the East side of town, at least the approach in climbing them. Sergio and Imalda were aware of that unusual situation. They decided to remove collar bells from the sheep to reduce noise and attention. Sergio, Don Nicola and Alvaro led the sheep across the creek. The water flow there was tolerable for everyone to either jump over or wade across. Behind the herd, the rest of the people followed, commanding the dogs to encircle the sheep. It looked like an authentic outing of a shepherd guiding sheep toward the mountains.

A sigh of relief could be seen on Imalda's face. The most difficult part of the trek was over. The uphill walk to the Castello was rather pleasant as Don Nicola and Alvaro enjoyed picking cactus pears along the way. They then encountered a fellow shepherd who was on the way to the high mountains with a team of guard dogs. Sergio recognized him and instructed, "You haven't seen anything." The shepherd replied in the affirmative with a chuckle. The only two who knew how to guide the sheep were Imalda and Sergio, as they positioned themselves to control the sheep with the dogs. Imalda warned the group not to sit on any big rock at the castle site but to keep going downhill on the other side. She went on to say that rattlesnakes might lie under the rocks. In her mind, being tired was not an option.

The big valley lies between Mount Vesuvius and Castello Normanno. The glen lies on the other side of the castle, hidden from the town of Avella. Courtesy of Morelli Salvatore.

Coming down on the other side of the castle, there were farmlands and grasslands between the castle and the high mountains. Shepherds took their sheep to graze and did some farming there. It looked more like a glen than a valley. The glen was well hidden from townies who resided at ground level, on the other side of the castle, as well as the few German soldiers camped further away. Shepherds owned the huts and farmhouses and they were loyal to Imalda, their matriarch. They were just as happy to get their sheep back that Imalda had borrowed for the excursion to their huts. They sensed the urgency of the situation and were happy to oblige, provide shelter to the group, and make a home for her friends. She would have made a great field marshal.

Sergio waited for the next day to return home. Again, he traveled in darkness to avoid locals in the street. The next morning, the same civilian policemen, who apprehended the teenager, showed up at Don Nicola's apartment knocking the entrance door down. They looked in and out of the apartment but no Don Nicola. By this time, Sergio and Sofia came out of their apartments into the courtyard, inquiring as to what the commotion was about. Shepherd neighbors also gathered at the entrance of the building wanting to know about the noise, especially coming from Imalda's building.

One of the undercover policeman turned to Sergio asking if he had seen Signore Nicola Celeste recently. From the way the policemen pronounced the word signore, Sergio could tell that these policemen were not Italian or Fascist thugs, but gestapo. For example, Neapolitans do not pronounce the ending, "re," as in the word signore. Sergio then sent the policemen on a wild goose chase by answering, "Nicola left for Avellino yesterday, because his daughter was in the Hospital of San Pellegrino with typhoid and his son worked in the Madonna Di Monte Vergine Church in Avellino," knowing full well that the Germans visitors were scared of typhoid. With tongue and cheek, he added, "Who shall I say is the one who damaged his door?" The gestapo left in a huff. They were lucky to get out alive with all those shepherds in the courtyard.

The next day, German troops disappeared just as they appeared in Avella, suddenly and without notice. The nightmare was over. This called for a celebration, but Sofia was in no mood to celebrate until she was in Mario's arms humming their song.

ELEVEN
Confusion Galore

It is instructive in digressing to review the ramifications and state of mind as a result of Italy signing the unconditional surrender pact with the Allies on September 8, 1943. It created many uncertainties and confusion among millions of people in the manner that it was done. The new Italian government of Pietro Badoglio flip-flopped by declaring that Italy would fight on the side of the Allies. That was an empty gesture because Germany occupied most of Italy and the rest of the Italian troops were dispersed north of the Alps and the Balkans under the supervision of the German Army. The new Italian government controlled only soldiers stationed in Southern Italy and most of them went home. Obviously, Badoglio must have learned to whistle Dixie for General Eisenhower. Forty-five days earlier he declared alliance with Germany after the incarceration of Mussolini.

General Dwight D. Eisenhower, Allied Commander in Europe, did not want to contend with Italian forces in mainland Italy. He wanted Italy to sign an unconditional surrender before the invasion of Salerno. In fact, General Giuseppe Castellano of the Italian Army signed a short surrender document on September 3 in Sicily. Hitler countered by threatening to send tanks to Rome and arrest the King, the crown prince, government officials, and Badoglio. There were German troops stationed not far from Rome, and, evidently, that raised havoc in Badoglio's mind. Badoglio still feared the Nazis would execute him and wanted to delay the formal signing of the accord. By September 8, twenty-five German divisions poured over the Alps that Badoglio failed to defend.

In signing the Armistice, Badoglio and the king made a bold move to hold on to power at the expense of Italian soldiers out in the fields of battle. Thus, it was no surprise that the people of Italy hated Badoglio more than Mussolini because everyone had a relative in some faraway place exposed to elements of war. Also, Italians felt that the king was being selfish in trying to form a government in which his son Umberto, would eventually take over. Absurdity and chaos ran amok in the minds of these two. British Prime Minister Churchill promised them the sky just to alleviate Eisenhower's concerns about having to fight two foes instead of one in Salerno. Churchill moved a mountain to rescue more than 350,000 soldiers at Dunkirk. These two Italian clowns didn't lift a finger to save more than two million Italian soldiers at the mercy of the German Army.

Within hours of the signing of the Armistice, the Allied Army invaded Salerno. The invasion of Salerno by the Allies had been planned long before the signing of the Armistice. Badoglio suggested that the Eighty-Second U.S. Airborne Division seize Rome before the Allies invaded any other place in Italy. His main concern, and that of the king, was to escape the wrath of Hitler. Ultimately, General Dwight Eisenhower decided to call off the landing, at the last minute. That was a wise move because the U.S. Eighty-Second Airborne Division planned to land only one regiment of paratroopers north of Rome. Without reinforcements, it would have been suicidal, since two or three German divisions were near Rome. Hence, the dash to Brindisi by Badoglio and the king.

The day after the signing of the Armistice, a frightened Badoglio and the king fled to Brindisi without alerting his ministers and giving no instructions to his generals concerning the defense of Rome. There was no bound to Hitler's wrath when he heard of the escape. In early September 1943, Princess Mafalda, daughter of King Victor Emanuel III, traveled to Bulgaria to attend the funeral of her brother-in-law, King Boris III. She was informed of Italy's surrender to the Allied Powers. On September 23, she received a telephone call from Major Karl Hass of the German High Command, who told her that he had an important message from her husband, who was imprisoned in Bavaria, Germany. On her arrival at the German embassy, Mafalda was arrested, ostensibly for subversive activities. She was transported to Munich for questioning, then to Berlin, and finally to Buchenwald concentration camp.

On August 24, 1944, the Allies bombed an ammunition factory inside Buchenwald. Some 400 prisoners were killed and Princess Mafalda was seriously wounded; she had been housed in a quarter adjacent to the bombed factory, and when the attack occurred, she was buried up to her neck in debris and suffered severe burns to her arm. The conditions of the labor camp caused her arm to become infected as a result, and the medical staff at the facility amputated it. She bled profusely during the operation and never regained consciousness. She died during the night of August 26–27, 1944. Her body was reburied after the war at Kronberg Castle in Hesse, next to her husband's grave.

Soldiers of the U.S. Fifth Army, under the command of General Mark Clark, cheered the news of the Italian surrender as the naval convoys approached the beaches of Salerno but were shocked by the speed and intensity of the German reaction to the landings. Four of the five German divisions in southern Italy were moved to Salerno to seal off and destroy the bridgehead. One of the German Army Divisions came from a camp in Avella, the Herman Goring Division. The battle hung in the balance for the next six days with little support from the Eighth British Army led by Field Marshal Bernard Montgomery. The Germans had skillfully delayed the Eighth British Army with demolitions and a slow withdrawal, though the British still managed and advanced 300 miles along the Adriatic Sea in seventeen days, away from Salerno. British official history claimed that transport problems and administrative difficulties hampered the Eighth Army and were the real barriers to rapid advancement. Few observers believe that transport problems were responsible for Montgomery's failure to press the advance toward Salerno with any sense of urgency. The Canadians, who were part of the British Airborne Division, were ordered to turn inland and advance toward Potenza, a road and rail junction fifty miles east of Salerno. Colonial British troops alleviated the British Army's need for more troops since the rescue at Dunkirk.

It is interesting to quote directly from British soldier Norman Lewis's diary about his experience during the invasion of Salerno. He was stationed on the beaches of Paestum, south of Salerno. Not much was happening there until September 12. From his diary entry on September 12, 1943:

"Suddenly, today, the war arrived with a vengeance. We were sitting outside our farmhouse, reading, sunning ourselves, and trying to come to terms with the acrid-tasting wine, when we noticed that a rumble of distant cannonades, present from early morning, suddenly seemed to have come closer. Soon after, a line of American tanks went by, making for the battle, and hardly any time passed before they were back. There were fewer of them, and the wild and erratic manner in which they were driven suggested panic. One stopped nearby, and the crew clambered out and fell into one another's arms, weeping. Shortly afterward there were cries of gas, and we saw frantic figures wearing gas masks running in all directions.

Chaos and confusion broke out on all sides. The story was that there had been a breakthrough by the Sixteenth Panzer Grenadier Division, which struck suddenly in our direction down to Battipaglia Road, with the clear intention of reaching the sea at Paestum, wiping out the Fifth Army Headquarters and cutting the beachhead in half. Rumors began to come in thick and fast, the most damaging one being that General Mark Clark was proposing to abandon the beachhead and had asked the Navy for the Fifth Army to be re-embarked. No one we spoke to believed that this operation was feasible, the feeling being that at the first signs of a withdrawal, the Germans would simply roll forward and drive us into the sea."

Thanks to the firepower of the U.S. and British Navies, the German Army was prevented from closing in on the Fifth Army. Rumbles from Mount Vesuvius usually meant to the people in the valley that bad news was imminent, but not this time. Rumbles were due to cannon shots from Allied ships. People could hear the shelling emanating from the Salerno coastline. People in Avella climbed rooftops to see what was happening on the other side of Vesuvius. They desperately wanted to confirm in their minds that indeed Allied ships were the ones shooting those cannon shots. American paratroopers landed all over the mountains of Avella, Cicciano, and Avellino, a distance of thirty miles apart between those towns. The target for the drop was to have been in the city of Avellino in order to sabotage the German supply line to Salerno.

From a military perspective, it was a failure, since most of the paratroopers were captured by German patrols. However, to the people in the valley, it was a huge success. The feeling that an American parachutist might land at their doorstep buoyed hopes immensely. If an American soldier knocked on the door of a house, a resident would have seen hope reincarnated. Hunger was just a matter of being able to sacrifice oneself to forage the farms, but hope was something else. It was needed to nurture aspirations in life. The American landing near Avella was not a total failure. American soldiers were able to set up a radio communication centered above the cave of San Michele. They communicated the location of German camps in Avella and German supply traffic to Salerno on Via Appia in Baiano.

As the battle for Salerno raged on, the paved road in Avella, from the camps to Via Appia in Baiano, was crammed with German tanks, troop-carrying trucks, and motorcycles. One could hear traffic night and day. Vehicles traveled on Via Appia to Nola, pivoting around Mount Vesuvius in an easterly direction and then South to Salerno. People in Avella were not allowed near the new paved road, only on the dirt road to the cemetery, which ran parallel and close to the paved road. The war in Salerno reached the skies of Avella. German and Allied planes engaged in a dog-fight above farmlands. One German plane was shot down very near the Roman Amphitheater and the new paved road. The area was cordoned off by soldiers for their entire stay in Avella. No one in town was allowed near the plane when scavenging for food on the farm, or for anything else edible, until soldiers left town.

The Maresciallo dared not show his face for fear of providing information to strangers or being interrogated by the gestapo. Don Nicola closed his studio but socialized with Sergio in the same building, and with Alvaro and Ramiro. Don Nicola was a marked man by the Fascist since the 1930s, but more so during the war. He was constantly reminded of that by the others. Sofia was frantic without Mario. As for the twin sisters, they still knitted sweaters at home to keep their hopes up as to the future of resuming dressmaking. The object was to lay low until something good might occur or, better yet, the soldiers left town.

The few German troops in Potenza played a pivotal role in repelling the British Army away from Salerno. Potenza, the largest city in the region of Basilicata, was founded in pre-Roman times as a village on the slope of a south-facing ridge above the Basento River. The poor agricultural land had led to the depopulation of the rural areas. However, Potenza had developed as a regional center around its twelfth-century cathedral. Beginning on September 13, the Allied air forces began attacks on the city's railroad yards and road junctions. Potenza, crowded with refugees from the Salerno battle area, was targeted by Allied heavy bombers on six consecutive days and much of the city was destroyed in these attacks with heavy loss of life. The first signs of a German withdrawal were noted on September 17, but no one ordered the Allied air forces to cease attacking a town or the railway yards that the Allies would soon need.

The Germans had planned to hold Potenza with a regiment of the First Parachute Division and remnants of the Fifteenth Panzer Division, which was partially camped in Avella. When the Canadian Royal Twenty-Second Regiment mounted an attack, using artillery, armor, and an additional infantry battalion, the German paratroopers withdrew. The Germans had already begun their withdrawal north, but they held onto Potenza with elements of the First Parachute Division. The battle for Potenza lasted until the afternoon of September 20 when the German Army withdrew to avoid being cut off. Canadian casualties at Potenza were very light compared to the standards of later battles: Six killed and twenty-one wounded. Canadian doctors treated sixteen wounded Germans as well as Canadians. However, the real tragedy of Potenza was the number of civilian casualties, estimated at over 2,000, including several hundred dead in air raids directed against a town that functioned as a railway center and route for reinforcements. Yes, few internees suffered casualties in the bombing. One building where they lived was destroyed.

There were German troops in Tito since it is located between Potenza and Brienza. Principally, the people of Tito refused to cooperate with the troops. Fortunately for the internees in those towns, they were able to mingle easily with the populace and hide among the locals. There was no food to be had since all livestock was moved to the nearby mountains, thanks to Strega. No one could be found at city hall, as the mayor and officials left their posts. All records were destroyed, thanks to Pasquale. The acting mayor, Bambolone, went back to the barbershop cutting hair, thanks to his wife. The Wolf family hoped and prayed that the soldiers' stay would be short. They dreamt of the day they would return to Avella and live in the comfort of the clan before going home to Vienna. The internees found it was easier to stay put than to escape to the hills and endure the pain of occupation momentarily. The main thrust of the German troops in that area was to hold on to Potenza as long as possible before leaving. The ordeal lasted approximately eight to ten days. By then, Mario and the two Ukrainians escaped to Naples, eventually partaking in another battle there against German occupation.

In Tito, they could hear cannon shots night after night. No more passeggiatas in the evenings and get-togethers in the piazza. A company of German troops loaded on two trucks led by a second Lieutenant in a jeep came to Tito in the middle of the night soon after the Allied invasion of Salerno. The first things that they laid claim to were the railroad station and city hall. Fortunately, soldiers found no one working at city hall and no paperwork trail in any place, totally void. Apparently, Bambolone's wife prevailed upon him to stop being a clown mayor for the Germans, if they came. Next, the soldiers raided every bakery and butcher shop for meat and white bread. They were tired of eating their food rations and stale dark bread.

Initially, they wanted to camp in the Colonna Palazzo, but the custodian had anticipated that move and closed the portone entrance with reinforced metal bars. Being an Italophile, the lieutenant suspected that this was not a typical hill town of Southern Italy. He had studied Italian art at the University of Florence and was very familiar with hill towns. No livestock at any place in the farms or streets; not possible he reasoned! He realized Tito being a shepherd town and, yet, no sheep to be found nearby in the hills when they came to Tito. The whole town makeup made no sense to him. He became highly suspicious of anyone there. He had a soft heart toward the locals and did nothing about it, partially because he didn't have the manpower to make a thorough investigation. He knew that it would take that kind of effort to unravel the secrets of the town. On one hand he was charmed by the locals, but, on the other hand, he didn't trust them. Obviously, they were hiding something. Yes, Strega did too good a job in setting the stage in Tito.

At that time there were about 200 internees in Tito. However, soldiers were not aware of that. Strega took it upon herself to shield and protect the Wolf family from inquiries and make food available to them, as she promised Ramiro. She advised Nanna and Ehrlich not to send Arya to school, because her blond hair would stand out among all those students with black or brown hair. Any peculiarities observed by soldiers may trigger unwanted attention and questions or worst some kind of personal inquiries. Arya was upset, as she enjoyed the company of Bambolone's children in school.

In lieu of the fact that the soldiers could not camp at the Colonna Palazzo, they camped in the courtyard of city hall located next to both Strega and the Wolf's apartments. This created a nightmare not only at night but also at daytime. She arranged a rendezvous with the doorman at city hall. Whenever soldiers went out on patrols, the doorman took a break from duty by walking toward the Piazza. A shepherd, waiting in Bambolone's barbershop, would bring food to Strega or the Wolf family.

However, one day the lieutenant paid a visit to the barber for a shave. Bambolone's ass tightened up, reminding himself to be careful with this officer. All along this time, Strega, her daughter, Ehrlich and Nanna were peering across the piazza when they noticed a military vehicle parked on the cobbled stone street in front of the barbershop blocking their view. As in Avella, the square is paved with asphalt, but near the buildings on both sides were cobbled stone streets. Strega had to see what was going on inside the barbershop. So, she darted across the piazza and veered off toward a convenience store, as she approached the vehicle. She could see that the lieutenant was getting a shave and, for the first time, Bambolone was not yapping. There was one big sigh of relief when Strega reported back to the others in the apartment.

After the shave, the lieutenant asked Bambolone, "Where is the mayor?" Bambolone calmly replied that because of the unbearable hot weather at this time of the year, the mayor and city hall staff had taken two-week vacations. The lieutenant knew that he had been had and no information could be gathered from the barber. With the help of Pasquale, Bambolone had locked up all of the Fascist members of the city council in the basement of the church. He didn't trust them with German troops snooping around town. During the troops' stay in Tito, the Viennese family stayed indoors the whole time.

During this period, guards at internment camps were more confused than ever as to what to do. Should they leave or stay at internment camps, since its creator, Il Duce was dwelling in jail someplace in central Italy. To make matters worse, Italian soldiers were being taken prisoners by German soldiers on Italian soil and sent to Germany to work in armament factories. The guards were not paid, since the new government was located in Brindisi and were not in a position to print new money. Rome was occupied by the German Army and payment to the guards was their least concern. Like the locals and the internees in town, the guards had mouths to feed in the family. They shirked their duties and joined the rest of the people in town to search for food. Besides, no one at city hall was going to hold them accountable, because city officials didn't want to be responsible for a Fascist program, especially when Fascism was passé then.

By then, most, if not all, Fascist mayors in Southern Italy had left their posts. They moved to other towns and returned after the war. Few ever made it back, as Communist partisans had them on their list to do away with after the war. In the interim period from July 25 to September 8, 1943, the registry of internees at the Magistrate Office was sloppily handled or filed away, never again to see daylight. However, records at Ferramonti di Tarsia and Campagna survived the war, but not in Potenza, Tito, and Brienza. Today, there is a museum commemorating the lives of internees at Ferramonti di Tarsia.

Like Ciano, Il Duce's son-in-law, the former Interior Minister Luigi Federzoni, was running for his life from Nazis and Fascists after July 25. This poses an interesting question: Who was running the internment camps in Italy from July 25 to September 8? Certainly not the prefects, since they were required to be apolitical. The next in line to run the internment camps in Southern Italy were city hall officials, which meant the podestas, but most of them left town. Thus, it was no surprise that guards left their posts in Campagna, Potenza, Tito, Brienza, and Ferramonti as well as at other internment camps, where the Allies occupied that territory. Some guards decided to assist the internees in whatever their needs, including their own families. Both the guards and internees were in the same boat—rowing upstream to avoid starvation. From the internees' perspective, they preferred to stay in the camps, since there was still a war north of the Alps. Hence, internees put their lives on hold through no fault of their own. They never lost hope that things would get better, knowing that locals cared about their plight.

The magistrate who was responsible for registering the internees at Potenza must have left city hall, together with the mayor and other officials, well before German soldiers showed up in Potenza around September 15. That may explain why there were no records of internees at the magistrate's office, only birth and death certificates. As such, future mayors and local historians were not aware of the existence of internees in Potenza. Like in Potenza, a small group of German soldiers was also stationed in Brienza, as witnessed by a German-speaking internee. The internee attracted the amorous attention of a German soldier which blossomed into a marriage after the war.

In Campagna, near Salerno, the carabinieri guards left the internment camp at the San Bartolomeo Convent on September 8. The number of internees decreased by then from about 450 to 150. Thus, about 300 internees escaped to freedom during this confusion period. On September 9, the convent again had a visitor from the German staff requesting a visit. This time, the remaining internees did not return to the convent having escaped the first time to the hillsides with the help of carabinieri and locals. Besides, there was a major battle taking place, right about the time of that visit, at Battipaglia, a town only five miles away from Campagna. They stayed out on the hills for the duration of the war in Salerno, roughly two weeks. Ferramonti's internment camp was liberated on September 8, as the guards left for good. Ferramonti was then under Allied control. However, some internees stayed there until 1945 when the war was finally over. From 1943 to 1945, the war was still raging in Europe, and news about the atrocities at the extermination camps reached Ferramonti. There was no incentive to hurry home to Northern Europe as Ferramonti was a lot safer.

With the demise of the Fascist government, subsidies ceased. The fact that internees survived is attributable to their will for survival and the compassion of the locals throughout their stay in Southern Italy. A story that illustrates the point is recounted in the book by Elizabeth Bettina, *It Happened in Italy*. A mother from Potenza breastfed her child and also a Jewish baby who was born in Potenza during the height of the battle in Potenza. The fact that the present-day mayor and local historians could not find a birth certificate of the Jewish child was inexcusable. Birth certificates at city hall were issued regardless of nationality, even during the war. Most likely, records of the internees at the Magistrate Office were destroyed. Some internees freed in Southern Italy found their way to Allied countries via Spain, Portugal, North Africa, and the Middle East, but not via Northern Europe.

At that time, Mario and the two brothers tried to appear as inconspicuous as possible to the German soldiers patrolling the streets of Naples. The fact that Mario was in Naples implied other internees were there as well since the islands of Capri, and Ischia offered some respite from the war. In Naples, anything was possible, as the Camorra operated freely. There was no city government to speak of. In Naples, there were better possibilities for leaving the war altogether. It was just a question of money. German soldiers mostly concentrated their posting near the train station and the port of Naples, about two miles from the Naval station. The routine of the trio consisted of fishing, and Mario wandering up to the San Carlo Opera House with the hope of seeing Don Nicola. By evening, they either got together with the scugnizzi to barter with them for food or to cook the catch of the day. By seven that evening a curfew was enforced.

On September 10, the Germans occupied Rome. Italian soldiers in Rome received no orders from Badoglio or the king in Brindisi and didn't know what to do. Germans captured many Italian soldiers and sent them to German camps and/or armament factories. Some Italian soldiers stripped their clothes off in the streets of Rome and put on old trousers. About 60,000 soldiers wandered in the streets begging for food in civilian clothes. German soldiers terrorized civilians in the streets, stole anything in sight, and many girls were violated. Major Herbert Kappler, head of the Gestapo in Rome, sequestered 120 tons of gold from the Bank of Italy and transferred it to Germany. See the books, *Bitter Chicory to Sweet Espresso* and *The Battle for Rome*.

There was an avalanche of Romans taking English lessons and wanting to welcome and cheer the Allies when they came to Rome. Roman men and allied prisoners were hiding in the city afraid to spend time in Italy or German labor camps. They hid in private homes, convents, seminaries, monasteries, and churches. Rome had never seen as many insanity cases in its history as when Italian soldiers, Allied prisoners, Roman and foreign Jews, OSS spies, and others began entering the asylum. Kappler forever chased these poor souls, as Romans pitched in to help in hiding them.

Under Pope Pius XII's balcony, on October 16, 1943, Jewish residents of the

Trastevere District of Rome were being transported by trucks to the railroad station in Tiburtina, and on their way to Auschwitz. Trucks stopped in front of Saint Peter Square so that soldiers could take pictures. How macabre that they should stop outside the "border" to the Vatican, a holy place. Those prisoners were more representative of Roman traditions than modern Romans. Roman Jews inhabited ancient Rome along the Tiber River long before Saint Peter appeared on the scene 2,000 years ago. Of the 1,023 deported, sixteen of them made it back home.

In Northern Italy, it was a whole different story. From Rome and North, internment camps were under the control of the German Army. Local administrations at city hall were accountable to Nazi officials. In effect, Nazi officials replaced the Fascist infrastructure from the minister of interior to the prefect. As such, guards had no other choice but to acquiesce to Nazi demands. With the return of a new Fascist government at Salo near Milan, Nazi officials still controlled the management of the internment camps in North Italy. There are very few records or stories about the disposition of guards or local administrators in Northern Italy but, clearly, they were under the watchful eyes of the SS troops or the like.

It is said that cats have nine lives. Mussolini must have had one extra life. On September 12, 1943, he escaped incarceration to torment the Italian people once again. He formed a new government under the banner of the Italian Socialist Republic in Salo, near Milan.

TWELVE
Wishful Thinking

The signing of the Armistice triggered a number of events. Hitler was hell-bent to free Mussolini from prison, reinstate him and start a new Fascist government in North Italy since he occupied North and Central Italy. It served his purpose to form a puppet government under his control to legitimize his occupation. Who was the sucker then? Definitely, not Hitler. Besides, he needed the same sucker to terrorize internees under his occupation. He justified to anyone who cared to listen that he was freeing a friend and a great modern-day Caesar. What a bunch of crock! Suckers love adorations. Those words were intended for Mussolini's ears and no one else's.

Another intent was to form a new Fascist government under Mussolini, allied to Germany for propaganda purposes. Eventually, Germany would annex part of Northern Italy bordering the Alps. He was still fighting WWI, when Italy took over the Dolomite Alps. In fact, the city of Bolzano was annexed during WWII by Germany and Mussolini did not resist that annexation. As such, Hitler assumed that there would be no resistance from anyone in the new Fascist government to his plan, the annexation of all the Dolomite Alps. Clearly, Hitler turned the tables on Mussolini. In their initial relationship, Mussolini was the hunter as he grabbed for colonies. This time, Hitler was the predator looking to annex the Italian Alps. He was just returning the favor. Thus, the jig was up and Mussolini knew it, being a former predator. Hence, Mussolini wanted no part of Hitler, as he was languishing in jail high up on the mountains of Abruzzo.

Since the main architects of internment camps in Italy, Mussolini and former Fascist Interior Minister Federzoni, were no longer in charge, local administrations in Southern Italy took matters into their own hands. They released, with the approval of the Badoglio government, carabinieri guards from internment camp duties and declared freedom for all internees in territories controlled by the new Italian government in Brindisi. Unfortunately, freedom did not come on a dish of spaghetti. It was no bargain to be free when internees had to scavenge for food much like the locals. What was the meaning of freedom, when all they could do was to walk out of their apartments, like anyone else in town, looking for food, and the war was all around them. They could not reclaim the lives that they had before nor the loss of valuable material things, properties, and other intangibles. They were stuck in a place for a while where they didn't want to be. At least, the guards or magistrates left them alone. In Northern Italy, they had a different worry, their lives were at stake. With the establishment of a new Fascist government, once again Mussolini restored internment camps under the guidance of German advisors. Thus, words from Badoglio about freedom were irrelevant to internees throughout Italy, especially north of Rome, just cheap talk.

In summary, the following events took place in rapid succession and in a more or less sequential order in Italy: On July 25, 1943, Mussolini was incarcerated; September 8, signing of unconditional surrender by Italy; September 8, guards leave internment camps in the South of Italy; September 9, Badoglio and the king leave Rome to form a new government; September 9, Allies invade Salerno; September 10, German troops occupy Rome; September 10, whereabouts of Mussolini discovered by gestapo; September 11, German military staff plan to rescue Mussolini; September 12, Mussolini was rescued. These events had significant impacts on the war, the internment camps in Northern Italy, and Mussolini himself.

Badoglio's government and the Allies also realized the relevance of a new Fascist government in the hands of the Germans. Strict measures to hide and secure Mussolini were taken by the carabinieri; he was moved several times and guarded by carabinieri troops. On July 25, Mussolini was arrested and brought to the carabinieri Headquarters in Trastevere, Rome; July 27, he was transferred to the island of Ponza in the Tyrrhenian Sea; on August 7, he was transferred to the island of La Maddalena, near the bigger island of Sardinia. Since August 28, he had been held at the Hotel Campo Imperatore, which was built on a remote and defensible mountain plateau 2,112 meters above sea level in the Gran Sasso d'Italia mountain range, Abruzzo region. A ski station was located next to the hotel, linked by a cable car. He was guarded by forty-three carabinieri officers and three undercover policemen, who protected their fortress with two heavy machine guns and rifles. One guard was always present in the apartment where Mussolini resided. However, Chief of the carabinieri Senise, advised the guards to exercise prudence, if the Germans attempted a rescue. This was contrary to Badoglio's order to shoot Mussolini if Mussolini were to escape. In any case, the carabinieri agreed among themselves that they would not put up a fight.

The three main summits of the Gran Sasso are Corno Grande, which, at 2,912 meters (9,554 feet) is the highest peak in the Apennines, followed by Corno Piccolo, and Pizzo d'Intermesoli, which is separated from the other two peaks by Val Maone, a deep valley. Corno Grande and Corno Piccolo's ash coloration come from their limestone and dolomite composition. The peaks are snow-covered for much of the year. Corno Piccolo is referred to as The Sleeping Giant. This is due to the appearance of a profile of a reclined face. Corno Grande and Corno Piccolo with their rough vertical walls provide serious rock climbers with challenges. In summary, it was a very remote place to hide Mussolini and very difficult to reach by foot. The defenders had all the advantages of the view of the valley below them.

German intelligence intercepted a coded Italian report which indicated that Mussolini was imprisoned somewhere in the Abruzzo Mountains. The Germans employed a ruse to confirm the exact location in which a German doctor pretended to establish a hospital at the hotel on the Gran Sasso. Major Herbert Kappler, in the Gestapo headquarters in Rome, used counterfeit money to obtain crucial Information from local informants. Hitler then selected a man to personally escort Mussolini back to Germany: Otto Skozeny. The overall planner of the rescue attempt was General Kurt Student. Major Skorzeny was born in Vienna in 1908. He trained as an engineer and became manager of a scaffolding business. He attended Vienna University about the same time as Ehrlich and Nanna. in 1939, he joined the Luftwaffe and later transferred to a crack SS military formation.

On September 12, 1943, Skorzeny and 160 SS troopers rescued Mussolini in a high-risk glider mission. Ten gliders, each carrying nine soldiers and a pilot, towed planes started from the Pratica di Mare Air Base, near Rome. Meanwhile, the valley station of the funicular railway leading to the Campo Imperatore was captured at 2:00 p.m. in a ground attack by two paratrooper companies which cut all telephone lines. At 2:05, the airborne commandos landed their ten gliders on Mt. Corno Piccolo near the hotel. One crashed and caused injuries. Mussolini and a carabiniere, Ferdinando Tascini, watched the landings from the little window of the Duce's apartment. However, he looked worried and commented, "This was not [what I] wanted." After the gliders landed, parachutists climbed out, dropping to the ground. Italian General Fernando Soleti of the Italian African Police, who flew in with Skorzeny, emerged, walking toward the Hotel Imperatore, where Mussolini resided. Soleti told the carabinieri to stand down. Behind Soleti walked Skorzeny carrying a machine gun. Parachutists followed Skorzeny.

After eighty years Ferdinando Tascini, who was then a carabiniere guard, explained what Mussolini meant by his wry comment. Mussolini confided much to Mr. Tascini as the two shared the same room much of the time during the incarceration period starting at Trastevere District in Rome. Mr. Tascini told the local media of Perugia, Province in Umbria, "Mussolini was expecting the Americans, but it turned out to be the Germans." Why would Mussolini say that? There are several reasons, but ultimately Mussolini came to the same conclusion as Ciano. Hitler and the rest of the Nazi hierarchy could not be trusted, especially when the end result was that Italy was gobbled up by the German Army. This was not what he envisioned for himself and Italy. Mr. Tascini was 101 years old when he died in 2024.

Mr. Tascini. Courtesy of Nancy DeSanti.

Thus, in summary: 1.) In late 1943, the reality of the situation was that the war would end soon with the Allies being victorious. 2.) Both Hitler and Mussolini were jockeying for negotiations after the war. The object was to keep as many territories after the war as possible. Hitler jockeyed to legitimize possessions of all German-speaking territories, Austria, Sudetenland, Danzig, and the Italian Alps. 3.) Mussolini wanted to rally Italian soldiers on the side of the Allies against German occupation of Italian territories. Sad, but both Fascist leaders were delusional.

Approaching the hotel, one carabinieri officer shouted: "Don't shoot!" Skorzeny entered the radio room and kicked the chair from under the operator interrupting transmission. Then, he ran upstairs, with a pistol in hand, and burst into Mussolini's suite. "Duce, the Fuhrer sent me to free you," Skorzeny said. "I knew that my friend Adolf Hitler would not have abandoned me," Mussolini replied. Il Duce followed Skorzeny outside the hotel and turning to a Carabiniere said, "I would have preferred to be freed by Italians." This comment is slightly different from the one stated by Mr. Tascini, but the tenor of it is similar, i.e. anyone else but Skorzeny. It was clear to all who witnessed the Duce's appearance that he was pale and sickly. His great friend, SS Colonel Eugen Dollman, who had often translated at Hitler-Mussolini meetings, said: "I believe that Mussolini would have preferred to remain on the Gran Sasso to admire the flight of eagles."

Mussolini was flown out by a special plane that had just arrived in the meantime. Although under given circumstances the small plane was overloaded, Skorzeny insisted on accompanying Mussolini, which endangered the mission's success. After an extremely dangerous but successful takeoff, they flew to Pratica di Mare airport, Rome. They then immediately continued to fly to Vienna, where Mussolini stayed overnight at the Hotel Imperial. The next day he was flown to Munich, where his family had been waiting for him. On September 14, he met Hitler at Führer Headquarters, in Wolf's Lair, near Rastenburg. By then, Mussolini was a shadow of himself. He was a broken man, mentally and physically—without the adoration of his countrymen in his future. He had an ulcer condition which kept him under a strict bland diet and other physical conditions.

German propaganda gave full credit for the rescue to Skorzeny. General Student, the main architect of the rescue, protested to Luftwaffe commander Hermann Goring about this, but Goring could do nothing because Hitler had accepted the story that Skorzeny was the principal hero. Goring suspected that SS chief Heinrich Himmler maneuvered to make Skorzeny the hero to promote the SS over the Luftwaffe. This was an argument between the two whereby jealousy overruled rational exchanges between the two.

Once at Rastenburg, Hitler got down to business with a stern message: "I don't doubt that you will agree with me in believing that one of the first acts...will be to sentence to death the traitors of the Grand Council...including Count Ciano. He is a traitor to his country,...to Fascism,...to Germany, and to his family... But I advise you: It is preferable that the death sentence be carried out in Italy."

"But you're talking of the husband of my daughter (Edda) who I adore and the father of my grandchildren," Mussolini protested. "All the more reason Count Ciano merits punishment in that not only has he failed in fidelity toward his country, but in fidelity to his family." Mussolini then told Hitler that his only desire was to leave public life and rest due to his sickness. Finally, Hitler insisted that Mussolini return to Italy and head a new Fascist government. If Mussolini refused, he would destroy Milan, Genoa, and Turin just as he intended to destroy London.

The threat from Hitler was somewhat hypocritical. On one hand, Hitler was implying that Italy was going to be treated like any other European country colonized or terrorized by Germany if Mussolini didn't do as told! On the other hand, Germany was already treating Italy as a colony, no different from other European countries occupied by Germany. It raped its women, robbed its resources, including priceless art, and indiscriminately killed all over Italy, including internees in Northern Italy. It could not have become any worse! Mussolini must have realized that the threat did not carry any weight, but there was not much he could do. Basically, he was under house arrest. Mussolini didn't call his bluff to ask the question, "What is the difference between now and what you intend to do?" Perhaps, Mussolini was too sick to point out the absurdity of Hitler's threats or, perhaps, he was of the same kindred spirit. More likely, Il Duce was worried for himself at the hands of this madman. Finally, the clown was intimidated and the gig was up.

Mussolini spent two weeks in Germany for medical exams, being reunited with his family and meeting Fascist Party and government officials who fled to safety in North Italy. Others fled to Spain. Mussolini, his wife Donna Rachele, and their two youngest children, Romano and Anna Maria were secured in Hirschberg Castle, fifty miles South of Munich. Ciano and Edda had been in Munich about three weeks before Mussolini arrived, but not of their own volition. This sad episode of Ciano's few remaining days of his life is repeated here verbatim, as described from Eugen Dollmann's book, *With Hitler and Mussolini*. The relationship between Dollmann and Ciano may be summarized from Dollmann's quotation in the book, "We never liked each other."

DOLLMANN'S VERSION

In order to present one point of view about events that took place in Rome in August of 1943, Eugen Dollmann is quoted verbatim from his book. However, to bring out the truth, a rebuttal is prepared by this author.

"The new Badoglio regime had placed the couple under house arrest in their elegant two-floor apartment in the Via Angelo Secchi, Rome. The clouds above their heads grew darker week by week, and anyone with experience of contemporary Italy knew that house arrest might easily be a prelude to something worse.... I received a visit from a smartly dressed man whose civilian clothes did not disguise the officer beneath. He handed me a note:

Dear Dollmann,

The bearer of this, a family friend, is instructed to convey my regards and a request which I should be grateful if you would fulfil.

Yours sincerely,
Edda Ciano-Mussolini

"I went for a stroll near the Ciano home with my faithful and unsuspecting dog. Unlike Ciano, Edda and her children enjoyed walking-out privileges. She emerged for a breadth of cool evening air. My car was waiting around the corner. I drove past, she climbed in, and we made for the home of some friends, a rendezvous which I had selected as being suitably unsuspicious. Mussolini's daughter behaved precisely as her intimates had expected her to behave when it came to a pinch. Questionable as some aspects of her married life had been in the past, she now became all wife and mother. For every thought and emotion was centered on a wish to save her husband and children, and the present fate of her father received only fleeting mention.

"The decision was that I should use my influence with Field Marshal Kesselring to secure the immediate availability of a special airplane for the Ciano's flight from Rome—a flight which would undoubtedly take them to Germany. I stressed this more than once.

"I further stressed that this exhausted my own powers of intervention. Herr Kappler and his experienced staff would be responsible for the technical aspect of the flight, its preparation, and implementation...Kappler and his aide-de-camp were present at our second meeting, which took place shortly afterwards. He was extremely grateful to me for entrusting him with a mission so dear to his own devious heart. Two days later, one of his men in civilian clothes came armed with a huge bouquet of flowers for the lady of the house. His actual job was to fill the capacious pockets of his overcoat with sundry articles of value which Cianos were particularly anxious to save.

"Early on the morning of 23 August,...the operation got under way. As always in such cases, the guards presented the main obstacle...Fortunately, this was Italy, and even the Ciano's sentry found it impossible to resist the wiles of Edda's maid indefinitely, especially when lured into a neighborhood park by promises of a seductive nature. The Carabiniere and the lady's-maid duly disappeared and Edda and her children set off on their morning walk...leaving the house deserted save for Ciano. ...a fast sports car drew up at the corner of the street. Wearing a pair of large, tinted glasses, Ciano made a last hurried exit from the house... The countess, who had meanwhile been picked up by another car, met him in the courtyard of the Deutsches Heim, and the whole family was loaded into a truck and conveyed to the airfield.

If Ciano had been thinking along the right lines, he would never have embarked on a journey which would take him into the domain of Ribbentrop, who was his mortal enemy, or Adolf Hitler, who despised him. The Cianos' escape from Rome, their subsequent stay in Bavaria, their meetings with Donna Rachele and Mussolini himself, ...I had no part in the grim drama which now unfolded under Benito Mussolini's supreme direction."

REBUTTAL

I argue that the sole purpose of Dollmann's description of the scenario, and perhaps the writing of this book, had to do with absolving himself of Ciano's grim drama or affair, leading to Ciano's demise. It has only confirmed the opposite. He double-crossed Ciano. The realities and facts surrounding the grim drama tell a different story. First, Herr Dollmann would have us believe that Count Ciano preferred death over life by preferring to go to Munich instead of Spain. That's absurd. As a bon vivant man of his time, he enjoyed life to the fullest. The Badoglio's government had no compulsion or desire to condemn Ciano to a death sentence in court. In view of his diary expressing opposition to an alliance with Germany and the fact that he voted against Mussolini on the vote of confidence, the Italian people would have lynched Badoglio for any attempt otherwise but freedom. However, the German hierarchy had every reason to put Ciano to death. Herr Dollmann didn't like Ciano as stated by him, Hitler despised him and Ribbentrop wished him dead. They all considered him a traitor to be put to death, period. The feelings toward the German leadership by Ciano were mutually expressed in his diary. Thus, Munich represented the last place in the world for Ciano to be after escaping the apartment in Rome and, worst of all, to meet his makers. Pure nonsense!

Second, the pilot, who flew the plane to Munich, was none other than Skorzeny, who was a replacement for the regular pilot at the last minute. The fact that Skorzeny was involved in this affair implied that Hitler must have heard of Ciano's plan. Clearly, Hitler had a hand in the grim drama. Hitler was fond of Skorzeny, because they were both Austrians and knew each other well and had direct access. Kappler couldn't have contacted Hitler directly unless violating protocol. Gestapo Chief Kappler in Rome could not make any move without the approval of Dollmann who outranked him. In order to contact Hitler, he needed approval from Dollmann, General Wolff, General Kesselring, and Himmler. That would have been time-consuming in view that the escape from the house arrest in Rome lasted hours, not days. So, the only other person involved in the drama that had direct contact with Hitler was Herr Dollmann since he served as a translator and interpreter at many meetings between Hitler and international government officials. Hence, Herr Dollman must have contacted Hitler. Myriads of scenarios may be envisioned as to what really happened, but not what Herr Dollman described in full detail in his book.

In summary, Herr Dollman double-crossed Ciano's family. Assuming that Ciano's family had reached Spain, a lot of heads would have rolled including the regular pilot, Kappler, Dollman, and anyone else involved with the grim drama. The only possible way to have succeeded was for the pilot to remain in Spain or Dollman to pilot the plane himself to Spain. Sooner or later, the long arm of Hitler would have reached either one of them in Spain. Dollman had no choice but to be the double-crosser if he valued his life. Ultimately, Hitler had his puppet, Mussolini, to do away with Ciano in Verona. According to Hitler, it was the only honorable thing to do by Mussolini.

On September 18, 1943, Mussolini made his first radio speech to the Italian people since the rescue. However, before the speech, Hitler had spoken to Mussolini about re-establishing an Italian Fascist state. Specifically, he suggested the name, Italian Fascist Republic, but Mussolini objected on the basis that the word Fascist might be a subject of discord among Italians. As of November 25, the new regime would be known as the Italian Social Republic (RSI). The name took him back to his past before he invented Fascism in the 1920s. In his speech, he contrasted Hitler's stable regime with the deceitfulness of the king. "It is not the Fascist regime that has betrayed...., it is the monarchy that has betrayed the regime," he said. "The state we want to establish will be national and social in the highest sense of the word...," he added.

Claretta Petacci heard the speech at an airfield near Bergamo, North of Italy, where she and her family had stopped en route to Merano, forty miles from Innsbruck which is very near the Alps. She was so overcome with emotion that she fainted, according to her diary. Three days after the incarceration of Mussolini, the Petacci family left Rome for Northern Italy. On the night of August 12, 1943, the Petaccis were arrested on orders of the Badoglio government and imprisoned at Novara, a city west of Milan. This was an interesting development at that time. The Badoglio government was located in Rome, well before the signing of the Armistice, and still allied with Germany. The government consisted of Badoglio, the king of Italy, and a handful of wannabe ministers. However, Novara was under German occupation, strange but true. One country occupying territories of its ally, no different than Italian soldiers under German command in Russia, Europe, North Africa, etc.

Let's put this in perspective. Badoglio did not have the time to warn Italian soldiers (millions of them) spread all over Europe to come home or scamper from the wrath of the German Army, and yet he had the time to track down the Pettacci family all over Italy (including Italian territories occupied by Germany) and prevailed on the local carabinieri to incarcerate her. Undoubtedly, this operation must have been conducted by the carabinieri secretly from the Nazis. So much energy was spent on one person at the expense of millions of Italian soldiers. In fairness to Badoglio, there were no carabinieri in Russia to warn Italian soldiers to come home, but there were other means to warn those poor souls, as Churchill did at Dunkirk. Obviously, Badoglio cared more about personal affairs than those soldiers stranded in faraway lands. On September 17, the Petaccis were freed in time for Clara to hear Mussolini's speech the next day.

Soon after the Petaccis settled in Marcello's villa, then SS Commander General Karl Wolff arrived and told Clara that he needed her help. He stated that Ciano must return to Italy. He told her that her influence could persuade Mussolini's government to issue an extradition of Ciano from Germany. He added, so far, that hasn't been issued. She replied that she was not in the service of the Reich. After about two months, on October 28, Mussolini and Clara met when he returned to Gargnano by the Garda Lake, Italy. When Clara returned to Merano, her mother pleaded with her to end her relationship with Mussolini. "...Our name has been compromised." Clara replied, "You are right, leave me alone."

From Merano, the Petacci family moved to Gardone Riviera, into the villa Fiordaliso, just six miles from the new Fascist government (RSI) at Gargnano. German and Japanese diplomats occupied the third and fourth floors of the villa and the Petaccis were on the first and second floors. Clara spent most of her time at the villa Fiordaliso swimming and sunbathing in the daytime. In the evenings, she stayed in, awaiting Mussolini's phone calls. Mussolini arranged trysts with Clara in the tower of a building across the road that had belonged to his friend, the poet Gabriele D'Annunzio.

The new republic, essentially a Nazi puppet state, claimed sovereignty over all of Italy, though it only controlled those territories in German hands in Northern and Central Italy. Effectively, Germany legitimized the occupation of Italy. Secondly, German troops and the nasty SS soldiers could do as they wished with internment camps/towns. On November 14, the RSI enacted eighteen policy guidelines, formally legitimizing the extermination of Jews pursued by Nazism. In particular, RSI (Italian Socialist Republic) Interior Minister Guido Buffarini Guidi ordered the arrest of all Jews present in the territory controlled by the RSI and transferred to special internment camps. In addition, RSI established the repossession of Jewish properties. With that order, the Nazi plans for extermination received crucial support. It is no coincidence that the German government hailed the Fascist anti-Jewish turn as being very timely. Starting that December, the RSI and Nazis began a manhunt for Jews with thorough sweeps carried out in the Venice area. About 150 Venetian Jews were captured. That took place the night between December 5 and 6. Moreover, December 6 was the day that a deportation train departed for Auschwitz from Milan, where the city prison of San Vittore operated as a gathering point for Jews swept up in the North.

With Mussolini back in power, at least in his mind, and the German Army in full retreat in Salerno, the war entered a new phase. No longer did the German Army dictate the pace of war to other combatants. The Allies and the Soviet Union dictated the pace of battles and the battlefields. The outcome of the war was inevitable, just a matter of time. Sooner or later, the Allies would occupy Italy, at least up to the Po River, which meant that the new Fascist government controlled very little territory. However, it exposed the diehards in the Fascist and Nazi movements, who refused to believe in reality. As to the internees in Northern Italy, they still were stuck there waiting for the end of the war, as the Nazis were hell-bent on extermination. The lucky ones waited it out in Southern Italy.

THIRTEEN

Enough is Enough

Mario and the two deserters Vladimir and Dimitri arrived in Naples about the same time as German troops, on or about September 1, 1943. Upon arrival, the German Army secured the railroad station in Naples to facilitate the deployment of troops in the area and prevent deserters and other young men from leaving Naples. The trio had no chance of making a run to the station. By then, Naples had already suffered 105 bombings from Allied planes, resulting in over 25,000 dead, tens of thousands wounded, 100,000 apartments destroyed, and incomparable cultural and artistic items dear to Neapolitans, obliterated. The city was left smoldering in ruins, with no water, no food, and a populace composed of women, children, the wounded, young men on the run from the occupiers, and the elderly. Other young ones had either fled or were in some distant land. To add to the misery, Vesuvius had erupted, after having been dormant for a long time.

Eruption of Vesuvius, 1943. Damaged buildings in Piazza Garibaldi can be seen due to bombings. Courtesy of Antonio Vittoria.

Neapolitans have seen invaders come and go for millennia. But it seemed at the moment that everything and everyone was conspiring against the people of Naples. Not only was Vesuvius acting up, but the random bombings of the city in the ensuing days, and the uncertainty created by a military takeover of the city only rattled their nerves and added fear and trepidation. They, by nature, do not frighten easily, because of their ability to adapt and survive invaders. But those times were very different from the past. They were hit from all sides: vagaries of nature, bombs from the skies, and attacks on the ground.

They had made peace with temperamental Vesuvius long ago. But Italian military generals, who were responsible for protecting Naples, abandoned it, having fled in civilian clothes. The city, left unprotected, was then at the mercy of a military force of 20,000 soldiers who were determined to follow Hitler's order to destroy it. The order was to reduce Naples to "cinders and mud" so that the arriving Allied forces could not use the port city as a strategic naval base. However, these invaders were different from the ones in the past; they were not about to spend time with Neapolitans to accommodate the wishes of the natives.

Naples consists of relics of different cultures, as reflected in the architecture. One district may have narrow streets full of vendors selling everything imaginable, reminiscent of a street bazaar in an Arabic country. Right next to it, there may be an avenue as wide as the Grand Canyon surrounded by buildings dating back to Spanish or French rule. In other districts, there may be a modern asphalt road leading to antique Roman Villas. Each district is divorced from the others in the sense that people living in a district have a unique characteristic different from the others, from the poor to the very rich and highly cultured.

It was inevitable that the street kids, the scugnizzi, would get themselves in trouble with the new invaders. Whereas scugnizzi strived for disorder in the streets to their advantage, the occupiers strived for the opposite. On September 10, the first bloody clash occurred. An Afrika Korp jeep on patrol was stuck in one of those narrow streets full of vendors while detaining a scugnizzo in the back seat. The boy was in his territory and, most likely, had lured the jeep there, knowing full well that he would be rescued from the German soldiers. A scugnizzo is no one's child but, also, everybody's child in Naples. Neapolitans blocked the path of the jeep, killing sailors and soldiers and freeing the scugnizzo. Retaliation for the insurrection came quickly; the Germans set fire to the National Library and opened fire on the crowd gathered there.

When the trio arrived at the Naval Military port, where once Mario was stationed, it looked abandoned and the building where he lived in 1935 was damaged by the extensive bombing by Allied planes. The ship in which he served also lay listless in shallow waters. His immediate need, and that of the two Ukrainians, was to rest. As they headed toward the damaged building of Officers Quarters, scugnizzi appeared out of nowhere to confront the trio. Their leader, Luigi, addressed the trio thusly, "There is not enough food to go around here, especially feeding those two gorillas." Fortunately, the Ukrainians didn't understand a word.

Mario diffused the situation by telling them that they would help in securing more food, because, as a former resident, he knew where to look. Also, he said that they were tired of running away from German troops and needed some rest. Often, scugnizzi were treated by family and Neapolitans with much disdain and outright hostility. They were not welcomed in Naples because there were more mouths to feed and usually trouble followed them. However, that was the first time an adult in Naples talked to them in a respectful manner and tried to be helpful, so they welcomed the trio. For one thing, they had common enemies— German troops and starvation. In time, the scugnizzi and the two "gorillas" became the best of friends and inseparable so much so that the Ukrainians learned dirty Neapolitan words and started to talk with a Neapolitan dialect. As a former military officer, Mario gave much thought to the predicament that they were in, besides food.

He asked the fundamental question to himself, "Why are the troops here?" Food? No, they have their own food. Why Naples? As Ehrlich pointed out to Mario and Don Nicola during Hitler's visit to Naples in 1938, appearances have nothing to do with intentions. Thus, Mario concluded that the troops in Naples were there to provide military support to a major battle taking place in Salerno on September 12. The brothers pointed out in Tito to the clan there that German troops were amassing in Potenza as well. Thus, German troops in Potenza and Naples provided support in securing the supply line from the North. The purpose, of course, was to affect an orderly retreat north through a corridor and keep the Allied Army in Italy, away from the North European theater. On a personal level, General Kesselring didn't want to readily relinquish his duties to his arch-personal enemy General Rommel once his Army reached Rome.

Being a Naval Officer, Mario appreciated the importance of military ports. He surmised that the troops would, sooner or later, try to bomb the port of Naples out of its existence to prevent the Allies from using it. By then, deportations of any man on two legs by SS troops were common knowledge. To Neapolitans, they could never adapt to that situation!

This presented quite a dilemma as to when the troops would raid the port. This meant that the trio and the scugnizzi needed, sometime later, to vacate the port and, therefore, be exposed to deportation, if they didn't find another place to hide. But when? As promised by Mario, he guided the scugnizzi to storage rooms hidden in the tunnels of Naples where a small amount of food was stored. In addition, the twins and the scugnizzi went fishing using homemade fishing rods. They even learned to pronounce the names of the "gorillas." At the end of the day, they gathered whatever little food and money that was available to eat. The trio didn't venture onto the streets, as things were not completely under their control. A revolt was building to a crescendo in the streets of Naples.

On September 12, numerous German soldiers were killed on the streets of Naples, while about 4,000 Italian soldiers and civilians were deported to Germany for forced labor. The populace refused to collaborate and rebelled. The same day, Colonel Walter Schöll assumed command of the military occupiers in the city, declaring a curfew and a state of siege, with orders to execute all those responsible for hostile actions against German troops, and up to 100 Neapolitans for every German were killed. The following proclamations appeared on the walls of the city on September 13:

With immediate action from today, I assume the absolute control with full powers of the city of Naples and the surrounding areas.

1. Every single citizen who behaves calmly will enjoy my protection. On the other hand, anyone who openly or surreptitiously acts against the German Armed Forces will be executed. Moreover, the home of the miscreant and its immediate surroundings will be destroyed and reduced to ruins. Every German soldier wounded or murdered will be avenged a hundred times.

2. I order a curfew from 8 p.m. to 6 a.m. Only in case of alarm will it be allowed to use the road in order to reach the nearest shelter.

3. A state of siege is proclaimed.

4. Within 24 hours all weapons and ammunition of any kind, including shotguns, hand grenades, etc., must be surrendered. Anyone who, after that period, is found in possession of a weapon will be immediately executed. The delivery of weapons and ammunition

shall be made to the German military patrols.

5.   People must keep calm and act reasonably.

These orders and the already executed reprisals have been necessary
because of the large number of German soldiers and officers who were
vilely murdered or seriously wounded while fulfilling their duties; indeed, in some cases the wounded have even been insulted and abused in
a manner unworthy of a civil population.

The orders were followed with the shooting of eight prisoners of war, while
a tank opened fire against students who were beginning to gather in the nearby
University of Naples. A young Neapolitan sailor was executed on the stairs of the
German Military headquarters, while thousands of people were forced by German
troops to watch. On the same day, 500 people were also forcibly deported to Germany and made to watch the execution of fourteen carabinieri policemen, who had
taken armed resistance against the occupying forces.

In other clashes, the people of Naples defended their city against the systematic destruction and looting by German troops. Each day, tensions were rising, with
some of the most beloved and precious treasures of the city destroyed by fire at the
University of Naples and the National Historic Archives. These acts of brutality
struck home with a population battered, but still proud of their past. The straw that
broke the camel's back occurred on September 22, when a decree was issued that
all males between eighteen and thirty-three years of age were to present themselves
to be deported and used for forced labor in Germany. Men were rounded up and
brought to the soccer stadium in the Vomero District to be deported.

Meanwhile, people living within 300 meters of the coastline were ordered to
evacuate in twenty hours; 35,000 families filled the streets while plans for blowing
up the houses were being finalized. This meant that about 240,000 people were
forced to leave their homes, taking refuge with other families, in public buildings,
or inside caves. Groups of citizens began to stock up on weapons stored in the carabinieri's barracks and in various stores. A manifesto from the city's Fascist prefect
called for compulsory work by all males in labor camps in Germany. However, only
150 Neapolitans, most likely Fascists, out of the planned 30,000, responded to the
call, which led Schöll to send soldiers into the city to round up and immediately
execute defaulting citizens. Neapolitans were not intimidated. They had reached the
threshold of tolerance.

This was the second and last incident that sparked the uprising; it was an impossible situation for Neapolitans to adapt to. About 30,000 Neapolitans were ready to engage soldiers in the streets, parks, beaches, in their barracks, and anywhere else in Naples. Another Churchill in Naples on the horizon? On September 26, an unarmed and screaming crowd saved young men apprehended by German soldiers for deportation. In response to this, an unarmed crowd poured into the streets to impede the Nazi roundups of the young men. The rioters were joined by former Italian soldiers who had kept themselves hidden so far. By then, German soldiers had looted big department stores in the main streets of Naples, undercutting the scugnizzi. A group of scugnizzi were raiding a department store, when German security police surrounded the store and demanded surrender.

Masaniello, leader of the scugnizzi, showed up with 200 to 300 scugnizzi and counter-demanded that the Germans surrender. What makes this story so remarkable is that Masaniello and a group of young scugnizzi stared right into two Tiger tanks. It was not clear whether Masaniello's response was an act of courage, foolishness, or simply a bluff. It was a life-or-death situation and this teenager was the epitome of calm. The name Masaniello is derived from a Neapolitan fisherman who became a hero in the 1640s, in a revolt against Spanish rule. It was a classic stalemate leading to only one conclusion, a shootout. Every street in Naples was barricaded and the people rallied behind the scugnizzi.

A fighting scugnizzo with a German helmet. Courtesy of Pomona Pictures.

The scugnizzi residing with Mario and the two deserters at the Naval military station were itching to join their scugnizzi friends as revolt was in the air. There was determination in their eyes and hunger to prove themselves to their mothers and relatives. Mario surmised that there must have been a cache of arms and ammunition someplace in the station. They didn't have to search very hard. The scugnizzi knew exactly where it was. In the armory, there were rifles, pistols, hand grenades, assortments of small arms, and, most importantly, benzene containers.

The eyes of the two deserters lit up. They knew how to make Molotov cocktails, which were very effective against tanks. The Molotov bomb consists of a bottle half full of benzene or gasoline topped with a cloth rag. The object is to light the rag with a match when a tank's fuel is most exposed and toss the bottle at it, hard enough to shatter the bottle resulting in an explosion. Russian soldiers used this technique during the Battle of Stalingrad. Molotov was the name of the Russian foreign minister then, whose name became affiliated with the bomb.

The two Ukrainian soldiers taught the technique to a very receptive audience. The scugnizzi practiced and practiced until they ran out of bottles. They went to a department store and raided a month's supply of bottles. The two Russians joined their fight and led them in a hunt for Tiger tanks. Their spirits were sky-high. Mentally, the twins were back in Stalingrad, but they were the hunters rather than the hunted. All the while, Mario set up an intelligence network. Tanks became most vulnerable when riding over the barricades. He would set up a network of scugnizzi at each barricade. They in turn passed the location to others as to when and where a tank was approaching. Molotov cocktails would then be thrown from roofs, windows, and barricades. While WWI rifles were the weapon of choice by the scugnizzi, not a scugnizzo died from tossing a Molotov cocktail, thanks to the training by the two Ukrainians.

The next four days, September 27 to 30, marked the turning point of the insurrection against German occupation. The defenders of Naples, comprise mainly of women, scugnizzi, elderly, deserters, young men, and the wounded, rose up. There had been no meetings or action plans, but the air was charged with rebellion and Neapolitans seized the moment. Clashes sprang up around the city. and they drove the German troops from the city; about 20 Tiger tanks were destroyed. It was the first revolt in any big city in Europe against the occupation of the German Army and the first city to expel the occupiers. It served as an example for other big cities such as Warsaw.

There was also a deep-rooted reason for the Neapolitans' revolt. After surviving so many invasions throughout their history, the people adopted a philosophy that can best be described as "Ci Arrangiamo," that they will adapt to survive their credo. This is a philosophy of avoiding confrontations whereby they and the invaders can live together in harmony even though they may disagree politically. As a result, Neopolitans are a-happy-go lucky people and easy-going. Only once before, in 1647, had they rebelled. It is not in their nature to resort to violence. Neopolitans would rather talk their way out of a difficult situation and co-exist.

In short, they are not born to be heroes. The fact that the German occupation provoked Neapolitans to their limit of what they considered humanly tolerable or adaptable speaks volumes to the brutality of the German occupation. Neapolitans reached a stage when dying was better than living. The invaders also didn't realize that the young Neapolitans, including their children, represented the heart and soul of the city, and were hell-bent on their mission to deport them. Thus, they made rebellion inevitable. There was no compromise for the second time in the history of Naples.

SEPTEMBER 27

The rounding up of men continued, as Neapolitans were deported to Germany. The populace was furious. Meanwhile, the Germans commenced to raid the University of Naples for students to deport. About 200 insurgents attacked the armory of Castel Sant'Elmo, near the Naval station where Mario was hiding. They subdued German counterattacks, confiscating arms and ammunition. About 200 men, plus a reinforcement of another fifty, attacked the soccer stadium in the Vomero District where young Neapolitans were interned to be deported. It was defended by a large group of German soldiers. There were violent shootings carried out with machine guns that fired from above the surrounding buildings. The clash lasted several hours. German troops stationed in the stadium had no way out. In the evening, the German commander came out with a white flag. Negotiations began which were also conducted at the German headquarters in Corso Vittorio Emanuele. The soldiers were released from the bad predicament that they were in. Again, Neapolitans preferred to talk rather than to fight, and alleviate misery for all. As usual, the invaders learned nothing from the episode. They continued to search for young adults to deport.

Scugnizzi dove into the Gulf of Naples to retrieve guns of WWI vintage which had been dumped there by the Germans. Caches of weapons were distributed throughout the city by the scugnizzi network. Knives, broom handles, toilets, and furniture were tossed from balconies aimed at soldiers below to block roads. The narrow and labyrinthine streets of Naples made it more easily defensible against the Germans' large unwieldy tanks. The underground cave network also made it easy to get from one place to another, leading to successful surprise attacks.

SEPTEMBER 28

Maddalena Cerasuolo, affectionately called Lenuccia, 23, was the eldest daughter of Carlo Cerasuolo, one of the leaders of the revolt in the Materdei District. She was tasked with procuring weapons for the insurgents in the carabinieri stations and barracks in her neighborhood. The Maresciallo of the barracks, appreciating the courage and determination of Lenuccia, proposed that she request German troops to surrender who were in the shoe factory on Trone Street. In exchange, the Maresciallo promised to give the weapons to the insurgents. Lenuccia accepted the challenge. She did not want to consider the dangers that she might encounter. German soldiers could have killed her instantly.

The building was surrounded by insurgents. They prevented the German soldiers from leaving the factory where they had gone to steal leather hides and valuables that were in the building. Lenuccia knocked on the door and handed the request for surrender to the soldier who had appeared at the door. Again, a preference for talking. The soldier refused to surrender with a disgusting grin. Immediately a shooting started between the men surrounding the building and the Germans. Lenuccia barely had time to take shelter. Insurgents and soldiers died in that battle. Eventually, the building occupants were forced to surrender.

Upon returning home, Lenuccia saw a German patrol on a jeep that had stopped to ask an old man directions to the Sanità Bridge. She immediately sensed that they intended to blow up the bridge. She ran at breakneck speed, reached her father Carlo, and told him of her fears. Carlo Cerasuolo gathered a few nearby insurgents and ran toward the bridge. Lenuccia ran through Via Santa Teresa to warn as many people as she could. She encountered a butcher who grabbed his two pistols, one for each hand, and ran to the bridge wasting no time.

Having gathered more insurgents, Lenuccia joined her father on one side of the Sanità Bridge. Three German soldiers came under fire; they had mined the bridge. As the Germans were about to trigger the explosion, one of the insurgents bravely slipped inside the trap door, where the explosives had been placed, and tore the wires connected to the detonator, saving the bridge from destruction.

Gennarino and his companions blew up a German truck with a grenade in Via Toscanella. Soldiers on the truck had been involved in a massacre in Miano, near Capodimonte. Then, they blocked another truck, loaded with soldiers that followed a short distance away. Gennarino, with a hand grenade, stood in front of the vehicle blocking it. The soldiers surrendered and were taken prisoner by that group of insurgents, made up of scugnizzi and other young men.

The fighting grew to a crescendo after more Neapolitans joined the rebellion. In the Materdei District, a German patrol, which had taken shelter in a civic building, was surrounded and kept under siege for hours, until the arrival of reinforcements. In the end, three Neapolitans had lost their lives in the battle. A group of forty men, armed with rifles and machine guns, set up a roadblock, killing six German soldiers and capturing four, while fighting broke out in other districts of Naples.

The soldiers launched other raids in the Vomero District, amassing numerous prisoners inside the Campo Sportivo del Littorio. Scugnizzi and Italian deserters attacked the Vomero sports field, freeing prisoners who were earmarked to be deported to Germany. Even in the heat of battle, German soldiers were hell-bent to deport Neapolitans. Talking alone was not going to dissuade the occupiers from carrying out their mission, no matter the cost of lives. Neapolitans had no other choice but to fight.

SEPTEMBER 29

On the third day of the riot, the streets of Naples experienced fierce clashes. As no connection could be established with national anti-fascist organizations, the insurrection was still without central direction, operations being in the hands of local leaders. In Giuseppe Mazzini Square, a substantial German group reinforced by tanks attacked fifty rebels, killing twelve and injuring more than fifteen. The workers' quarter of Ponticelli suffered a heavy artillery bombardment, after which German units committed several indiscriminate massacres among the population. Other fighting took place near the Capodichino Airport in Piazza Ottocalli, in which three Italian airmen lost their lives.

In Via Santa Teresa, a group of scugnizzi armed with rifles and hand grenades opposed German tanks that advanced along the road. The most courageous boy was Gennarino Capuozzo. He was only eleven years old, a cousin of Lenuccia. Despite his young age, he already worked in the shop, since his father had been drafted and left for Libya in 1941. He had joined a group of scugnizzi who fled the reformatory to fight the Germans. The scugnizzi brigade took up positions on the terrace of the building that housed the Istituto delle Maestre Pie Filippini, a hundred meters from the museum. The youths fired from the institute's terrace at German tanks that attempted to leave the city. A grenade, thrown by one of the tanks, hit Gennarino in full, killing him instantly. The sacrifice of Gennarino Capuozzo, too early a hero, was one of the last acts of the armed struggle. That same evening, the Germans began negotiations with the insurgents to leave Naples before the arrival of the Allied Forces. Finally, the locals had persuaded the invaders to talk, which had been their aim all along.

At this point, explosives, delayed or otherwise, had been planted all over the city. It was just a matter of time for the Germans to plant explosives at the Naval station. The curtain was about to come down on the German troops and this meant that Mario needed to get his ass in gear. He gathered Luigi and the Ukranians. He explained, "Within two to three days, we will have visitors planting explosives all over the station to blow it up. So, let's hide in tunnels until we hear explosions. If we don't hear anything, Vladimir and Dimitri will be able to disarm the mines." Both Ukrainians specialized in planting explosives and Molotov bombs. The next day, a loud explosion could be heard miles away. When they returned to the station, they discovered every ship was damaged, blocking any entry to the port. Railway tracks in the station and buildings were also destroyed. However, it made fishing easier and sleeping accommodations a bit uncomfortable. At last, freedom.

SEPTEMBER 30

During their retreat, the Germans burned everything in sight—museums, libraries, houses, everything. On October 1, the Allies entered Naples, welcomed by cheers. Close to 170 lives were lost during those four days among the 1,589 partisans and 159 among the civilians. However, cemetery records noted 562 deaths. The armed insurrection against the Germans prevented the occupiers from making Naples "ash and mud" as Adolf Hitler had explicitly commanded, and the mass deportations of citizens of Naples were avoided as much as possible. To this day, it is not clear how many were deported to Germany but not the 30,000 initially planned. It is estimated the number ranged between 4,000 and 5,000.

Although the Germans were about to leave Naples, some Fascists still resisted against their own in the city. They shot treacherously from the windows at the civilian population. Some of these had barricaded themselves in a building in Materdei and shoot wildly at passers-by. Lenuccia, together with other resistance men, tried to flush them out of their lair. An American officer arrived with a jeep, replacing the insurgents with his soldiers. He disarmed the insurgents by breaking their rifles. Lenuccia said to the officer that she would have liked to keep her musket. The soldier with a smile told her to keep the rifle and added "Go home!"

The next day Lenuccia was invited to the Royal Palace where she met General Montgomery. He, having heard of her bravery, had wanted to meet her. Montgomery hugged and kissed her forehead, thanking her for what she had done. The city of Naples was awarded the Gold Medal for Valor, the highest honor of the Italian State. Also, four scugnizzi, who lost their lives in the fighting, were awarded the Gold Medal for Valor: Gennaro (Gennarino) Capuozzo, 12; Filippo Illuminato, 13; Pasquale Formisano, 17; and Mario Menechini, 18.

Before the Germans left Naples, their demolition squads went around the city blowing up anything of value or in operation, including the telegraph building, post office, and department stores. There was no water or electricity; Naples smelled of charred wood. People tried cooking with seawater and tried to distill it. Neapolitans were deprived of things that justify a city's existence and adapted themselves to a life in the Dark Ages. Even the upper class and royal families were suffering.

There was no food so Neapolitans went to nearby farms in the valley to search for edibles. Neapolitans fondly refer to the valley as their backyard. There were about fifteen different kinds of plants that were edible, but bitter in flavor. Inexplicably, no boats were allowed to fish in the fall of 1943. Germans planted delayed-action explosive devices in Naples before departure. As a result, several buildings were pulverized in late October of 1943, about three weeks after they left. Colonel Scholl of the German army had mined buildings located 300 meters from the coastline. A million and a half people left their houses and crowded into the streets to avoid potential explosions in their respective buildings and streets. Fortunately, the bombs never exploded along the coastline, but they did at other places. In late fall, most restaurants in Naples were open but the clientele were mostly Allied officers.

The two Ukrainians warned Mario that there was a strong possibility that the German troops planted delay bombs at the Naval station based on recent delayed explosions nearby. They advised Mario to search for these bombs and defuse them. The thought that one of these bombs might explode at any moment haunted Mario to the point that he couldn't sleep at night. Initially, Vladimir and Dimitri made a thorough search of all the damaged ships at port, but nothing turned up. Mario didn't accompany the two Ukrainians in the search. He never dealt with explosive devices in the Navy. Then, they inspected all the buildings at the station. Again nothing. That brought some relief. However, Mario recalled that, in Naples, underground tunnels connect various parts of the city from the sea to the train station. Thus, the search narrowed down to an entry point to a tunnel underneath the station. The twins discovered enough explosives to blow up the whole station.

What's more, Allied soldiers were charged by the carabinieri for looting antique art objects. Officers of England's King's Dragoon Guards, who entered Naples first after the Germans left, removed paintings from frames in museums and made off with fine pottery collections. These items were created and shipped to England, never to be returned.

The black market reigned supreme and prices were outrageous. At the famous restaurant Zi Teresa, the price for a fish dinner was priced at 10,000 lire. That is equivalent to about $1,000 today. The black market was controlled by the Camorra in collaboration with the local Maresciallo who wielded tyrannical power in towns as well as in cities like Naples. The Camorra was an organization of thieves, equivalent to the Mafia in Sicily. People were stealing wires and selling the copper to small shops to melt. In the town of Cicciano, near Avella, Allied Military Government caught many wire cutters in the act of stealing copper wires and sent them to military prison. At least, the prisoners had something to eat regularly. If there was plunder to be had, the Camorra was first in line. They tolerated the carabinieri, because they kept the small-time robbers away from the big spoils and eliminated the main competition. The brigands operated mostly in the surrounding hill towns in the valley.

North of Naples, the Camorra was concentrated in towns like Afragola, Acerra, Aversa, and Casoria, although they controlled all illicit trades or legal business throughout Naples and neighboring towns in the valley. The Camorra lived by their own secret set of rules, whether or not Germans were in the city. The Camorra today is one of the biggest underground syndicates operating all over the world rivaling the Mafia. It is one of the legacies of WWII. The book, *Hidden in Plain Sight*, chronicles the growth of the Camorra, Mafia, and Ndrangheta as indirect collateral damage.

U.S. General Mark Clark came to Naples to take credit for conquering Naples.

The fact that he was the youngest field general and declared himself the liberator of Naples should tell you something about his ambition and vanity at the expense of the people of Southern Italy. The general had become the destroying angel, prone to panic, as at Paestum, and then to violent and vengeful reaction, occasioned by the sacrifice of the village of Altavilla. The town was shelled out of existence in the fear that it might have contained a few German soldiers. He never acknowledged the role that the scugnizzi or anyone else in Naples played in the liberation, as Field Marshal Montgomery did. To General Clark's thinking, the scugnizzi's efforts in war counted for naught. The historical fact remains that there was not a single German soldier in sight when General Clark entered Naples. The only thing that he captured was a destroyed city and a starving populace. Nevertheless, a celebration of the liberation was called for at the restaurant, Zi Teresa, by where all the ships were sunk by Allied bombing.

The problem with General Clark's visit to Zi Teresa was that there was no meat or fish to offer the general. One astute chef had a brilliant idea. He went to the aquarium located at city hall, about a mile from the restaurant, and raided a large bass fish. He then cooked it with vegetables and, voila, a dinner was served to General Clark. According to the general, it was the best fish meal that he ever had. The resourcefulness of the people of Naples in those starving days was truly remarkable. When the whole population was starving and the scugnizzi were pimping even their sisters and mothers, they produced a four-star meal for a three-star general. The general was so egocentric and pompous that he didn't have the capacity to see the misery and starvation of the people all around Naples. However, to General Clark's credit, his presence in Naples prevented a bloodbath. Without the Allied Army advancing to Naples, the German Army would have fought to the last soldier to carry out their mission and, unfortunately, the Neapolitans would have obliged. It was a confrontation of willpower.

SUMMARY

With roughly one Army division and thirty Tiger tanks, the Germans tried to impose their will on the people of Naples. They took what little food there was; fraternized with local women; looted museums, specialty stores, and libraries; and enjoyed the scenery, the wine, and the music. But when it came to deporting their young men to Germany, Neapolitans reached a threshold where it was no longer tolerable or acceptable behavior. Neapolitans realized that the bullshit talk was not going to get anywhere with the invaders. They also realized that the ones deported might never return and, in fact, never did. They rose spontaneously to oppose German occupation and deportation. In confronting the invaders, Neapolitans didn't see bullets and tanks coming their way. They saw a void in their lives without their young ones which spurred them to fight to the end. The confrontation was not about manpower, rifles, and bullets, but of willpower. Those modern-day invaders underestimated the will of the locals because they misinterpreted the locals' laissez-faire* lifestyle as a weakness. It turned out to be just the opposite. To the Neapolitans, it was a way of life in which they were not willing to compromise and were more than willing to sacrifice themselves. It pitted Nazi oppressors against a populace that was drunk on that indomitable lifestyle of theirs or that spirit called freedom.

*This is a common expression in Naples dating from the Middle Ages "Lasci-Fa" in Neapolitan dialect, means to let go. The "ci" is rarely pronounced. Today, the sentiment of the word has degenerated into the expression, "Forget about it" or "Frigetz," as in some Italian communities in the United States. Most likely, the French adopted the original Neapolitan expression into their language, laissez-faire, when they occupied Naples in the Middle Ages.

FOURTEEN
Coming Home

By the beginning of October 1943, the German Army was in full retreat heading northward to Rome, well away from the beaches of Salerno and Naples. One of the main escape routes was by the old Via Appia built about 2,000 years ago. There must have been at least 200 Tiger tanks passing through Baiano, heading north. Soldiers looked tired and distraught. A lot of them were injured, riding on trucks or other forms of transportation. Some still had sand on their faces from the beaches of Salerno. Residents of Sperone, Baiano, and Avella stood on the side of the highway staring at the soldiers, avoiding eye contact. The soldiers trudged along as though they were not there; their only concern was to get a ride.

Two of the ten German divisions consisted of veteran soldiers involved in the Russian and African campaigns. They were replaced by younger and younger inexperienced soldiers, barely out of high school. German troops retreated to form defensive positions from the Tyrrhenian to the Adriatic Seas, referred to as the Winter Line, anchored at the San Pietro-Venafro area and later, the Gustav Line, anchored at Monte Cassino. The German army maneuvered itself, under the stewardship of General Kesselring, to the high ground and forced the Allied Army to move in terribly wet and soggy terrain along narrow uphill corridors in wet weather. In places, the mud was knee-high. That's because the rainy season was in full swing. The mostly dry Clanio Creek in Avella became a river and it flooded the towns of Avella and Baiano. German soldiers left camps in Avella and Baiano just in time to avoid the monsoon rain of late October. They were prepared for that, as they bypassed the muddy road in front of the cemetery and traveled on the paved one, built by them when they first arrived in Avella, to Via Appia in Baiano.

It seemed that the only reason people from Avella and Baiano went to Via Appia was to confirm that the German soldiers were indeed leaving for good. They could not very well show delight or display the "V" sign if they weren't sure. The locals felt that they deserved a break after putting up with the occupation. At least, they could dream about what their lives could be without soldiers all around town—without the trash heaps from the camps; the lack of food; the stranded and charred trucks, jeeps, and motorcycles; and the benzene containers. Not to mention the farms were pockmarked with huge craters from the Allied bombings, and the greenery was charcoal black. The German plane shot by Allied planes at the beginning of the Salerno invasion was also left behind. The dead pilot was buried in the Cemetery of Avella. Despite it all, everyone in town pitched in to clean up the mess. People scavenged the camps for food as well, but there was none to be had. Shepherds began to drift into town slowly but surely. At least, people could search for some edibles on the farms near the abandoned camps.

During that terrible ordeal in Tito, the Wolf family was not aware that Mario and the two Ukrainian brothers were stuck in Naples and involved in the revolt. German troops left Potenza and, therefore Tito, in the latter part of September, as the battle of Salerno winded down. The Wolf family could breathe a sigh of relief as the battleground moved north. They looked forward to comparing notes with the Avella clan about their experience. Strega, Bambolone, Pasquale, and their children were so sad to see them go. So many beautiful memories and struggles to survive together.

Back in Naples, Mario's thoughts turned to Sofia, the children, family, and friends. Finally, he promised the Ukrainians a big welcome in Avella. As for the Ukrainians, they had seen enough war to last them a lifetime, especially in Tobruk, Libya, and Stalingrad, Russia. They needed to start thinking about what they wanted in life now that freedom was won. Going back to Ukraine was out of the question. There was still a war in Russia after all. Peasants in the farms had only one choice under the Stalin regime, to be happy with misery. That was the reason they left the Russian Army in the first place and joined the German Army. But as it turned out, Hitler's regime was more despotic than Stalin's. Besides, they loved sunny Naples and the spirit of Neapolitans. The Neapolitan spirit matched their desire to get away from the war and all that misery to live life to the fullest. Also, the two liked the fact that when confronted, Neapolitans were not intimidated by the German Army; their spirit rose to the occasion instead. They also recognized in Mario a special person who could be trusted to guide them in their endeavors in Avella.

Mario distinguished himself in the uprising in Naples as a master tactician. As such, they had the greatest respect for him and vice versa. The Ukrainians looked upon Mario more like a father figure rather than a military strategist.

Mario wanted to send word to Sofia as to when he would be home. As the three of them approached the entrance to the post office, a tremendous explosion took place. The German soldiers had planted a delayed-action explosive under a statue before they left town. As in most public buildings in Naples, the entrance door was decorated with attractive glass figurines. Upon explosion, shards of glass flew in the air, as in a wave, toward the three, with Mario closest to the entrance. Mario's face was a total mess, unrecognizable and bloody. The two Ukrainians laid Mario on the ground protecting him with their lives. They wouldn't let anyone near him. As usual, scugnizzi showed up. Anytime there was a crowd, scugnizzi appeared on the scene. This time it was different. They quickly recognized their heroes, cordoned off the crowd, and secured a carriage from a fruit vendor. They didn't ask for permission. They just grabbed it from the vendor and told him to get lost. The Ukrainians and the scugnizzi gently laid Mario onto the carriage and hurried to the nearest hospital.

Mario's face was bandaged by evening. Luckily, the shards of glass barely penetrated his chest area, as his jacket shielded him. In the surgery room, doctors removed small fragments of glass from Mario's face. The Ukrainians refused to leave the surgery and the recovery rooms. That evening, Mario waved the two of them to his bedside. He asked for them to go to Avella and contact his wife, Sofia. He added that Erminio would take them to Sofia and that he could be found at a wine store next to the train station in Avella.

The Ukranians had no idea where the station in Naples was located and even less about Avella. Again, they relied on the scugnizzi to take them there, at least to catch the train In Naples. However, they had no money. No problem, the scugnizzi absconded two tickets from the station clerk. They used the Ukrainians as the go-between to transfer the tickets from the station clerk to the Ukrainians. However, the station master had seen that stunt before. So, he just handed two more tickets to the Ukrainians and told them to get lost. On the way to Avella, they observed buildings nearly destroyed by Allied bombardments. Squatters all over those buildings appeared like rats running in and out of their broken balconies. Destroyed train wagons were pushed aside to make room for undamaged tracks. In Nola, a 1,000-pound unexploded bomb was pushed on top of a wooden plank. Only the Americans built bombs that size. The devastation from those bombs must have been unfathomable.

On the train, there were no first-class wagons. It was first come, first served. Farmers, shepherds, women, and professional men were riding the train. Farmers and shepherds were returning home after setting up shop at various towns where a market was scheduled. Women were most likely returning home after working in brothels in Naples. They all gawked at the size of the Ukrainians. Farmers would have loved to package them in a box and put them to work on their farms. Allied soldiers stationed in Naples were more concerned about syphilis than where they were going to be shipped for the next battle. About 10 percent of the professional men on the train were peddling medicine controlled by the Camorra to cure syphilis. The remaining professional men were lawyers who represented women who petitioned the Allied Military Government office for a license to marry an Allied soldier or petitioned Allied consulates for immigration visas. The conductor never checked for tickets. Most likely, he was rewarded by the farmers. As such, farmers and shepherds never bought train tickets.

At the train station in Avella, the Ukrainians inquired about the wine store, although they needn't look far. The winery was the only building near the station. Without Mario, they panicked, but their confidence perked up as they saw a big sign, "Erminio's Winery" atop the building. They made their way over as Erminio sat at a small table in the courtyard in awe of these two giants. As they approached the store, Erminio wondered who they could be. For sure, they were not from the area. "Signore Erminio?" they asked. At this point, Erminio panicked. "How did they know my name?" he wondered. The Ukrainians mentioned Mario. That was the magic word. Erminio's ears perked up because the town hadn't heard a word from Mario for about a year or so and everyone in town worried about their beloved son.

Erminio tried to strike up a conversation but his mind and words were coming out so fast that the Ukrainians couldn't possibly understand a word. They spoke some words in Neapolitan dialect. The two parties simply could not communicate until one of the Ukrainians mentioned the name Sofia. Erminio put two and two together and rationalized that he had better get Sofia, as it may be important. Erminio cupped his hand and gesticulated it toward his mouth, as if to say, "Are you hungry?" That much they understood and responded, "Si." Erminio quickly brought them smoked shepherd cheese, salami, bread, tomatoes, and wine. Again, he used hand gestures to indicate that he would be back. Their eyes were fixated on the food, not noticing that Erminio left the winery. They more than welcomed a salami sandwich, as fish was now coming out of their ears.

Erminio drove to Sergio's building inquiring about the whereabouts of Sofia.

In the courtyard, Erminio told Sergio about the two giants who knew Mario. Don Nicola overheard the commotion and ran down his apartment's steps wanting to know more. They wanted so much to believe that Mario was alive. Sergio, Don Nicola, Imalda, Felicia, and Alvaro crammed into a car and drove to the dress shop, where Sofia and the twin sisters worked. When the girls saw their parents and Don Nicola, they imagined the worst. Erminio reassured them and said that these two giants, who are now at his winery, have news about Mario. The girls jumped with joy and pleaded with Erminio to take them to those two men. Sofia turned to Sergio and company and said, "We will let you know."

By the time the car arrived at the winery, the two Ukrainians had finished eating everything in sight, including the crumbs. In Erminio's absence, Dimitri sketched a picture of Mario in bed with bandages on his face inscribing the word, vivo, meaning that Mario was alive. The girls were so happy that all three embraced them. Immediately, Sofia declared, "Let's go to Naples now and visit him. No reason to wait until tomorrow." Erminio interjected by asking the two Ukrainians if they wanted some fruit from the garden and to take some back to Mario—apples, pears, figs, and plums were there for the taking.

Then Ramiro's Maserati 500 showed up with the two sets of parents and Don Nicola. They, too, had heard the good news. Everyone in town seemed to be anxious to know, as they were standing in the streets asking each other about the whereabouts of Mario. Don Nicola also insisted on coming along. In the late afternoon, Sofia, the twin sisters, Vladimir, Dimitri and Don Nicola boarded the train to Naples. Imalda and Felicia told their two grandchildren all about their papa and that he would be coming home soon. The children stood guard at the portone waiting for papa. Nothing in the world would have dislodged them from there.

Since the tracks for the tram rail line had been bombed by Allied planes during the German occupation of Naples, they walked to the San Paolo hospital, where they found Mario in very good spirits, so much so that he suggested to Sofia that they pack up and go home. Although he was sensitive to anyone touching his face, he had no problem eating the figs or kissing Sofia. He didn't care how painful it was going to be. They told him that by now the whole town was aware of his ordeal. Even though neighbors didn't hear the full story, it didn't stop them from making up one or embellishing it. The girls wanted to know more about the two Ukrainians and how he got to know them. Mario recounted everything and that, without them, he would never have made it alive. The two men knew that Mario was talking about them and they blushed, turning sheepishly toward the sisters. Although their body frames were huge, their behavior was akin to little boys wanting to be liked, especially by the sisters. Sofia, Mario and Don Nicola noticed the special attraction between the sisters and the two brothers.

Mario recovered after a couple of days in the hospital. In the meantime, the three girls stayed in the apartment in the San Carlo Opera House with Don Nicola. Maintenance people and stage managers welcomed him back to San Carlo and told him that rumor had it that he was being considered as the orchestra conductor. He was expected at San Carlo well before the opening of the opera season on April 18, 1944. They added, "Now that you are here, Mario can stop coming looking for you." Mario's devotion and loyalty to Don Nicola deeply moved him to the point of hiding a tear. This also meant that Mario would soon be employed since the conductor would have a lot to say about the hiring of an accountant manager.

In the afternoon, Don Nicola was the tour guide for the group. He took them for a stroll to the Vomero Hills that overlooked the Bay of Naples and the valley to the mountains of Avella. Then, Don Nicola recounted the historical background of the many invasions in the valley and the Bay. He then took them to San Carlo and showed them his and Mario's former offices and pictures of the tenor, Enrico Caruso.

The brothers were extremely interested in the history of Naples and, in particular, of the Arab and Jewish influences on the Neapolitans, their songs, and their architecture. They couldn't ask for a better guide. Don Nicola spoke a little Russian to keep the conversation going. The girls were impressed, especially the sisters. Vladimir asked the sisters if they could teach the Ukranians proper Italian. The scugnizzi taught them only swearing and dirty words in the Neapolitan dialect and conversed strictly in the Neapolitan dialect. That was nothing more or less than an invitation for the four of them to be together. Before Serafina could answer, she whispered to Don Nicola, "Are they Jewish?" He replied with a grin, "There was one way to find out." On the way back for dinner, Sofia could see out of the corner of her eye that the two couples were holding hands.

The next day, Mario was up bright and early and ready to go home. The stitches were removed and his face was full of scars. He was now on a mission to make up for lost time. Then, straight home. On the train, he noticed Serafina and Filomena cozying up to the two Ukrainians and asked Sofia, "What gives?" Sofia shrugged her shoulders and smiled. After all, she was the architect of it all. In the old days, he and Don Nicola would talk and talk, but not this time. He wanted to hear only from Sofia about everything: the children, the family, and their friends. He had a lot to catch up on. Meanwhile, Don Nicola beamed just like a conductor pleased with an orchestra's performance. Mario knew Don Nicola well enough to know when he was up to something mischievous. That smile and that far-away look was a dead giveaway. His mind started wondering about what it could be.

Erminio was nervous, as he looked at his watch every minute waiting for the train to arrive in Avella. As the train appeared around the corner, Erminio rushed to his winery. No one was waiting for the train, but Don Nicola suggested that the group stop at Erminio's winery to get something to eat. All the while, Mario was suspicious. There was no one around, it was eerie. Usually, there were passengers at the station, especially in the morning. As the group approached the winery, the children darted to jump into the arms of Sofia and Mario. Then, Don Nicola popped out of nowhere with a stick in his hand to conduct a chorus consisting of Erminio, Alvaro, Felicia, Sergio, Ramiro, Imalda, and friends singing their favorite ballad, "Parlami D'Amore, Mariu." Mario and Sofia began to cry. No one noticed Mario's scarred face. Love beautifies and forgives everything.

A few days after Mario's celebrated return, Bambolone, his children, and the Wolf family arrived in Avella looking for Erminio's place. Peeking through a string curtain, Erminio saw a group of people heading toward his shop. As typical of the mindset of people in small hill towns in Italy, he started wondering about who they were. In Avella, visiting strangers pose a challenge to locals trying to identify the visitors or why visit. Usually, it is a collective effort whereby locals compare notes and, most often, their hunches are correct. In the case of Erminio, he appeared to be familiar with one couple, the Wolfs, but could not place the other adult couples. He thought that Bambolone walked and smelled like a goat or a shepherd. As the group entered the premises, Erminio remembered that there was once a Viennese couple living in one of Sergio's apartments for a couple of years, but he didn't know or forgot their names.

By the hand of God, they stopped at Erminio's place, as they were tired and hungry after their long trip. When Bambolone asked Erminio for directions to Imalda's place, it just confirmed that his hunch was right. Erminio must have felt like Saint Peter opening up the gates of heaven. He knew very well the ordeal that the Wolf family went through. Happy times were just around the corner in his mind for the visiting family. He told them, "Relax and eat whatever is displayed on the counter and I will be right back; it's on the house." Ermino then drove his car like a race driver right through the portone entrance right into the middle of the courtyard. He then shouted at the top of his lungs, "The Viennese couple is here in my store!" Everyone ran down the steps. Happiness would not describe the situation, more like relief that the madness was over for the Viennese couple.

Erminio returned to the store with as many people as he could squeeze in his car. Bambolone, forever the showman, said to Imalda, "Imalda, I have a message from Strega." He came over to Imalda, hugged her, and gave her a gentle kiss on her forehead. "That's from her." Don Nicola then upstaged Bambolone and said, "Please convey the same exact message to Strega and many thanks for her help. She is one brave woman, but you are not going to get a kiss from me." Ehrlich and Nanna added, "Amen." They all recognized in Strega that inner strength and pride to over-come anything in life. Nothing phased her. That got everyone there relaxed and in the mood to chit chat about their experiences over the past two to three years. They had a lot of catching up to do. In a short time, the children turned the shop up-side down, but Erminio didn't mind it at all. He loved the festive mood and happy people, especially in those days. But it was time to go home. Sergio saved the same apartment for the Wolf family just in case they ever returned to Avella.

Don Nicola corralled the Wolf family to walk back home with him. He admired and respected Ehrlich as a great musician. Don Nicola thought that Ehrlich's reper-toire and knowledge of Mozart's music would complement Italian opera music. In his mind, he was grooming a cello player, like himself, to be a future conductor at the San Carlo to keep the cello tradition alive. Ehrlich responded by saying, "I know where you are headed, but, my friend, my intent is to return to the Vienna Opera House one day, hopefully soon."

"At least, in the meantime, we will have the pleasure of you being at the San Carlo," Don Nicola replied. He went further by warning Ehrlich not to go back too soon, because there was still a war north of Rome and, that while he was interned in Tito, extermination camps north of the Alps were built and unimaginable atrocities took place in Poland and Russia.

Any commotion surrounding Imalda and Sergio's building always attracted at-tention from the shepherd community in the neighborhood. Soon enough, they gath-ered in the courtyard of the building. Mario, Sofia, and Sergio mingled among the crowd explaining the special occasion. Everyone there in waiting wanted to take a peek at the Viennese couple treated as important dignitaries. Bambolone, Mario, Ehrlich, and the shepherd's children wanted no part of that adult talk. They just roamed all over the courtyard and the adjacent field next to the courtyard. It was pure bedlam. To say that Nanna and Ehrlich were overwhelmed by the reception was an understatement. Ehrlich stared at Don Nicola, as if to say, "You planned this, didn't you?" and Zi Nicola shrugged his shoulders and smiled at Ehrlich admitting as much.

Serafina and Filomena introduced their new friends, Vladimir and Dimitri, to their parents, Alvaro and Felicia. Of course, the parents were pleased in view of the fact that there were very few bachelors of eligible age in Avella or any other town nearby. As with most parents, they wanted to know whether it was love or desperation. They didn't care what they did for a living, but they wanted a good-hearted person in their midst.

Sergio took Vladimir under his wing as a mountain patrol assistant. Many times, he repaired makeshift bridges, removed trees, and irrigated the land. Sergio could use Vladimir to do the heavy maintenance while he concentrated on the paperwork required by the central office of the mountain police force in Naples. Vladimir mingled freely with the shepherds; philosophically and spiritually they were his kind of people. Dimitri was artistically inclined as the sisters realized when he sketched a portrait of Mario on the hospital bed. Nicola Jr., Don Nicola's son, was already a well-recognized artist, and his reputation was growing by leaps and bounds. However, he was not cut out to build scaffolds in churches. Dimitri didn't mind doing that and learning from the master. Eventually, he branched out to become a great sculptor.

The Ukrainians eventually rented one of the empty apartments in Imalda's building. Lena and Imalda chaperoned the lovers in their passeggiata on Main Street. That was the time for Italian lessons for the two Ukrainians. Most times Lena, Imalda's granddaughter, left the lovers alone to stop at a local café for gelato. Imalda loved to spoil her grandchildren and to incessantly talk to them about that special shepherd spirit. Imalda, Paolo, and Lena would sit by the fireplace in the wintertime, as Imalda recounted ancient shepherd fables of Avella, shepherd heroes, ghosts, and whatnot. The children were mesmerized by the old tales as they ate roasted chestnuts.

The town was going through major changes politically and in many other ways. There was no mayor. The last one left before the German Army arrived in town. Alvaro resumed his duty as the magistrate of city hall and retrieved all records of people. Former employees eventually returned and the bureaucracy was back in business. The post office resumed delivering mail and providing telegraph and phone service. The Ramiro family, as always, was immune to war, since they belonged to the Colonna's vast empire, extending throughout Europe since the seventeenth century. It was financially and, in effect, a political empire.

Whatever political activity was on Main Street, it was organized by the Communists. Partisans, mostly communists, were busy chasing former Fascists whose deaths were preordained. They visited Don Nicola in an attempt to obtain a list of Fascists who harassed him at the height of Fascism. Don Nicola did not comply for the simple fact that he was not equally sympathetic to Communist ideals and, also, he was not a revengeful person. He learned a lot about Communism as practiced in Russia from the Ukrainians to reject any idealism proposed by the locals. There was nothing to admire about the government controlled agricultural system deployed by their leaders. In many ways, Don Nicola was a naive dreamer as much as previous Socialists of the 1930s, like Carlo Levi and others. The Socialist Party in 1943 was allied with the Communist Party in Italy promising a better life for the peasants. Don Nicola didn't buy into this strange alliance. He remained a die-hard Socialist.

When Vladimir and Dimitri came to the dress shop for their Italian lessons, they were in love. Filomena and Vladimir formed one pair and the artist, Dimitri, and Serafina the other. They were soon married at city hall, where Alvaro officiated the wedding. For their honeymoon, they went to Posillipo, Naples. The scenery impressed the married couples as they rode on a horse-drawn carriage. The driver then began to sing old Neapolitan songs reminiscent of better times. To the surprise of their wives, the two brothers hummed along harmonizing with the driver. The Italian lessons were working.

The sisters were on a pilgrimage to visit the Naval station since it possessed so much family history. Mario and Sofia lived there before the war and now their new husbands and Mario lived there during the worst of times. When they arrived there, the station looked the same as before, during the days of the revolt. The apartment where the trio stayed was still unoccupied and in total disarray. Scugnizzi still dominated the landscape, except for the older scugnizzo, Luigi, who was fishing on the dock using Vladimir's homemade fishing rod. Luigi jumped for joy as soon as he saw Vladimir. He couldn't stop talking to the sisters about the heroics of the two brothers and Mario during the insurrection.

The episode shed a whole new light on the brothers never appreciated before by the sisters. The brothers were more Neapolitan than they appeared to be. They absorbed the spirit of Naples as if they were born there. There was no return to Odessa in their minds. It established a whole new relationship and understanding between the sisters and their husbands.

FIFTEEN

Visitors from Hell

By the end of October or early November 1943, the rainy season reached its peak. The Clanio Creek often overflowed. Children, of course, loved the occasion to waddle in water. Unfortunately, they often got sick as a result of influenza, typhoid, and yellow fever. With penicillin in short supply, it caused much grief in small towns like Avella. By then, the German occupation was long forgotten. However, the landscape was about to change fairly soon. The British troops arrived in Avella just as the rains stopped. The locals in the east end of town began to hear bagpipe music from a distance.

A contingent of the British Army marched in an orderly fashion from a side street, past Saint Peter's Church, led by Scottish soldiers playing the bagpipes. To the locals, it was a beautiful sight, because the town needed some levity, men in dresses. The soldiers were marching toward the foothills. No one paid attention as to exactly where they were heading, as people were resigned and fed up with soldiers from any origin, friends or no friends. People assumed that the British troops were going to take over the German camp on the hill, well away from town and farms. No such luck. The British camped very near to the Roman amphitheater, about 100 meters from Sergio's building, accessible to few locals. The farmer who owned the farm was unaware of the camp in his farm, until his elder farmhand informed him about it.

The end result was that the farmhand was out of a job and the owner was bribed with one loaf of white English bread every day of the occupation. By the time the owner parceled out the bread to the rest of the family, only one slice of bread remained for himself. At that time, it was a bargain for anyone in town, because they hadn't seen a loaf of bread in two years, and lived on polenta the whole time. It was truly tormenting to smell the aroma of the kitchens in the camping grounds. One could tell from the aroma what they were cooking and the locals dreamt what life could be like.

At that time, few in town knew that a Roman colosseum or amphitheater existed nearby, except for Sergio. That was where Sergio dug up antique art pieces. For centuries, farmers grew vegetation and trees to hide the amphitheater from the public. They had a lot to lose, if the central government ever discovered the site. British soldiers must have also discovered the site, because much art was sold by them to museums in London and elsewhere.

The amphitheater in Avella with Monte Avella in the background. The entrance to the amphitheater with the large door is shown at the opposite end. The British camp was about 50–70 yards to the left of the entrance beyond the trees. The town of Avella is on the left of the camp, about 100 meters. The cave of San Michele is above the gorge separating Monte Avella and the smaller hill. The German camps were located to the right of the large door on the small hills. Courtesy of Anmarie Vittoria.

Historically, Emperor Sulla of Rome built this colosseum or amphitheater in 89 BC as a reward to the people of Abella (Avella) for being loyal to Rome in their battle against the Samnite tribe of Nola. The Colosseum in Rome can hold 50,000–60,000 spectators; the one in Avella seated 20,000–30,000. Besides colosseums in Avella and Rome, others were built in Verona, Pompeii, Naples, Pola, Nimes, Arles, and El Djeem or Carthage. The amphitheaters were adaptations of Greek theaters which were considerably smaller, often referred to as amphitheaters rather than colosseums. The one in Rome is referred to as a colosseum. The others are referred to as amphitheaters, where gladiators entertained the masses.

Unbeknown to the locals, the tranquility and peaceful existence between the locals and the British soldiers was about to go through a dramatic change, not for the better. In the middle of the night, colonial troops from North Africa referred to as Goumiers, came incognito in mid-November of 1943 and made camp on a farm located in between the British camp and Sergio's apartment building. The locals soon discovered what hell must be like on Earth, and it was nothing like that of Dante Alighieri's abstract world. The Goumiers were not allowed on French territory in the Allied invasion of France, although they were part of the French Expedition Force, consisting of Algerian, Tunisian, and Moroccan soldiers. Their behavior gave a new meaning to the word atrocious. They raped anything on two legs. To them, young, old, male or female mattered none. Supposedly, they had uniforms but they rarely used them. Besides the Goumiers, colonial troops from Australia and Canada camped in farms near the other two. Thus, different Allied camps brought different shades of misery to the people of Avella. The only remedial part of the unwanted visitors was the thought of a life without Fascism and Nazism.

The Goumiers appeared in town in bizarre uniforms, unlike the British and German soldiers. Their uniform looked like a loosely fit pajama with vertical brown and white stripes. However, their behavior was unlike that of the British and German soldiers. Typically, a group of Goumiers would enter a wine shop, consume all the wine in the store, and not pay. To add insult to injury, the Goumiers' payment consisted of raping the owner or clients who were on the premise. It was shocking behavior and defied all standards of civility. The reputation of these soldiers quickly circulated town and, of course, people tended to embellish the worst behavior. Fortunately for Erminio, his store was sufficiently far away from the Goumier camp. Nevertheless, he closed the shop. He didn't need the hassle. He sold directly to wine conglomerates and used the shop mostly to socialize with his friends. The Goumiers were definitely not his friends.

Goumiers marched in the streets brandishing their knives. Often, they would come from the pool, built by the British, nude, and run up a farm road to their camp. Dante Alighieri described in his book, *The Divine Comedy*, heaven, purgatory, and hell as abstract concepts. People in Avella felt like they were in purgatory, not here or there, with the presence of German and British troops, waiting for better times. They assumed that the transition would be from purgatory to heaven with the arrival of Allied troops, but instead pure hell arrived on this earth with the coming of the Goumiers. The shepherds in the neighborhood were apprehensive because their matriarch lived next door to their camp. Once again, Sergio's residence was converted into a fortress whereby, besides the usual residents, the Da Alia family moved in with the newly married couples. The Ukrainians could have taken matters into their own hands, but they acquiesced just to please their wives. Mario, Ehrlich, and Don Nicola's families were already living in the building. Sergio double-locked the portone every evening by adding two metal bars across the large door.

At the west end of Main Street, everything seemed to be normal; people were out and about shopping or relaxing at a café. However, Sofia, Filomena, and Serafina had seen enough to shut their shop in the piazza. They didn't want to be caught by the Goumiers on their way to the shop. Also, they didn't want to provoke any incidents involving their husbands and the Goumiers on the way to the shop, as the husbands would have escorted them there. For the same reason, Alvaro closed city hall until the Goumiers left town to protect the workers. Ramiro's palazzo in the piazza was protected by two carabinieri and custodians. Whatever terror generated by the Goumiers, it was mostly localized near their camp in the east end of town.

However, it didn't stop the Goumiers from roaming around the high mountains. Sergio and Vladimir spotted them trying to domesticate wild horses at the base of the mountains. It was clear to Sergio that the purpose of domesticating the horses was to ride them to their camp and butcher them. That was sacrilegious not only to Sergio but to the whole shepherd community. Wild horses have been in that area of the mountains ever since the Stone Ages. It was useless to report to the Maresciallo as he was intimidated by the Goumiers. Still, people complained to him since he was the only authoritative official in town. His response: he stopped taking his usual walks on Main Street, especially in the piazza. Before the arrival of the Goumiers, he would walk around the piazza like a peacock in heat. He fancied himself as a Don Juan. Suddenly, with the arrival of the Goumiers, he thought of himself more as prey and avoided them. He was never the same after the war.

Sergio instead informed Imalda, who was upset, to say the least. She and a group of shepherds went straight to the commander of the Goumiers. She complained that the behavior of his troops was not representative of nomads like her shepherds and his troops. Her parting comment, "We will not tolerate that behavior in our community."

Unfortunately, the Goumiers had no qualms about slaughtering sheep, goats, or horses—whatever they could find in the mountains. But their actions did not go unnoticed. They woke a sleeping giant in return: the shepherd community, who laid out a trap for them. Two Goumiers were enticed to visit a shepherd family in the hills for wine, roast goat, and sex. The Goumiers were drugged as more shepherds joined the so-called festivities. The two Goumiers were then tied onto a table where they were castrated and allowed to bleed to death. The shepherds subsequently carried the dead bodies back to the entrance of the Goumiers' camp. The message was delivered and clear, as both the shepherds and the Goumiers understood the same unwritten language of nomads.

Soon after that incident, the Goumiers left the mountains, unnoticed by anyone. People in the village were stunned by what occurred, to say the least. Once they recovered their equilibrium, they were in a hurry to get back to normal life. To begin with, people began to assemble in the piazza to socialize and see who survived the awful ordeal. Sofia, Filomena, and Serafina wanted so badly to get back to their dress shop. They began to use pre-war fashion designs, with minor modifications, to make dresses. By then, Lena was becoming a beautiful young lady of fourteen who modeled the dresses. However, most of their clients needed alterations, a little tuck here or there, or more room in places.

SIXTEEN
A Diary Revealed

It was a bitter cold winter in Avella in 1944. For anyone who couldn't remember, it snowed for the first time since the beginning of the century. Children ran out in the streets to grab the snowflakes before they hit the ground. The war was effectively over in Avella as well as in the rest of Southern Italy. The German Army was entrenched at Monte Cassino, about one hundred miles north of Naples, holding the high ground next to the Abbey. Allied planes bombed the Abbey of Monte Cassino, reducing it to rubble and powder in order to prevent German soldiers from possibly hiding there. However, as in Avella, the soldiers hid in the caves within walking distance of the Abbey. Colonial and Polish soldiers of the Allied Army had an insurmountable task to gain the high ground by fighting uphill in muddy terrain. A huge cross on Monte Cassino has been dedicated to remind the world of the sacrifice made by the Polish soldiers.

The Goumier troops were dispatched east of Monte Cassino to flush out German soldiers from the high ground by attacking from behind enemy lines. It didn't stop them from committing unspeakable atrocities in towns on the way to Monte Cassino. After the battle, the Goumiers regrouped in Cancello, a town ten miles north of Naples. This area was referred to then as the Zona di Camorra—the Camorra's headquarters. Again, the Goumiers' behavior was uncivilized. It is not clear from historical books who was responsible for the castration of five Goumier soldiers who were buried in a cabbage field. But it marked the end of their barbaric escapades in Southern Italy and Europe. The Goumiers were shipped back to their homes soon after.

By 1944, the main focus of the Allied Army shifted from the Italian campaign to north of the Alps. This meant that the warring factions left sufficient numbers of soldiers and armaments in Italy to reach a stalemate. However, the devastation in Italy continued as before for the rest of the war, resulting in more direct collateral damage than in any other country in Europe. Mussolini formed a new government stationed at Garda Lake. The Italian people were not surprised by another absurdity from the Duce. Badoglio and the king of Italy did the same by forming another Italian government in Brindisi, Southern Italy. Both governments supposedly represented the Italian people, although neither one was elected, as there was no national election that year. The Badoglio government didn't print money to rev up the economy. Nor did the Badoglio government see the necessity to bring young men home from the war to work on the farms to produce food for the starving nation.

As for the shepherds in Avella, they returned from the mountains to their neighborhood. The war was now a long distance away and they felt safe to resume their lives. The carabinieri were not chasing them in the hills, as in the previous war. Imalda and Sergio were happy to have them and Nino back, as some of them were related to the matriarch. Another reason that the shepherds returned early was due to the inclement weather up in the high mountains. Sometimes, it is so cold there that the snow melts as late as July. Also, they wanted to take advantage of the wet season to replenish the pond with water so they could shear their sheep after dumping them in the pond. Water was collected in the pond by rerouting it from the Clanio Creek. Before the war, this was an annual ritual to rid the sheep's wool of ticks and fleas in the wool.

As for the farmers, they had a mess in their hands. All those army vehicles from occupying armies dug trenches all over their farms. They had to re-plow furrows in their land to plant seeds. The most troublesome concern was all the large craters they needed to refill with dirt. The craters were the result of the Allied forces' bombing of the German camps in the foothills. All of this was on top of one major hurdle: there was no one around to help get all of this work done. Labor of any kind was in short supply, not only in Avella but all over Italy. What's more, even if a farmer succeeded on his own to get the land ready for farming, there was no protection from the brigands roaming the hills of Avella foraging for food. As such, farmers were just as content to plant corn seeds in a relatively small patch of land as polenta was still the main meal of the day.

Lawlessness and corruption throughout Southern Italy didn't have to wait for spring to germinate like weeds. It was there all the time. The Maresciallo was as corrupt as the brigands and the Camorra or Mafia. Italian and American deserters and common thieves made up the core of the brigands. Their favorite targets were bakeries, all-purpose stores, butcher shops, and pharmacies. In small towns like Avella, pharmacies were short on penicillin. But, somehow, brigands would show up every time a shipment arrived. As such, it pitted the Camorra against the brigands, since the Camorra controlled the shipments of penicillin throughout the valley and Naples. The Maresciallo was on the take from both sides.

Politically, the Communists were taking over the streets, as they paraded every so often on Main Street, carrying the hammer and sickle red flag. They campaigned by indoctrinating anyone in the streets about Communism for the next election, although no election was expected that year. Communists draped the statue of Garibaldi with the red flag in the piazza. By then, Don Nicola abstained from politics so that he could concentrate on the coming opera season. He was promoted to be conductor of the orchestra. Mario returned to his former job as an accountant at the San Carlo.

Political confrontations in the streets of Avella between Communists and Fascists gave way to another form of confrontation. With the establishment of a naval base in Naples by the United States, the black market flourished not only in Naples but also in the valley. Approximately one-third of American goods at the base were sold on the black market. American cigarettes were the most popular among the populace followed by U.S. Army-issued blankets. The thought that the locals didn't have to roll that harsh tobacco into a cigarette drove them to pure ecstasy. They saved whatever little money they had so that they could buy one measly American cigarette. It didn't matter what brand, but they preferred Camel cigarettes. Neapolitan housewives were very inventive in turning Army blankets into luxurious coats and jackets. The Camorra controlled the black market but were impartial as to where they operated in the valley, including Avella.

The Camorra yielded tremendous political power over city halls throughout the valley and Naples. Most, if not all, Fascist mayors of small and big towns were replaced by mayors appointed by the Allied Military Government (AMG). Vito Genovese, the former underboss of the New York City Mafia, made all the recommendations for those posts and, of course, the appointments were filled by camorristi throughout Southern Italy. In Sicily, Mafiosi, or members of the Sicilian Mafia, were appointed as mayors. Salvatore "Lucky" Luciano was the Mafia boss in NYC despite being incarcerated. Vito was born in Tufino, very near Naples, and enjoyed protection no less from the U.S. Army through the AMG.

The ramifications of the appointments were far-reaching. For one thing, the Maresciallos had to toe the line with the appointed corrupt mayors and be subservient to them. Their main role was to keep the brigands away from the spoils and corruption at all levels. The Camorra had the first pick of the spoils. Any murder of brigands in the streets were white-washed by the local authorities, as, for example, in a town like Avella. With an abundance of soldiers and sailors in Naples, it attracted sex workers as well. Thus, penicillin was in high demand. As such, the Camorra also controlled the distribution of penicillin and vaccine for smallpox. At that time, there was an outbreak of typhoid, smallpox, and influenza.

As the Allied Army advanced toward Rome, more towns were liberated under the yoke of Fascism. Fascist officials crossed the battlefronts into towns freed from German occupation. They would wait in liberated towns until it was safe to return to their former towns where they held official titles. In ancient Roman days, dictators, generals, and politicians escaped from Rome toward Greece or the Middle East in order to avoid the so-called proscription list. Any Roman was welcome to murder the ones named on that list and take all of the material possessions of the deceased, including villas, farms, and sheep. The escapees traveled on Via Appia to the city of Brindisi. From there, it was a short boat ride to Greece. They would return when another ruler, favorable to them, appeared on the scene in Rome. Nothing had changed in two thousand years.

With summer fast approaching, the shepherds, including Imalda, were itching to get back to their routine before the war. The wool generated in the spring was made available to Sofia, Filomena, and Serafina, enough to keep the dress shop open for that year. Imalda had a full assortment of cheeses to unload in the next couple of months. Sergio and Vladimir advised the shepherds to take their sheep grazing in the hills toward the town of Campagna around Vesuvius since the hills of Avella were infested with brigands. Both of them decided to lay low until the hills in Avella became safer. In the meantime, they cultivated the garden by growing more corn. As for Dimitri and Nicola, they were busy renovating paintings in churches. Churches had the financial means to pay them, a rarity in those days. In the Communist section of town, commercial activity perked up as a new café opened in anticipation of the passegiata resuming soon with Christmas approaching fast.

Between September 1943 and the end of 1944, Ferramonti was home to one of the largest and most active Jewish communities in liberated Italy. It was at this point that Jewish self-governance first took shape during the internment. It quickly developed into a vital infrastructure, including the setup of all social and cultural services, media, education, small businesses, and, above all, a social fabric fostering entrepreneurship. Many internees transferred to other camps located in better areas, especially from Puglia and Sicily. Others found their way to Africa, Palestine, and the United States.

On May 26, 1944, 254 former internees left Ferramonti for Palestine on the first emigration transport authorized by the British mandatory government. On July 17, 1944, a little over 1,000 Jews from Ferramonti, Campagna, Potenza, Tito, and other internment towns in Southern Italy set sail from Naples for the United States. By the end of World War II, the facilities at Ferramonti had been abandoned. In the following decades, its memory has been kept alive solely through former internees and their families, and by some local residents. There is little evidence in towns like Potenza and Tito that Jewish internees lived there, although in Campagna living quarters of internees have been preserved to this day.

The war was very much alive in people's minds in Northern Italy. The Nazis wanted to keep Mussolini on a short leash. As such, they chose the headquarters of a new Italian Fascist government close to the German border so that they could be close enough to control Mussolini and the new government. However, not that close would give an appearance of subjugation to the rest of the world. They chose a small town on Lake Garda, Gargnano, near the German Army headquarters of Field Marshal Kesselring. Finally, Kesselring got his wish to replace his arch-rival Rommel as supreme commander of the Italian territory, only because Rommel was put in charge of the coastal defense against an impending Allied invasion in Normandy, France. Reluctantly, Mussolini accepted the town as his capital. He settled in the nineteenth-century Villa Feltrinelli, on the shores of the lake. It functioned as Mussolini's office and home, but the office was transferred later on to Villa delle Orsoline also in Gargnano. He never learned to like the thirty-seven rooms in Villa Feltrinelli. According to him, it was too dark and hostile. The doorways to the Villa were guarded by one SS guard and one Blackshirt Fascist and SS men surrounded the grounds.

Three days following Mussolini's rescue in the Gran Sasso raid, he was taken to Germany for a meeting in Hitler's headquarters in Rastenburg in East Prussia. While Mussolini was in poor health and wanted to retire, Hitler advised him to return to Italy and start a new Fascist State under the protection of the Wehrmacht. When Mussolini balked, tired of the responsibilities of the war and unwilling to retake power, Hitler told him the alternative would be a German military administration that would treat Italy no different from other occupied countries. Hitler also threatened to destroy Milan, Genoa, and Turin, unless Mussolini agreed to set up a revived Fascist government. Reluctantly, Mussolini agreed to Hitler's demands. In retrospect, it was all a lie by Hitler, because Northern Italy was already treated as occupied territory like other European countries. Mussolini never saw through the bluff.

However, Hitler's motives were entirely different from what he expressed to Mussolini. First, he wanted to legitimize Germany's occupation of North Italy with the eventual annexation of all the regions in the Alps. He had already annexed Bolzano. Second, Hitler wanted direct access to internment camps in North and Central Italy in order to carry out his brutal extermination of Jewish internees. The new Fascist government would be held responsible for the extermination; a future cover-up for their demonic deeds. Finally, Hitler had a personal message for Mussolini; he wanted to convey to him that the only clown between the two of them was Mussolini. Mussolini attempted to create an illusion in Hitler's mind that Italy, too, had internment camps. However, Hitler and other Nazi officials never bought into that picture. They felt that only clowns create illusions and that was Hitler's message. In effect, Hitler created a replica of internment housing, Italian style, similar to the ones created in Southern Italy in remote hilly towns.

The only time Mussolini was free from the German guards was when he went to the bathroom. Even when he visited his mistress, Clara Petacci, in town, he needed permission from the guards to escort him. Thus, Mussolini lived in a town internment, much like the internees in Tito and Potenza. Mussolini complained as much to his daughter, Edda, and wife, Donna, stating, "I am under house arrest."

After an absence of three months, Mussolini was reunited with Clara Petacci. Mussolini sent a car driven by a German officer to take her from Merano to Villa Feltrinelli. His wife was still in Munich, Germany. Petacci planned to move to Gargnano soon after. Donna Rachele rejoined the Duce together with their two youngest children, Romano, 16, and Anna Maria, 14, soon after the mistress showed up in Gargnano. The local police estimated that about 200 Mussolini's relatives were living around Gargnano.

The return of Donna Rachele and their children was not a happy one. Mussolini and Rachele often passed each other in their residence without speaking. She took pride in her peasant background and her practical management of household affairs. She often ironed clothes, although the family had five servants. She was uncomfortable in public appearances. According to a friend of the family, "She knew how to handle her man."

While Mussolini was busy setting up a new government, his son-in-law, Ciano, was languishing in jail in January 1944. Hitler had Ciano sent to a jail in Verona after house arrest in Munich. The plan to go to Spain was not Ciano's idea, but his wife, Edda's She was the oldest and favorite child of Mussolini. Also, she was in a good personal relationship with Hitler. She simply miscalculated her power to influence people at the top of both governments. Ultimately, Ciano's family was double-crossed by SS Colonel Eugen Dollmann. Dollman had lived in Italy since 1927. His family had served the royal courts of Bavaria and Austria. He went to Italy to research Renaissance history, and earned his living as a translator and writer. He moved in both Roman and German aristocratic and clerical circles and was not the type to become an SS officer. In 1937, Dollman returned to Germany, with a group of Fascists, serving as an interpreter. When Hitler's interpreter fell ill, Himmler asked him to substitute. Dollmann impressed the Nazi hierarchy such that Himmler made him his private SS interpreter. He seldom wore the SS uniform so as not to embarrass his Italian artistic friends. Dulles described him as "an intellectual, highly sophisticated, somewhat snobbish and cynical," and a man of almost effeminate gestures. An ideal double agent? See my book, *Bitter Chicory to Sweet Espresso*.

Basically, Hitler washed his hands of the whole affair by shipping Ciano to Verona, and letting Mussolini do the dirty work for him. In a way, Il Duce, had no choice. He himself was under house arrest. However, he did have many options, as Edda tried, in vain, to explain to him. Either he was too sick or too cowardly to exercise any of them. One straight-forward option would have been to order the guards to release Ciano from jail or to demand a fair trial. Either way, Hitler would have done away with him, as well as Ciano. The only other option would have been to leave the country altogether with Ciano's family, but that would have been somewhat difficult because of his internment. However, Mussolini was too delusional to even think about it, let alone carry it out.

While Ciano considered how to leverage his diary to save himself, opportunity knocked on his jail door. The SS assigned an attractive young woman agent, Hildegard Burkhardt Beetz, to induce Ciano to reveal where he had hidden the diary. The Nazis were concerned about revelations of their demonic behavior. Ciano, a notorious womanizer, won her sympathy. She served as an interpreter for Ciano during discussions with German officials and already had developed a soft spot for him. Mrs. Beetz smuggled Ciano's letters out of prison and turned them over to Edda. On December 12, Emilio Pucci, a former lover of Edda, helped to smuggle Ciano's three children, Fabrizio, 12; Raimonda, 9; and Marzio, 6; across the border into Switzerland. On December 18, Edda saw her father and he told her that there was nothing he could do to save her husband. "You are all mad, you are all mad!" she shouted at him. The final coup between the two came when she declared, "Between us, it is finished, finished forever..." Edda never saw her father thereafter.

Through Mrs. Beetz, Ciano smuggled out a letter to Edda instructing her to get a hold of the diary hidden in the train station in Milan. Edda and Pucci put in place a plan for Edda to escape to Switzerland. On January 8, Edda slipped out of the Ramiola clinic through a cellar door, and walked across fields to join Pucci, who was waiting in his car. The next day, SS and gestapo units discovered that Edda left the clinic. The race was on, with Edda having a day head start. In the early evening of January 9, Edda crossed into Switzerland with Pucci's help. With Germans in sight, he pushed Edda onto Swiss ground. Then he said, "Go now." She carried Ciano's diary in a pajama shirt under her dress, fashioned by Pucci so the bulge would make her look pregnant. Pucci later became one of the premier Italian fashion designers of women clothing, rivaling the Dior house. The Swiss guards were shocked to see Edda and, the next day, she joined her children. Pucci was later discovered by the SS units only to be beaten almost to death. Somehow, he recovered from his skull being fractured in several places. In late 1944, he managed to join Edda. Mussolini was deeply hurt by Edda's estrangement, and he would later send an emissary to Switzerland, a priest who had known Edda for many years, to try to persuade her to return, but to no avail.

The trial of Ciano and his co-defendants began on January 8, in Verona, Italy. The trial lasted two days. A kangaroo court found Count Ciano guilty of treason and the judge condemned him and others to death by the firing squad: Giovanni Marinelli, Carlo Pareschi, Luciano Gottardi, Tullio Cianetti, and Emilio De Bono. That evening the condemned men signed a petition to Mussolini for pardon. They were all executed on January 11, 1944, in the fort of San Procolo in Verona. Each one was tied to a chair with their backs to the shooters. At the very moment of the shooting, Ciano turned his face around to shout, "Viva L'Italia!" Mussolini never telephoned the prison to find out if pardon requests were in route to him, an omission that was no doubt deliberate.

New long-range rockets developed by Germany in 1944 had little effect on the outcome of the war or the people, when aimed at London. The Allies liberated Rome and Paris, the Russian Army approached the German border from the east and the Allies from the west. The Allies would see Ponte Vecchio, as they occupied Florence. It was just a matter of time for the curtain to come down on Nazi Germany. However, there was another war raging in the Feltrinelli household. Donna Rachele fumed over the affair between her husband and Petacci. The rumor circulated throughout the town. There was no peace in the household at the Feltrinelli residence. The constant bickering between Il Duce and Donna Rachele about the affair dominated whatever conversation in the house. Finally, Rachele reached her threshold and decided to confront Petacci.

In November 1944, Donna Rachele informed her husband that she was going to Villa Fiordaliso, Petacci's residence. She demanded that Interior Minister Buffarini accompany her. Mussolini telephoned Petacci to warn her of the storm that was about to occur: "She is coming to you... Don't let her in...she may be armed." Clara summoned an SS guard to close the gate, but Donna Rachele began to climb over it with Buffarini tugging her skirt to hold her back. After the verbal confrontation between the two, and no resolution, Rachele returned to Villa Feltrinelli and swallowed bleach inducing a terrible sickness and constant vomiting. Mussolini took care of her and patched up their differences.

By early 1945, Mussolini broke free from internment. German troops were recalled home to defend their country. Russian and Allied troops breached the German defenses at the borders. Partisans were all over Northern Italy chasing Fascists. The Partisans trapped Mussolini in Milan. While south of Po Valley, by consent, Allied troops faced enough German troops to force a stalemate. Partisans then got more brazen and roamed the hills surrounding major cities like Milan, as the Allied Army advanced north of the Po River in the vicinity of Milan.

A meeting on April 24, 1945, was arranged by Cardinal Schuster, of the Milan diocese, among Mussolini, his associates, partisans, and aspirants to future governments. At that meeting, the Duce declared that he and 5,000 die-hard Fascists were ready to fight to the end. Cardinal Schuster asked, "And so you intend to continue the war in the mountains?" Mussolini replied, "Yes, for a little while, but then I will surrender." Cardinal Schuster shot back, "Don't deceive yourself, Duce, ... only three hundred at most... as you believe." Again, the Duce deluded himself. Only a handful of Fascists followed him to the area of Lake Como.

Discussions in the presence of the cardinal pertained only to terms and conditions for surrender by the Fascists to the partisans. The meeting broke up with Mussolini promising to respond to the terms of surrender offered by the partisans. But the next day, he left for the city of Como on Lake Como with a caravan of twenty to thirty Fascists. Arrangements were made to reinforce the Mussolini group with 5,000 more Fascists. But those troops only existed in his mind, as the cardinal asserted. Mussolini arrived near Lake Como, only one mile from the Swiss border—a twenty-minute walk at most—but he never crossed the border. He didn't have the courage to cross it on foot. That cost him his life.

Mussolini was caught by the partisans at Dongo, twenty-five miles north of Como, dressed as a regular German soldier. He and his mistress Clara Petacci were shot to death by a special Communist agent Walter Audisio on April 28, 1945, with the explicit order from the Communist leadership to kill Mussolini. Two days later, Hitler heard the news and decided that he was not about to be taken alive by Russian troops like Mussolini had been by the Communists. He and Eva Braun decided to take cyanide pills and shoot themselves. Their bodies were found on May 5, 1945 in the underground bunker, where they died by suicide.

That historic day, May 1, 1945, was a beautiful sunny spring day with grape vines blooming that special sky-blue color all over town. People streamed toward the piazza in Avella. There was an enthusiastic celebration when the news broke that Mussolini was dead. No one showed any remorse. The same group of people, partisans and Communists who had paraded a year before with their red flags all over the piazza, carried a loudspeaker blaring the news of Mussolini's death. A two-man band also played a tambourine and trumpet and sang Communist revolutionary songs. The mood was jubilant and engaging. By this time a café had opened at one corner of the piazza. The aroma of sweet espresso could be smelled for the first time—espresso brewed using roasted coffee beans rather than dried leaves and buds of chicory. And the espresso wasn't bitter since sugar was now available. People patiently waited in line for an espresso and took in the atmosphere and all the commotion around them. They sensed a truly historic moment. A page had been turned, they were all about to enter a new chapter in their lives—they were no longer on hold. Nevertheless, food was still the main preoccupation, but they were happy for a change.

SEVENTEEN

It's Not My Bed

The Union of Italian Jewish Communities reported that, in general, most confiscated assets were returned to their owners or next of kin, except in cases when the latter could not be identified. However, government institutions did not follow up in identifying survivors or their heirs entitled to unclaimed property. In December 1998, the Italian government created the Anselmi Commission, a technical body whose mandate was to investigate the confiscation and restitution of Jewish assets during the Holocaust. The Commission discovered evidence of at least 7,847 local and national government decrees expropriating Jewish assets during the Fascist era and analyzed 7,187 of them. The decrees affected approximately 8,000 individuals and 230 companies.

The Anselmi Commission released its final report and recommendations in April 2002. The report's findings showed, in general, that assets were returned to deported survivors who submitted claims, but those survivors or heirs who did not submit claims were not proactively traced and compensated. The Commission recommended that Italian authorities investigate unclaimed assets to identify survivors and heirs who may not have filed claims and highlighted, in particular, the need to investigate the unclaimed assets stored in the Italian investment bank, Cassa Depositi e Prestiti, which provided financing services for public-sector investments in Italy. Government institutions have not, in most cases, followed up on these recommendations. Furthermore, Italian Jews sold their assets at below market value during the Holocaust due to dire and life-threatening circumstances. In fact, post-war trauma and fear caused many Holocaust survivors and heirs not to pursue compensation for many years.

The Jewish community in Rome, now comprising almost half of the country's Jewish population before the war, successfully hid many historical artifacts, but some items in the community's archive were confiscated or destroyed. In 1943, the Nazis seized the contents of two libraries located in Rome in the same building: the library of Rome's Jewish community which contained 4,728 books, 28 incunabula, and 183 books printed in the sixteenth century, and the library of the Italian Rabbinical College, a collection originally from Florence but later transferred to Rome comprising 6,580 books and 1,760 booklets. The libraries contained prayer books, documents, prints, and manuscripts from all periods of Jewish history in Italy. The rabbinical library's collection was recovered in Germany after the war, but the majority of the contents in Rome's libraries were never found.

The Jewish internees, about 200, in Tito disappeared just as they had appeared in town before the war, happy to resume their lives and thankful to the locals. They waited until after the war to leave Tito. From September 8, 1943 to May 1945, they were free to leave, but it was too dangerous to go home, north of the Alps. There was still a war. Some went home to conditions no better than those in Tito; others went to the newly declared state of Israel via Brindisi, the old Roman route to the Middle East. Most likely, internees in Campagna, Ferramonti, Potenza, and Brienza pursued the same route to Palestine. However, some stayed behind to return to their homes in Central Europe or emigrated to the United States. All registration records of the internees at Tito's city hall disappeared. How they disappeared is still a mystery. Unfortunately, the only one who would have known, Pasquale, the chief magistrate, also disappeared after the war. He emigrated to the United States and never contacted anyone about the documents. In fact, most Italian American expatriates who were stuck in Tito and many other towns during the war returned to the United States after the war.

According to Elizabeth Bettina's book, *It Happened in Italy*, the only paper evidence that Jewish internees lived in Tito during the war are birth and death certificates stored in city hall. This was not a unique situation in Tito. Most likely, towns like Tito purposely burned or got rid of official records for fear that they might fall into the hands of SS officers. This poses an interesting question: What if there were no birth or death certificates discovered in Tito or Potenza or many other towns like them; would the world forget or ignore the existence of Jewish internees in those towns? We do know that the mayor of Potenza denied, long after the war, the relevance of his town to Jewish internees until a birth certificate was shoved in his face.

In many ways, the internees and the locals had much in common. Both understood their special predicaments relative to their respective governments. As Carlo Levi pointed out in Aliano the local peasants had been ignored and neglected by the central government for centuries to the point of denying civilization not only for the peasants but also for the upper class residing in the same town. It didn't matter that many of the Jewish internees were well-educated, upper-class people. They were rejected, harassed, persecuted, and exterminated by the Nazi government. Both the townies and internees shared something in common: their governments rejected them. Whereas the central government of Rome turned a blind eye to the very existence of peasants in small towns, the Nazi regime hunted Jewish internees all over Europe to eradicate them. As far as their governments were concerned, they didn't exist. Hence, there was much empathy between the visiting Jewish internees and the local peasants. Besides, they were in the same figurative boat when it came to surviving the war and resuming their lives. Jewish internees, who came there as strangers, left with deep feelings of gratitude and friendship toward the locals on their return visit. They survived the Nazis and the world recognized their existence.

Soon after the war, Nanna gathered her children in her bedroom to say, "What would you like to hear: the good or the bad news first?" Both Arya and Werner replied, "both". "The good news is that we are going home and the bad news is that we are leaving Avella," Nanna proudly announced. Understandably, the children were confused and shouted, "This is home!" For more than six years, the Wolf family made Avella their mainstay. Besides, the children befriended many other children in the area and they had no desire to leave them behind. It was part of who they were. They even found it easier to converse in Italian. Soon, the word about their departure spread throughout the neighborhood, and sadness prevailed among the neighborhood children.

But the news didn't surprise the clan of friends. As in life, there are good and bad moments. They preferred to remember the good times that they shared with the Wolf family and not the war. They tried to make the departure as painless as possible for the children and family. However, their somber looks could not be erased from their faces. Don Nicola no longer tried to recruit Ehrlich to San Carlo. Until departure, Don Nicola, Mario, and Ehrlich still took the 8:11 a.m. train to Naples on the way to the San Carlo. On the train, the topic of conversation was about the city and the people of Vienna. The neighborhood children still played together like old times forgetting everything about Arya and Werner's departures. There would not be a get-together in Sergio's garden because the clan didn't want to celebrate the departure in any shape or form. They just wanted to enjoy the family while they were there. They felt one of their own was about to leave. There was nothing to be happy about.

Nanna imposed on Ehrlich to return to Tito and give thanks to both Strega and Bambolone for their wonderful hospitality. Another reason was to appease their children who got along very well with Bambolone's children. While there, she thought that she might as well have Bambolone style her hair with the latest hairdo. At this point, Ehrlich just wanted to resume their lives, not to prolong the sad moment. "What the heck, let's go," Ehrlich muttered. Mario, Sofia, and their children came along for the train ride. After all, Mario received much help from those two, Strega and Bambolone, as well as Pasquale. Interestingly, Tito was not recognized as a historic internment town during WWII, until Elizabeth Bettina paid attention to it in her book, *It Happened in Italy*.

Once in Tito, the women and children took over the agenda of the day. Mario and Ehrlich's children shot out of the train like a cannon and ran up Main Street over to Bambolone's barber shop in the piazza. Bambolone was taken aback with surprise, waving and shouting at his wife across the piazza to let their children romp with the others there. As usual, the children disappeared out of sight, but the parents didn't worry. They knew that the children would come back at chow time. Finally, Sofia met the two masterminds, Strega and Bambolone, who were responsible for protecting Mario and the Wolf family during the internment. In an emotional moment, Strega embraced all the visitors. Sofia inquired about Pasquale's whereabouts. "He is at city hall busy making life miserable for Bambolone," replied Strega. She added, "He is the new mayor. The two of them have a game of upmanship since Bambolone was briefly the acting mayor in 1943."

Without knocking on the door to the mayor's office, Bambolone in a serious tone declared to Pasquale, "Get off your ass, because the Nazis are back and are looking for you." For a split second, Pasquale panicked but quickly recovered his equilibrium. "Ma fa a Napule, guaglione!" he shouted back, a derogatory expression. Bambolone explained gently that Sofia and the Viennese couple were waiting for you down in Strega's place. Like old times, Pasquale organized a dinner in the reception room at city hall only among people in Strega's apartment.

As expected, the children returned just in time. After lunch, Mario spoke on behalf of all the guests thanking the hosts for the critical help and support during their stay in their towns. He stated that without their help, it would have been nearly impossible to survive the conditions of internment. "Pasquale, you are right, when you said to Sofia that she was part of you all. The truth of the matter is that all of you are part of us. Bambolone, you see life in its naked form. You cover it up with your levity. In those days, and especially today, that's needed. My beautiful Strega, your heart is as big as those mountains surrounding the town. You moved them to help us."

"Don't you ever tell that to Ramiro," Strega snapped. "He already knows," replied Mario. They all laughed. Mario didn't mention that the Wolf family was returning to Vienna, because he didn't want to spoil the good feelings of all at that moment. After Bambolone styled the ladies' hair, the visitors returned to Avella.

The Wolf family took the 8:11 a.m. train in Avella for the last time. They didn't pack much, because while in Avella they didn't collect many material things. Imalda took care of transferring money to a bank of the Wolf family's choosing. Other than that, they were ready and excited to go home to Vienna. The family was accompanied by Don Nicola and Mario to the train station in Naples. From there, straight to Vienna with a few stops in Rome and Milan. At the station, there wasn't much to say other than embracing and bidding goodbyes. Arya embraced Don Nicola and in a perfect Neapolitan dialect, "Te vogli bene, Zio," I love you, Uncle. Don Nicola was deeply touched. Mario and Don Nicola resumed their usual trek walking to the San Carlo and reminiscing about the Wolf family.

In Vienna, the Wolfs discovered their neighborhood in the Dobling District totally pulverized by Russian tanks or Allied planes. It didn't matter which Army did what damage to their neighborhood. Damages don't come with labels. It must have been a devastating feeling to see one's home vanish just like a flick of the finger. Fortunately for them, they heard about the work of the Swedish Red Cross in Vienna. Many survivors ended up in the displaced persons (DP) camps set up in Western Europe under Allied military occupation at the sites of former concentration camps. There, they waited to be admitted to places like the United States, South Africa, Palestine, and Scandinavian countries. These countries were in need of skilled labor. Count Folke Bernadotte, who was chairman of the Swedish Red Cross, and the Danish government sponsored thirty-six "white" buses to transport Jewish internees to their countries, Denmark, Sweden, and Norway.

The Wolf family arrived in Odense, Denmark, where they were provided with an apartment subsidized by the Danish government. Ehrlich was employed as an accountant at an architecture firm owned by Mr. Kerman Ticka, who was a former resident of Vienna. He left Vienna soon after the occupation of Austria by Germany in 1938. Four or five years later, the Austrian government restored the Dobling neighborhood almost to its original condition. But the Wolf family decided to settle in the Innere Stadt District in Vienna to be closer to the Vienna Opera House. Nanna was well aware of the many properties that her father, Harold, and uncle, Herbert, owned in Vienna, the suburbs, and other European countries. The big concern was whom to contact and proceed with the recovery of properties as well as valuable items. She postponed the problem by contacting her father in Switzerland and uncle in New York City.

In addition to Jewish internees, many soldiers from various warring countries were dispersed all over Europe. In particular, an uncountable number of Italian soldiers were imprisoned in concentration camps or gulags in Russia, never to make it home. Some remained behind and started families and assumed new lives. For Fascist soldiers, it was too dangerous to return home with Communists searching for them. Of the 600,000 Italian troops deployed in the Russian campaign, 5,000 to 10,000 soldiers returned to Italy after the war. There is no accountability for Italian youth deported to German factories and for more than 600,000 Italian soldiers stranded in the battlefields of Central Europe and the Balkans. In addition, an uncountable number of Italian soldiers were released by the British Army in Libya. Most of them chose not to return to Italy and started a family there.

Soldiers throughout Europe, peasants and gentry, and illustrious people, who were close to decision-makers caught in the whirlpool of the war, hungered for a normal life. During her husband's spectacular and bombastic political career, Donna Rachele remained in the background, caring for their five children and running her household. After the war, Donna Rachele spent most of her time on her farm in Predappio, a small town near the Adriatic Sea in the Emilia region of Italy, the district where she and Mussolini were born and where they first met. Despite the ruin spawned by Mussolini's public career and the infidelities that marked his private life, Donna Rachele honored his memory to the end of her days.

She insisted that his body be returned to her by the Italian government, and in 1956 it was. She saw to it that he received a Christian burial in the cemetery in Predappio. She insisted that part of his brain that had been taken to the United States be returned, and it was. She fought for the return of his personal belongings, all of which had been confiscated after the war, and many of them were given back. She insisted on her rights to a pension as the widow of a former soldier and government official; in 1968, the government capitulated and granted her a sum equal to $200 a month. A large portrait of Il Duce was displayed in her house. A smaller picture, taken when he was a young socialist newspaper editor, graced a table in her room.

Donna Rachele managed a restaurant, La Caminate, at the hilltop near her home, where Mussolini once had a villa, popular with tourists, curiosity seekers, and neo-Fascists. It is said that the only one of her husband's belongings that she refused to accept was a large walnut bed. When the government offered it together with other furniture, she turned it down, reportedly saying, "Claretta used it." Donna Rachele often visited her husband's grave. Beside him lie the bodies of two of their children, Bruno, an Air Force pilot killed in a crash during World War II, and Anna Maria, who died in 1968. Donna Rachele had a granite coffin prepared for herself that lies next to the body of Mussolini. She professed little interest in politics. "I was sorry that Mussolini went into politics," she once said. "He had a newspaper; he was the editor. He should have stayed there. You can't be happy in politics, never, because one day things go well, another day they go badly." Donna Rachele was survived by three children, Vittorio, who had a successful business career in Argentina before returning to Italy in 1968; Edda; and Romano, one of Italy's leading jazz pianists and the former husband of Sophia Loren's younger sister. Donna Rachele died in 1979 at the age of eighty-nine.

Mussolini and his mistress, Claretta Petacci, were executed in 1945 by Italian partisans and Communists. Petacci's corpse and those of the other fifteen shot in April 1945 were taken to Milan. Her body was exposed in Piazzale Loreto on April 29 together with those of Mussolini and others, which hung upside down. Around 3 p.m., the American military command ordered the nineteen bodies to be taken by lorry to the municipal morgue in Via Ronzo, lot one. Petacci's body was then taken to the Maggiore Cemetery and buried as unknown in a field of sixteen, where those of Mussolini and others were already. In March 1957, Clara was buried in the family tomb at the Verano Cemetery in Rome, thanks to the permission given by Interior Minister Fernando Tambroni.

Edda Ciano escaped to Switzerland on January 9, 1944, disguised as a peasant. She managed to smuggle out her husband's, Count Galeazzo Ciano, wartime diaries. During the War, Pucci was a lieutenant in the Italian Air Force but later found fame as a fashion designer. War correspondent Paul Ghali of the *Chicago Daily News* learned of her secret internment in a Swiss convent in Neggio and arranged for the publication of the diaries. They revealed much of the secret history of the Fascist regime between 1939 and 1943 and are considered a prime historical source.

After returning to Italy, Edda was arrested and held in detention on the island of Lipari. On December 20, 1945, she was sentenced to two years imprisonment for aiding Fascism. At that time Badoglio was still the prime minister of the new Italian government in Brindisi. It is noted that Captain Erich Priebke and Colonel Herbert Kappler of the Gestapo headquarters in Rome were found guilty after the war of murdering 335 civilians during the German occupation. The killings were in retaliation for partisans killing thirty-three German security policemen. The irony of it all was that those policemen were Italian citizens before the war. None of the remaining policemen took part in the retaliation. Yet, Priebke and Kappler did not spend one day in prison, because it was considered a harsh punishment for them to endure. The British Military ended up interfering with many of the court decisions of the Italian courts after the war.

An Italian film was dedicated to the incarceration of Edda in Lipari and her relationship with a young Communist guard. After the war, Mrs. Edda Ciano settled quietly in Rome. She broke her public silence on wartime events in a 1975 book, *My Testimony*, and several years before her death she attended a public mass in memory of her father. She never reconciled with her mother, Donna Rachele. Her mother blamed Mrs. Ciano's husband, Galeazzo, for being responsible for the fall of Benito Mussolini. Alessandra Mussolini, the wartime dictator's granddaughter who was a member of parliament for the right-wing National Alliance, told Reuters: "My aunt was born a woman but lived like a man. Not only did she stand up to her father over the man she loved; she stood up to Il Duce, which is something altogether different."

Edda died in Rome in 1995. She forgave her father, Mussolini, just before she died for having her husband, Count Ciano, shot on January 11, 1944. Her relationship with her mother, Donna Rachele, was at best strained and uncomfortable. Her love relationship with the fashion designer Emilio Pucci ceased soon after the war, because their lives and careers went separate ways.

EIGHTEEN

Post-Political Landscape

With all the schemes and make-believe scenarios by Mussolini, its modern-day Caesar, Italy lost all of the colonies and Italian territories gained in WWI. In the months of April and June 1946, the people of Italy were preoccupied with the coming election of the General Assembly on April 19, 1946, and the vote of a referendum on June 2, 1946, about the disposition of the monarchy. The main purpose of the assembly was to draft a new constitution, and they had two years to do it. A yes vote in the referendum implied that the monarchy, or King Victor Emmanuel III, could form a post-war government similar to the British one. A no vote implied that the monarchy or the king would be exiled from Italy. The Communist and Republican parties were active against the king. The Communist Party in Avella moved the headquarters next to city hall. They held a rally almost every day up and down Main Street and would carry their red flag, singing Communist revolutionary songs, and a trumpeter to get people's attention. As many as thirty to forty Communists roamed the streets raising the noise.

The outcome was inevitable and the referendum did not carry. The no vote barely won in Southern Italy, but Northern Italy voted overwhelmingly no. That was an unpredictable result, as the king hailed from Northern Italy. The king and his wife, Queen Elena, were exiled to Egypt where he died on December 28, 1947, of pulmonary complications. Their son, Umberto II, was exiled to Cascais, Portugal. He reluctantly accepted the result of the referendum. People were afraid that he might incite a civil war. The following year, 1947, the new constitution was drafted and passed by the General Assembly with a vote of 452 for, 63 against.

The feeling among the people of Avella became almost euphoric. For the first time in a long time, they had the freedom to pursue their dreams and aspirations. But there was a new threat in town: A mini civil war was brewing in the streets of Italy in which Communists and former Fascists were at each other's throats. Newspapers shied away from reporting it for fear of inciting one. However, people in Italy were fed up with politics and in a hurry to catch up with the rest of the world, joining the twentieth century in exploring new ideas, fashion, and lifestyles. The United States was an exciting place to live and, for the most part, it was the first choice of where refugees wanted to emigrate.

Local and national elections took place throughout Italy. There were two candidates for mayor in Avella, the former apolitical mayor, who left the office when German troops came to town, ran under the banner of the Christian Democratic Party; and a candidate from the west end of Avella who ran under the Communist Party. Immediately, the local politics became nasty. The local Communist Party of Avella accused Imalda of taking bribes from the leaders of the Democratic Party. Like most shepherds, Imalda had no political leaning one way or another, but she felt that, with Communists in charge, the town would regress to the old days and she had enough of that. It would have only generated more strife between the classes. Like her community of shepherds, she detested the Communist Party with a passion. She felt that, although her community might be poor, they worked hard to carve out a living; local Communists were forever looking for handouts from the church, government, business, the wealthy, etc. She decided to do something about the coming election. Imalda spent much time with shepherds teaching them to sign their names on the ballot which was a requirement to vote.

The Catholic priests got involved in the election as well only because the church feared losing their extensive land holdings in town. Communists were campaigning on the promise to break up farms owned by the churches into smaller plots and distribute them to poor farm workers, and loyal Communists. The Communists paraded on Main Street with red bandannas around their necks similar to the one Giuseppe Garibaldi wore during the revolutionary days of the 1850s, implying that Garibaldi was a founding father of the Communist Party. Of course, that was a false claim, as the party didn't exist until after the Russian Revolution in 1918. That stunt garnered some votes, but not enough to win the election. Karl Marx began preaching Communist ideologies around the 1850s, not enough time to influence anyone at that time in Italy. Labor issues were not the main preoccupation at that time.

The Democratic candidate was elected with a majority of 56 percent versus 42 percent for the Communist candidate and 2 percent for one other write-in candidate, Luigi the Drunk. This result surprised everyone since the towns surrounding Avella, Baiano, Sperone, Cervinara, and Cicciano, voted for Communist mayors. The surprising result was due mostly to Imalda's efforts in the shepherd community. The Communist Party put up a candidate who lived on the outskirts of town, near the Castle of Avella, and no one in town knew or was aware of him. Rumor had it that the Communist Party of Avella brought in an outsider for the election. However, even if people knew who the man was, it would have not made any difference. The shepherd community was then the largest one in Avella.

One of the first acts of the new mayor was to fund a road project toward the picnic grounds, the Fusaro area, which included the swimming pool built by the British Army. The rationale for the paved road was that, in case of a potential surge of visitors to the annual spring festival at the Fusaro, they would be ready for the large crowd. Before WWII, visitors from the city of Naples and towns in the valley made their pilgrimage to the picnic grounds and the Church of Montevergine on the high mountains. Imalda suggested that the mayor hire Dimitri and Nicola Jr., Don Nicola's son, since there was a shortage of construction workers in the valley and no one qualified as a civil engineer. The three of them, including the mayor, planned the construction of the road. They had no clue where to begin. They were aware that the Germans built a paved road near the cemetery during the war. If only they could obtain those construction plans, they thought. However, the Communist mayor in Baiano possessed the road plans and he outrightly refused to release them to a Democratic mayor. How they got a hold of those plans is a mystery to this day. Everyone knew that they had them, as there were much road constructions in Baiano.

The mayor of Baiano let it be known that he would be happy to deal with a Socialist like Don Nicola, since the two of them were orchestra members of the San Carlo. The two artists thrashed out a deal, a palatable bribe for both sides. Both being Neapolitans, it was a foregone conclusion that they would do so. Most of the laborers on the road construction were to be members of the Communist Party who had never worked on road construction and were unskilled residents of Baiano and Avella. The political implications were obvious. The day-to-day operation was handled by Dimitri. Nicola Jr. kept tabs on who should be paid on the project. The project to pave about two miles of road that ran from downtown Avella to the Fusaro picnic area was finished in a year. The mayor left office soon after the road was built as he was promoted to a judgeship position, replacing a Fascist judge.

An out-of-town person was installed as the new mayor. The people of Avella never knew where he came from and what his party affiliation was. The fact that there were not many crimes in Avella at that time, attested to his representing the Camorra's interests. The mayor kept to himself and didn't do much of anything for the rest of his term. In the following local election, Imalda stayed out of the campaign. By this time, Don Nicola also stayed out of politics and remained very busy with his studio and San Carlo. Whatever little time he had, he preferred to spend with his group of friends, the clan of old. The local pharmacist ran for mayor against the Communist Party candidate. The pharmacist ran under the Republican Party. There was no candidate from the Democratic Party. The pharmacist easily won and was able to stay in the office as mayor for four years. People wanted to be in good terms with the pharmacist, as they would need medicine in the future.

The picnic festival at the Fusaro fields resumed after a hiatus of seven or eight years, having been postponed during the war. A contingent of Neapolitan families made the pilgrimage to the Fusaro picnic grounds, located at the foothills of Mount Avella. Neapolitans have been fixated every spring with coming to the Fusaro area for a picnic, although there are many other similar places nearby. Neapolitans claim that they love the cool and clean mountain air compared with the congested living conditions in Naples surrounded by charred buildings. This tradition goes back 600 years. Usually, Neapolitans and people in the valley came on the first Saturday in May and the people of Avella scheduled their own picnic on the following Saturday.

The picnic was a two-day event. On the second day, mule, donkey, and horse riders lined up for a race. If Hannibal's descendants could have been there, probably elephant and zebra riders would also have lined up for the race. Jockeys were ordinary people representing different districts of town, much like the Palio horse race in Siena. The mule was usually ridden by someone representing the farmers. The donkey was ridden by a bride pulled by the groom. There were a few aficionados of the horse. This type of diversification in four-legged animals would not be allowed in Siena. Sergio and Vladimir served as the official timekeepers of the race; they also provided order and safety in the picnic area, which was part of their duties as mountain policemen. They walked up and down the foothills, all the way to the Church of Montevergine, Avellino, frequented mostly by Neapolitans. From the picnic grounds to Montevergine was straight uphill, through treacherous terrain. Surprisingly, city folks from Naples trekked through it all! And when they arrived at the church, they would get on their knees and struggle to get inside the church still on their knees. Strange ritual!

On the outskirts of Avellino and the church, they followed a difficult and circuitous route to avoid stranded, charred, and destroyed German tanks, cannons, trucks, jeeps, motor scooters, and benzene containers spread all over the road. The destroyed vehicles appeared to be heading toward Salerno, probably as a supply convoy, and were bombed by Allied planes. If Dante Alighieri were there, he would have labeled the road as the Inferno road. The smell of benzene was so powerful that it was difficult to breathe even two years later. Interestingly, a medical survey reported that thyroid cancer patients in old people were most pronounced in the Avellino area. The grass was charcoal black and did not grow back for a couple of years. Yet, Neapolitans were not fazed by the terrain and the terrible smell. They kept their pace to arrive at the church for the evening mass. Sergio and Vladimir were happy that the Neapolitans headed back to Naples by bus the next day with everyone accounted for.

North of the Alps, Allied troops occupied Austria just about the time the curtain came down on the two Fascist and Nazi leaders, Mussolini and Hitler. Russian troops occupied the eastern region of Austria reducing Vienna to rubble, especially downtown and nearby suburbs. British, French, and American troops occupied the western part of Austria. Occupation forces included about 150,000 Soviet troops, 55,000 British, 40,000 American, and 15,000 French. Similarly, Vienna was subdivided into four zones. In particular, American troops occupied the Dobling and part of the Innere Stadt districts. Initially, occupation costs were paid by the Austrian government which was about to be organized. Eventually, the occupying forces shared in the occupation costs.

Remarkably, Communist agitators in Vienna and other big cities in Austria did not hunt down Fascists or Nazis in the streets to do away with them in contrast to what was happening in Italy where political disagreements were still settled by a hit list as in times of the proscription list in Roman times. The only difference was that in Roman times killing was rewarded but not in modern times.

With the consent of the occupying forces, former Chancellor Karl Renner formed a provisional government consisting of Social Democrats, Christian Socialists, and Communists proclaiming the establishment of the second republic in Austria. One-third of Renner's Cabinet members were staffed by Austrian Communists. However, on November 15, 1945, a national election resulted in the

Communist Party receiving about 5 percent of the votes. The coalition of Christian Democrats and Social Democrats gathered 90 percent of the votes. The Christian Democratic Party, also known as the Austrian People's Party, returned eighty-five members to Parliament, seventy-six Social Democrats, and four Communists. Renner was elected president. With the consent of parliament, he appointed Leopold Figl as chancellor of Austria. Stalin's government responded with massive expropriation of Austrian assets. They confiscated much industrial equipment valued at $0.5 billion then. Total war reparations taken from Austria by the Soviet Union amounted to more than $2 billion. The American high commissioner complained about the Soviets' thievery—the onset of the so-called Cold War of the 1950s and thereafter.

Not only was the capacity to return to normalcy in Austria reduced with the disruption of the Soviets stealing their industries, grains, and oil from the Eastern zone under Soviet control, but food was not forthcoming to the rest of Austria. Hence, food remained the worst problem. In 1945–1946 Austria was on a near starvation diet. In 1947, the U.S. government issued $300 million in food aid and invited Austria to join the Marshall Plan. Austrians were gracious in granting 8 percent of the Marshall Plan aid to the eastern region of Austria. The Austrians regarded financial aid to the Soviet Zone as a lifeline to keep the country together. As in Italy, most of the aid was earmarked for heavy industry in the western zone. No European nation benefited more from the Marshall Plan than Austria, as they were the recipient of $1.5 billion plus $300 million in returning occupation money back to Austria. In addition, heating depended on supplies of German coal shipped by the United States.

On December 31, 1950, Renner died. By then, Austria had returned to normalcy so much so that the Austrian and U.S. governments signed the Fullbright Agreement, which facilitated student and scholar exchanges between the two countries. These types of exchanges prevailed throughout Europe and Asia. About 200 students in Austria attended universities in the United States between 1951–1952. Renner's dream of uniting all the zones under one umbrella came true. The state's treaty on crude oil was signed by representatives of the four occupying powers and Austria and formally established the Austrian Second Republic as an independent and democratic state. Britain, France, and the United States relinquished all property, rights, German assets, and war booty to Austria. The USSR or Russia received as compensation $152 million and 10 million metric tons of grains. The treaty became effective as of July 27, 1955; thereafter, all occupation forces left Austria. The USSR demanded Austrian neutrality, similar to Switzerland, before leaving their occupied zone. Thus, a constitutional law of perpetual Austrian neutrality was promulgated to complement the Austrian Constitution of 1920.

In summary, by the year 2000, there were 8,000 Jewish residences, around a quarter of a percent of the population of Vienna, settled mostly in the Leopoldstadt District compared to 200,000 or around ten percent before WWII spread throughout Vienna.

NINETEEN

Sweet Smell of Freedom

In some sense, those were the golden days for the people in the valley. Hope sprang up like the seeds in farms in spring. It seemed like the whole world wanted to forget about the war and make up for lost time despite Europe's devastation. Today, damages due to bombing and warfare are often referred to as direct collateral damage. However, there was more damage from indirect or hidden collateral damage as detailed in the book, *Hidden in Plain Sight*, due to the resurgence of Mafia-like syndicates. Instead, Europeans looked to the United States for the latest diversions: movies, theaters, fashion, new appliances, television, etc. The most popular outlet for the people of Avella was the cinema theater, built in the winter of 1946. The cinema in Avella was called Sala Azzurra or Blue Room. The people were enthralled by the new diversion. It played mainly American Westerns; children sat on the ground, in front of the first row, cheering for their heroes, Randolph Scott and Buster Crabbe, every time they appeared on the screen. Before long the kids made wooden pistols to use in gun duels out in the streets.

In order to appease the adults, sentimental Neapolitan movies, such as *Anema e Core* or *Heart and Soul* were shown. The film industry was beginning to rise from the ashes in Italy. Initially, favorite operas were filmed for the public. It was not until the early 1950s that the industry produced world-class directors and actors. They aimed to inject more realism into the movies, and soon they began to replace the American movies at the cinema. Italian audiences were receptive to the new vision of films and so was the rest of the world. The comedian Toto or Antonio De Curtis and actress Sofia Loren began to appear in slapstick movies about that time. Director Federico Fellini introduced escapism from realism with the famous movie, *La*

Strada or *The Road*. People needed that diversion from all the destruction that still surrounded them in the 1950s.

In towns like Avella, people no longer wanted to be tied down to farming and shepherding. The world around them was moving faster than they liked. They wanted to be part of that evolution. The dress shop, owned by the three women, began to expand their fashion line to a younger generation in addition to the older traditional clientele. The Pucci and Dior fashion lines and American casual clothes were popular with the young and old. The dress shop expanded to add apprentices to the shop while maintaining excellent rapport with their former mentor. Lena was as beautiful as ever modeling the new fashion designs. Her aspiration was beyond Avella. She had a dream of becoming a model.

As the dress-making business expanded, the girls were spending too much time together on the road to Nola to purchase various types of fabrics, as new dress fashions and fabrics were becoming available in local shops after the war. Sofia was designated to take over the role of purchasing fabrics and selecting new fashions, since she could coordinate fabrics with styles. Besides, like her mother Imalda, she was the best negotiator. In a way, negotiations were another form of socializing. With the coming of summer, Sofia and Mario decided to buy an apartment in a building that also housed the dress-making shop. It was convenient for both Sofia and Mario to be closer to the train station and the dress shop. Their apartment was located within the common courtyard adjacent to the shop. Five residents shared that courtyard which was connected to the piazza by a sixty-foot-wide tunnel. Usually, tunnels were closed off by a large portone, but not this one.

Sofia once rented an apartment at the Naval station before the war near a well-to-do district of Naples—the Posillipo and Vomero areas. When they lived there, they came in contact with aristocrats. As the famous French writer Alexandre Dumas discovered, most aristocrats in Naples were pretenders of wealth. Only a small percentage had access to real wealth and the means to afford the latest fashions. Sofia could discern whom to contact for future business. However, soon after the war, it wasn't safe for her to contact them. That district drew too much attention from scugnizzi, Communists, and sex workers. Naples was becoming a no-man's land. Chaos and lawlessness reigned there as in other districts of Naples. The best option for Sofia was to bide her time until better days, because the will to survive and live life to the fullest was and is inbred in every Neapolitan.

Sofia and the sisters would re-design or modify a style to fit the shape of a customer. They would cut the fabric based on the new modified design. Lena would often model dresses after school. She blossomed into a beauty, like her mother. The boys in the neighborhood certainly took notice. As time went by, business improved steadily to the point that the women needed help from another dressmaker in town, their former teacher and mentor. Business was thriving in Avella, not because of the Marshall Plan, but because people escaped the yoke of Fascism and were free to express themselves in many ways. Shipments of food from the Marshall Plan and money from relatives in the United States spurred small businesses all over Southern Italy.

Cafés were open for business in the piazza as well as in the poorer sections of town. The topic of conversation now in the piazza revolved around who made it alive from the war and who was missing. In the east end of town, two soldiers made it home. One returned from the Russian front having been at the battle of Stalingrad. The other soldier was imprisoned in Libya by the British and released after the war. Often he would sit in the piazza wanting to tell people about his experiences during the War, but no one wanted to listen to him. People were afraid to get near him because his monkey, acquired in Libya, would attack anyone who approached him. Overall, less than 2 percent returned to Avella from the war. Farm owners congregated in the piazza for the purpose of recruiting farmhands or anyone with two hands and legs to work in their farms. The shepherd community was unscathed by the war. However, more and more of them returned to their neighborhood in the east end of town.

A café and bar opened for business for the first time on the east end of Main Street. The new feature of this bar was the billiard room and spumone gelato. The bar was located across from Saint Anthony Church, and it was centrally located on the passeggiata route to the piazza. Espresso aroma wafted all the way to the piazza, about two blocks away. In the morning, workers, on the way to the train station, would stop to buy a pastry and an espresso. In the afternoon, teenagers found a way of unwinding from schoolwork and socializing with their friends. The Giro D'Italia, the bicycle tour race of Italy, and the Tour De France, were broadcast live on the radio. Teenagers were glued to the radio. Their favorite riders were Gino Bartali and Fausto Coppi who competed against each other for more than a decade. In the evening, teenagers, replaced by adults, played cards for serious money. The aroma from the espresso coffee could be smelled all along the passeggiata route. People felt like floating on air, as they walked past the café. In short, people were intoxicated with the feel and smell of freedom.

Farmer's Market Day returned to Avella in the winter of 1946, after a hiatus of five years due to the war. The market combined the usual food products found in a farmer's market and home products in flea markets in the United. The market was scheduled for each Monday except for holidays, such as Easter and Christmas. It extended from east to west of Main Street, for about ten blocks. Every imaginable fruit and vegetable in season were sold, along with shoes, purses, bracelets, umbrellas, etc. However, it was more of a social gathering than a shopping day. Money was still a scarce commodity. Imalda welcomed the market. It made life a lot easier for her since she could sell food items such as ricotta, hard and soft goat cheese, and goat milk, as well as cheesecloth, wool, and other items. People from neighboring towns came to Avella to shop. Psychologically, they needed that outing or large gathering, just to confirm that this was a real happening, not their imaginations, and to find out who came back from the war.

Below that aristocratic look of Ramiro, was a soft-hearted sentimentalist, willing to take risks for others. During the German occupation of Avella, he offered Alvaro's family shelter in his palazzo. Alvaro refused only because he didn't want to endanger his good friend. Thanks to Imalda, he was able to escape the gestapo's entrapment of the whole family. Alvaro returned to city hall once the British camped in town. However, Ramiro hid the local mayor in his vast palazzo until after the war. The former mayor was in a strange predicament; when the Germans camped in Avella, the apolitical mayor feared that the local Fascists might have branded him as a Socialist or Communist to the Gestapo police. However, when the British showed up, he feared that the Communists would brand him for being a podesta or a Fascist mayor. Either way, he would have paid the price for being apolitical. Blame would have come from all directions. After the war, the former mayor became active politically in the Democratic Party.

However, the most dangerous undertaking of Ramiro was to hide two American paratroopers of the 509th Battalion. During the Salerno invasion, the paratroopers were to be dropped in the city of Avellino in order to sabotage the German supply line to Salerno through Avellino. However, the paratroopers were dropped from Avellino to Avella, thirty miles away from the intended target. Local partisans steered the two stranded American paratroopers to Ramiro's palazzo where they wore the garments of farmers, just in time for the fall crop season. Coming from the farms of the midwestern United States, the paratroopers felt as though they were home.

Along Main Street, about a block from the palazzo, a combination of pasta factory and bakery opened for business for the first time. It was managed by the two paratroopers who hid in the palazzo. By then, they were fluent in Neapolitan dialect and adopted the mannerisms of the locals. They had decided to stay and assumed a new life in Avella, as they married local women. Pasta production occupied a large building and supplied dry pasta to all the grocery and pastry stores in Avella, Baiano, Sperone, Cicciano, and other towns in the vicinity; the pasta factory was owned by Ramiro. Besides these two businesses, he owned a factory that produced virgin olive oil which he shipped all over Italy and abroad. The farm was located immediately behind these three businesses and his residence and was surrounded by a twelve-foot wall. The farm was cultivated for wheat, corn, and olives. In addition to these thriving businesses, Ramiro owned a cement and brick factory located near the creek. These factories are still in place in Avella. Prior to the brick factory, bricklayers made their own bricks and cement powder by heating rocks and pulverizing them.

The two Ukrainians were settling nicely in Avella. Dmitri branched out into sculpture, complementing the work of Nicola Jr. in churches. Nicola Jr. was a classical painter specializing in religious themes in churches. He regarded painting or repairing canvasses in churches as work that paid the rent. However, he saw an opportunity to spark the interest of churches in sculpture as well as in paintings, since Dimitri loved sculpturing. Nicola Jr. and Dimitri were impressed with the wave of impressionist paintings, but a Renoir painting would not have complemented any of their work in churches. Nevertheless, both were excited by expanding their repertoire in art by branching out into impressionist works in their studio and the outdoors.

The team of Nicola Jr. and Dimitri was doing exceptionally well. They were getting church commissions, not only from local churches but also from churches in neighboring towns. Their reputations grew rapidly as artists who could repair famous paintings from the Middle Ages damaged by Allied bombings during the invasion of Salerno. Also, they were well-equipped to repair the structures of the churches and install church bells. Dimitri became part owner of the local cinema as well. They had no interest in going back to Ukraine and resuming farming there under the brutal Communist regime of Stalin. The same could be said of many Italian soldiers who started families in Russia and elsewhere in Europe. That may be considered another outcome of WWII, the intermixing of nationalities.

As for Vladimir, he felt at home being in the mountains with the shepherds. Sergio allowed him more and more responsibility in taking over the role of the inspector. As Sergio was getting older, he spent more time with paperwork, tax records of lands on the mountains, and presentations to headquarters in Naples. By now, both Dmitri and Vladimir were fluent in Italian, but they preferred to speak in the Neapolitan dialect at home. Their size and light complexions indicated that they were not from the area. People didn't care. Both Serafina and Filomena gave birth to baby boys. Signore Alvaro resumed his post as chief magistrate at city hall, ensuring that the bureaucracy was running at full capacity. Once a month, the four musketeers got together. However, the gatherings of the families grew bigger and bigger as Erminio's family joined the group. However, the four musketeers needed their privacy to play scopa, a card game, under a trellis covered with grapevines in Erminio's backyard, and to sip wine flavored with fresh seasonal fruits. A bomb could have exploded next to them and they would have not budged an inch. In the summertime, family get-togethers gathered either at the palazzo or at Sergio's garden.

When the Wolf family returned to Vienna, they discovered that not only their home was pulverized by the bombings during the Russian invasion of Vienna in April 1945, but also the beloved Vienna Stadtoper or Vienna State Opera House. Its reconstruction was completed in 1955. Although they enjoyed their stay in Denmark and were thankful for the hospitality, the whole family wanted to return to Vienna and make a go of it. The Vienna Opera House welcomed Ehrlich back to the orchestra with open arms to resume playing the cello. In the interim, performances of the state opera were held at the Vienna Volksoper and the Theater an der Wien. They lived in a modern-day apartment in downtown Vienna within walking distance of the Folk Opera building. Vienna was going through a major reconstruction period—getting back to its former condition, clearing the streets of mines and unexploded devices, and rebuilding apartment complexes of old.

Being away for more than twelve years, Nanna was in a hurry to get back to establishing family contacts, future permanent housing, schooling, financial accounts, and, most important, being aware of any Nazis in the streets. Like her mother, everything had to be meticulously just so to her liking, no more make-do. She ventured into a nearby farm, where her sister Suzanna hid during the war. The farmer gave Nanna the address of Suzanna in New York City which happened to be that of her uncle Herbert. One big sigh of relief could be seen in Nanna's face knowing full well that her uncle acted as the clearing house for all family contacts. All she had to do was to contact Herbert by phone to obtain all the contacts and she did.

Nanna learned that Suzanna held a position as a lecturer, just below that of an assistant professor rank, in the sociology department at Princeton University. Also, it put her in touch with her parents in Switzerland. She didn't ask or request but demanded for her parents to return to Vienna to take care of their grandchildren. Of course, they were more than happy to oblige, since they missed being with Werner and Arya whom they hadn't seen in years. Besides that, they missed their beloved Vienna. Nanna couldn't wait fast enough to get back to normalcy. Again, her Uncle Herbert was the glue that bonded the family together.

In Nanna's communication with Herbert, he encouraged her to take over the accounting of the family's financial situation, especially in retrieving the family properties, paintings, and expensive items, since she lived in Vienna. Also, he suggested that she contact his dear friend Bernhard, who moved to Innsbruck because of the heavy bombings in Vienna, to help her retrieve properties. Basically, Bernhard wanted to get away from the Communist zone of Austria. She postponed the retrieval part. Schooling for the children preoccupied her mind more at that time. Children's language skills in German were relatively poor; it didn't help that they were more fluent in a Neapolitan dialect. But, by the end of summer, the children picked up enough German to be adequately prepared for schooling.

The reconstruction of the state opera building was completed near the Innere Stadt District financed by taxes, contributions, and the Marshall Plan. The Wolf family bought a large apartment next to her parent's apartment and near the opera house. Nanna successfully retrieved some of the properties in Switzerland, France, and Italy but none in Austria, Poland, and Germany. Bernhard advised her to wait and to submit requests directly to the courts in Germany and Poland, but eventually properties will be retrieved to the rightful owners, Harold and Herbert. Like her mother, Nanna collected rent and did the accounting and deposited the money in a common bank account. She was meticulous in her dealings with family holdings, because eventually inheritance issues would come up.

TWENTY
Vita Bella

Carlo Levi and other scholars dwelled on the disparity of the economic classes after the War in Italy. They proposed that the peasant class have a parliamentary representation irrespective of electoral results and, therefore, a voice in the government's decision-making. Laws would then be enacted to benefit peasants and elevate them to the middle class, eliminating peasantry and unemployment in Southern Italy. The problem with that idea is: Who chooses the people representing the peasant class in parliament? If the upper class or elitists represent the poor class, then the lower class is at the mercy of the upper class. After the war, the Marshall Plan just accentuated the disparity in the economic standing of agricultural Southern Italy and the industrial North. The clash between classes is a result of the fact that natural resources in a given country are finite and one class hoards most of the natural resources.

This means that the intrinsic or absolute wealth of a country will not change, because natural resources don't grow with time. Northern Italy has gobbled up most of the natural resources in Italy because of their industrial base. The electoral process has not been able to redistribute natural resources from North to Southern Italy, helping to create an industrial base in the South as well. Still, it was an interesting proposal by Levi's group but not practical in terms of how to implement it equitably via the parliamentary process. Another problem to overcome is that the peasantry comes in different shades or levels of poverty.

Politicians are not in the business of sharing power. They practice the art of telling people what they want to hear. However, governing is the art of telling people what they don't want to hear. In short, the old system of voting is not conducive to solving the problem of redistributing wealth equitably. One possible idea is to draw non-politicians or people within the poor class from a random lottery system and have them serve for a short time in parliament representing the interests of peasants. Two separate elections may be held. One for candidates chosen by the party system and the other by the lottery system not affiliated with a party. The number of lower-class parliamentary representatives would be equal to the percentage of those ranked as poor in Italy.

In the 1950s, tourism alleviated some of the unemployment in Southern Italy. Also, new technologies appeared on the horizon, such as: TV, jets, computers, autos, medicine, etc. For example, before the war, there may have been no more than four telephone lines in Avella. After the war, most if not all of the gentries had one while others aspired to get one. The first item bought by one immigrant to the United States from Avella was a telephone. Old customs, as reflected in men and women's fashion, hairstyles, music, movie compositions, etc. changed dramatically from prewar times.

The dress shop owned by Filomena, Serafina, and Sofia expanded their fashion line to include a younger clientele in addition to the older, traditional one. The Pucci and Dior fashion lines also attracted both the young and old. Templates of fashionable current styles were being sold at stores in the piazza. The three seamstresses modified the templates to fit the latest fashionable dresses onto customers with various shapes and sizes.

However, the tradition of art in churches paid the rent for the two artists. Nicola Jr. and Dimitri received a commission to paint a giant mural in the biggest church in Avella. The mural was to be painted on the ceiling portion of the main entrance, much like the Sistine Chapel in Rome. The two artists graduated from touch-up jobs in churches to full-blown original paintings. However, Dimitri's interest was still in sculpting marble statuettes while also delving into impressionist and modern paintings. This new project required all the skills they possessed and more. The enormity of it would have chased many artists away, but they took on the project with feverish energy. The two artists burned midnight oil to organize the project. For one thing, it required building a wooden scaffold to stand on or lay on to paint. The bishop in Nola suggested that the subject of the painting be the Archangel Saint Michael. The two artists went through many proposals of the painting until the bishop agreed to the proposed sketch.

Don Nicola had never been inside a church but every day he would sneak in a side door of the church to take a peek at what the artists were doing. He didn't want to distract them. He just couldn't help himself. Church or no church, he had to see what they were doing. He was not the only one. Everyone in town had to take a peek at the mural. It became everybody's project. The two artists complemented their talents. One had the temperament of Herbert, the adventurous type with wild and new ideas. The other was more conservative, like Harold, in evaluating new ideas within a traditional framework. Usually, the end result was stupendous to the eye and a clear message to the audience. As to who contributed the most was irrelevant. Both did.

By this time, the Wolf family returned to Vienna. They owned an apartment in the Innere Stadt District of Vienna so that Ehrlich could be closer to the Vienna opera house, where he advanced to be the main cello player in the orchestra. Major construction took place firstly in downtown and then to the suburbs. As noted earlier, Harold and wife Sarah decided to return to Vienna from Switzerland to be closer to their grandchildren. They hadn't seen their grandchild Werner since birth in Tito, he was almost a teenager by then. Yes, life was beautiful. Vita bella once again, just like the days before Hitler appeared on the scene.

Harold's daughter, Suzanna, survived the occupation of Austria by Nazis by working in a farm near Vienna, posing as one of the farmer's daughters. With the help of her uncle Herbert, she emigrated to New York to work in a bakery preparing Viennese pastries to supplement her poor salary as a lecturer at Princeton University. She taught introductory courses in sociology and served as a substitute teacher. She refused financial help from Uncle Herbert, being strong-willed and one fiercely independent woman—a trait in the family. She rented a studio apartment on her own for thirty dollars a month. Eventually, she went on to become one of the leading authorities in the field of Sociology at Princeton University, commanding much respect from the community. Her husband developed a national policy in inner-city development and later served as an adviser to President Lyndon Johnson.

Don Nicola read about Ehrlich's promotion to the regular position as a cello player in the Vienna orchestra. Opera news traveled fast, as there were not too many big-time opera houses operating at that time. The war destroyed most of them in Europe. He called to congratulate him on the promotion, because it implied a future position as a conductor. Don Nicola added that he wanted Ehrlich and his family to come to Avella and see the other Sistine Chapel painting. Ehrlich visualized Don Nicola bubbling all over the phone about his son's painting. Without hesitation, "Yes, of course, it will be a pleasure to see the painting during a break in the opera season and to visit my old friends. Is there enough room for us in Sergio's building because there may be a lot of us?" he answered. "If not, the sheep will have to vacate some apartments," replied Don Nicola.

Initially, Herbert rented a three-room suite inclusive of a kitchen in a luxury hotel in downtown Manhattan. The living room had impressionist paintings covering from wall to wall. His income from investments in the United States supported his luxurious lifestyle. The building became a cooperative and he bought it for about $5,000–$7,000. Today, it may be worth $5–10 million. After running around all over the globe for many years, he settled down with his wife. His legitimate daughters remained in Palestine raising their own families. However, he was itching to get back into a new business enterprise. That spirit defined his persona. In the past, he needed Harold to counter his wild spirit and enthusiasm in pursuing new business ventures. Most times Herbert's hunches were right on the mark, but, sometimes, foolish. Most importantly, Herbert trusted Harold's advice and he needed him now.

Herbert had a dream. He wanted to establish an art gallery in New York, but he didn't know beans about how to go about it. In the interlude, both cousins lived in two separate continents. So, they spent most of their time on the phone, searching for deeds and documents of holdings and properties to recover properties located from Berlin to Ravello, Italy. That just drove Herbert mad. Fortunately, Nanna also worked to recover their properties, because she was relentless at it. It was time to do something together with his business partner, Harold. For one thing, he needed to get in touch with Nanna and organize the old businesses into one folder.

After all those dreadful years, Herbert cherished the thought of getting together once again with Harold, like old times, in pursuit of a new business venture, hopefully the last hurrah. Herbert still had that hunger. However, Harold was somewhat reluctant, because he was burned in a couple of business ventures in Switzerland. During one of their telephone conversations, they agreed to take on a sure shot, at least, in recovering their house in Ravello overlooking the Amalfi coastline. The only obstacle in releasing it was that the Italian government passed a squatter law which stated that any squatter or occupant residing in a property for more than seven years may claim that property. The resident of the house lived there for more than ten years.

During the war, many squatters took over the farmlands of people who emigrated to the United States before the war. This presented one major problem in reclaiming the farms by Italian Americans returning to Italy. Harold suggested that on the way to Ravello, they stop by the cozy town of Avella and look over some interesting art produced by local artists. He added that his son-in-law, Ehrlich, be-friended the artists as well as the rest of their families during the two years that he spent in an internment camp in Southern Italy and a number of years in Avella. He went on to add that Ehrlich was successful in hiding his family from Nazis for more than six years. The people there opened their hearts and homes to Nanna's family. As if struck by a lightning bolt, he saw an opportunity to realize his ultimate dream of an art gallery in New York City. The only problem he had was to get Harold to join him in this venture. So, he decided to travel with Harold on this trip to see the second Sistine Chapel. At least, it will get the motor started with Harold.

Harold promised that he would make all the arrangements to visit Avella and Ravello. Wow, Herbert was excited to join up again with Harold taking the initiative this time. Plus, what better place to vacation in Southern Italy—Amalfi, Ravello, Positano—the Sorrentine Peninsula. Yes, Herbert had been there before many times and loved the people and scenery. He didn't envision any problems with the present owner or resident of the house in Ravello, because before the war the owner was the regular gardener in need of a place to stay temporarily. Being a scholar of art and wanting to initiate a new business in the art gallery, he welcomed the visit to Avella, as confessed to Harold. That was the seed to get Harold involved. Harold sensed as much and liked the idea. He knew Herbert's tendencies. Their roles reversed. Harold was the instigator of a new business venture in art. Herbert enjoyed every bit of it.

In mid-May, the beautiful sky-blue flowers turn into small green grapes. Yet violets continue to grow all over the surrounding hills of Avella. The dark blue flowers of chicory plants begin to wither away, no longer picked by the locals to make coffee or edible food. Coffee beans replaced dried chicory buds, and sugar became available. Espresso coffee no longer tasted bitter. People were floating on air in the piazza smelling the coffee aroma emanating from the cafes. It reflected the times after the war. It seemed like the whole valley was changing colors making way for the coming growing season just in time to welcome the guests from Vienna.

They arrived late in the afternoon at the train station in Naples—all eight of them—the Wolf family, Herbert, Harold, and their wives. Don Nicola and the two artists, Nicola Jr. and Dimitri, received them at the station. The rest of the Avella clan stayed home to prepare a three-star Neapolitan dinner and get the apartments ready for the guests. Remarkably, the bulk of the two clans of friends got together to enjoy each other's company wishing better things to come for all.

The next day, Don Nicola and the two artists accompanied their guests to Saint Peter's Church in Avella to view the huge painting on the ceiling wall painted by Nicola Jr. and Dimitri. Herbert and Harold were more interested in the mechanics of how the feat was accomplished rather than the composition. They returned to the art studio in Sergio's courtyard to view marble statuettes of Dimitri and impressionist paintings on canvas by both artists. Most importantly, it showed the range of talents of the two, from classical to abstract art. Yes, very impressive. Herbert and Harold looked at each other and Herbert said, "Do you see what I see?" Harold replied, "Yes, an art gallery in New York." For once, they agreed right from the start. The rest of the group in the studio wondered, "What the hell were they talking about?" Harold and Herbert knew. Next, onto Ravello.

Don Nicola drove Harold and Herbert to Ravello. As soon as the gardener saw the party of three approach the house, he ran out to greet Herbert. He embraced Herbert, handing him the deed of the house and land in the original name and said, "It's about time you showed up. I can't afford to stay here." He added, "Recently, vultures were hovering around the property ready to pounce on it. If they showed up again, I was going to shoot." Apparently, the tax assessor and the tax collector asked too many questions about the property. Herbert was moved to tears for the first time in his life. Not so much for the honesty displayed by the gardener, but for his will to fight for the property on his behalf. He thanked the gardener profusely.

However, the gardener asked if he could stay in the property to take care of the garden and cultivate the land as a farm. Herbert realized that the gardener was loyal and deserved an opportunity to improve his lot. Herbert promised to build a farmhouse and a barn on the surrounding land for the gardener and his family to move in and manage the property. Sometimes, heaven can be found on earth, as the gardener did. Finally, Herbert informed the gardener to expect friends of the family to visit the house any time of the year.

This called for a celebration. He inquired if Sebastiano's small restaurant was still operating down on the waterfront. "No, he moved to a bigger place on the same waterfront, as tourists keep coming to Amalfi and Positano," replied the gardener. After a sumptuous lunch, the trio of them headed back to Avella taking the spectacular coastline drive around the Sorrentine Peninsula.

Back in Avella, Ramiro escorted the Viennese crowd and the rest of the clan of friends to the newly discovered amphitheater in town, very near Sergio's building. It was no longer a well-kept secret for centuries hidden by farmers. With Canadians and British troops camping within a stone's throw from the amphitheater, the secret was out as some of the art confiscated now resided in museums throughout the world. Indeed, the government in Rome got involved in restoring the art discovered there: statues, paintings, seating arrangements, strange rooms perhaps for gladiators, etc. Since then, it has been discovered that farmers hid more than just an amphitheater, but also a complete town buried below ground under their farms.

Herbert later arranged for Dimitri and Filomena, and Nicola Jr. and his girlfriend, to visit him in New York City to put plans together for an art gallery. His dream had always been that someday he may be surrounded by art pieces from wall to wall, besides in his apartment. He was getting old and determined to go out with a bang. He felt that both Dimitri and Nicola complemented each other very well, and they would be ideal artists to manage such an undertaking. They represented a cross spectrum of art, from classical to abstract art and in between, as well as sculpture. Besides, he had enough impressionist paintings in his apartment to attract an audience, if necessary.

Filomena didn't sleep the whole night. She was so excited about attending a fashion show the next day on Forty-Second Street and Fifth Avenue, the center of the garment industry, exhibiting the latest American sportswear and dressmaking. She was enamored with Americans' casual style and adored the variety of fabrics they used. It was a fashion spirit not imaginable in Italy or anyplace else in Europe then. The dress styles from Paris and Milan tended to be formal and expensive catering to a certain class of people, especially the new jet-set crowd. In Southern Italy, especially in a town like Avella, the clientele demanded practicality and price flexibility. In contrast to Northern Italians, Southern Italians loved to negotiate or haggle for prices. Clearly, the wave of the future in clothes was the casual American fashion style. She thought to herself, "America, here I come."

The 1950s witnessed one of the most important developments in the American fashion industry: the birth of modern sportswear. Capable of being freely mixed and matched by the consumer, sportswear—or separates—was the quintessential work of the contemporary American designer. Linked to more casual lifestyles that emerged as the American population moved out of cities like New York and into the suburbs, the creation of sportswear also set off the search for cheaper labor. Indeed, this fashion trend happened to coincide with the control over wage scales, forcing upon manufacturers a new consideration: Why keep paying skilled tailors to do the unskilled work required for the sportswear boom? In fact, standardized sportswear required more section work and, therefore, more space. This was one fashion trend that did not match the limitations of a zoned Garment District, where space was at a premium. Alternative places of production developed soon after.

Filomena couldn't wait to get home and tell Sofia and Serafina all about the new explosion in the fashion industry. The girls wanted to hear about the fashion show, in particular, what drew the most attention. Sportswear and shorter dresses fitted tighter. The color of the fabrics in the show were outstanding, according to Filomena. They asked Filomena how they could be identified with this new wave of dressmaking. Filomena had an idea. She could emigrate to America and keep them posted with new developments. That surprised Sofia and Serafina. Filomena explained that it was not a done deal but close to it. She owed the other two an explanation of what she meant. After all, they were still business partners.

Filomena implored Dimitri and Nicola Jr. to accept without hesitation Herbert's offer as an opportunity of a lifetime. She rationalized that they have the freedom to pursue their art to their hearts' content and make a bundle of money. Obviously, Imalda's negotiation skills must have filtered down to her as well as to Sofia and Serafina. She asked her husband, Dimitri, categorically, "Are you allergic to money because you are an artist?" Then told him, "As for me, I want to pursue the new wave of dressmaking in America. That is where it is nowadays." Her passion and determination truly overwhelmed Dimitri. He never saw that side of her, but he loved it. His only hesitation was that for the first time he would be separated from his twin brother. However, Don Nicola encouraged his son to pursue his art. "Besides, I will get to see you more often, since traveling by jet is a lot easier," he added jokingly, but crying inside.

The Immigration Law passed during the Truman Administration authorized the entry of 200,000 displaced persons over the next two years. However, in 1950, the entry increased to 415,000 displaced people. Clearly, Dimitri qualified as a displaced person but not Nicola. No problem for Herbert, as he was well acquainted with immigration laws and how to bypass them. He hired the best immigration lawyer in the world and, presto, Nicola qualified as a displaced person. It came down to the interpretation of displacement and Nicola's whereabouts during the war. Herbert employed the same lawyer to circumvent the immigration law to allow Suzanna to emigrate to the United States as a displaced person. As before, it came down to the interpretation of the law or, perhaps, bribing the right person.

Soon after the arrival of Suzanna in New York City, uncle Herbert rented a studio apartment for Suzanna on Sixty-Fifth Street and Fifth Avenue for a reasonable price of fifty dollars a month. Suzanna loved the apartment. It allowed her to be in the greatest city in the world at that time and continue her studies. Today, the same apartment may be rented for thousands of dollars. Suzanna accepted a post-doctoral position at Princeton University in the sociology department. The appointment was for two years with the potential to advance into a lecture position which may lead to full-time professorship. After the two-year stint, Princeton University hired Suzanna as a lecturer. However, the pay was no more than what the university paid a graduate student. She supplemented her salary by working part-time at a bakery store which her uncle Herbert often frequented in the morning for coffee. Most likely, Herbert put in the good word for Suzanna to the owner. His nonchalant attitude toward the owner didn't fool Suzanna, but she needed the money.

Before the arrival of the two couples from Avella, Herbert rented an abandoned warehouse from the city to convert it into an art gallery, a large studio, and an office. The warehouse in the Upper East Side was located on Second Avenue and Sixty-Fourth Street. Rentals for an apartment in Manhattan were relatively expensive even then for someone starting a new job. So, Herbert decided to reserve two apartments for the two couples in the borough of Queens across from Roosevelt Island on a dead-end street near Queens Bridge Park and Forty-First Avenue. The artists could easily take local transportation to the art gallery or walk across the bridge. Avenues in the Queens Borough run perpendicular to the ones in Manhattan. Thus, Sixty-Fifth Street in Manhattan coincides with Forty-First Avenue in Queens. He named the gallery, The Triple H Art Gallery, for Harold and Herbert Herzog.

The new immigrants traveled by sea first-class to New York City, courtesy of Herbert, on the American ship, Constitution. Of course, the whole clan showed up at the port in Naples to bid their goodbyes to the departing couples. On disembarking in New York, they were quickly introduced to Ellis Island, formerly a jail house for hardened criminals. Various vaccines against diseases such as tuberculosis, smallpox, and typhoid were administered to all of them. They sat there like a bunch of zombies not knowing what was next until one customs official waved for them to leave the port.

Herbert and his wife drove the new arrivals in his new Cadillac around Manhattan before finally stopping at the warehouse. Herbert explained roughly where the studio, gallery, and office may be located. Then gave his final instruction, "Make it happen, baby!" The artists replied in unison, "Si, Si, padrone!" or "Yes, Yes, boss!" Herbert then drove them to their apartments, each furnished with one television, telephone, bed, bathroom supplies, and a refrigerator full of food. Compared to living conditions in Avella, they thought to themselves, "This must be heaven."

EPILOGUE

Let's compare the personalities of the make-believe modern-day Caesar with the real one. The personalities and characters of Mussolini and Caesar were worlds apart. Mussolini was a coward; he wilted under pressure, had no principles, was unfaithful to women, including his wife, was one-dimensional in his aims, highly opinionated, easily intimidated, had no clue how to wage wars, and was completely disloyal to those around him—even to his children and grandchildren. Mussolini ranked as a corporal in WWI and connived his way to the top Army rank to become, in his mind, the modern-day Caesar of WWII. The real Caesar was a courageous man, cool-headed in crisis, a man of principles, forever faithful to his wife, had a talent for improvisation, was rigorous in his analysis of a situation, was a man who feared nothing, was ready for everything, knew the proper time for waging war, was tireless, attentive to details, and earned unshakeable loyalty from centurion guards to generals.

The only similarity between Mussolini and Hitler was that both rose from the rank of Army corporal, one as Caesar and the other as Napoleon. Whereas Mussolini was determined and overconfident to the point of becoming delusional to achieve from the outset. Hitler was convoluted and troubled, suffering from an inferiority complex. There are many theories to explain his complex mindset, but we will not delve into that because there is nothing to be learned from a deranged man. Some scholars claim that he was influenced by outcasts and extreme characters who bolstered his battered self-image.

As time went on, Hitler gained a following of deviants in Germany, and his intentions became more outlandish and harrowing. He had no imagination or was completely unaware of how to start an original political movement, so he copied the one started by Mussolini in the early 1920s. Now instead of one misguided political movement, there were two. The blind led the blind. Mussolini caved under pressure in the middle of WWII and Hitler held on until the end when he died by suicide. The real tragedy was that they left the world in a mess and millions of families without their parents, children, and relatives, and survivors of the Holocaust burdened with pure agony for the rest of their lives.

The relationship between Mussolini and Hitler went beyond ordinary contact via ambassadors, ministers, and diplomatic protocols. According to new findings discovered in the making of this book, they colluded together in ways to enhance their standing among peers. For example, any communication between the two was never revealed to others in the diplomatic core, as protocol required.

The case in point was the Dunkirk pause. In my previous book, *Hidden in Plain Sight*, only two communications out of four were confirmed in regard to the pause at Dunkirk. The first communication between Churchill's war cabinet and the Italian ambassador in London, Giuseppe Bastianini, and the fourth between Hitler and his generals. The second between Bastianini and the Foreign Office in Rome and the third one between the Foreign Office in Rome and Hitler has been confirmed in this book only via direct communications between Mussolini and Hitler. Thus, the two leaders communicated directly at critical times in history, bypassing protocol. Most likely, there may have been many other communications between the two never to be revealed in the future.

The basic question that begs to be asked is, "Did King Victor Emanuel III and German President Paul von Hindenburg learn anything from the history of WWI?" Apparently not! The Italian king appointed Mussolini as prime minister and President Hindenburg did the same to Hitler in Germany. If both the king and the president had done their homework about these two characters, they would have discovered that both appointments were fraudulent, based on their history in WWI. Incompetency is a mild word to describe their appointments. This raises another interesting question. Historical facts may be 100 percent true, but, if not utilized, history will indeed repeat itself. Nevertheless, we need to maintain a high standard of factual information about historical events so that future leaders may be able to learn from history. Collateral damage, either hidden or otherwise, has increased exponentially since 1800. Thus, the world cannot afford to repeat the failures of WWII.

It is interesting to note the contrast and similarities in the treatment of Italian and Austrian Jewish people by Fascist and Nazi regimes:

Before March 12, 1938: Fascist thugs, wearing black shirts, harassed and intimidated Communists and Socialists in the streets of Italy regardless of faith affiliations. The aim was to prevent other political influences on the populace. The harassment reached a peak in the late 1920s to early 1930s. By 1938, the harassment began to ebb. In Vienna, the harassment and intimidation by stormtroopers focused explicitly on the Jewish population with the local support of the rest of the population. The harassment occurred in streets, workplaces, schools, and universities. Physical violence was very common. The harassment started in full swing in the mid-1920s and built to a crescendo in 1938 and beyond.

Before November 17, 1938: Although the Blackshirt Fascists continued their harassment and intimidation of political dissidents, Italian Jews were still employed in government jobs, banks, and professional jobs. Incarceration of political dissidents required a trial. By April 10, 1938, the situation in Vienna deteriorated from intolerable to catastrophic for the Jewish population in Vienna, because the Nuremberg Racial Laws, enacted in Germany in 1935, were applied only to Jews throughout Austria. Nazis harassed, persecuted, incarcerated, forced into labor camps, deported, taxed, and singled out Jewish people in Austria only because they were Jewish. Incarceration did not require a trial. As a result, the Jewish population decreased from 10 percent to less than 1 percent in Vienna. Austrian Jews were forced to leave the country, pay an exorbitant amount of money in taxes and, most times, leave their properties behind. The Nuremberg Laws were strictly enforced by Nazis in their occupied territories.

From November 17, 1939 to June 10, 1940: Fascist racial laws were enacted in Italy. Italian Jews could no longer hold on to government jobs or the equivalent. The racial laws were mostly enforced in large cities. By and large, the laws were not supported by Italians and the Catholic Church during the time of Pope Pius XI. Again, Fascist thugs mainly harassed Socialists, Communists, and political dissidents. Italian Jews were not singled out per se. There was no extortion of money or deportation because they were Jewish. A person, regardless of religion, would have been incarcerated, if considered a political dissident. A trial was required to incarcerate. According to the Fascist regime, a political dissident represented a grave security risk to the regime. The Italian racial laws were circumvented most of the time, especially in small towns, because Jewish residents were the glue that bonded the town together. Most times, a Jewish resident may have resided longer in a town than anyone else. Hence, there was no need for the Jewish population to leave Italy, pay taxes to leave Italy, and leave their possessions behind.

From June 10, 1940 to January 20, 1942: In Italy, foreign Jews were sent to internment camps or towns throughout Italy without trial. Many European Jews emigrated to Italy because no visa was required for entry. Italian Jews who were convicted by trial of political activities against the state were sent to internment towns. Otherwise, they were left alone, especially in small towns. The internment camps consisted of housing people in town settings or Catholic convents and monasteries. Even the very few camps that consisted of barracks had no fence surrounding the premises. All Jews in Austria, regardless of nationality, were deported without trial to forced labor camps. Not many survived the harsh living conditions and unhealthy quarters in these camps. The internment camps were guarded night and day by guards and dogs. The camps were surrounded by fences.

From January 20, 1942 to July 26, 1943: The population of internees in Italian internment towns remained the same as before. Few died of sickness due to malaria, typhoid, and influenza. Jews in German camps were sent to extermination camps. However, even before January 20, the Nazis sent Jewish prisoners to occupied territories for extermination. After January 20, unimaginable atrocities and killings were committed throughout the occupied territories.

From July 26, 1943 to September 8, 1943: The architect of internment towns in Italy, Mussolini, was put in jail by the king. Hence, confusion reigned galore. Basically, internees and local residents of remote hilly towns were in the same boat, trying to survive the War. In Nazi-occupied territories, the extermination of Jewish people, regardless of nationality, increased.

From September 8, 1943 to May 1, 1945: All internees in Southern Italy were set free. However, Nazis raided internment camps and towns in Northern Italy to deport only Jewish people for extermination. The policy of extermination of Jewish people continued unabated north of the Alps.

May 10, 2024: What have we learned from the history of WWII? Apparently, not much. After eighty-six years, Jewish students still are prevented from attending classes at major universities throughout the United States. In some cases, they have been physically assaulted on campus. We, as writers, can only spotlight the facts as they occurred or were discovered, with the hope that the words see daylight.

Let's examine the deposition made by the only witness to this day regarding the incarceration of Mussolini by the king—Ferdinando Tascini. It is well known that

German paratroopers rescued Mussolini at the Gran Sasso in Abruzzo on September 12, 1943. Mr. Tascini recently died at the age of 101 years. He represented one of many carabinieri guards employed then by the new government of Badoglio and the king of Italy to guard the building where Mussolini was incarcerated. In particular, his duties included guarding the room where Mussolini was located. According to Mr. Tascini, Mussolini shared many feelings and thoughts with him. However, Mr. Tascini released only one statement, "Mussolini wished the Americans had rescued him instead of the Germans." Very revealing.

Clearly, from Ciano's diary, Mussolini and his son-in-law disagreed strongly about the alliance with Germany. So much so that Mussolini banished his son-in-law from his government. On the one hand, Ciano and the rest of Italy, at least most Italians, felt that the alliance was an unnatural one because he felt that, given the many meetings with high-ranking Nazi officials, they were untrustworthy. On the other hand, Mussolini felt that he made a personal commitment to Hitler and he should honor it. Despite his actions, Mussolini identified himself as representing the wishes of Italians. His mindset went beyond conceit, more like delusional. He put personal commitments over the wishes of the people. It is concluded here that sometime during the incarceration period, he began to believe that his son-in-law and the people of Italy were right.

Whatever thoughts, feelings, and political schemes Mussolini had regarding an American rescue, went out the window once the Germans rescued him. In twenty years, the relationship between Hitler and Mussolini went from Mussolini being the main cog to a servant to Hitler, which included killing the father of his grandchildren. Ultimately, his ego did him in.

The stage for the killing of Ciano was set up by none other than Hitler himself. Details of setting the stage for Hitler may be found in the book by Eugen Dollmann listed in the references. Two witnesses have come forward to describe Dollmann's character. In 1952, a Central Intelligence Agency (CIA) archive report described Dollmann as infamous for his blackmail, subterfuge, and double-dealing. The other witness, CIA director Allen Dulles, described Dollmann as a "slippery customer." Dollmann requested an explanation of the word slippery from Mr. Talbot. He was told that it was someone who was shrewd, cunning, and Machiavellian. Dollmann smiled and replied, "Oh! That's a compliment for me." Also, Mr. Talbot confirmed that Dollmann was a double agent for the Office of Strategic Services (OSS), the future CIA, and German Intelligence.

Most likely, Herr Dollmann is smiling from his grave, because he lived forty more years after Ciano's fiasco. Ultimately, it came down to him or Ciano.

CHRONOLOGY

PIVOTAL TIMES IN ITALY DURING WWII

May 7: Tunis falls to the British 7th Armored Division, and Bizerte, the last remaining port in North Africa in Axis hands, is taken by troops of the U.S. II Army Corps.

May 13: Axis forces in North Africa surrender to the Allies. Some 250,000 German and Italian soldiers are taken as prisoners.

July 9: Operation Husky, the Allied invasion of Sicily, begins under the overall command of General Dwight D. Eisenhower.

July 19: More than 500 Allied bombers strike Rome for the first time, hitting the San Lorenzo freight yard and steel factory, as well as the Littorio and Ciampino airports.

July 22: Troops of Patton's Seventh Army take Palermo.

July 24–25: A majority of the Fascist Grand Council approves a motion of no confidence in Benito Mussolini.

July 25: King Victor Emmanuel III meets with Mussolini, removes him from office, and has him arrested. Marshal Pietro Badoglio, former chief of the Italian general staff and member of the Fascist Party, replaces Mussolini as prime minister and declares on the radio that Italy would remain loyal to Germany.

August 1: The hardest fighting of the entire campaign in Sicily sees the U.S. First Infantry Division, "The Big Red One," under the command of Major General Terry de la Mesa Allen Sr., "Terrible Terry," as he is known to his men, battling the German Army for the town of Troina, centrally located in Sicily. With the Germans on the high ground and U.S. forces under enemy observation for the duration of the battle, U.S. losses are heavy, but the Americans grind forward.

August 5: First secret negotiations between Eisenhower and the Badoglio government take place to arrange an Italian unconditional surrender to the Allies.

August 6: The U.S. First Infantry Division takes Troina as German troops evacuate and continue their retreat to the northeast of Sicily toward the Strait of Messina.

August 7: Major General Allen relinquishes command of the U.S. First Infantry Division to Major General Clarence R. Huebner. Two days later *Time* magazine features Allen.

August 11: German soldiers begin evacuation at night from Sicily across the Strait of Messina. The bulk of the German forces on Sicily escapes.

August 17: Allies enter Messina, ending the conquest of Sicily.

September 3: Field Marshal Montgomery's Eighth Army launches Operation Baytown, an amphibious operation at Reggio Calabria, the toe of the Italian peninsula. The Badoglio government secretly signs an armistice of unconditional surrender with the Allies.

September 8: General Eisenhower announces that the Italian government under Badoglio agrees to an armistice with the Allies—General Giuseppe Castellano signed the armistice in Cassibile, Sicily—and that Italy will have the status of a "co-belligerent" against Nazi Germany. German forces carry out Operation Axis, occupying Italy using troops already in the country in conjunction with forces newly arriving via the Brenner Pass. Hitler orders that Italy be treated as an occupied country. Field Marshal Erwin Rommel is given responsibility for the occupation of Italy and for disarming the Italian armed forces. General Albert Kesselring is then put in charge of Central and Southern Italy. He plans to take over Rome and organize the resistance to the Allied landing at Salerno. In addition, German forces move to disarm Italian garrisons in France, Yugoslavia, Albania, and Greece.

September 9: General Mark Clark, commander of the U.S. Fifth Army, initiates Operation Avalanche—Allied landings on the Italian peninsula at Salerno.

September 10: German units, especially the 16th Panzer Division, launch fierce counterattacks at Salerno, which for a time, threaten the integrity of General Clark. Admiral Alberto da Zara surrenders the Italian fleet to British Admiral Andrew Cunningham, commander-in-chief of the Mediterranean fleet in Malta.

September 10: German troops occupy Rome.

September 11: Germans begin to move troops from Sardinia to Corsica.

September 12: German paratroopers and SS men, brought in by glider and led by SS-Hauptsturmführer and Otto Skorzeny, carry out a raid, freeing Mussolini from imprisonment in the Gran Sasso Mountains of the Abruzzo region. Mussolini met Adolf Hitler in Rastenburg, Germany, two days later.

September 13: The Italian Thirty-Third Infantry Division resists the Germans on the Greek island of Cephalonia. Fighting continues until September 21. More than 1,300 Italians are killed in battle and over 5,100 are massacred. Some 3,000 members of the division perish when the German ships are sunk by Allied aircraft.

September 14: Allied troops land on Sardinia.

September 15: The Allied Army secures the beachhead at Salerno, thanks to the skillful use of artillery and massive naval and air support.

September 16: Canadian Troops of the British Eighth Army spearheads, moving from Calabria through Potenza, meet troops of Clark's Fifth Army in the beachhead near Salerno.

September 19: Confrontations between Italian partisans and German soldiers ensue.

September 23: Mussolini is coerced by Hitler to form a new Fascist government.

September 25: Reichsführer SS Heinrich Himmler notifies Herbert Kappler, head of the intelligence gathering branch of the SS in Rome, to make preparations for the immediate deportation of Jews from Rome.

September 26: Without authorization from Himmler, Kappler orders Dante Almansi and Ugo Foà, two leaders of the Jewish community in Rome, to give him fifty kilograms of gold to save Rome's Jewish population from deportation. They comply with Kappler's demand.

September 27: What's known as the Four Days of Naples occurs; four days of uprising in the city. On the first day, martial law is enacted by the Germans. The townspeople erect barricades and attack German soldiers in response. More than 660 Neapolitans perish during these four days.

October 1: Allied troops enter Naples.

October 3: German troops complete evacuation of Corsica, after battling free French troops and resistance fighters.

October 6: Adolf Eichmann's subordinate, Theodor Dannecker, arrives in Rome with a group of Waffen-SS personnel to organize the deportation of Roman Jews.

October 13: Italy declares war on Germany. The declaration, signed by Victor Emmanuel III, is transmitted to Berlin through the Italian Embassy in Madrid.

October 16: Dannecker's team, with support from Wehrmacht troops, arrests more than 1,200 Jews in Rome. Two days later, 1,023 Jews, a majority of them women, and 200 of them children are deported to Auschwitz, where most of them are murdered immediately. Only sixteen survived the war.

October 18: The Allied Military Government (AMG) announces control over the zones of combat in Italy and the region of Naples, with its indispensable port.

November 6: Hitler orders Field Marshal Rommel to leave Italy and go to France to prepare defenses there against an expected Allied invasion.

November 20: Field Marshal Kesselring becomes supreme commander of German forces in Italy—from Rome to the Alps.

November 22: The British 8th Army starts an offensive on the Sangro River, Field Marshal Montgomery's final battle in the Mediterranean theater.

November 23: Mussolini announces the creation of the Republican Socialist Italian (RSI) Party with Mussolini as both chief of state and prime minister of the new RSI government.

December 2: At the Cairo Conference U.S. President Franklin D. Roosevelt informs British Prime Minister Winston Churchill that he has chosen General Dwight D. Eisenhower to lead the Allied invasion of France. Italy increasingly becomes a secondary theater of Allied operations.

December 24: Lieutenant General Sir Oliver Leese succeeds Field Marshal Montgomery as commander of the British Eighth Army.

PIVOTAL TIMES IN AUSTRIA DURING WWII

1919: Austria becomes the first republic.

1921: An anti-Semitic mob parades in Vienna.

1930: An economic depression takes over Austria.

1933: The Enabling Act gives Hitler legislative control.

September 15, 1935: The passage of Nuremberg Racial Laws.

March 12, 1938: German troops enter Austria.

March 13, 1938: Germany incorporates Austria.

April 10, 1938: The Anschluss Referendum vote annexes Austria.

July 31, 1938: German officials collected 7 billion reichsmarks from Jewish people in Austria, which is equivalent to almost $100 billion today.

November 9, 1938: Kristallnacht, or what is known as the Night of Broken Glass, occurs in Vienna.

September 1, 1939: The German Army invades Poland.

January 20, 1942: During the Wannsee Conference the decision by the Nazis to exterminate the Jewish People takes place.

April 13, 1945: Russian troops occupy Vienna.

ACKNOWLEDGMENTS

In contrast to scientific research, the search for unpublished historical events is equivalent to a treasure hunt. It's basically a hit-or-miss proposition. I was fortunate to have my friend, Professor Giuseppe Balestrino, University of Rome (Tor Vergata), guide me on where to look in the archives of Rome and I want to thank him. In addition, I want to thank Professor Emilio Gentile of the University of Rome (Sapienza) who helped me narrow down the search in the Foreign Office archive during WWII from April 9 to June 10, 1940 (300 pages in Italian). In another search, I want to thank Nancy DeSanti for making me aware of comments made by a former police (carabiniere) guard during the incarceration of Mussolini in 1943. Finally, I want to thank my dear Reginella (my wife) for being the cheerleader and inspiration of my books and for editing this one.

ABOUT THE AUTHOR

Carmine Vittoria received his Ph.D. in applied quantum physics from Yale University in 1970. He is currently a professor at Northeastern University, where he has established a world-class research laboratory in the development of new microwave films deposited at the atomic scale. He is a fellow of the American Physical Society and IEEE.

REFERENCES

*The bibliography follows a time sequence of historical events consistent
with the table of contents.*

HISTORICAL BACKGROUND

1. Chisholm, Hugh, "Avella," Encyclopedia Britannica (11th ed.), Cambridge University Press; Bunbury, Edward, *Abella*, (https://books.google.com/books).

2. Kamen, Henry, *The Spanish Inquisition: A Historical Revision*, Yale University Press (1998). ISBN 9780300075229.

3. Colletta, Pietro, *The History of the Kingdom of Naples*, I. B. Tauris. ISBN 9781845118815.

4. Maltby, William S. Alba, *A Biography of Fernando Alvarez de Toledo, Third Duke of Alba*, University of California Press (1983). ISBN 0520046943.

5. Montanile, Nicola, *The Baronial Palazzo: History, curiosities, nobles, and benefactors*, to be published and private communication.

6. Payne, Stanley G., *Fascist Italy and Spain, 1922–45*, Mediterranean Historical Review 13, p. 99 (1998).

7. Leopold von Ranke, *History of the Popes*, Wellesley College Library Volume III, 2009.

8. Dodge, Theodore, *Hannibal*, Da Capo Press (1891), Cambridge, MA, ISBN 0306813629

9. Bradley, Keith R., *Slavery and Rebellion in the Roman World, 140-70 BC*, Indiana University Press (1989), ISBN 0253312590.

10. Gruen, ErichS., *Jews Amidst Greeks and Romans*, Harvard University Press (2009).

11. Gunther, R. T., *Pausilypon, the Imperial villa near Naples*, Oxford University Press (1913).

12. Isaia, Roberto, Marianelli, Paola and Sbrana, Alessandro, *Caldera unrest prior to intense volcanism in Campi Flegrei at 4.0 ka B.P.:* "Implications for caldera dy-

namics and future eruptive scenarios," Geophysical Research Letters 36, 2009.

13. E. T. Salmon, *Samnium and the Samnites*, Cambridge University Press, Cambridge (2010).

14. A. Everitt, *Cicero*, Random House, Inc., New York (2001).

15. USA Today, May 21, 2018 Issue.

POST-WORLD WAR 1 POLITICAL EVENTS

1. Englestein, Laura, *Russia in Flames: War, Revolution, and Civil War, 1914-1921*, Oxford University Press (2018).

2. Morselli, Mario, *Caporetto, 1917: Victory or Defeat?*, Routledge Pub. (2001), ISBN 0714650730.

3. Brundage, J. F. and Shanks, G. D., "What Really Happened During the 1918 Influenza Pandemic? The importance of bacterial secondary infections," *The Journal of Infectious Diseases* 196, p. 1717 (2007).

4. Taubenberger, J. K., 1918 "Influenza: the mother of all pandemics," *Emerging Infectious Diseases* 2, p.15 (2006).

5. Feldman, Gerald D., *The Great Disorder: Politics, Economics, and Society in the German Inflation, 1914-1924*, Oxford University Press (1996). ISBN 0195101146.

6. Gregor, James A., *Young Mussolini and the Intellectual Origins of Fascism*, University of California Press (1979). ISBN 9780520037991.

7. Bernardo, Francesco, *Il Diavolo e L'Artista. Le passioni artistiche dei giovani Mussolini, Stalin e Hitler* (*The Devil and the Artist. The artistic passions of young Mussolini, Stalin and Hitler*), Tralerighe Pub. (2019). ISBN 978883287079.

8. Rieber, Alfred J., *Stalin as Georgian: The Formative Years*, Cambridge University Press (2005). ISBN 9781139446631.

9. Hafner, Sebastian, *The Meaning of Hitler*, Harvard University Press, Cambridge (1979). IBSN 978067455778.

10. Gruber, Helmut, *Red Vienna: Experiment in Working-Class Culture 1919-1934*, Oxford University Press, New York (1991).

EVOLUTION OF FASCISM AND NAZISM

1. Shirer, William, *The Rise and Fall of the Third Reich*, Simon & Schuster, New York (1960).

2. Young, Anthony J. G., *Mussolini and the Intellectual Origins of Fascism*, University of California Press. ISBN 9780520037991.

3. Ciano Galeazzo, *Diary, 1937-1943*, Enigma Books (2008). ISBN 9781929631025.

4. Mollo, Andrew, *The Armed Forces of World War II*, I. B. Tauris & Co. Ltd. ISBN 9780517544785.

5. Marino, James I., *Italians on the Eastern Front: From Barbarossa to Stalingrad*, Warfare History Network (Nov. 17, 2018).

6. Speer, Albert, *Inside the Third Reich*, Weidenfield & Nicholson (1995). ISBN 9781842127353.

7. Zimmerman, Joshua D., *Jews in Italy Under Fascist and Nazi Rule, 1922-1945*, Cambridge University Press (1980). ISBN 9780521841016.

8. Zuccotti, Susan, *Italians and the Holocaust*, Basic Books Inc., New York (1987).

9. Standenmeyer, Peter, "Racial Ideology Between Fascist Italy and Nazi Germany," *Journal of Contemporary History* 55, p. 473 (2019).

10. Bosworth, R. J. B., *Mussolini's Italy: Life Under the Dictatorship 1915-1945*, Allen Lane, London (1998).

11. Moseley, Ray, *Mussolini: The Last 600 Days of Il Duce*, Taylor Trade Publishing, Dallas (2004).

12. Mussolini, Rachele, *Mussolini: An Intimate Biography*, Pocket Books (1970). ISBN 0671812726.

13. Pugliese, Stanislao G., *Fascism, Anti-Fascism and the Resistance in Italy: 1919 to Present*, Rowan and Littlefield (2004). ISBN 0747531236.

14. Lyttelton, Adrian, *The Seizure of Power: Fascism in Italy, 1919-1929*, Routledge (2003). ISBN 0714654736.

15. Silvestri, Carlo, *Matteotti, Mussolini e il Dramma Italiano*, Ruffolo, Roma (1947). Translation: *Matteotti, Mussolini, and the Italian Drama*.

16. Dornberg, John, *Munich 1923: The Story of Hitler's First Grab for Power*, Harper Row, New York (1982).

17. Gordon, Harold J. Jr., *The Hitler Trial Before the People's Court in Munich*, University Publications of America (1976).

18. Kershaw, Ian, *Hitler: 1889-1936*, Penguin Books, New York (2001).

19. Hitler, Adolf, *Mein Kempf*, Houghton Mifflin, New York (1999).

20. Pastore, Stephen R., *The Art of Adolf Hitler*, Grand Oaks Books (2013).

21. Fulda, Bernhard, *Press Politics in the Weimar Republic*, Oxford University Press. ISBN 9780199547784.

22. Goeschel, Christian, *Mussolini and Hitler: The Forging of the Fascist Alliance*, Yale University Press. ISBN 9780679446958.

23. Irene Pipes, Personal chronicle of her family in Warsaw from 1925 to 1945.

24. Wasserman, Janek, *Black Vienna: The Radical Right in the Red City, 1918-1938*, Cornell University Press, New York (2014).

25. Boissoneault, Lorraine, "A 1938 Nazi Law Forced Jews to Register Their Wealth" ..., *Smithsonian Magazine*, SmithsonianMag.com.

26. Beller, Steven, *Vienna and the Jews, 1867–1938: A Cultural History*, Cambridge University Press, London (1990).

27. Knaur, Peter, *The International Relations of Austria and the Anschluss 1931–1938*, University of Wyoming Press, Wyoming (1951).

POLITICAL DISSIDENTS AGAINST FASCISM

1. Levi, Carlo, *Christ Stopped at Eboli*, Farrar, Strauss and Giroux, New York (1974).

2. Casanova, Antonio G., *Matteotti: Una Vita il Socialismo* (*A Life in Socialism*), Bongianni Pub. (1974).

3. Canali, Mauro, *Il delitto Matteotti* (*The Murder of Matteotti*), Il Mulino (2004).

4. Moorehead, Caroline, *A Bold and Dangerous Family: The Rosellis and the Fight Against Mussolini*, Chatto and Windus (2000).

5. Amendola, Eva Kuhn, *Life with Giovanni Amendola*, Parenti (1960).

6. Colarizi, Simona, *The Democrats in Opposition: Giovanni Amendola and the National Union*, Il Mulino (1973).

7. Ward, David, *Piero Gobetti's New World: Antifascism, Liberalism and Writing*, University of Toronto Press (2010).

8. Ciano, Galeano, Diary, Ibid.

9. Moseley, Ray, *Mussolini's Shadow: The Double Life of Count Galeano Ciano*, Yale University Press, New Haven (1999). ISBN 97800300209563

RACIAL LAWS IN FASCIST ITALY

1. Sarfatti, Michael, *Characteristics and Objectives of the Anti-Jewish Racial Laws in Fascist Italy*; Joshua D. Zimmerman, *Jews in Italy Under Fascist and Nazi Rule, 1922–1945*, Cambridge University Press (2005). ISBN 0521841011.

2. Livingston, Michael A., *The Fascists and the Jews of Italy: Mussolini's Race Laws, 1938–1943*, Cambridge University Press (2014). ISBN 0333760646.

3. Kertzer, David I., *The Pope at War: The Secret History of Pope Pius XII, Mussolini and Hitler*, Random House, New York (2022).

4. Kertzer, David I., *The Secret History of Pope Pius XI and the Rise of Fascism in*

Europe, Random House, New York (2004).

5. Bradsher, Greg, "The Nuremberg Racial Laws," *Prologue Magazine*, The National Archives and Records Administration 42, (2010).

6. Burleigh, Michael, *The Racial State: Germany 1933–1945*, Cambridge University Press (2000). ISBN 9780521398022.

7. Longerich, Peter, *Holocaust: The Nazi Persecution and Murder of the Jews*, Oxford University Press (2000). ISBN 9780192804365.

8. Eisner, Peter, *The Pope's Last Crusade*, Harper Collins, New York (2013).

INTERNMENT CAMPS IN FASCIST ITALY

1. Capogreco, Carlo S., *I Campi del Duce. L'Internamento Civili nell'Italia Fascista* (*Il Duce's Camps. Civil Internments in Fascist Italy*), *1940–1943*, Einaudi, Torino (1993).

2. Klinkhammer, Lutz, *L'Occupazione Tedesca in Italia* (*German Occupation of Italy*), *1943–1945*, Bollati Boringhieri, Torino (1993).

3. Zuccoli, Susan, *Holocaust Odysseys: The Jews of Saint-Martin-Vesubie and Their Flight through France and Italy*, Yale University Press, New Haven (2007).

4. Bettina, Elizabeth, *It Happened in Italy*, Thomas Nelson, Nashville (2009).

5. Freidberg, "An Account of the S.S. Pentch and the Italian Internment Camps at Rhodes and Ferramonti," *The Israel Philatelist*, XV (No. 8 and 9), p.112 (1964).

6. Watson, James, "History and Memory of the Italian Concentration Camps," *Historical Journal* 40 (#1), p. 169 (1997). Cambridge University Press.

7. Museum of Ferramont di Tarsia, (http://www.museoferrmonti.it).

8. Goeschel, Christian and Wachsmann, Nikolaus, *The Nazi Concentration Camps 1933-1939: A Documentary History*, University of Nebraska Press. ISBN 9780803227828.

9. Healey, Dan, "Lives in the Balance: Weak and Disabled Prisoners and Biopolitics of the Gulag," *Kritika* 16 p. 3. (1980).

10. Blatman, Daniel, *The Death Marches: The Final Phase of Nazi Genocide*. Harvard University Press. ISBN 9780674059191.

11. Hinnershitz, Stephanie, *Japanese American Incarceration*, University of Pennsylvania Press. ISBN 9780812299953.

TURNING POINTS IN WORLD WAR II

1. Wilhelm, Adam and Ruhle, Otto, *With Paulus at Stalingrad*, Penn Sword Books (2015). ISBN 9781473833869.
2. Bell, P. M. H., *Twelve Turning Points of the Second World War*, Yale University Press, New Haven (2011).
3. Craig, William, *Enemy at the Gates: The Battle of Stalingrad*, Penguin Books, New York (2000).
4. Ban, Niall, *Pendulum of War: The Three Battles of El Alamein*, Overlook Press, Woodstock (2000). ISBN 9781585617382.
5. Greene, Jack and Massignani, *Alessandro, Rommel's North African Campaign: September 1940–November 1942*, Da Capo, Cambridge (1994). ISBN 97815809970181.
6. Blumenson, Martin, *Kasserine Pass*, Houghton Mifflin, Boston (1966).
7. Badoglio, Pietro, *Italy in The Second World War, Memories and Documents*, Oxford University Press (1948).
8. Badoglio, Pietro, *The War in Abyssinia*, Methuen Publishers, London (1937).
9. Smith, Dennis M., *Italy and Its Monarchy*, Yale University Press, New Haven (1989).
10. Bastianini, Giuseppe, Memoirs, Vitigliano, Rome (1959); *Volevo Fermare Mussolini* (*I Wanted to Stop Mussolini*), BUR Saggi, Rome (2005).
11. Guderian Heinz, *Hitler's Momentous Order to Stop*, Panzer Group Leader, Da Capo Press (1952, 2001). ISBN 9780306811012.
12. Lord, Walter, *The Miracle of Dunkirk*, Allen Lane, London (1983).
13. Thompson, Julian, *Dunkirk: Retreat to Victory*, Acade, New York (2011).
14. Richardson, Mathew, *Tigers at Dunkirk and the Fall of France*, Pen Sword, Barnsley (2010). ISBN 9781848842106.
15. LS-I, "I Documenti Diplomatici Italiani, Nona Serie (1939–1943)," Volume IV (Aprile 9–Giugno 10 1940).
16 Ferdinando Tascini, online site, ndesanti7@gmail.com (Nancy DeSanti).

GLOBALLY ORGANIZED CRIME SYNDICATES

1. Vittoria, Carmine, *Once Upon a Hill*, Purpo, Inc., Key Biscayne (2022). ISBN 9780578320014.
2. Nicasio, Antonio and Lamothe, Lee, *The Global Mafia: The New Order of Organized Crime*, MacMillan of Canada (1995). ISBN 0771573111.

3. Saviano, R., *Gomorrah*, Arnoldo Mondatori Editore, Milan (2008).

4. Frasca, D., *Vito Genovese: King of Crime*, Avon Books. New York (1963).

5. Gosch, M. A. and Hammer, R., *Lucky Luciano*, Little Brown and Company, Boston (1975).

6. Raab, S., *Five Families*, Saint Martin Press, New York (2005).

7. Reavill, G., *Mafia Summit*, Thomas Dunne Books, New York (2013).

8. Dickie, John, *Mafia Republic: Italy's Criminal Curse. Cosa Nostra, Ndrangheta and Camorra from 1946 to the Present*, Hodder and Stoughton, New York (2013). ISBN 97814444726435.

9. Behau, Tom, *The Camorra*, Routledge (1996). ISBN 0415099870.

10. Letizia, Paoli, *Mafia Brotherhoods: Organized Crime, Italian Style*, Oxford University Press, New York (2003).

11. Varese, Federico, "How Mafias Migrate: The Case of Ndrangheta in Northern Italy," *Law and Society Review*, June 2006.

RELEVANT LITERATURE

1. Atkinson, R. A., *The Day Battle in Sicily and Italy, 1943–1944*, Henry Holt, New York (2007).

2. Bertoldi, S., *Badoglio*, Rizzoli, Milan (1982).

3. Branko, B., *Spy in the Vatican*, Vita, London (1973).

4. Hapgood D. and Richardson D., *Monte Cassino*, Congdon & Weed, Inc., New York (1984).

5. Katz, R., *The Battle for Rome*, Simon & Schuster, New York (2003).

6. Posner, G., *God's Bankers: A History of Money and Power at the Vatican*, Simon & Schuster, New York (2015).

7. Stille, A., *Benevolence and Betrayal: Five Jewish Families Under Fascism*, Summit Books, New York (1991).

8. Tompkins, Peter, *Una Spia a Roma (A Spy in Rome)*, Il Saggiatore, Milan (2002).

9. LaFarge, John, *Interracial Justice as a Principle of Order*, Catholic University of America Press, Washington D. C. (1937).

10. Goldhagen, D. J., "What Would Jesus Have Done?" *The New Republic*, New York (2002).

11. Castellano, Giuseppe, *How I Signed the Armistice of Cassabile*, Mondatori, Milan (1945).

12. Churchill, Winston, *Closing the Ring*, Houghton Mifflin, Boston (1951).

13. Mikolashek J. B., *General Mark Clark*, Casemate, New York (2013).

14. Falconi, Carlo, *The Silence of Pius XII*, Little Brown, Boston (1970).

15. Dollman, E., *Roma Nazista*, Longanesi, Milan (1949); *Call Me Coward*, William Kimber, London (1956); *The Interpreter*, Hutchison, London (1967).

16. Harris C. R. S., *Allied Military Administration of Italy, 1943–1945* (HMSO, 1957).

17. Croce, Benedetto, *The King and the Allies*, Allen & Unwin, London (1950).

18. Everitt, Anthony, *Cicero*, Random House, New York (2001).

19. Bimberg, E. L., *The Moroccan Goums: Tribal Warriors in a Modern War*, Greenwood Press, Westport (1999).

20. Carter, R. S., *Those Devils in Baggy Pants*, Signet, New York (1999).

21. Montgomery, B. L., *The Memoirs of Field Marshal the Viscount Montgomery of Alamein, K. G.* Companion Book Club, London (1958).

22. Clark, M. W., *Calculated Risk*, Harper & Brothers, New York (1950).

23. Newark, T., *The Mafia at War: Allied Collusion with the Mob*, Greenhill Books, New York 2007).

24. Passelecq, G. and Suchecky B., *The Hidden Encyclical of Pius XI*, Harcourt Brace, New York (1997).

25. Kesselring, A., *A Soldier's Record*, Morrow, New York (1954).

26. Casanova, A.G., *Matteotti*, Bombiani, Milan (1974).

27. Battistelli, Pier Paolo, *Tobruk 1941*, The History Press, New York (2012).

28. Hellbeck, J., *Stalingrad,* Public Affairs, New York (2015).

29. Patton, G. S. and Harkins, P. D., *War As I Knew It*, Houghton Mifflin, Boston, (1995).

30. Newness, G., "Appian Way," *Chambers' Encyclopedia*, 1, p.149, London (1961).

31. Eisenhower D. D., *A Crusade in Europe*, Doubleday, New York (1948).

32. Smith R. H., *OSS*, Lyons Press, New York (1972).

33. Stalin, Joseph, *The Road to Power*, University Press of the Pacific, New York (2003).

34. Cawthorne, W., *The History of the Mafia*, Arcturus, New York (2011).

35. Hogan, Michael J., *The Marshall Plan*, Cambridge University Press, Cambridge (1987).

36. Orlando, L., *Fighting the Mafia*, Encounter Books, San Francisco (2001).

37. Stille, Alexander, *Excellent Cadavers*, Random House, New York (1995).

38. Vittoria, Carmine, *Hidden in Plain Sight*, Munn Ave. Press, Lebanon, NJ,

(2023).

39. Dollmann, Eugen, *Nazi Fugitive*, Skyhorse Publishing, New York (2017). This book was previously published in 1956 as *Call Me Coward* by William Kimber & Co.

40. Dollmann, Eugen, *With Hitler and Mussolini*, Skyhorse Publishing, New York (2017). Originally published in 1967 as *The Interpreter* by Hutchinson & Co.

41. William, Bader, *Austria Between East and West*, Stanford University Press (1966), ISBN: 0-8047-0258-6.

42. Bischof, Gunther, *Austro-Corporatism: Past, Present, Future*, Transaction Publ. (1996), ISBN: 1-56000-833-4; *Allied Plans and Policies for the Occupation of Austria, 1938–1955*, Transaction Publishers (2009), ISBN: 1-4128-0854-5.

43. Gimbel, John, *The Origins of the Marshall Plan*, Stanford University Press (1976).

44. Kesselring, Albert, *A Soldier's Record*, Morrow, New York (1954).

45. Larson, Erik, *The Splendid and the Vile*, Random House, New York (2020).

46. DeSanti, Louis A. *The U.S. and Mussolini*, The Millenium Publishing Co., McLean, VA (2001).

47. Guareschi, Giovanni, *Comrade Don Camillo*, Pilot Productions, N. Yorkshire (2017).